W9-BKV-932

For a complete listing of books by Diana Palmer, please visit www.dianapalmer.com.

DIANA PALMER

UNTAMED

HQN™

ISBN-13: 978-0-373-78940-5

Recycling programs for this product may not exist in your area.

Untamed

Copyright © 2015 by Diana Palmer

Printed in U.S.A.

Dear Reader,

Stanton Rourke has been one of my favorite characters since he showed up in *Tough to Tame*, helping protect Cappie Drake from her abusive ex-boyfriend. Since then, he's been in a lot of books. Bits and pieces of his life have emerged, most especially in *Courageous*, when he went to help General Emilio Machado face down a usurper.

It was there that Clarisse Carrington, whom he called Tat, was introduced. His feelings for her were mixed and obviously violent. In this book, the reason becomes clear. It is a tapestry of love and loss, selfishness and unselfishness, and, at the last, sacrifice. I have rarely loved a hero as much. I hope that you enjoy reading his story as much as I have enjoyed writing it. There has been one odd side effect from the writing process. I have a sudden yen to learn how to tango…

As always, your biggest fan,

Diana Palmer

For Dr. Sherry Maloney,
who took such wonderful care of our son
when he was small, and who painted
the most beautiful canvases I have ever seen.
You brought joy to so many lives. May God hold you
safely in the palm of His hand and lead you home.

CHAPTER ONE

IT TOOK FOREVER to get anywhere, Stanton Rourke fumed. He was sitting at the airport on a parked plane while officials decided if it was safe to let the passengers disembark. Of course, he reasoned, Africa was a place of tensions. That never changed. And he was landing in Ngawa, a small war-torn nation named in Swahili for a species of civet cat found there. He was in the same spot where a small commercial plane had been brought down with a rocket launcher only the week before.

He wasn't afraid of war. Over the years, he'd become far too accustomed to it. He was usually called in when a counterespionage expert was wanted, but he had other skills, as well. Right now he wished he had more skill in diplomacy. He was going into Ngawa to get Tat out, and she wasn't going to want to let him persuade her.

Tat. He almost groaned as he pictured her the last time he'd seen her in Barrera, Amazonas, just after General Emilio Machado had retaken his country from a powerful tyrant, with a little help from Rourke and a company of American mercs. Clarisse Carrington was her legal name. But to Rourke, who'd known her since she was a child, she'd always been just Tat.

A minion of the country's usurper, Arturo Sapara,

had tortured her with a knife. He could still see her, her blouse covered with blood, suffering from the effects of a bullet wound and knife cuts on her breast from one of Sapara's apes, who was trying to force her to tell what she knew about a threatening invasion of his stolen country.

She was fragile in appearance, blonde and blue-eyed with a delicately perfect face and a body that drew men's eyes. But the fragility had been eclipsed when she was threatened. She'd been angry, uncooperative, strong. She hadn't given up one bit of information. With grit that had amazed Rourke, who still remembered her as the Washington socialite she'd been, she'd not only charmed a jailer into releasing her and two captured college professors, she'd managed to get them to safety, as well. Then she'd given Machado valuable intel that had helped him and his ragtag army overthrow Sapara and regain his country.

She did have credentials as a photojournalist, but Rourke had always considered that she was just playing at the job. To be fair, she had covered the invasion in Iraq, but in human-interest pieces, not what he thought of as true reporting. After Barrera, that had changed.

She'd signed on with one of the wire services as a foreign correspondent and gone into the combat zones. Her latest foray was this gig in Ngawa, where she'd stationed herself in a refugee camp which had just been overrun.

Rourke had come racing, after an agonizing few weeks in Wyoming and Texas helping close down a corrupt politician and expose a drug network. He hadn't wanted to take the time. He was terrified that Tat was really going to get herself killed. He was almost sweating with worry, because he knew something that Tat didn't; something potentially fatal to her and any foreigners in the region.

He readjusted the ponytail that held his long blond hair. His one pale brown eye was troubled, beside the one wearing the eye patch. He'd lost the eye years ago, in a combat situation that had also given him devastating scars. It hadn't kept him out of the game by a long shot, but he'd turned his attention to less physical pursuits, working chiefly for K. C. Kantor's paramilitary ops group as an intel expert, when he wasn't working for a covert government agency in another country.

K.C. didn't like him going into danger. He didn't care what the older man liked. He suspected, had long suspected, that K.C. was his real father. He knew K.C. had the same suspicion. Neither of them had the guts to have a DNA profile done and learn the truth, although Rourke had asked a doctor to do a DNA profile of his assumed father.

The results had been disturbing. Rourke's apparent father had been K.C.'s best friend. Rourke's mother had been a little saint. She'd never cheated on her husband, to Rourke's knowledge, but when she was dying she'd whispered to the doctor, Rourke's friend, that she'd felt sorry for K.C. when the woman he loved had taken the veil as a nun, and things had happened. She died before she could elaborate. Rourke had never had the nerve to actually ask K.C. about it. He wasn't afraid of the other man. But they had a mutual respect that he didn't want to lose.

Tat was another matter. He closed his eye and groaned inwardly. He remembered her at seventeen, the most beautiful woman he'd ever seen in his entire life. Soft, light blond hair in a feathery cut around her exquisite face, her china-blue eyes wide and soft and loving. She'd been wearing a green dress, something slinky but demure, because her parents were very religious. Rourke had been teasing her and she'd laughed up at him. Something had snapped inside him. He'd gathered her up like priceless treasure and started kissing her. Actually, he'd done a lot more than just kiss her. Only the sudden arrival of her mother had broken it up, and her mother had been furious.

She'd hidden it, smoothing things over. But then Tat's mother had taken Rourke to one side, and with quiet fury, she'd told him something that destroyed his life. From that night, he'd been so cold to Tat that she thought he hated her. He had to let her think it. She was the one woman on earth that he could never have.

He opened his eye, grinding down on the memories before they started eating him alive again. He wished that he'd never touched her, that he didn't have the shy innocence of her mouth, her worshipping eyes, to haunt his dreams. He'd driven her into the arms of other men with his hatred, and that only made the pain worse. He taunted her with it, when he knew it was his own fault. He'd had no choice. He couldn't even tell her the truth. She'd worshipped her mother. She had passed away from a virus she'd caught while nursing others. Now Tat was alone, the tragic deaths of her father and young sister still haunting her months after they'd drowned in a piranha-infested river on a tour of local villages.

Rourke had been at the funeral. He couldn't help the way he felt. If Tat was in trouble, or hurt, he was always there. He'd known her since she was eight and her parents lived next door to K.C., who was by that time Rourke's legal guardian, in Africa. Since Tat was ten years old and Rourke was fifteen, and he'd carried her out of the jungle in his arms to a doctor, after letting her get bitten by a viper, she'd been his. He couldn't have her, but he couldn't stop taking care of her. He knew his attitude puzzled her, because he was usually her worst enemy. But let her be hurt, or threatened, and he was right there. Always. Like now.

He'd tried to phone her, but he couldn't get her to answer her cell. She probably knew his number by heart. She wouldn't even pick up when he called.

Now she was here, somewhere close, and he couldn't even get information from his best sources about her condition. He remembered again the way she'd been in Barrera, bleeding, white in the face, worn to the bone, but still defiant.

The steward walked down the aisle and announced that the rebels who held the airfield were allowing the passengers to leave after a brief negotiation. He even smiled. Rourke leaned over and unobtrusively patted the hide gun in his boot. He could negotiate for himself, if he had to, he mused.

HE CALLED HIS CONTACT, a man with a vehicle, to drive him to the refugee camp. This man was one of his few friends in the country. It was Bob Satele, sitting beside him, who had given him the only news of Tat he'd had in weeks.

"It is most terrible, to see what they do here," the man remarked as he drove along the winding dirt road. "Miss Carrington has a colleague who gets her dispatches out. She has been most sympathetic to the plight of the people, especially the children."

"Ya," Rourke said absently. "She loves kids. I'm surprised that Mosane hasn't had her killed." He was referring to the leader of the rebel coalition, a man with a bloodthirsty reputation.

"He did try," his contact replied, making Rourke clench his teeth. "But she has friends, even among the enemy troops. In fact, it was one of Mosane's own officers who got her to safety. They were going to execute her…"

He paused at Rourke's harsh gasp.

Rourke bit down hard on his feelings. "NATO is threatening to send in troops," he said, trying to disguise the anguish he felt. At the same time he didn't dare divulge what he knew; it was classified.

"The world should not permit such as this to happen, although like you, I dislike the idea of foreign nations interfering in local politics."

"This is an exception to the rule," Rourke said. "I'd hang Mosane with my own hands if I could get to him."

The other man chuckled. "It is our Africa, yes?"

"Yes. Our Africa. And we should be the ones to straighten it out. Years of foreign imperialism have taken a toll here. We're all twitchy about letting outsiders in."

"Your family, like mine, has been here for generations," the other man replied.

"We go back, don't we, mate?" he said, managing a smile. "How much farther?"

"Just down the road. You can see the tents from here." They passed a truck with a red cross on the side, obviously the victim of a bomb. "And that is what hap-

pens to the medical supplies they send us," he added
grimly. "Nothing meant for the people reaches them,
yet outsiders think they do so much good by sending
commodities in."

"Too true. If they're not destroyed by the enemy,
they're confiscated and sold on the black market." He
drew in a breath. "Dear God, I am so sick of war."

"You should find a wife and have children." His
friend chuckled. "It will change your view of the
world."

"No chance of that," Rourke said pleasantly. "I like
variety."

He didn't, actually. But he was denied the one
woman he did want.

THE REFUGEE CAMP was bustling. There were two people
in white lab coats attending the injured lying on cots
inside the few big tents. Rourke's restless eye went
from one group to another, looking for a blond head of
hair. He was almost frantic with worry, and he couldn't
let it show.

"She is over there," Bob said suddenly, pointing.

And there she was. Sitting on an overturned crate
with a tiny little African boy cradled in her arms. She
was giving him a bottle and laughing. She looked
worn. Her hair needed washing. Her khaki slacks and
blouse were rumpled. She looked as if she'd never worn
couture gowns to the opera or presided over arts ceremonies. To Rourke, even in rags, she would be beautiful. But he didn't dare let his mind go in that direction.
He steeled himself to face her.

Clarisse felt eyes on her. She looked up and saw
Rourke, and her face betrayed her utter shock.

He walked straight to her, his jaw set, his one brown eye flashing.

"Look here," she began before he could say a word, "it's my life..."

He went down on one knee, his scrutiny close and unnerving. "Are you all right?" he asked gruffly.

She bit her lower lip and tears threatened. If she was hurt, in danger, mourning, frightened, he was always there. He'd come across continents to her, across the world, around the world. But he didn't want her. He'd never wanted her...

"Yes," she said huskily. "I'm all right."

"Bob said you were captured, that they were going to kill you," he ground out, his scrutiny close and hot.

She lowered her eyes to the child she was feeding. "A necklace saved my life."

"That cross..." he began, recalling that her mother had given it to her and she never took it off—except once, to put it around Rourke's neck in Barrera, just before he went into the capital city with Machado and the others, for luck.

"No." She flicked open the top button of her blouse. She was wearing a seashell necklace with leather thongs.

He frowned.

"This little one—" she indicated the child in her arms "—has a sister. She was dying, of what I thought was appendicitis. I commandeered a car and driver and took her to the clinic, a few miles down the road. It was appendicitis. They saved her." She took the bottle away from the child's lips, tossed a diaper over one shoulder, lifted the child and patted him gently on the back to make him burp. "Her mother gave me this necklace, the little girl's necklace, in return." She smiled. "So the captain whose unit captured me saw it and recognized it and smuggled me out of the village." She cradled the child in her arms and made a face at him. He chuckled. "This is his son. His little girl and his wife are over there, helping hand out blankets." She nodded toward the other side of the camp.

He whistled softly.

"Life is full of surprises," she concluded.

"Indeed."

She looked at him with eyes that were quickly averted. "You came all this way because you thought I'd been kidnapped?"

He shook his head curtly. "I didn't know that until I got here."

"Then why did you come?" she asked.

He drew in a long breath. He watched her cradle the child and he smiled, without sarcasm for once. "You look very comfortable with a child in your arms, Tat."

"He's a sweet boy," she said.

His mother came back and held out her arms, smiling shyly at Rourke before she went back to the others.

"Why did you come?" she asked him again.

He stood up, jamming his hands into his khaki slacks. "To get you out of here," he said simply. His face was taut.

"I can't leave," she said. "There isn't another journalist in this part of the country. Someone has to make sure the world knows what's going on here."

"You've done that," he said shortly. He searched her eyes. "You have to get out. Today."

She frowned. She stood up, too, careful not to go close to him. He didn't like her close. He backed away if she even moved toward him. He had for years, as if he found her distasteful. Probably he did. He thought she had the morals of an alley cat, which would have been hilarious if it hadn't been so tragic. She'd never let anyone touch her, after Rourke. She couldn't.

"What do you know, Stanton?" she asked softly.

His taut expression didn't relent. "Things I'm not permitted to discuss."

Her eyes narrowed. "Something's about to happen…?"

"Yes. Don't argue. Don't hesitate. Get your kit and come with me."

"But…"

He put his finger over her lips, and then jerked it back as if he'd been stung. "We don't even have time for discussion."

She realized that he knew about an offensive, and he couldn't say anything for fear of being overheard.

"I'm taking you home," he said, loudly enough for people nearby to hear him. "And no more argument. You've played at being a photojournalist long enough. You're leaving. Right now. Or so help me God, I'll pick you up and carry you out of here."

She gave him a shocked look. But she didn't argue. She got her things together, said goodbye to the friends she'd made and climbed into the backseat of the car he and Robert had arrived in. She didn't say another word until they were back at the airport.

HE SEATED HER beside him in business class, picked up a newspaper in Spanish, and didn't say another word until they landed in Johannesburg. He bought her dinner, and then she got ready to board a plane for

Atlanta. Rourke had connections back to Nairobi, far
to the northeast. They got through passport control,
and Clarisse stopped at the gate that led to the international concourse. "I'll get on the next flight to DC
from Atlanta and file my copy," she told him as they
stood together.

He nodded. He looked at her quietly, almost with
anguish.

"Why?" she asked, as if the word was dragged out
of her.

"Because I can't let you die," he bit off. "Regardless
of my inclinations." He smiled sarcastically. "So many
men would grieve, wouldn't they, Tat?"

The hopeful look on her face disappeared. "I as-
sume that I'll read about the reason I had to leave
Ngawa?" she asked instead of returning fire.

"You will."

She drew in a resigned breath. "Okay. Thanks," she
added without meeting his eye.

"Go home and give parties," he muttered. "Stay out
of war zones."

"Look who's talking," she returned.

He didn't answer her. He was looking. Aching.
The expression on his face was so tormented that she
reached up a hand to touch his cheek.

He jerked her wrist down and stepped back. "Don't
touch me," he said icily. "Ever."

She swallowed down the hurt. "Nothing ever
changes, does it?" she asked.

"You can bet your life on it," he shot back. "Just for
the record, even if half the men on earth would die to
have you, I never will. I do what I can for you, for old
time's sake. But make no mistake, I find you physi-

cally repulsive. You're not much better than a call girl, are you, Tat? The only difference is you don't have to take money for it. You just give it away."

She turned while he was in full spiel and walked slowly from him. She didn't look back. She didn't want him to see the tears.

He watched her go with an expression so full of rage that a man passing by actually walked out of his way to avoid meeting him. He turned and went to catch his own flight back to Nairobi, nursing the same old anguish that he always had to deal with when he saw her. He didn't want to hurt her. He had to. He couldn't let her get close, touch him, warm to him. He didn't dare.

HE FLEW BACK to Nairobi. He'd meant to go to Texas, to finalize a project he was working on. But after he had to hurt Tat, his heart wasn't in it. His unit leader could handle things until he got himself back together.

He drove out to the game ranch with his foreman from the airport in Nairobi, drooping from jet lag, somber from dealing with Tat.

K. C. Kantor was in his living room, looking every day of his age. He got to his feet when Rourke walked in.

Not for the first time, Rourke saw himself in those odd, pale brown eyes, the frosty blond hair—streaked with gray, now—so thick on the other man's head. They were of the same height and build, as well. But neither of them knew for sure. Rourke wasn't certain that he really wanted to know. It wasn't pleasant to believe that his mother cheated on his father. Or that the man he'd called his father for so many years wasn't really his dad...

He clamped down on it. "Cheers," Rourke said. "How're things?"

"Rocky." The pale brown eyes narrowed. "You've been traveling."

"How gossip flies !" Rourke exclaimed.

"You've been to Ngawa," he continued.

Rourke knew when the jig was up. He filled a glass with ice and poured whiskey into it. He took a sip before he turned. "Tat was in one of the refugee camps," he said solemnly. "I went to get her out."

K.C. looked troubled. "You knew about the offensive?"

"Ya. I couldn't tell her. But I made her leave." He looked at the floor. "She was rocking a baby." His eyes closed on the pain.

"You're crazy for her, but you won't go near her," K.C. remarked tersely. "What the hell is wrong with you?"

"Maybe it's what the hell's wrong with you, mate," Rourke shot back with real venom.

"Excuse me?"

The pain was monstrous. He turned away and took a big swallow of his drink. "Sorry. My nerves are playing tricks on me. I've got jet lag."

"You make these damned smart remarks and then pretend you were joking, or you didn't think, or you've got damned jet lag!" the older man ground out. "If you want to say something to me, damn it, say it!"

Rourke turned around. "Why?" he asked in a hunted tone. "Why did you do it?"

K.C. was momentarily taken aback. "Why did I do what, exactly?"

"Why did you sleep with Tat's mother?" he raged.

K.C.'s eyes flashed like brown lightning. K.C. knocked him clean over the sofa and was coming around it to add another punch to the one he'd already given him when Rourke got to his feet and backed away. The man was downright damned scary in a temper. Rourke had rarely seen him mad. There was no trace of the financial giant in the man stalking him now. This was the face of the mercenary he'd been, the cold-eyed man who'd wrested a fortune from small wars and risk.

"Okay!" Rourke said, holding up a hand. "Talk. Don't hit!"

"What the hell is wrong with you?" K.C. demanded icily. "Tat's mother was a little saint! Maria Carrington never put a foot wrong in her whole life. She loved her husband. Even drunk as a sailor, she'd never have let me touch her!"

Rourke's eyes were so wide with shock and pain that K.C. stopped in his tracks.

"Let's have it," he said. "What's going on?"

Rourke could barely manage words. "She told me."

"She who? Told you what?"

Rourke had to sit down. He picked up the glass of whiskey and downed half of it. This was a nightmare. He was never going to wake up.

"Rourke?"

Rourke took another sip. "Tat was seventeen. I'd gone to Manaus on a job." Rourke's deep voice was husky with feeling. "It was Christmas. I stopped by to see them, against my better judgment. Tat was wearing a green silk dress, a slinky thing that showed off that perfect body. She was so beautiful that I couldn't take my eyes off her. Her parents left the room." His eyes closed. "I picked her up and carried her to the sofa. She didn't protest. She just looked at me with those eyes, full of... I don't even know what. I touched her and she moaned and lifted up to me." He drew in a shaky breath. "We were so involved that I only just heard her mother coming in time to spare us some real embarrassment. But her mother knew what was going on."

"That would have upset her," K.C. said. "She was deeply religious. Having you play around with her teenage daughter wasn't going to endear you to her, especially with the reputation you had in those days for discarding women right and left."

"I know." Rourke looked down at the floor. "That one taste of Tat was like finding myself in paradise. I wanted her. Not for just a night. I couldn't think straight, but my mind was running toward a future, not relief."

He hesitated. "But her mother didn't realize that. I can't really blame her. She knew I was a rake. She probably thought I'd seduce Tat and leave her in tears."

"That could have happened," K.C. said.

"Not a chance." Rourke's one eye pinned him. "A girl like that, beautiful and kind..." He turned away. He drew in a long breath. "Her mother took me to one side, later. She was crying. She said that she'd seen you one night at your house, upset and sick at heart because a woman you loved was becoming a nun. She said she had a drink with you, and another drink, and then, something happened. She said Tat was the result."

"She actually told you that Tat was your half sister? Damn the woman!"

Rourke felt the same way, but he was too drained to say it. He stared at his drink. "She told me that. So

I turned against Tat, taunted her, pushed her away. I made her into something little better than a prostitute by being cruel to her. And now I learn, eight years too late, that it was all for a lie. That I was protecting her from something that wasn't even real."

He fought tears. They played hell with the wounded eye, because it still had some tear ducts. He turned away from the older man, embarrassed.

K.C. bit his lip. He put a rough hand on Rourke's shoulder and patted it. "I'm sorry."

Rourke swallowed. He tipped the last of the whiskey into his mouth. "Ya," he said in a choked tone. "I'm sorry, too. Because there's no way in hell I can tell her I believed that about her mother. Or that I can undo eight years of torment that I gave her."

"You've had a shock," K.C. said. "And you really are jet-lagged. It would be a good idea if you just let things lie for a few days."

"You think?"

"Rourke," he said hesitantly. "The story she told you was true," he began.

"What! You just said it wasn't…!"

K.C. pushed him back down on the sofa. "It was true, but it wasn't Tat's mother." He turned away. "It was your mother."

There was a terrible stillness in the room.

K.C. moved to the window and stared out at the African darkness with his hands in his pockets.

"I got drunk because Mary Luke Bernadette chose a veil instead of me. I loved her, deathlessly. It's why I never married. She's still alive and, God help me, I still love her. She lives near my godchild, her late sister's only living child. I told you about Kasie, she married into the Callister family in Montana. Mary Luke lives in Billings."

"I remember," Rourke said quietly.

He closed his eyes. "Your mother saw what I was doing to myself. She tried to comfort me. She had a few drinks with me and things…happened. She was ashamed, I was ashamed…her husband was the best friend I ever had. How could we tell him what we'd done? So we kept our secret, tormented ourselves with what happened in a minute of insanity. Nine months later, to the day, you were born."

"You said…you weren't sure," Rourke bit off.

"I wasn't. I'm not. I don't have the guts to have the test done." He turned, a tiger, bristling. "Go ahead. Laugh!"

Rourke got up, a little shakily. It had been a shocking night. "Why don't you have the guts?" he asked.

"Because I want it to be true," he said through his teeth. He looked at Rourke with pain in his light eyes, terrible pain. "I betrayed my best friend, seduced your mother. I deserve every damned terrible thing that ever happens to me. But more than anything in the world, I want to be your father."

Rourke felt the wetness in his eyes, but this time he didn't hide it.

K.C. jerked him into his arms and hugged him, and hugged him. His eyes were wet, too. Rourke clung to him. All the long years, all the companionship, the shared moments. He'd wanted it, too. There wasn't a man alive who compared to the one holding him. He respected him. But, more, he loved him.

K.C. pulled back abruptly and turned away, shaking his head to get rid of the moisture in his eyes. He shoved his hands back into his slacks.

"Don't we have a doctor on staff?" Rourke asked after a minute.

"Ya."

"Then let's find out for sure," Rourke said.

K.C. turned after a minute, looking at the face that was his face, the elegant carriage that he knew from his own mirror.

"Are you sure?"

"Yes," Rourke said. "And so are you."

K.C. cocked his head and grimaced as he looked at Rourke's face.

"What?"

"You're going to have a hell of a bruise," K.C. said with obvious regret.

Rourke just smiled sheepishly. "No problem. It's not a bad thing to discover that your old man can still handle himself," he chuckled.

K.C. glowed.

CHAPTER TWO

ROURKE SPENT THE night getting drunk. He was out of his mind from his father's revelations. Tat had loved him. He'd pushed her away, for her own good, but in doing so, he'd damaged her so badly that he'd turned her into little better than a call girl.

He remembered her in Barrera, her blouse soaked in blood that even a washing hadn't removed, the stitches just above one of her perfect small breasts where that animal, Miguel, had cut her trying to extract information about General Emilio Machado's invasion of the country.

Rourke had killed Miguel. He'd done it coldly, efficiently. Then he and Carson, a fellow merc in the group that helped Machado liberate Barrera, had carried the body to a river filled with crocodiles and tossed it in. He hadn't felt a twinge of remorse. The man had tortured Tat. He would probably have raped her if another of Arturo Sapara's men hadn't intervened. Tat, with scars like the ones he carried, with memories of torture. He closed his eyes and shuddered. He'd protected her most of her life. But he'd let that happen to her. It was almost beyond bearing.

He got up, nude, and poured himself another whiskey. He almost never drank hard liquor, but it wasn't every day that a man faced the ruin of his own life.

He'd been protecting Tat from a relationship that was impossible, because he'd been told that there was blood between them, that Tat was really his half sister. And it was a lie.

He'd never even questioned her mother's revelation. He'd never dreamed that the religious, upright Mrs. Maria Carrington would lie to him. She loved Tat, though. Loved her dearly, deeply, possibly even more than she loved Matilda, her second child. The woman had been a pillar of the local church, never missing Mass, always there when anyone needed help, quick with a check when charity was required. She was almost a saint.

So when she told him that K.C. had seduced her in a drunken stupor, he'd believed her. Because he believed her, he pushed Tat away, taunted her, humiliated her, made her hate him. Or tried to.

But she wouldn't hate him. Perhaps she couldn't. He put the whiskey glass against his forehead, the cold ice comforting somehow. When he'd gone with the others to invade the capital in Barrera, Tat had pulled him to one side and linked the cross she always wore around his neck, asking him to wear it for luck. The gesture had hurt him. He wanted to pull her against him, bury his hard mouth in hers, let her feel the anguish of his arousal, show her how much he wanted her, needed her, cared for her. But that was impossible. They were too closely related. So he'd worn the necklace, but when he'd given it back, he was deliberately cold, impersonal.

When he'd left Barrera, what he'd said to her had shuttered her face, made her turn away, hurting. He'd hurt her more with his venomous comments at the airport in Johannesburg after he'd taken her out of Ngawa.

And that, all that, was for nothing. Because there was no blood between them. Because her mother had lied. Damn her mother!

He barely resisted the urge to slam the glass of whiskey through his bedroom window. That would arouse all the animals in the park, terrify the workers. It would bring back memories of another night when he got drunk, the night after Maria Carrington's revelation. He'd gone on a week-long bender. He'd trashed bars, been in fights, outraged the small community near Nairobi where he lived. Even K.C. hadn't been able to calm him, or get near him. Rourke in a temper was even worse than K.C. They'd stood back and let him get it out of his system.

Except that it wasn't out. It would never be out. He finished off the whiskey and put the glass down on the bureau. The tinkle of ice against glass was loud in the quiet room. Outside a lion roared softly. He smiled sadly. He'd raised the lion from a cub. It would let him do anything with it. When he was home, it followed him around like a small puppy. But let anyone else approach him, and it became dangerous. K.C. had said he needed to give it to a zoo, but Rourke refused. He had so few amusements. The lion was his friend. There had been two of them, but a fellow game park owner had wanted it so desperately that Rourke had given it to him. Now he had just the one. He called it Lou—a play on words from the Afrikaans word for lion, *leeu*.

He closed his eyes and drew in a long breath. Tat would never forgive him. He didn't even know how to approach her. He imagined Tat's mouth under his, her soft body pressed to his hardness, her hands in his thick hair as he loved her on crisp, white sheets. He groaned aloud at the arousal the images produced.

And just as quickly as they flashed through his mind, he knew how impossible they were. He'd spent eight years pushing her away, making her hate him. He wasn't going to be able to walk into her home and pick her up in his arms. She'd never let him close enough. She backed away now if he even approached her.

He thought of her with other men, with the scores of them he'd accused her of sleeping with. His fault. It was his fault. Tat would never have let another man touch her if she'd ever really belonged to Rourke; he knew that instinctively. But he'd pushed her into affairs. Her name had been linked with several millionaires, even a congressman. He'd seen photos of her in the media, seen her laughing up into other men's faces, her body exquisite in couture gowns. He'd pretended that she was only playacting. But she wasn't. She was twenty-five years old. No woman remained a virgin at that age. Certainly not Tat, whom he'd baited and tormented and rejected and humiliated.

But he had to get near her. He had to know if there was any slight chance that she might not hate him, that he could coax her back into his life. She'd never let him in the door in Maryland, where her home in the US was located. She had security cameras—he'd insisted on them—placed all around the house she owned there, the house that had belonged to her father.

Tat's father had worked for the US Embassy. His people had been wealthy beyond the dreams of avarice. He'd married Maria Cortes of Manaus, a woman who had Dutch and highborn Spanish heritage who was also an heiress. It had been a marriage of true love. They had houses in Africa and Manaus and Maryland. Tat had inherited the lot, and their combined fortunes. Tat had loved her mother. It had devastated her when Maria died of a fever she caught nursing a friend.

He knew how Tat revered her mother. How could he tell her what the woman had done? It would shatter her illusions. But he would have to tell her something, to try and explain his behavior.

How to get near her, near enough to make her listen, that was the problem. His eye fell on an invitation on top of the stack of mail one of the workers had left on the bureau for him to go through. He frowned.

He picked it up and opened it. Inside was a formal invitation to a gala awards ceremony in Barrera. It was a personal invitation from General Machado himself. Now that his country was secure once more, all the loose ends tied up, it was time to reward the people who had helped him wrest control away from the usurper, Sapara. Machado hoped that Rourke could come, because he was one of several people who would be so honored. He went down the list of names on the engraved invitation listing the honorees. Just above his name was that of Clarisse Carrington.

His heart jumped. Machado had promised that she would be recognized for her bravery in leading two captured college professors to safety and giving the insurgents intel that helped them recapture Barrera's capital city and apprehend Sapara.

Tat was going to be in Barrera, in Medina, the capital city. She would certainly go to the awards ceremony. It was a neutral place, where he might have the

opportunity to mend fences. Certainly he was going
to go. The date was a week away.

He took the invitation back to bed with him, scan-
ning it once more. Tat would be in Medina. He put the
invitation on the bedside table and stretched out, his
hands behind his head, his body arching softly as it
relived the exquisite memory of Tat half-naked in his
arms, so many years ago, moaning as he touched her
soft breasts and made the pretty pink nipples go hard
as little rocks.

The memories aroused him and he moaned. Tat in
his arms again. He could hold her, kiss her, touch her,
have her. He shuddered. It would take time and patience, much patience, but he had a reason to live now.
It was the first time in years that he felt happy.

Not that she was going to welcome him with open
arms. And there was the matter of her lovers, and there
had to have been many.

But that didn't matter, he told himself firmly, as
long as he was her last lover. He'd bring her here, to
the game park. They could live together…

No. His expression was grim. Despite her diver-
sions, Tat was still religious. She would never con-
sent to live with him unless he made a commitment.
A real one.

He got up from the bed and went to the wall safe.
He opened it and took out a small gray box. He opened
it. His hand touched the ring with tenderness. It had
belonged to his mother. It was a square-cut emerald,
surrounded by small diamonds, in a yellow gold setting. Tat loved yellow gold. It was all she wore.

He closed the case, relocked the safe and tucked the
ring into the pocket of a suit in the closet. He would

take it with him. Tat wasn't getting away this time, he promised himself. He was going to do whatever it took to get her back into his life.

He lay back down and turned out the lights. For the first time in years, he slept through the night.

THREE DAYS LATER, K.C. came into the living room, where Rourke was making airline reservations on a laptop computer.

"You're going to Barrera, then?" K.C. asked.

Rourke grinned. "You'd better believe it," he chuckled. "I've got my mother's engagement ring packed. This time, Tat's not getting away."

K.C. sighed and smiled tenderly. "I can't think of any woman in the world I'd rather have for a daughter-in-law, Stanton."

Something in the way he said it caught Rourke's attention. He finished the ticket purchase, printed out the ticket and turned toward the other man.

"Something up?" he asked.

K.C. moved closer. He was looking at the younger man with pride. He smiled. "I knew all along. But the doctor just phoned."

Rourke's heart skipped. "And...?"

K.C. looked proud, embarrassed, happy. "You really are my son."

"Damn!" Rourke started laughing. The joy in his eyes matched the happiness in his father's.

K.C. just stared at him for a minute. Then he jerked the other man into his arms and hugged him. Rourke hugged him back.

"I'm sorry...about the way it happened," K.C. said heavily, drawing back. "But not about the result." He searched Rourke's face. "My son." He bit down on a surge of emotion. "I've got a son."

Rourke was fighting the same emotion. He managed a smile. "Ya."

K.C. put a hand on Rourke's shoulder. "Listen, it's your decision. I'll do whatever you want. I was your legal guardian when you were underage. But I would like to formally adopt you. I would like you to have my name."

Rourke thought about the man who'd been his father, who'd raised him. Bill Rourke had loved him, although he must have certainly thought that Rourke didn't favor him. Bill had been dark-haired and dark-eyed. The man he'd called his real father had been good to him, even if there hadn't been the sort of easy affection he'd always felt for K.C.

"It was just a thought," K.C. said, hesitating now.

"I would...like that very much," Rourke said. "I'll keep my foster father's name. I'll just add yours to it."

K.C. smiled sadly. "Your father was my best friend. It tormented me to think what I did to him, to your mother. To you."

"I think it tormented her, too," Rourke said.

"It did. She loved me." His face hardened. "That was the worst of it. I had nothing to give her. Nothing at all. She knew it."

Rourke's one good eye searched his father's. "Nobody's perfect," he said quietly. "I have to confess, I wished even when I was a boy that you were my real father." He averted his eye just in time to miss the wetness in K.C.'s. "You were always in the thick of battles. You could tell some stories about the adventures you had. I wanted so badly to be like you."

"You're very like me," K.C. said huskily. "I worried about letting you work for the organization. I wanted to protect you." He laughed. "It wasn't possible. You took to it like a duck to water. But I sweated blood when you left me and went with the CIA." He shook his head. "I agonized that I'd let you get US citizenship, even though you kept your first citizenship."

"It was something I wanted to do." Rourke shrugged. "I can't live without the adrenaline rushes." His good eye twinkled. "I must get that from my old man."

K.C. chuckled. "Probably. I still go on missions. I just don't go on as many, and I'm mostly administrative now. You'll learn as you age that your reaction time starts to drop. That can put your unit in danger, compromise missions."

Rourke nodded. "I've had so many close calls that I've been tempted to think about administrative tasks myself. But not yet," he added with a grin. "And right now, I have another priority. I want to get married."

K.C. smiled warmly. "She's really beautiful. And she has a kind heart. That's more important than surface details."

Rourke nodded. His face hardened. "It's just, the idea of those other men…"

"You've had women," K.C. replied quietly. "How is that different?"

Rourke looked vaguely disturbed. He turned away with a sigh. "Not so very, I suppose."

"Tell Emilio hello for me," K.C. said. "I knew him, a long time ago. Always liked the man. He's not what you expect of a revolutionary."

Rourke chuckled. "Not at all. He could make a fortune as a recording artist if he ever got tired of being President of Barrera. He can sing."

"Indeed he can."

Rourke turned at the door and looked back at the man who was the living image of what he'd be, in a few years.

He smiled. "When I get back, maybe you could take me to a ball game or something."

K.C. picked up a chair cushion and threw it at him. "Get stuffed."

Rourke just laughed. He picked up the cushion and tossed it back.

"You be careful over there," K.C. added. "Sapara has friends, and he's slippery. If he ever gets out of prison, you could be in trouble. He's vindictive."

"He won't get out," was the reply. "Just the same, it's nice that my old man worries about me," he added.

K.C. beamed. "Yes, he does. So don't get yourself killed."

"I won't. Make sure you do the same."

K.C. shrugged. "I'm invincible. I spent years as a merc and I've still got most of my original body parts." He made a face as he moved his shoulder. "Some of them aren't up to factory standards anymore, but I get by."

Rourke grinned. "Same here." He searched K.C.'s hard face. "When?"

"When, what?"

"When do you want to do the paperwork?"

"Oh. The name change. Why not get it started to-morrow? Unless you're leaving for Barrera early?"

"Not until Thursday," Rourke replied. His face soft-ened. "I'd like that."

K.C. nodded.

Rourke went back to his room to start packing.

THE PAPERWORK WAS UNCOMPLICATED. The attorney was laughing like a pirate.

"I knew," he said, glancing from one to the other. "It was so damned obvious. But I knew better than to mention it. Your old man," he added, to Rourke, "packs a hell of a punch."

Rourke fingered his jaw, where there was only a faint yellow bruise to remind him of his father's anger when he'd accused him of being Tat's real parent. "Tell me about it," he laughed.

K.C. managed a bare smile. "I need to have a few classes in anger management, I guess," he sighed.

"No, Dad," Rourke said without realizing what he'd said, "you'll do fine the way you are. A temper's not a bad thing."

K.C. was beaming. Rourke realized then what he'd said and his brown eye twinkled.

"Nice, the way that sounds, son," K.C. said, and his chest swelled with pride.

"Very nice."

"Well, I'll have this wrapped up in no time," the attorney told the two men. "You can check back with me in a few days."

"I'll do that," K.C. said.

ROURKE WALKED OUT the door of his house with a suit-case and a suit bag, in which he had a dinner jacket, slacks, shirt and tie. He was going to look the best he could. He was so excited about the day to come that he hadn't slept. Tat would be there. He'd see her again,

but not in the same way he'd seen her for eight long
years. Tomorrow night was going to be the best of his
life. He could hardly wait.

THE FLIGHT TO Barrera was long and tedious. Rourke
caught the plane at the Jomo Kenyatta International
Airport in Nairobi. It was sixteen hours and eight minutes to the Eduardo Gomes International Airport in
Manaus. He tried to sleep for most of the flight, only
fortifying himself with food and champagne in between. He was impatient. He had to conduct this like
a battle campaign, he thought. Tat wasn't going to be
welcoming, and he couldn't blame her. He'd spent years
tormenting her.

Finally the plane landed. The tropical heat hit him
in the face like a wet towel, and it was something he
wasn't accustomed to. Kenya was mild year-round.

He went through passport control and customs, with
only the carry-on bag and his suit bag. He always traveled light. He hated the time spent waiting for luggage
at baggage claim. Much easier to travel with only the
essentials and buy what he needed when he arrived.
He didn't advertise it, but he was quite wealthy. The
game park kept him in ready cash, from tourism. Not
to mention what he'd made for years as a professional
soldier, risking his life in dangerous places. It was wonderful that K.C. was his father, but Rourke didn't need
his father's financial support. He'd made his own way
in the world for a long time.

He walked through baggage claim and looked for
the appropriate sign, which would be held up by a limo
driver he'd hired from Nairobi on his cell phone. He
could easily afford the fees and he hated cabs.

The man spotted him and grinned. Rourke, dressed in khakis, tall and blond and striking, with the long ponytail down his back could never be mistaken for anyone except who he was. He looked the part of an African game park owner.

He smiled as he approached the man.

"Senhor Rourke?" the small dark man asked with a big grin.

Rourke chuckled. "What gave me away?" he asked.

"You do not remember?" the little man asked, and seemed crushed.

Rourke had an uncanny memory. He stared at the man for a minute, closed his eye, smiled and came up with a name. "Rodrigues," he chuckled. "You chauffeured me around the last time I was in Manaus, just after the Barrera offensive. You have two daughters."

The man seemed to be awash in pleasure. "Oh, yes, that is me, but, please, you must call me Domingo," he added, wringing Rourke's hand. Imagine, a rich cosmopolitan man like this remembering his name!

"Domingo, then." He drew in a breath. Jet lag was getting to him. "I think I need to get a hotel room for the night. I'm flying out to Barrera in the morning. General Machado is having an awards ceremony."

"Sim." The man nodded as he climbed in under the wheel. "Several people are to be honored for their part in overthrowing that rat, Arturo Sapara," he added. "My cousins were tortured in Sapara's prison. I danced with joy when he was arrested."

"So did I, mate," Rourke replied solemnly.

"One lady from Manaus is to be awarded a medal," Domingo said with a smile. "Senhorita Carrington. I knew her mother. Such a saintly lady," he added.

"Saintly," Rourke said, almost grinding his teeth as Domingo pulled out in traffic.

"Creio que sim," Domingo replied, nodding. "She was kind. So kind. It was a tragedy what happened to her husband and her youngest daughter, Matilda," he added.

Rourke drew in a long breath. "That was truly a tragedy."

"You know of it?" Domingo asked.

"Yes. I've known Tat... Clarisse," he corrected, "since she was eight years old."

"The *senhorita* is a good woman," Domingo said solemnly. "When she was younger, she never missed Mass. She was so kind to other people." His face hardened. "What that butcher did to her was unthinkable. He was killed," he added coldly. "I was glad. To hurt someone so beautiful, so kind..."

"How do you know her?" Rourke asked.

"When my little girl was diagnosed with lymphoma, it was Senhorita Carrington who made arrangements for her to go for treatment at the Mayo Clinic. It is in the United States. She paid for everything. Everything! I thought I must bury my daughter, but she stepped in." Tears clouded his eyes. He wiped them away, unashamed. "My wife and I, we would do anything for her."

Rourke was touched. He knew Clarisse had a kind heart, and here was even more proof of it.

"You will see Senhorita Carrington in Barrera, yes?" Domingo asked with a wise smile.

Rourke nodded. "Yes, I will."

"Please, you tell her that Domingo remembers her

and he and his family pray for her every single day, yes?"

"I'll tell her."

Domingo nodded. He pulled up at the best hotel in Manaus and stopped. "What time shall I come for you tomorrow, *senhor*?"

"About six," Rourke said. "I've got a ticket for the connecting flight to Medina." He yawned and signed the slip Domingo handed him, retrieving his credit card and sliding it back into his expensive wallet.

"Sleep well," Domingo said as he carried the bags to the bellboy's station inside the luxury hotel.

"Thanks. I think I will."

ROURKE HAD STRANGE DREAMS. He woke sweating, worried. There had been a battle. He was wounded. Tat was standing far away, crying. Tears ran down her cheeks, but not tears of joy. Her face was tormented, the way it had looked at their last meeting. She was pregnant…!

He got up and made coffee in the small pot furnished by the hotel. It was four in the morning. No sense in going back to bed. He swept back his hair, disheveled from the pillow. He took off the hair elastic and let his hair fall down his back.

Absently, while the coffee was brewing, he ran a brush through it. Probably he should have it cut completely off, he was thinking as he looked at himself in the mirror. He'd worn it that way for years, partly out of nonconformity, partly because he shared some beliefs with ancient cultures that there was good medicine in long hair. He'd been superstitious about cutting it. But he looked like a renegade, and he didn't want to. Not tonight. He was going hunting, for lovely prey.

Perhaps cutting his hair might show Tat that he was changing. That he was different.

HE POSTPONED HIS flight for five hours and had Domingo take him to an exclusive hair salon. He had his hair cut and styled. He was impressed with the results. It had a natural wave, which fell out when his hair was halfway down his back. The wave was prominent. The cut made him look distinguished, debonair. It also made him look amazingly like K.C., he thought, and chuckled as he studied himself in the mirror.

Domingo raised both eyebrows when he walked out of the salon.

"You look very different," he said.

Rourke nodded.

Domingo smiled, but it wasn't a happy smile. He opened the door of the limo for Rourke, and then climbed in under the wheel.

"What's bugging you?" Rourke teased.

"It is that you have cut your hair," he remarked. He laughed self-consciously. "I'm sorry."

"You think I've damaged my 'medicine,'" Rourke said with pursed lips and a twinkling eye.

Domingo flushed over his high cheekbones. "I am a superstitious man. What can I say? But you are a modern man, *senhor*," he laughed. "You do not believe in such things, I am sure. Now we go to the airport, yes?"

Rourke was feeling something similar to Domingo's apprehension as he ran a hand through his short, thick hair. In all the years he'd been a merc, there had been precious few close calls. He'd been shot a few times, never anything serious, except for the loss of his eye. He'd always felt that his hair had something to do with that. It was a primitive superstition, though. He was sure he was just being dumb.

"Yes, Domingo," he said, and smiled. "To the airport. I have a busy day ahead." And a busier night, he was hoping, if he could coax Clarisse into bed with him.

His hand felt in his pocket for the ring. It was still there. He knew she wasn't going to be easy to convince, especially about the bed thing. But he had an ace in the hole. He was going to propose first.

He hoped he wasn't going to have to go back to Nairobi alone. But, then, whatever it took, he was going to do it. If he had to follow her back to Manaus and court her like a schoolboy, he would. He was never going to let her get away from him. Never.

MEDINA, BARRERA'S CAPITAL, was like most other South American cities, cosmopolitan and remote at the same time. The people were a mixture of races, and the official language was Spanish.

There was a regional airport and a bus terminal. There were no limousines here. Not yet. The general was only beginning to repair the damage to the infrastructure that Sapara had caused. The usurper had done a lot of damage during the time he'd been in power. Most of the money had gone into his own pockets and he'd spent lavishly on himself. The presidential mansion was worth many millions. Machado had wanted to tear it down, but the grateful populace, much of which he'd rescued from Sapara's prisons, wouldn't hear of it. Powerful foreigners would come here to help rebuild the country, one of his advisers had said.

A luxurious presidential residence would reinforce the notion that Barrera was worth aid.

He didn't agree at first, but he finally gave in. If he demolished it, he'd have to spend the money to rebuild it. He did, however, have all the solid gold fixtures that Sapara had imported melted down and minted. That had earned him much praise, especially in light of the social programs he'd implemented to give free health care to the poor. Machado was a good man.

Rourke checked into the only luxury hotel in the city. He wondered if Tat would be staying here, too. He hoped so.

He put his suitcase down and unpacked his dinner jacket. He smiled as he thought of the evening ahead. It was going to be the best night of his life.

FIVE DOORS AND a floor away, Clarisse Carrington was looking at the dark circles under her eyes as she thought about the night to come. Rourke's name was on the list of honorees, but she was certain that he wouldn't show up. He hated society bashes, and he was a modest man. He wouldn't be interested in having people make him out to be a hero, even though he was one.

Clarisse had hero-worshipped him from the age of eight, admired his courage, loved him to the point of madness. But Stanton Rourke hated her. He'd made it crystal clear for years, even without the horrible things he'd said to her when he got her out of Ngawa.

He was never going to love her. She knew that. But she couldn't help the way she felt about him. It seemed to be a disease without a cure.

She studied her face in the mirror. The bullet wound

had left evidence of its passage in her scalp, but a little careful hair-combing hid it well. The scars on her left breast were less easy to camouflage. Sapara's henchman, Miguel, had put a knife into her, over and over again while trying to make her tell about General Machado's offensive. She hadn't talked. That was why she was getting a medal tonight. For bravery. Because she'd survived the torture and rescued not only herself, but two college professors, as well. They said she was a heroine. She laughed without humor. Sure.

She was standing there in a long slip. It would go under the elegant white gown she'd bought from a boutique for the event. It had simple lines. It fell to her ankles. The bodice wasn't even suggestive. It was high enough to cover the scars on her breast. It had puff sleeves that reminded her somehow of a gown she'd seen in a period movie about the Napoleonic era. She looked good in white.

She thought how Stanton would have laughed to see her in the color. He would think it should be scarlet. He thought she was little better than a call girl. That was ironic, and it would have been amusing except that it was tragic.

She'd never been with a man in her life. She'd never been intimate with anyone, except Stanton, one Christmas Eve long ago, when she was seventeen. She'd loved him then and every day since, despite his antagonism, his mockery, his taunting.

She knew he hated her. He'd made it obvious. It didn't seem to make any difference, though. She couldn't get him out of her mind, any more than she could permit any other man to touch her.

She'd made a play for Grange, the leader of Mach-

ado's insurgent troops. But that had been an act of
desperation, and mainly due to antianxiety drugs that
she'd taken after the tragic deaths of her father and
her little sister, Matilda. Her life had been shattered.

Rourke had come running, the minute he heard
about it. He'd handled the funeral arrangements, organized the service, done everything for her while she
walked around numb and brokenhearted. He'd put her
to bed, holding her while she sobbed out her heart. He'd
called a doctor, her doctor, Ruy Carvajal, and had him
sedate her when the crying didn't stop.

She thought of Ruy and a question he'd asked her
before she came here. She'd invited him to come, too,
just on the chance that Rourke might show up. He'd
had to go to Argentina, to treat a longtime patient
who was also a friend. But he'd asked her to consider
marrying him; a marriage of friends, nothing more.
He knew how she felt about Rourke, that she couldn't
permit another man to touch her. It wouldn't matter,
he assured her, because he'd been badly wounded in
a firefight on a mission with the World Health Organization. Because of the wounds, he could no longer
father a child. He was, he added solemnly, no longer
a man, either. He was unable to be intimate with a
woman. This had led to many suspicions among his
people, who revered a man's ability to beget children
above all other attributes.

He would be happy to put an end to the gossip. He
could give Clarisse a good life. If she was certain, he
added, that Rourke would never want her.

She told him that she'd consider it, and she had.
Rourke didn't want her. She couldn't want anyone else.
She was twenty-five, and Ruy was kind to her. Why

not? It would give her some stability. She would have a friend, someone of her own.

It sounded like a good idea. She thought she might do it. It might sound like an empty life to some people. But to Clarisse, whose life had been an endless series of tragedies, the prospect of a peaceful life was enticing. She didn't need sex. After all, she'd never had it. How could she miss something she'd never experienced?

She mourned Rourke, but that would end one day, she thought. She gave her reflection a grim smile. Sure it would. When she died. She turned and went to put on her gown for the gala evening.

CHAPTER THREE

CLARISSE WALKED INTO the building where the awards were being held, and several pair of male eyes went immediately to her slender, beautiful figure in the clinging white dress she wore. Her blond hair curled toward her face like feathers, emphasizing her exquisite bone structure, her perfect skin and teeth, her wide blue eyes. She was a beauty. In the gown, she looked like some Grecian goddess come down to earth to taunt mortals.

She didn't even notice the attention she was getting. Her eyes were on the podium where the general would speak. There was an orchestra. It was playing soft, easy-listening sort of music while people gathered in small groups to converse. Most of the conversation was in Spanish here, not Portuguese, because Spanish was Barrera's official language.

She smiled sadly at the little cliques. To Clarisse, who was always alone, it seemed like just one more gathering where she'd stand by herself while men tried to entice her. Sometimes she hated the way she looked. She didn't want male attention.

She paused by a table where drinks were being served when her arm was taken by a tall man she recognized as one of General Machado's advisers. He smiled at her. "We were hoping that you would come,

Miss Carrington," he said in softly accented English. "We have the other honorees backstage. The awards ceremony will be first, followed by dancing and drinking and utter pandemonium." He chuckled.

She smiled up at him. "The pandemonium sounds nice. They shouldn't have done this for me," she added. "I didn't really do anything except get shot and captured."

He turned and smiled down at her. "You did a great deal more than that. All of us who live here are grateful to you and the others, for giving us back our country."

"Are Peg and Winslow here?" she asked hopefully.

"Alas, no," he replied solemnly. "Her father had to have surgery, just a minor thing, but they were both uncomfortable with the idea of not going to sit with him."

"That's like Peg," she said softly, and smiled. "She's such a sweet person."

"She thinks quite highly of you, as well, as does her husband. And El General, of course," he added with a chuckle.

"Where is the general?" she wondered.

He nodded his head toward where a tall, distinguished Latin man in a dinner jacket towered over a tall brunette in a striking blue gown.

"It's Maddie!" she exclaimed. "She treated Eduardo Boas, who was shot before I was kidnapped."

"Yes. She and the general are, I believe, getting married soon," he whispered, laughing at her delighted smile. "But you must not mention this. I am not supposed to know."

She smiled up at him. "I know absolutely nothing. I swear," she added facetiously.

"Not true, Tat. You're plenty smart enough," came a deep, husky voice from behind her.

Her blood froze. Her heart started doing the tango. She didn't want to turn around. She hadn't dreamed that he'd show up.

"Señor Rourke will escort you to where the others are gathered backstage," he said, nodding and bowing. Then he deserted her.

"Aren't you going to turn around, Tat?" he asked very softly.

She took a deep breath and faced him. He looked different. She couldn't understand why at first. Then she realized it was because his hair was short. He'd cut his hair. She wondered why. It had been in that long ponytail for years.

"Hello, Stanton," she said quietly. "I didn't expect you to be here."

He looked down at her intently, his one eye narrowed and piercing as he drank in the sight of her, the memory of her in his arms making his heart race. There were no more barriers. He could have her. He could hold her and kiss her. He could make love to her...

He shook himself mentally. He had to go slow. "I was at a loose end," he said carelessly.

"I see." She was uneasy. She kept looking around, as if she wanted to be rescued. In fact, she did.

He looked around, too. "Did you come alone?" he asked suddenly, and there was a bite in his voice.

She swallowed. "I'd asked Ruy to come with me, but he had to fly to Argentina to treat an old friend."

"Ruy... Carvajal, your doctor friend."

"That's right."

He scowled. "You aren't dating him, for God's sake?" he asked curtly. "My God, Tat, he's twenty years your senior!"

She couldn't meet his eyes. "He's older than I am, yes."

He felt his muscles tighten from head to toe. She couldn't be getting involved with the doctor. Surely not!

His silence coaxed her into looking up. His expression confounded her. In another man, it would look like jealousy. But Rourke would never be jealous of her. He hated her.

She moved restlessly. "We should go backstage."

"Are you going to be here overnight?" he asked as they walked.

"I fly back to Manaus in the morning," she replied.

"I'm here overnight, as well."

She didn't say anything. She knew that he was going to avoid her like the plague, as usual.

"Which hotel are you staying in?" he asked abruptly.

"Why? Do you want to make sure you can get one at least half the city away from it?" she burst out.

He stopped dead. "I've got a lot to make up to you," he said solemnly. "I don't even know where to start. I've done so much damage, Tat," he added in a husky tone. "Far too much."

She looked up at him, shocked.

He reached out toward her face, only to have her jerk back from him and avert her eyes.

It hurt more than he'd ever dreamed anything could.

"Tat," he whispered roughly, wounded.

"Don't you remember?" she bit off. "You told me… never to touch you. You said that I was repulsive…"

Her voice broke. She walked around him and moved blindly to the back, where a man in a suit was motioning to them to get with the other honorees. She didn't look to see if Rourke was coming behind her. She didn't want to see him.

He followed her, his heart torn out of his body at her words. Yes, he'd told her that; he'd been brutal with her. How could he have forgotten? He'd hurt her so badly. Now, after years of tormenting her and himself, he finally had a chance to start over with her. But judging by what she'd just said, it was going to be a very hard road back.

THE AWARD CEREMONY was lengthy. General Machado made a speech. His director of the interior made a longer one. The presenter made an even longer one. By the end of it, Clarisse's feet hurt. She was glad she was wearing low-heeled shoes.

One by one, the honorees went out to receive their awards, made a short speech and shook hands with the general. Clarisse did the same, smiling up at him as he bent to kiss her cheek, the medal in its velvet case held tightly in one hand.

"Thank you for coming," he whispered in her ear.

"Thank you for inviting me," she whispered back.

She shook hands with him and carried her award off the stage.

She waited while the others received their medals. Rourke joined her, somber and quiet. He hadn't liked the general kissing her. He was fuming inside.

Clarisse saw his expression and felt her heart sink. He was angry at her again. It was familiar, though. Nothing really changed, least of all Rourke's bad opinion.

SHE LEFT HER award with her coat in the cloakroom and nursed a rum drink. She'd already refused half a dozen requests to dance. She bristled at the thought of strange hands on her skin, and the dress was low cut in back. So she stood by herself, watching other people enjoy the music on the dance floor.

She felt heat at her back and stiffened. She always knew when Rourke was close. She wasn't sure how. It was rather uncanny. She turned, her whole posture defensive.

"You've never danced with me, Tat," he said, his voice deep and velvety as he drank in the exquisite sight of her.

She sipped the rum, for something to do. "Have you had all your shots?" she asked with quiet sarcasm.

There was a pause. He drew in a breath. "How about a truce, just for tonight?"

She studied him with apprehension, her face wary, her eyes wide and worried.

"I won't hurt you," he said. His face was taut, and not with revulsion. He looked as if he was hanging in midair, waiting for her to answer. At his side, his big hands were curled into fists. "Just for tonight," he repeated in a voice so soft that she had to strain to hear it.

He'd tormented her for so long. The pain, the memories, were in her wide blue eyes, in her sadness. She bit her lower lip, hard, and twisted her small evening bag into an unrecognizable shape in her cold hands.

He moved a step closer, so that he was almost right up against her. His breath caught as he breathed in the floral perfume she wore, just a hint of it. His hands came up, very slowly, and went to her waist. He was hesitant.

"Trust me," he said at her forehead. "Just this once."

"You don't like me to touch you," she managed in a choked tone.

His eye closed on a wave of pain. "I lied." He looked down into her shocked face. "I lied, Tat," he whispered. "I want your hands on me. I want you close, as close as I can get you." He drew in an unsteady breath. "Humor me."

She hesitated. It would start the addiction off, all over again, just when she was thinking that she could finally get over him.

"Come on." He took the drink from her cold hands and put it on the table. Then he caught the other small hand in his, linking his fingers into hers, and led her into the large room where the orchestra was playing. Couples were moving slowly to a bluesy tune.

He turned and curved one long arm around her waist. He slid his fingers in between hers and rested them over his spotless white shirt. He moved closer and led her, to the rhythm of the music. He could hear her breath catch, feel the tenseness in her young body slowly give way to the seduction of the slow movements.

"That's more like it," he said roughly at her temple.

She thought she felt his mouth there. Surely he wouldn't do that, though, she reminded herself. She should pull away. She should run. He was going to hurt her. This was the way it always was. He was kind, or seemed to be. Then he pushed her away, taunted her, tormented her...

She pulled back and looked up at him with anguish in her face.

"No," he whispered, wincing as he read the apprehension there. "I meant it. I swear to God, I won't hurt you, Tat. Not with words, not any other way. I give you my word."

That was serious business with him. If he made a promise, you could bet money on his keeping it. She searched his hard face. "Why?"

He let out a breath from between chiseled, very masculine lips. His gaze went over her head to the wall beyond. "I...heard some gossip, years ago. Malicious gossip. Long story short, I thought we were related by blood."

She stopped dancing. She gaped at him. "Wh... what?" she asked, and started to jerk away from him.

His arm curled her into his tall, muscular body and held her there. "It wasn't true," he said. "I had it checked out. Your mother's blood type was O positive," he said through his teeth. "And your father's blood type was B positive. I'm AB Negative, like K.C. You're B positive." He hesitated. "I had a covert DNA scan done from a sample of your blood. Don't ask how I got it," he said when she opened her mouth. "I'm a spy. I have ways. I spoke to a geneticist. There is no way in hell we could be related. Not even in the most distant way."

She was standing very still. All of a sudden the past eight years made absolute sense. He'd behaved sometimes as if it was tormenting him to be near her, as if he wanted her but he wouldn't permit himself to touch her, or her to touch him.

The realization made her face change, made her expression change.

His jaw tautened as he looked down at her. "Oh, God, don't you think I wanted you, too?" he whispered in anguish. "Wanted you, ached for you, for years! And I couldn't... I didn't dare even touch you...!"

Tears welled up in her eyes. It was like dreams coming true. She couldn't believe it.

"Oh, baby," he whispered, and suddenly dragged her body against his, holding her. He started shivering, from the force of desire, so long denied.

She pulled back abruptly, her eyes horrified. "Are you all right, Stanton?" she asked at once. "You're shivering! It isn't the malaria recurring?" He'd had it years ago. She'd nursed him through one bout of it when she was a child, in Africa. She reached up hesitantly to touch his face. "You do feel a little warm..."

He was almost in shock. He was shivering with desire and she didn't know it. But she was experienced. She'd had men. How could she be ignorant of something so basic?

He scowled. Impulsively, his hand slid down to the base of her spine and pulled her very close, letting her feel the sharp, immediate arousal of his body.

She went scarlet and tried to get away from him, struggling to escape the intimate contact, which she'd only ever felt once, the Christmas Eve that she'd almost given in to his ardor. No man had been allowed to touch her that way since. It was still embarrassing.

Rourke felt as if Christmas had come. He let her move away, but his one good eye was brimming with joy, with exultation.

He bent his head a little, so that he was looking right into both of her eyes. "You're still a virgin, aren't you, Tat?" he asked in a rough whisper.

"Stan...ton!" she choked, and averted her eyes.

He slid his cheek against hers. He shivered again.

"I don't have malaria," he whispered. "That part of me is looking for a soft, warm, dark place to hide in."

It took her a minute to work that out. When she did she colored even more. She hit his chest. "Stanton!"

He laughed softly, with utter delight, nuzzling his face against hers. "You couldn't do it with anyone else, could you, Tat?" he teased.

And there it was. Assumptions. Arrogance. He knew how she felt. He'd said it would be a truce, but it really wasn't. He was moving in for the kill. Now that he knew what she really was, he'd never relent. He'd stalk her until he seduced her. He might sound pleasant; he might even sound as if he cared about her. But at the end of the day, he just wanted sex. He'd desired her for years, but thought he couldn't have her. Now he knew that he could. And it was true. She had no defense. Except one.

"Ruy asked me to marry him," she said quietly, without looking up at him.

He went very still. "What?"

She swallowed. "He may be much older than I am, but he's a good, kind man." She closed her eyes. "I said yes, Stanton," she lied. It was the only protection she could give herself from a one-night stand that she didn't want, couldn't bear. She loved him too much. "So if you're thinking in terms of a night in bed with me, think again. I won't cheat on my fiancé."

His whole world exploded. He stared at her with anguish that he couldn't even hide. He started to speak, but before he could get a word out, General Machado appeared beside them with Maddie beaming at his side.

"We are getting married," Machado said, laughing softly as Maddie actually blushed. "I wanted you both to know." He shrugged. "I am years too old for her, but what the hell. I love her." He looked at the pretty brunette with eyes that worshipped her.

"Almost as much as I love him," Maddie tried to joke, but her eyes were eating him.

"Congratulations," Rourke said, hiding his own misery. He shook hands with the general and kissed Maddie on the cheek. "I'm happy for both of you."

"So am I," Clarisse choked, repeating his gestures. "I hope you'll be so happy together."

"Same here," Rourke added.

They smiled, then laughed, then talk revolved around the awards and how they came to be. The general mentioned that his son, San Antonio police lieutenant Rick Marquez had wanted to come, but his wife was in the early stages of pregnancy and wasn't doing well; Rick couldn't bring her with him, or leave her, so he sent his regrets via Skype. The general and his son spoke often these days.

Rourke went through the motions of paying attention, but he was dying inside. He was too late. Tat had finally given up on him. She was going to marry the damned doctor in Manaus.

HE WANDERED AWAY. Tat noticed him dancing with a ravishing blonde, laughing down at her. She smiled sadly to herself. Why did she ever expect things to change? There was Rourke, being himself, coaxing women to his bed. She imagined the ravishing blonde would give him what Clarisse wouldn't, a single night of pleasure.

It disturbed her that he'd found a replacement so quickly. Well, what had she expected? That when he realized she wasn't a blood relation, he'd declare eternal love and produce a wedding ring? Fat chance of that ever happening. She'd had a lucky escape, because it wouldn't have been possible for her to refuse him. She loved him too much, despite everything.

She turned with a sad little smile and went out of the building, caught a cab and went back to her hotel room. It was just as well not to trust in dreams.

SHE WAS SLEEPING. She woke suddenly, just after an attack of some sort, bombs going off, a rifle shot. She was wet with sweat, even in the air-conditioned room. She still had nightmares from her ordeal in Barrera. The phone was ringing off the hook.

She answered the phone, noting that it was three o'clock in the morning. "Yes?" she asked, surprised at the call at this hour.

"Miss Carrington? It's O'Bailey. You remember me?"

She searched her memories. "You're the computer hacker. You were with us when General Machado led the counterrevolution."

"That's me, ma'am." He cleared his throat. "The general said you were here for the awards ceremony. I was, too, but I arrived late. I heard a commotion downstairs and when I looked in the bar, well, it's really bad. He's going to kill somebody or get himself arrested. That would really upset the general with all the international press here, and I thought..."

"He?" Clarisse asked.

"Rourke," he replied. "He's totally out of control. I've only ever seen him drunk a time or two, and he's dangerous when he drinks. Somebody has to get him out of there, or the general's policemen are going to arrest him and put him in jail." He hesitated. "There are reporters in the hotel, too. If one of them sees him…"

"Rourke is drunk?" She was dumbfounded. "O'Bailey, he doesn't drink hard liquor. Well, maybe he drinks, but he never has enough to make him lose control…"

"Ma'am, he just threw one of the bouncers through a glass window."

"Oh, good Lord!" she exclaimed.

"I was wondering if you could come down here and maybe talk to him."

She hesitated. She was afraid of Rourke in a temper.

"Ma'am, there's always one person that a drunk person can be controlled by. With my dad, it was my little sister. She could just lead him by the hand, when he'd kill another man for trying to make him stop drinking. I don't think Rourke would ever hurt you. But I'll be there if he tries to. Please?"

"Are you downstairs?" she asked.

"Yes, ma'am."

"I'll meet you in front of the bar." She hung up.

She put on slacks and a yellow pullover blouse. She didn't wait to make up her face. She met O'Bailey outside the lounge downstairs, where a vicious loud voice was cursing in Afrikaans. She winced.

"He'll listen to you," he said. "I know he will."

She gave O'Bailey a grim look. "I'll try," she said.

She walked into the bar. There was another man, one who looked about half as drunk as Rourke. He spotted her and got up, grinning from ear to ear.

"Well, look what a pretty little fairy just walked in

the door," the man exclaimed. He caught her by the arm and tried to pull her to him. "Precious, how about coming up to my room...?"

In an instant, Rourke had him by the throat. His one eye was dark with rage. "You touch her again and I'll kill you!" he said through his teeth. He threw the man backward. He fell over a table and picked himself up and ran out of the lounge, holding his throat.

"Stanton," Clarisse said softly.

He looked down at her. He was breathing roughly. He reeked of whiskey. He peered at her, frowning. "Why are you here, Tat?" he asked in almost a whisper.

"I came to get you." She slid her cold, nervous hand into his. He'd frightened her when he grabbed the man by the throat. But he didn't look violent at all now. "You have to come with me."

"Okay," he said easily.

She tugged on his hand. He let her lead him right out of the room, to where O'Bailey was waiting. She could hardly believe it. The bar was a wreck. Men, big men, were against the wall, behind tables, as if they were hoping Rourke wouldn't notice them. Grown men were afraid of him, but he was following along with Clarisse like a lamb.

"I'll talk to him. Is he staying at this hotel?" Clarisse asked the Irishman, grimacing as she noted the bartender just peering over the bar and looking hunted. "He'll pay for the damage," Clarisse said.

O'Bailey nodded. "Rourke's in room 306. I imagine the key's in his pocket."

"Thanks," she said.

"No, ma'am, thank you!" he replied, and she smiled.

He nodded, grinned, gave Rourke an apologetic smile and went into the lounge.

Rourke looked down at Tat. "Why are you here?" he asked angrily. "Won't your fiancé miss you?"

"He's in Argentina with a patient," she reminded him. "He won't be home for several weeks."

"What a tough break for him," he said, looking down at her with barely hidden hunger. "God, you're a knockout," he said huskily. "I ache just looking at you!"

She flushed. She turned and led him into the elevator. They rode up in silence to the third floor. He was watching her with unnerving intensity.

She led him to his door. "You need to get out the key card," she said.

He leaned against the door. "No."

"Stanton," she groaned.

"Once I open the door, you'll leave," he said heavily.

She nibbled her lower lip.

"I can always go back to the bar," he said cagily, shouldering away from the door frame.

"No!"

"Promise you'll stay with me until I fall asleep, then," he said, his voice only slightly slurred. "Give me your word, Tat."

She ground her teeth together. He wasn't quite in control of himself and she was afraid of him. Not of his temper, but that he might try to continue where they'd left off when she was seventeen. That had been a near thing. Not until she was in her twenties did she realize just how near.

"I won't...do anything you don't want," he promised.

She drew in a slow breath. "I'll hold you to that, Stanton."

He smiled. He drew out the card and pushed it into the lock. There was a click and a tiny green light went on. He pulled the card out and slipped it back into his pocket. He opened the door. "After you."

She walked into the room, a poem about spiders and flies teasing around the edge of her mind.

The room flooded with light as he touched a switch.

She turned to him. He looked harder than she'd ever seen him. His handsome face was tense with some powerful emotion as he stared down at her with his one good eye.

She looked back, wincing at the eye patch.

He misread the look. "Ya," he said coldly. "I'm disabled. That what you're thinking?"

"I was remembering when it happened," she said softly.

The tension grew worse. "I'd just…been told something that upended my life," he said evasively, avoiding her quiet gaze. "Like a rank beginner, I walked right into an ambush." He laughed coldly. "Lost an eye, took a bullet in the chest…" His eye cut back around to her face. "You were there, sitting by the bed when I came out from under the anesthesia."

"K.C. called me," she said. She lowered her eyes to his chest. "He was scared to death, and he didn't want to start gossip all over again by sitting with you. Nobody thought it unusual that I did. I knew most of the hospital staff in Nairobi."

He drew in a breath. He felt sick. Sweaty. "There was a lot of gossip after that."

"I never noticed. Neither did you."

He studied her downcast face. "As soon as the

stitches came out, I invited Anita out to the game farm
and sent you home to DC."

She bit her lip. "Yes."

He closed his eye, anguish in his whole body as he
recalled that act of cruelty. "I didn't even thank you,
for what you did. I wanted to die when they told me
I'd lost an eye, that I might go blind. You made me
want to live."

She didn't say anything, but her posture was elo-
quent.

He swayed a little. She caught him as he reeled.

"I'm drunk, Tat," he managed with a breathy laugh.

"You don't do this much."

"Only rarely," he agreed as she helped him toward
the bed. "I don't like being out of control."

"You never did."

He eased down onto the bed, shoes and all. He
looked up at her quietly. "Help me undress. I can't
sleep in my clothes."

She stared at him while the soft plea made her flush.

He held out a big hand. "Come on, chicken," he
said with a faint smile. "Tat, I'm drunk," he reminded
her when she hesitated. "I can't get hard. If I can't get
hard, I'm no threat."

The flush got deeper.

He laughed huskily. "And all these years, I thought
you'd had one man after another," he said. His face
twisted. "Damn me for what I did to you!"

She didn't understand the anger. She didn't understand his change of attitude. She didn't really trust it,
either.

"Don't," he said, seeing the debate going on in her

mind. He shifted and winced. "Help me, Tat. I just want to sleep."

She moved closer to the bed. Hesitantly, she pulled off his shoes, and then his socks. He had beautiful feet, for a man.

He sat up. She dropped down onto the bed beside him, still wary. He pulled her hands to the buttons of his shirt. He stared into her wide eyes. "Take it off," he whispered, his voice like deep, soft velvet.

She felt her heart run wild. It had been years since she'd been this close to him, since he'd wanted her this close.

"Come on," he whispered again, coaxing her fingers to the first button while his mouth hovered just above her eyes.

The tone, the proximity, got to her. She worked buttons out of buttonholes, noting the thick hair that covered his bronzed chest as she pushed the shirt back over his broad shoulders. There was a raised place just to the left of his breastbone, where he'd been shot when he lost his eye. It was hardly noticeable now.

He felt his body going taut as the shirt fell off. Her eyes were so expressive. She loved looking at him. He loved letting her. He was getting aroused, despite his protests to the contrary. So many years. A lifetime.

"You can…do the rest, I'm sure," she said, and tried to get up.

"No, I can't." He smoothed her cold hands to his belt. "Help me, Tat," he whispered.

He lay back down. When he did that, she relaxed, just a little.

She managed a shaky smile. "I've never undressed anybody except myself," she blurted out.

She unfastened the belt and pulled it out of the loops, noting the expensive leather it was made of as she dropped it into the chair beside the bed. She hesitated.

He pulled her hands to the fastening of his slacks. "I can't sleep in my best clothes," he said gently. "Keep going."

"Rourke…"

"Shhh," he coaxed. His hands smoothed hers down on the fastenings. "Just a little more. That's it. Now put your hands under the waistbands and pull. That's all you have to do."

His voice was seducing her. She shouldn't. She should get up and run. She was embarrassed and nervous. Her hands were shaking.

"You can't be…that drunk," she began.

"Hold on to that," he said softly, and he lifted his hips and pushed both waistbands down.

She was looking at him without realizing what she was seeing for several shocked seconds. During them, he slid out of his slacks and boxer shorts and lay back down on the bed, his eyes on her wide-eyed, shocked face as she looked and looked.

He laughed with pure delight. He was aroused. Very aroused, despite the liquor. Her eyes were enhancing what was already a magnificent hunger. He shifted on the clean sheets and groaned softly.

"I've dreamed of this," he whispered huskily. "Of letting you look at me like this, feeling your eyes on me."

She was too shocked to reply or even to try to leave.

"Tat, at your age, you've surely seen photographs of

men like this, even if you haven't seen the real thing," he chided.

"Well...yes," she said in a choked tone.

"But...?"

"None...none of them looked like...like that," she whispered, fascinated. "You're...you're beautiful," she blurted out.

His face changed. He shifted again on the sheets and shivered.

"I should... I should...go," she choked.

One long arm snaked gently around her waist and pulled her across him and down on the bed beside him.

He wasn't aggressive. He didn't demand. He unbuttoned her blouse and pulled it aside. His fingers went to the front catch of the lacy little bra and unfastened it. He moved it away and looked at her beautiful, pink-tipped breasts, the crowns hard.

"You were beautiful at seventeen like this," he said quietly. "But you're more beautiful now."

She couldn't even manage words. Her heart was beating her to death.

"What...are you going to do?" she asked with helpless apprehension, because she knew that she couldn't stop him, didn't want to stop him. She was almost shivering with a hunger that had eight years of abstinence behind it.

"I'd very much like to put my mouth on your breast and suckle you until I made you come," he whispered. "The way I did when you were seventeen. Remember, Tat?" His voice was soft and sensual as he looked at her bare breasts. "You were shocked at first, and after you went over the edge you cried. I kissed you and moved on top of you. I had your lacy little panties halfway down your legs and my pants unzipped. And we heard footsteps."

She was trembling. "Yes."

"I hurt like hell. I never thought I could stop, even then." He drew in a long, unsteady breath. "I lived on that night for years."

"Before or after you started going through beautiful women like tissues?" she asked with weary cynicism.

He wasn't going to get into that. "You don't understand what it was like," he said quietly. "Have you ever wanted someone so much that it was like physical torture to be near them at all?"

Her head rocked on the mattress. "Not really," she confessed.

"I wanted you to the point of madness, Tat," he said softly. "And I couldn't even touch you." He smiled, but it was a hollow smile.

"So that was why…"

"That was why." He drew in another breath. He stared down at her relaxed body, at the taut little breasts open to his eye. "So beautiful," he whispered.

"You…haven't touched me," she said.

"I know. I'm not going to."

Her expression wasn't easily read. "Is it…because of the scars?"

His eye went to the scars, faint white lines where that butcher, Miguel, had cut her when she was a prisoner in Sapara's jail. His face was dangerous. "I killed him, Tat. I wish I could have spared you what happened."

Her fingers went up to his mouth and pressed there. They were cold.

He kissed them tenderly. "Those scars are marks of

honor," he whispered. "And I want very much to kiss them. But I can't."

"You…can't?"

He moved away from her, just a little, and coaxed her eyes down to the raging masculinity below his belt line.

She flushed.

"I can't," he repeated. "Because our first time isn't going to be when I'm too damned stinking drunk to do justice to you."

He sat up, tugged her up and put her bra and blouse back on. He nuzzled his nose against hers, but he didn't kiss her. "Don't take this the wrong way. But get out of here."

She got to her feet. He pulled the sheet across his hips and lay back with a smile.

She didn't know what to say. He wasn't offering anything but a sensual experience at some point in the future. He could take her and walk away. She would die a thousand deaths.

She bit her lip. "Stanton, I'm engaged…"

He studied her intently. "You want me," he whispered. "I want you. How is the beloved physician going to feel when we go at each other like starving wolves?"

"That won't happen," she said, clenching her teeth.

The tension left his face. He looked at her quietly. "It will. And you know it. I can't walk away from you again, Tat. I'm not even going to try. I'll sober up in the morning." It was almost a threat. His eye narrowed. "And when I do, there won't be any place on earth you can go to get away from me."

"I'm going…to be married," she said harshly.

"To a man you neither love nor want," he said.

"You've never really seen how aggressive I can be when I want something. You're going to find out."

She flushed. The past few minutes had been entirely too stimulating. "I'm going home!"

He nodded slowly. "For now."

She turned and almost ran from the room. He watched her, his eye full of longing as she closed the door firmly behind her. He smiled to himself.

ALL THE WAY to Manaus, Clarisse kept going over the night before in her head. Rourke wanted her. It was almost unbelievable that he'd let someone convince him that she and he were related. She tried to see it from his point of view. She grimaced. If that had been reversed, if she'd thought they were related... Her eyes closed on a wave of pain. She'd have done the same. She would have wanted him to hate her, so that she didn't give in to her hunger, so that she didn't slip.

He'd been different last night. Tentative, when Rourke was never tentative. Then he'd treed a bar. She couldn't recall that he'd ever done anything like that. He'd threatened the man who came on to her; he'd been violent. She'd never seen him so out of control. Why had he been drinking in the first place?

Then she remembered. She'd told him she was marrying Ruy Carvajal. Had that set him off?

And was it just that he wanted her? Could he feel something for her, too, something powerful and overwhelming, the way she felt about him? She laughed silently. No. Rourke didn't love her. He was fond of her, of course; they had a long history. And he certainly wanted her. He'd gone hungry for eight years, so now that the barriers were down, he was full of expectation, full of plans to seduce her. She wanted him, too, but once he had her, he'd go on to the next conquest. It wasn't that he wanted her so much, it was that she'd been inaccessible to him.

But he'd had her in bed with him, half-naked, and he hadn't even touched her. She flushed, recalling what he'd shown her, how aroused he'd been. Surely if it had been only physical, he'd never have hesitated. Of course, he'd been drinking...

She took the glass of champagne the stewardess offered and drained the glass. It made the hurt a little easier. She'd told Rourke no. Now she was going home to get married. She'd tell Ruy when he came home. He'd said he'd be away for three weeks. She'd tell him when he got back. He would be delighted. She'd help him regain his status in his community. She'd protect herself from being tempted to give in to Rourke's hunger. It would benefit everyone.

The stewardess offered a refill. She accepted it. She drained the second glass. She was pleasantly numb. She didn't drink, so the champagne affected her strongly. She closed her eyes, drifting away. Rourke wanted her, at last, at long last. But all he really wanted was one night in bed with her, after which he'd walk away and probably be just as abusive, just as taunting as he'd ever been in the past. Except this time he'd have real ammunition. He would be able to taunt her with giving in to him, if she was crazy enough to let him into her bed. She'd become what he'd always accused her of being.

Her heart jumped when she remembered what he'd said to her, while they were dancing and later, in his room. He knew she was innocent. But he'd known when they were dancing. How had he known?

She closed her eyes and let herself drift away. She was going home. She would marry Ruy. Rourke would return to Nairobi. She would be safe. Yes. Safe.

WHAT SHE DIDN'T know was that a tall, blond man with a bloodshot pale brown eye was even at that moment buying a plane ticket to Manaus.

CHAPTER FOUR

CLARISSE TOOK A cab to her small house, the one that her parents had bought so many years ago. She'd been staying at hotels when she was in the country, when she'd brought Peg Grange here, because the memories were too stark. But she had to face the past someday. The house was part of it.

She put down her suitcase and purse and walked into the living room. She'd replaced the couch where Rourke had almost seduced her eight years ago. But the memories were still there, so exciting, so hot, that she flushed just recalling them.

It had been Christmas Eve. She was seventeen years old. Rourke had been in Manaus on a job, and he came by to pay his respects to Clarisse's parents. He and her father had been friends, despite the difference in their ages. Her parents and K. C. Kantor had been close since Clarisse was a child, playing with Rourke when her father was stationed in Kenya.

Rourke had teased her while they decorated the Christmas tree. She'd been wearing a slinky dress that her mother hadn't approved of, but she knew Rourke was coming by the house and she'd wanted so much to look grown-up, to make him see her as a woman.

And he had. He'd looked and looked. While they

spoke, while he teased her, while they put the ornaments on the tree.

Her father and sister had been doing last-minute shopping. Her mother had been home, but a neighbor had come by and asked her to step next door and look at a small child with a fever. Maria had been a nurse and she was still the last refuge of people with little money. Reluctantly, because she knew Rourke's reputation, she'd let herself be talked into leaving the house.

Clarisse could still see the expression in Rourke's brown eyes, because it was before he'd lost one of them, as the front door closed behind her mother. He'd moved toward her with intent, for the first time since she'd known how she felt about him.

Without a word, he'd lifted her off the floor in his strong arms and his mouth had settled with exquisite tenderness on her trembling lips.

He brushed them softly with his and smiled when she looked at him from wide blue eyes. "You've never done this," he whispered.

She shook her head.

"Lucky, lucky me," he whispered back, and bent again to her lips. "Don't be afraid, Tat. I won't hurt you. I promise."

He'd spread her out on the couch while he unbuttoned the silk shirt he was wearing and pulled it out of his slacks. She watched him like a cat, with wide-eyed wonder.

He slipped out of his shoes and slid alongside her on the long leather couch.

"Mama," she whispered worriedly. "She won't be gone long…"

"I'll hear her," he promised.

While she was worrying, his big hands went to the wide straps that held up the dress and slid them with sensual mastery right down over her soft little breasts. She opened her mouth to protest and his mouth went down right on one breast and began to suckle it.

She had to bite her lip almost through to keep back the helpless cry of pleasure as she felt desire for the first time in her life. It was more than desire. She arched up to his lips, clutched at the back of his head, where the hair was thick, and tried to bring his mouth even closer. The suction increased suddenly and she threw back her head, arched her back and climaxed in his arms.

She cried then. It shocked her that she was abnormal. But Rourke had only laughed, softly, with pure delight, and comforted her. She loved him, he whispered, that was why. It made her extremely sensitive to his lovemaking.

Her eyes had opened wide as his body slowly overwhelmed hers. He let her feel the slow, building tension of his body, let her feel it swell against her flat belly. That, too, he whispered, was the most natural thing in the world. And how would she like to feel it inside her?

She flushed, but his mouth covered hers and she shivered, her legs parting as he moved between them, her voice breaking as she encouraged him. She felt his hands under her dress, moving the lacy little briefs down, touching her in a place and a way she'd never been touched in her life. And all the while, he fed on her breasts, working the hard crowns with his tongue. She was pleading then, begging him. His hand moved between them in a heated rush as he felt for the zipper and tugged at it with something like desperation…

And they'd heard the door open and her mother's footsteps.

Barely in time, they were dressed and apparently putting decorations on the tree when she walked in. But Clarisse's mother could see quite easily what had been going on. She hadn't approved—that was obvious. She'd lectured her daughter after Rourke had left, minutes later, without a word to Clarisse or even a backward glance. That man, Maria said coldly, had a string of lovers, and he was not adding her precious chaste daughter to them! She would make sure of it.

Clarisse didn't think of Rourke that way. Not until Rourke had been wounded soon afterward in a conflict that cost him his eye and almost his life. She'd flown to Nairobi and sat by his bedside for days, nursing him, forcing him to live, to cope with the loss of the eye. His reaction to her had been heartbreaking. He'd been ice-cold, withdrawn. He acted as if he hated her. The minute he was allowed to leave the hospital, he took an old girlfriend home with him and didn't even thank Clarisse for being there when he needed her most.

But that was only the beginning. Later that year, he flatly refused her invitation to a party in Manuas. Even then, she didn't get the idea. He stopped answering her letters and refused to pick up the phone if she was on the other end.

Not until the next time they met, at some fund-raiser in Washington, DC, when he was so cold and mocking about her behavior that she was certain he hated her. He called her an immoral little tramp who was any man's. Nothing had ever hurt so much. He was the only man she'd ever been intimate with. Had her behavior with him made him think that she was any man's, that she was immoral? Was that why he suddenly hated her? She hadn't known. She hadn't understood. But his hateful attitude had caused her to avoid him, off and on, ever since.

But every time there was a tragedy in her life, he was there. It had never made sense. Now, perhaps, it did. He'd wanted her beyond bearing and he'd heard gossip that they were related. She couldn't help wondering if her mother had anything to do with that gossip. Then she swept aside the suspicion. The mother she loved would never have been that cruel, even to save her daughter's innocence. Of that she was certain.

Perhaps K.C. had told Rourke something. He seemed to like Clarisse, but perhaps he had someone else in mind for his employee—or his son, some people said. Rourke and K.C. were so alike that she'd wondered for years if they weren't related.

Well, it didn't matter now. Rourke was not going to take her to bed and walk away. Whatever she had to do to protect herself, even if it meant marrying Ruy, she would do.

She loved Rourke far too much. She'd just gone on the endangered list, if he'd meant what he said. So she had to start making plans. She didn't love the Manaus physician, but he was kind and she could live with him as long as there were no physical demands. It would protect her from Rourke, who would never coerce a woman into forsaking her marriage vows. He was quite old-fashioned in that sense. There had never been a single instance when he'd been seen with a married woman, not even one who was separated from her husband. He was, in his own way, something of a Puritan.

Besides all that, she thought that it had just been

the alcohol talking. Rourke had been very inebriated. Probably he was just teasing her, as he had for years.

SHE THOUGHT THAT until she answered a knock at the door that evening and found an amused, blond man leaning on the door frame facing her.

She caught her breath.

"And you thought I didn't mean it," he mused, smiling through bloodshot eyes. "Come dancing, Tat."

She was all at sea. "We danced last night," she began.

He smiled. "There's a Latin Club in town. It just opened." He leaned toward her. "I can do the tango."

She flushed. It was her favorite dance. She'd been dancing it with a handsome Latin at a club in Osaka, Japan, one night when she'd gone to a society wedding to which Rourke was also invited. The club was where the crowd had gone for supper after a rehearsal dinner. Rourke had shown up there with a date. He hadn't danced with Clarisse, of course; he was his usual mocking, sarcastic self. But he drew his date onto the dance floor and Clarisse watched with wide-eyed wonder as he held the audience enthralled with his skill. She thought she'd never seen anyone dance like that in her life. He hadn't said a single word to Clarisse, much less danced with her.

"Come on. Give in," he teased. "You know you want to."

"I was going to watch television…"

"Put on something sexy and come dancing. You can watch television when you're alone."

She opened the door, with obvious apprehension. "I'll have to get dressed."

He tilted her face up to his with a thumb under her chin. His expression was very solemn. "I'll make you a promise, Tat. I won't touch you, in any way, until you tell me you want me to."

She colored. "That's new."

"Isn't it?"

"I'll get dressed," she said.

SHE CAME BACK into the living room dressed in a black cocktail dress with sequins around the hem, with strappy tango shoes and carrying a small black purse.

"Leave the purse here," he said, smiling at the picture she made. "I've got money."

"Okay." She tossed it onto the side table. "Oh, my house key…"

She dug it out and looked at herself. The dress fit closely and there were no pockets.

He took the key from her and slid it into the expensive slacks he was wearing with a black silk shirt open at the neck and an expensive dark jacket.

His fingers linked into hers. "Do you mind?" he asked softly.

She tingled all over. "No," she faltered. "It's all right."

He smiled and led her to a stretch limousine that she hadn't even noticed in her excitement.

"Oh, it's Domingo, isn't it?" she exclaimed when the driver got out to open the back door for them. "How is your family? Your daughter…?"

"Doing very well, thanks to you, *senhorita*," he said with feeling. "I am happy to see you again!"

She grinned at him and let Rourke ease her into the seat.

"Where are we going?" Domingo asked when he climbed in under the wheel.

"El Jinete," he said, laughing. "An Argentina native runs it. We're going to teach the locals how to tango."

"Ah, such a dance," Domingo said with feeling. "My mother is from Argentina, you know. She and my father, they danced it together. Not like these silly movies you see…"

Which brought up another subject of conversation, and that took them all the way into Manaus.

THE LATIN CLUB was decorated with images of flamenco and furnishings that were reminiscent of both Spain and Latin America.

A young woman wearing a red flamenco dress escorted them to a table near the dance floor and left menus with them.

"They serve food, too," Rourke said with a grin. "I'm starving!"

She laughed. "Me, too," she confessed.

They had seafood salads followed by a fruity dessert and coffee.

"I've almost forgotten how to dance," she confessed when he took her onto the dance floor.

"So have I," he replied. He was remembering the club in Osaka and the hurt look on Clarisse's face. "I got drunk after you left the club that night in Osaka."

"Wh…what?" she faltered.

He drew her against him. "Do you think I enjoyed hurting you?" he asked huskily. He averted his gaze to the far wall. "I was scared to death to let you get this close."

She was fascinated by his expression.

He looked down at her hungrily. "You've never been much good at hiding how you feel, Tat," he said as he began to move her to the lazy, seductive rhythm. "It was a very good thing that I'd had so much to drink last night."

She flushed and lowered her gaze to his throat.

"Of course, I was still capable," he mused, and laughed when she stiffened. He hugged her close, with rough affection. "I don't deserve it. But I feel ten feet tall."

"You do? Why?"

His mouth teased her ear. "Because you're still a virgin, Tat."

His arm brought her closer as he turned her.

"Couldn't you, with another man?" he asked.

She swallowed. "You're a hard act to follow," she managed.

His chest rose and fell a little unsteadily. "If your mother had waited another ten minutes to come back home…"

"I'd have gotten pregnant, most likely," she interrupted him. "That would have been the end of the world, for you."

"Why?" He lifted his head and looked into her wide eyes. "I love kids, Tat. So do you." He smiled. "I remember you giving a bottle to that little boy at the refugee camp," he said. "It was so poignant that I had to grit my teeth to keep from reaching for you, all the way to the airport."

He was confusing her. She didn't understand.

"Don't look so worried," he said, brushing his lips over her hair. "We've just met. I'm a former secret agent. I have a game park and a pet lion in Africa named Lou. I love beautiful blue-eyed blondes, and I enjoy dancing the tango."

She laughed. "Do you have one of those permits, too? So you can shoot people…?"

"I never shoot people." He hesitated. "Almost never."

She was recalling Miguel and the feel of the knife at her breast. Involuntarily, her fingers went to her bodice.

His arm tightened around her. "He'll never hurt another woman."

"He was scary," she recalled with a tiny shiver. "A big man, very muscular…"

He pursed his lips. "So am I, Tat."

"Yes, but he had sloppy muscles. You're…" She recalled how he looked under his clothes and she blushed. "I can't believe I let you talk me into that."

He laughed. "I can't believe it, either. I'll carry that memory around with me for the rest of my life."

"Why?"

"Because of the way you looked at me," he said. He averted his gaze. "I'm touchy about my disability, Tat," he said. "When you looked at me, you weren't seeing it."

"I never see it," she said. "Stanton, there are men missing arms and legs, in all sorts of conditions, coming home from wars and conflicts. Many of them are married or in relationships. People cope, you know?"

"I had a woman tell me once that it would be creepy to go to bed with a one-eyed man," he said, trying to make a joke of it.

She stopped dancing and winced.

"I didn't," he said at once, because he knew why she winced.

"Because she wouldn't?" she asked.

"No. Because I...couldn't," he said. He drew her close again and danced.

She didn't understand.

His big hand grew caressing on her back. "While you were under the influence of those anxiety meds, you thought you wanted Grange. But would you have slept with him?"

"No," she said at once.

"Why?"

She drew in a shaky breath. "I can't... I don't..." She closed her eyes.

"Because you only want me, that way," he whispered for her.

"Yes," she said miserably, her pride gone.

He tilted up her chin and searched her blue eyes. He wasn't smiling. "And I only want you, that way."

"Pull the other one," she laughed. "That was a gorgeous blonde you were dancing with at the awards ceremony when I left the room..."

"She's married to the presenter," he said quietly.

"Oh."

"Why in the hell do you think I went out and got drunk?" he asked at her ear.

"Because I wouldn't go to bed with you," she bit off.

He lifted his head. He sighed. "We've got a long way to go," he said after a minute. "But, then, I knew it wouldn't be easy."

"I don't understand."

"Dance," he said, smiling. "There's only tonight."

"Really?"

"Well, not really. I thought I'd take you on a tour of Manaus tomorrow," he added. "We'll go look at the opera house and see some of the street performances. We might take in a show. I'll see what's in town."

"You're not going right back to Africa, then?"

"No."

She followed his steps so easily, as if she could read his mind and knew exactly what he was going to do next. But it wasn't that way except for dancing. "When?" she asked.

"How long is your fiancé going to be out of town?" he asked.

"Three weeks, he said."

He lifted his head and looked into her eyes. "I'm going to be here for three weeks," he said.

"Stanton…"

"When I take you home tonight, I'm going to leave you at your front door," he said quietly. "But I'm going to kiss you in such a way that you'll lie awake all night wanting me."

Her lips parted on a husky breath.

"Of course, I'll also lie awake all night wanting you," he mused, and laughed to break the tension.

The music ended. He took her back to their table and ordered champagne.

"Are we celebrating something?" she asked when the waiter poured it into flutes.

"Yes," Rourke replied, smiling tenderly. "To beginnings."

Well, that was innocuous enough, she supposed. He didn't really look threatening. She smiled and raised her glass to touch to his.

DOMINGO WAITED IN the car while Rourke walked Clarisse to her door.

He paused just in front of her, producing her house key. She unlocked the door, leaving the key in it.

"I had a lovely time," she said. "Really lovely. Thank you."

"I did, too. I don't get out much these days," he confessed. "Never dancing. I'm usually up to my neck in some project overseas."

That brought back to mind what he did for a living, and she felt uneasy. "You're always at risk."

He shrugged. "I can't live without it, sweetheart," he said softly, smiling when she flushed a little at the unaccustomed endearment. He never used them to her. Not in the past. "I have to have those adrenaline rushes."

"I suppose it's like men who play sports or go into law enforcement work."

"Something like that."

She searched his face with quiet, resigned eyes. "Try not to get killed. I hate funerals."

He chuckled. "I'm sure I'd hate my own. But you'd look gorgeous in black lace, Tat. I used to dream about you in a long, lacy see-through black gown. I'd wake up sweating."

That was surprising. "You dreamed about me?"

"Just as you dream about me," he said, as if he knew.

"It was eight years ago," she began.

"No. It was yesterday." He looked down at her. "This may get a little rough," he said apologetically as he drew her slowly to him. "I don't mean it to, okay?"

"I don't understand," she faltered, already on fire from just the contact with his powerful body.

"I've kept to myself…for a while," he whispered as he bent to her mouth. His hands slid to her hips and drew her against him. He shivered as his body reacted immediately, explicitly, to just the touch of her. "Sorry," he added unsteadily.

"It's all right," she said. She stood very still as his head bent, his mouth coming to brush hers very softly. He nudged her top lip away from the lower one and teased it with brief, soft little kisses that made her body go tense.

He felt that. He felt her nails biting into his upper arms as she held him.

"I'll bet—" he breathed into her mouth "—that your nipples are like little stones right now, Tat…"

She opened her mouth, shocked, and his went down against it with furious hunger. His hands on her hips were hurting but he didn't move them, he didn't try to bring her closer. He just kissed her, with hunger, almost with desperation.

He groaned against her lips. "I'm going to die when I have to step away from you," he said huskily.

He pulled back, shuddering.

"I'm sorry," she said.

"What for?"

"Making you hurt," she said, wincing at the strain on his face.

He straightened a little jerkily. "It will go down eventually," he said with graveyard humor. "An ice pack might help…"

She burst out laughing. "You're horrible!" she exclaimed, flushing.

He laughed, even through the pain. "Yes, I am," he

agreed. He bent and brushed his mouth over her nose. "Go to bed. I hope you don't sleep a wink."

"I'll sleep just fine, thanks."

"In a pig's eye," he mused. He winked at her. "I'll be over about nine. Too early?"

She shook her head. Her eyes were soft for a few seconds, then her expression grew somber.

"You think I'll hurt you again," he said, reading the apprehension he saw. "I won't. But I'll have to prove it, won't I?"

"I'm afraid so."

He smiled slowly. "We're going down a different path this time, my baby," he said with tender affection. "No more nasty remarks. No more insults."

She drew in a breath. "Okay."

"See you tomorrow."

"Tomorrow."

He winked and danced down the steps, whistling as he went back to the limousine. He paused at the door, turned and waited.

She realized, belatedly, that he wasn't leaving until she was safely inside. She pulled out the key, went inside, locked the door and turned off the porch light. He got into the vehicle and left.

SHE DIDN'T SLEEP a wink, just as he'd predicted. But when he showed up at her door the next morning, his own eyes were bloodshot, as well.

"No, I didn't sleep." He chuckled, and grinned at her. "Come sightseeing."

She looked past him. A late-model rental car was sitting in the driveway.

"The limo attracts too much attention," he explained

when she was sitting beside him in the car. "I want us to be just typical tourists for a few days. That suit you?"

"That suits me very well."

He reached out and captured her small hand, linking his strong fingers with it. The contact was electric.

"How about the botanical gardens first?" he asked.

"That would be lovely."

THEY STROLLED THROUGH the exquisite vegetation, stopping to smell flowers and look at small creatures in the undergrowth.

"Careful," he said, when she went off the path. "There are probably snakes here, even if they aren't part of the exhibit."

She moved back quickly. She laughed. "You know, that place where the snake bit me still swells up every year about the same time." She shook her head. "Nobody can tell me why."

"I remember that time with absolute terror," he said grimly. "I carried you in my arms, running, to the clinic. I was afraid I wouldn't get you there in time. You could have died. It would have been on my conscience forever."

"It wasn't your fault," she said, surprised by the emotion in his deep voice. "Stanton, I rushed ahead of you. I remember that you called to me, trying to stop me. I didn't listen. I was always headstrong, in those days."

"Headstrong. Spirited." He sighed, clasping her hand in his. "I knocked the spirit right out of you, Tat. I didn't want to hurt you. I just…couldn't risk letting you get close to me."

The clasp of his strong fingers was almost pain. She stopped and looked up at the rigid lines of his face.

He looked down at her, wincing. "If you only knew," he said in a rough whisper, "what it did to me to say those things to you, to make you hate me…" He looked away. His body was like stone.

Why, he cared! She hadn't believed it possible. But of course he cared. In any crisis in her life, he was always the first one there.

"When my father and Matilda died," she said softly, "you were there just after it happened. You took care of everything." The memory of the loss still hurt a little. "In Barrera, you couldn't wait to get to me when you knew I'd been hurt. In Africa, you came all that way to get me out before the offensive in Ngawa…"

He looked down at her. "I don't have a life without you," he said simply.

She bit her lower lip and tears overwhelmed her blue eyes.

He averted his. "Don't," he said unsteadily. "I can't bear it when you cry."

His fingers loosened their tight grip and became caressing. "Come on. Let's look at the flamingos, precious, and look like we're enjoying ourselves."

Precious. She beamed. She laughed.

He looked down at her with warm affection in his one good eye. "A bit of news I forgot to tell you," he said as they started walking again. "K.C. had the DNA test done."

She stopped walking. "And?" she asked excitedly.

He smiled. "He really is my dad," he said. "I'm having my name legally changed to Kantor. I'm keeping the Rourke part, though. I loved the man I thought was my father, just the same."

"I'm so happy for you," she said. "K.C. is a wonderful man."

He pursed his lips. "Until you make him mad," he agreed. He laughed. "I accused him of…" He didn't dare say what he'd accused K.C. of. She loved her mother. "Well, I made him mad. He popped me one on the jaw and knocked me over a couch. He was coming right for me when I apologized quickly enough to head him off." He roared laughing. "God, my old man packs a punch!"

She laughed. "I'm glad that you finally know. I suspected it, for a long time. You're the image of him, Stanton. Even more so with your hair cut like that."

"I sort of miss the length," he confessed. "Domingo was vocal when he saw me. He said I'd hurt my 'medicine' by having it whacked off."

"Jungle people are superstitious," she said, but felt a cold chill when he told her what Domingo had said. Rourke was in a dangerous line of work. Very dangerous.

"Don't you start," he murmured drily, smiling down at her.

"I like it," she replied, her blue eyes searching over his hard face, up to the wavy blond hair. "I think you look very distinguished."

He drew in a breath. His hand touched her cheek. His thumb moved tenderly over her full lower lip. "I want to back you into the trunk of a tree and kiss you until I stop aching," he whispered. He looked around, oblivious to her faint flush. "Damned people everywhere…!" he muttered with frustration.

"You're very…forthright," she managed.

He looked down at her. "Very blunt, you mean. Yes, I am," he replied. His pale brown eye narrowed. He studied her face. "I shocked you the other night, when I coaxed you into undressing me."

The flush went ballistic.

He didn't make fun of her. He touched her soft cheek. "It was glorious," he whispered. "Having your eyes on me. If I hadn't been so damned drunk, you really would have been in trouble."

She kept her eyes on his broad chest. "You're…impressive," she managed.

He chuckled. "Thank you." He brushed his lips across her forehead. "So are you," he whispered. "I could get drunk just looking at your breasts. I'll bet," he added as his mouth brushed against her eyebrows, "that your nipples are standing at attention right now."

"Stanton!" she gasped.

"I've got something that's standing at attention, as well," he murmured at her ear. "It's still looking for a place to hide, too."

"I will hit you," she threatened, stepping back, flustered.

He laughed with pure delight. "My Tat," he said softly. "Bright and beautiful. God, how I've missed having you in my life!"

He wasn't joking. That was real emotion on his face.

"I've…missed having you in mine," she confessed.

"We go back a long way, don't we, honey?" he asked quietly. "Your father lived next door to us when you were just a little girl. We were friends from the day we met, even though I was five years older."

"I loved hanging around with you. The boys made fun of you for letting a girl tag along."

"I didn't mind. You were a cute kid, all legs and hair." He searched her eyes. "You had pigtails," he recalled. "I remember when you were about sixteen, I saw you in Nairobi with your parents. Your hair was down to your waist in back, like a pale gold curtain. You were wearing a simple little pink dress. It hurt me to look at you."

"Why?"

"Because I got hard as a rock when I looked at you," he said simply.

Her lips fell apart. "Even...then?"

"Yes, Tat, even then," he said quietly. "You're the only woman in my life that I ever wanted that badly, and never had."

She swallowed, hard, and averted her gaze to the gorgeous tropical vegetation. "That's just sex."

"Just!" he scoffed.

She shrugged. "I don't know a lot about it," she confessed.

He drew in a breath. "I guess not." He caught her hand back into his and they walked some more. "But you're not totally innocent." He glanced down at her. "I've never forgotten how it felt, to feel you come, watch you, that night at your house, when you were seventeen."

She felt her face go scarlet.

He stopped walking and turned her to him. "Don't make it into a sordid memory. It was beautiful," he whispered. "You were...the sweetest candy I ever tasted. I would have died for you, even then."

Her eyes lifted to his, full of curiosity.

"Do you think it was ordinary, for me? That I felt that way with other women? Because I never did, Tat."

CHAPTER FIVE

CLARISSE LOOKED UP at him with her heart in her eyes. "Yes," she confessed. "I knew you were experienced. Everybody did, in our circle of friends. You had women and threw them away."

He grimaced. "Yes, I did." He drew in a heavy, rough breath. "I thought men did that, I thought it was how a man was supposed to behave. K.C. was furious with me. He said that I was taking terrible chances with my health, and that what I was doing would come back to haunt me one day." He shrugged. "I didn't believe him, of course. And I was ticked at him, because he interfered so much in my life. My parents had been dead since I was ten years old. I'd lived in an orphanage and been on my own for a good while by then. K.C. had been out of the country when my mother was killed. But he came back a few months later. He took me out of the orphanage, looked out for me, took me in, was responsible for me until I was of legal age. But I thought that nobody except a blood parent should presume to lecture me, and I told him so." He shook his head. "God help me, I had no idea." His expression was full of remorse. "Yes, I had women," he said. "But it would never have been like that with you, especially at your age. You were only seventeen, honey."

"You weren't going to stop," she whispered.

"I couldn't stop!" he returned. His face was rigid as his pale brown eye searched both of hers. "It had never been that way with a woman. Never! Even now, I go crazy when I remember how it felt." His eye closed and he shuddered. "Eight damned long years I went without you because of a lie. I could kill someone...!"

"Stanton!" Her hand reached up and hesitated at his cheek.

He felt the heat of it and opened his eye. He winced as he recalled what he'd said to her at the airport, the last time they'd met before the awards ceremony. He knew why she was reluctant to touch him.

"I lied, baby," he said softly, drawing her palm to his mouth. "I want your touch. I ache for it!"

Her cold fingers touched his hard cheek, moving up to just under the eye patch, where a small scar ran vertically from under it.

"It's still pretty messy under that, despite the surgery," he said stiffly.

She looked up into his face. "I saw it when you were recovering. It didn't bother me, except that it hurt me to see how much pain it caused you."

He frowned.

"I expect," she said, averting her gaze, "that you've never taken it off with a woman when you..."

He was rigid.

"Sorry," she said, and started to remove her hand.

He clasped it to his cheek. "Look at me," he said huskily.

She looked up again.

His face was taut, his eye blazing with feeling. He wanted to tell her then, how long it had been since he'd had a woman. He wanted to make her understand what devastation the lie had caused him. But it would serve no purpose now except to hurt her. She'd been hurt enough already.

"You're still the most beautiful woman I've ever known," he said in a soft, deep voice.

"I have scars…"

"So do I," he replied. "I let you see them, the night I got drunk."

She flushed and averted her eyes.

"You can't imagine how it feels to me," he whispered roughly. "To know that you've never done it with a man." He laughed shortly. "You thought I had malaria because I was shaking when I had you in my arms. I was shaking because I want you to the point of absolute madness. I can just look at you and get hard enough to put it through a damned tree trunk…!" She flushed. He groaned and averted his gaze. "Sorry," he bit off. "I'm really sorry. That was crude, even for me."

"But that's, I mean, it's natural with men," she faltered.

He let out a breath and moved a step closer. He caught her shoulders and leaned his forehead against hers. "No. It's not. It isn't like that for me, with anyone except you."

She frowned. "I don't understand."

His eye closed. He drank in the scent of her body. "You give me peace," he whispered. "The only time I've ever known it is when I'm close to you." He laughed softly. "And that's surprising, Tat, because you shake me up, too."

She let out a sigh. He drew her completely against him and stood just holding her, his forehead touching hers, his coffee-scented breath on her mouth.

"You don't trust me," he murmured quietly.

Her heart jumped. "Stanton..."

His cheek slid against hers. "I can't hide how much I want you," he whispered. "But I give you my word that I absolutely will not touch you with intent until and unless you ask me to."

She drew back. He was serious. There was no teasing light in that one pale brown eye, watching her so intently.

She drew in a breath. She swallowed. "Okay," she said finally.

He kissed her eyelids. "Let's go see the street performers." He took her hand, linked her fingers with his, and drew her along the path toward the exit.

THERE WERE STREET performers downtown. One had a guitar and he sang like an angel. Rourke and Clarisse sat on a bench, enjoying the sound of his deep voice as he crooned a love song in Spanish.

Rourke's fingers smoothed over hers. "Lost love," he mused when the last notes of the song faded slowly away. "So many songs have been written about it. Nothing quite captures the pathos, though."

"Sometimes things don't work out for people," she said noncommittally.

He looked down at her. "And sometimes they do."

Her eyes searched his. "You're not a marrying man, Stanton," she said quietly. "At the end of the day, that's the bare truth. And I don't play around."

"I know that."

She averted her gaze to people passing by.

"You used him."

Her head came up, shocked.

His expression was quiet. Intent. "You needed some way to keep me at arm's length. Carvajal was it. You think I'll keep my distance because you're engaged."

She didn't quite know what to say. He looked odd.

"You don't know how it is with me, Tat," he said softly. He smiled gently. "I've gone hungry for years, and I'm sitting next to a banquet. Do you really think even an engagement is going to continue to keep me at bay?"

"You respect a binding relationship..."

"I would if you loved him. You don't." He searched her wide, wounded eyes. "You love me, Tat. You've loved me at least since you were seventeen. Maybe even longer. It's the only reason you'd ever have let me touch you the way I did, that Christmas Eve so long ago."

Her cheeks flushed. She wanted to deny it. She couldn't.

His chest swelled with pride. He'd been guessing, hoping. Now he knew the truth. It made the world bright and beautiful. She belonged to him.

His fingers slid sensually around hers, lightly touching, exploring. The way he smiled at her then wasn't smug or arrogant. It was with a tenderness she'd rarely seen in him.

"We know so much about each other," he said softly. "Things we never share with other people." He looked down at her soft hand. "You know how my parents died." His face tautened. "I never talk about it."

"You told me a lot of things, when you lost your eye," she recalled. Her fingers slid in between his and closed on them. "You've had such a hard life, Stanton."

He drew in a breath. "It made me the man I am,"

he replied. "K.C. was good to me, but I resented what people said about him. I loved my mother and the man I thought was my father. I didn't like having them gossiped about."

"Not that many people gossiped," she replied. "They were too afraid of K.C."

"He's still formidable," he mused. "My old man." He shook his head. "I used to live for him to come home, so he could tell me about the things he did, the places he saw. He knew all sorts of people, in dangerous places. I dined out on adventure tales."

"You lived them, too," she recalled.

"Ya, with an ammunition belt strapped around my chest, carrying an AK-47 when I was just ten years old. I went into battle with the insurgents. K.C. was horrified. He was still active in those years, off from one little war to another, leading men into battle. But he couldn't believe I'd been rash enough to sign on with a bunch of mercs." He laughed. "He was furious. He dragged me back to Kenya and formally became my guardian. I didn't have much say in the matter, at that age. I resented him, for a long time. You see, I loved my mother," he added quietly. "And my father. I hated the insinuation that my mother was a loose woman."

"She loved K.C.," she reminded him. "That didn't make her a loose woman. I don't think she could help it. He loved another woman and lost her to the church."

"Ya. Got drunk and my mother felt sorry for him. And here I am." His fingers tightened around hers.

"People pay for mistakes, Stanton," she said softly, tugging at the hard pressure of his strong hand around hers.

"Sorry, love," he said, loosening his hold at once. "Bad memories."

"I know."

He looked up at her. "You never left me, while they fought to save my eye," he recalled. "You made me fight."

"You'd never have given up, even if I'd gone home," she said with a sad smile. "Anita would have been there…"

He put his fingers over her mouth. "She was just a friend," he said. "I never slept with her."

Her high cheekbones colored.

"I wanted you," he whispered roughly. "If you'd stayed around when they let me go home, I would have…" He bit down on the words and averted his face. "I couldn't risk it. I had to make you leave."

She swallowed down the pain. "I wish…you'd told me."

"I couldn't. It was my burden."

"It was mine, too. It would have made it easier…" Her voice broke on the word.

He stood up, tugging her with him.

She could barely see where she was going for the tears. He didn't speak. He just walked, faster, until they reached the car.

He put her inside, started it and drove back to her house in a silence alive with tension.

When they got to the front porch, he picked her up in his arms and carried her to the door.

"Unlock it," he said through his teeth.

She fumbled the key out of her pocket and opened the door. He retrieved the key, relocked the door and carried her straight toward the bedroom.

"Stanton…no," she choked.

He was blind, deaf, dumb, so overcome with his hunger that he couldn't even think. He placed her onto the coverlet of the big bed and went to lock the door. He leaned his forehead against it, shuddering.

Clarisse, watching him, was stunned.

"I gave you my word," he choked. "I'm trying… damned hard…to keep it. I really am."

She sat up in the bed, staring at him with faint surprise. "I don't understand," she whispered. "I don't understand, Stanton."

He turned and moved toward the bed. He stopped beside it. His face was almost chalk white as he looked down at her. His tall, powerful body was shivering with desire.

"Tat," he said in a haunted tone, "I haven't had a woman…in eight years."

The enormity of the confession shocked her speechless. She stared at him with wide blue eyes, her lips parted as she tried to breathe normally.

"Eight…no," she faltered. "No, it isn't possible…!"

"You haven't had a man," he said roughly. "Why isn't it possible?"

"Eight years…!" she said unsteadily.

"I can't do it with anyone else," he said harshly.

All her protests were quite suddenly gone. She could see the raging arousal that he made no effort to hide. She could see the tension in his tall, powerful body, the anguish that drew his face taut with pain.

She lay back on the bed, her hands beside her head on the pillow. She just looked at him with quiet, soft blue eyes. He'd robbed her of the last defense she had with that confession.

His gaze went from her head down her body, over the taut nipples that showed under her blouse, down her long legs to her small feet in strappy sandals. She was the most beautiful creature he'd ever seen in his life.

"I don't have anything to use," he said unsteadily. "But even if I did, I wouldn't want to use it," he added. "I want, very badly, to make you pregnant with my baby."

She gasped. Her body reacted to the words by arching, shivering.

"You want it, too," he said, surprised.

"I want it...more than anything in the world," she stammered, and flushed.

He slipped out of his shoes, unfastened his belt and tossed it to one side. His big hands were unsteady as he flicked at buttons and stripped himself out of the silk shirt. He unzipped his trousers and stepped out of them, letting her watch.

He was so aroused that it was impossible to look anywhere else.

"Try not to look at that for a few seconds," he said with graveyard humor as he sat down beside her on the bed, "or I'll explode before I can even get inside you."

She was watching him like some elegant little cat, her eyes wide and soft and curious on his face as he began to undress her.

"Just...from looking?" she whispered.

"Just from looking."

"Gosh."

He eased her out of the blouse and bra and sat gazing at her beautiful little breasts. He touched the scars tenderly and winced. "I would have given my life to spare you that pain," he whispered.

She moved restlessly on the cover as he unfastened her slacks and pulled them, and her lacy pink briefs, down her legs and tossed them aside.

"Will it...hurt?" she asked huskily.

"It may," he said quietly. "But you won't notice."

Her eyes were opening even wider.

He smiled gently. "You have no idea, do you?" he asked, his voice tender and slow. "None at all."

"Well, I remember...what it's like, a little," she replied.

He nodded, recalling the torrid interlude her mother had interrupted. His hand went to her soft thigh and touched it, traced it, hearing her breath catch. His fingers moved up, teasing at her hip, across her flat belly, up to her taut breasts. He touched the hard tip, very gently. She arched up to tempt his hand closer.

He traced around the tender flesh, feeling her shiver.

"I don't...even know what to do," she wept.

"I'm going to teach you that." He slid alongside her, drawing her gently onto her side so that they were facing each other. He pulled her close, so that her hard-tipped breasts buried themselves in the thick hair over the hard muscles of his chest. He caught his breath at the exquisite sensation.

"Be still, love," he whispered, shivering at the contact. "This first time, I have to be very careful. You mustn't knock me off balance. All right?"

"All right, Stanton," she managed unsteadily.

His mouth touched around hers, teasing the bottom lip away from the upper one. All the while, his hands were smoothing her hips against the hard thrust of him.

"I've dreamed of this," he said in a husky, deep tone. "Years and years of dreams."

"So have I."

He lifted her into a more intimate position and heard her soft gasp as he paused at the soft moist veil of her. His mouth traced her lips, teasing them to open. His lips closed on them, hungry and hard. She moaned.

"Don't close your eyes when I go into you, Tat," he whispered unsteadily. "Let me watch. All right?"

She shivered as she felt him moving hungrily against her. "All…all right."

His hand slid down her soft body, to the most tender place of all, and he began to touch her.

She shivered again, her lips falling apart in a soundless gasp as her body shuddered with pleasure she'd never experienced.

"I'd like to take hours with you," he breathed against her mouth. "But I'm too aroused. I have to make you hungry enough, quickly enough, before I lose control."

Her eyes opened like saucers as he started inside her.

He had to bite back a laugh at the shock he saw there. "Now you know, honey," he whispered. "This is what happens."

"It's…very…" She swallowed, lost for words to describe what he was doing to her. It was slow and sweet and very intimate. She stiffened, but his fingers moved, caressing away the faint stab of pain, making her wild, making her hungry.

His hand flattened at the base of her spine and pulled her, positioned her, as one hair-roughened leg went between both of hers and he pushed harder.

She cried out. But she was pushing toward him, not pulling away. Her eyes began to dilate. He felt her body, warm and soft, accepting the slow, soft invasion of his, moving with him, moving toward him.

His teeth ground together and he shuddered. "Dear... God!" he cried out, gasping for breath as he saw her eyes go almost black.

"Stanton...?" Was that her voice, that high-pitched almost-unrecognizable whisper of sound.

"My darling," he groaned. He rolled her onto her back and moved between her long, soft legs. His powerful body strained down toward hers. He shuddered with each motion of his hips, his face contorted with the anguish off desire. "My darling," he whispered huskily. "Oh, God, baby, baby, baby...!" He ground out the words with each movement of his body on hers. His voice broke with the violence of it, his hips grinding down into hers with hard, quick, stabbing thrusts. He lifted his chest. "Look. Look down...!" he bit off. "Watch!"

Her eyes slid down to the hardness of him, the muscles rippling over his chest, down his flat stomach, to the intense motion of his body as it plunged inside hers.

Her nails stabbed into his upper arms as he drove into her, almost sobbing with the pleasure as it grew and grew.

"Stanton!" she cried out, feeling her whole body go so taut that she thought she might tear apart under him as the heat began to explode in her.

"Oh, God... I love you," he whispered hoarsely. "I love you...more than my own life...!"

She arched up, shuddering with delight as the heat burst and exploded into shards of pleasure so great she thought she might die.

He looked into her eyes and watched, overcome

with joy as he convulsed over and over again, giving himself to the incredible climax, letting her see, letting her watch.

He cried out finally as the pleasure almost tore him in two. He arched down into her with his last breath of will, feeling his body shatter, his hips tense until it was almost painful, as he endured the sweet agony of satisfaction.

She held him, savored his warm, damp weight on her body, loved him, in the aftermath of something she'd never dreamed she could ever feel.

"Oh…my goodness," she choked at his ear.

"That, by God, was an orgasm," he said heavily, his voice drowsy in the aftermath. "A real, honest-to-God orgasm. I've never had one in my life."

"Oh."

He lifted his head and looked down into her soft, loving blue eyes, with wonder. "I thought I'd never be able to have you," he whispered. "It was hell. Pure hell." He traced her soft mouth with fingers that weren't quite steady. "I wanted to take a lot longer, our first time. I was so aroused, I couldn't manage it. I'm sorry."

"Sorry!" She shivered. "I thought I was going to die," she whispered, her eyes searching his with wonder. "I never believed women felt the things I read about. It was…it was…" She searched for words and couldn't find any.

He bent and brushed his mouth tenderly over her eyes. "It was almost sacred," he whispered. "I thought about making a baby while we did it."

"So did I," she whispered.

He let out a long sigh and relaxed. "Am I too heavy, darling?"

"No. I love the way it feels."

"So do I."

Her arms slid under his, holding him to her. They were still intimately joined. She closed her eyes. She felt him draw in a long breath. Incredibly, they fell asleep.

SHE SMELLED COFFEE. She opened her eyes and Rourke was sitting beside her, wearing just his slacks, holding a cup of coffee under her nose.

He smiled tenderly. She smiled back.

"I made eggs and bacon," he said. "Burned the toast."

"I don't care."

His eyes slid over her nudity. "You are much more beautiful than Venus, my love," he said quietly. "And I love you quite madly. More than ever after what we did."

"Me, too."

He let her hold the coffee and sip it while his hands cupped her breasts. "Beautiful," he said softly.

She laughed softly.

He let go of her and stood up, reaching for his jacket. He pulled a jeweler's box out of the pocket and opened it.

"Here." He took the coffee cup and put it on the bed-side table. He slid an emerald-and-diamond ring onto the third finger of her left hand. He kissed it. "That will have to do for an engagement ring. We'll have some-thing to eat and start the paperwork. I'd like to marry you in church, if we can manage it."

"Marry me?"

"Of course," he said simply.

She could barely believe it. She looked at him with her heart in her eyes. Tears stung them.

"I told you I loved you, while I was making love to you," he reminded her with a slow, sweet kiss. "Did you think I said it because I was out of my mind with desire?"

"Yes," she confessed.

He chuckled. "I love you more than my life, Tat," he said, searching her eyes. "I'll never stop."

She let the tears fall. "I've loved you all my life, Stanton," she whispered. "Even when you hated me…"

He caught her up close and kissed her with all the years of hunger in his hard mouth. "I loved you, and I thought I hadn't the right," he ground out as he buried his face in her throat. "Loved you hopelessly, deathlessly, wanted to die because I couldn't have you. For eight long, damned, endless years…!" His mouth slid onto hers, hard and hungry. "But I've got you now, and I'll never let go. Never!"

Her arms tightened around his neck. She held him, shivered against him. "Maybe I'm dreaming," she managed tearfully.

"Maybe you're not."

He moved away, but only to unfasten his slacks and throw them aside. He was even more aroused than he had been the night before.

She caught her breath as she looked at him.

He sat up against the headboard and pulled her gently over his hips.

"What…are you doing?" she asked with a gasp.

He chuckled wickedly. "Teaching new concepts of

pleasure?" He moved her against him and caught his breath. "I can go deeper this way, love," he whispered, loving the way she blushed.

"Oh."

"Much deeper."

"Oh!" That exclamation wasn't an answer to his teasing remark. It was an expression of pleasure so sweeping that it was accompanied by the ripple of her entire body in his arms as she arched and pushed down helplessly.

"Yes," he ground out. "Yes, yes…!"

He dragged her down onto him, loving the way she clung to him, loving the way her body melted into his, the way she sobbed as he carried her far beyond the pleasure she'd felt their first time, into heights that she'd never dreamed could exist.

He was over her then, under her, all around her as they went from one side of the bed to the other in such a heat of need that even when the climax came, it wasn't enough. He was insatiable. It was dark when he could finally lift away from her.

THEY ATE IN SILENCE. She was in his lap, wearing a gown. He was in his slacks and nothing else.

She couldn't bear to stop touching him. Every time her eyes met his, the love in them almost blinded him.

He fed her eggs and bacon, fresh ones that he'd just cooked, his one good eye loving her all the while.

"Nothing in my life was ever like this," he said softly. "Even in my misspent youth, I wasn't able to feel what I feel with you."

She flushed a little with pride and embarrassment.

She opened her mouth as he coaxed another bite of scrambled eggs into her mouth.

He looked down at her with an odd expression. There was deep affection, hunger, but something else, something much deeper there.

"Why are you looking at me like that?" she asked softly.

"I keep having this damned weird dream," he said in a subdued tone. "Stupid, I know. You're crying, and pregnant, and I can't get to you…"

"Nightmares never make much sense," she interrupted. Her fingers went to the thick hair at his temple and savored its coolness.

"I suppose not." He laughed. "Domingo's got me being superstitious now. Maybe I shouldn't have cut my hair," he added with a grin.

She laughed, too. "I like the way you look. I sort of miss the ponytail, though," she confessed.

He fed her the last of the bacon and held the coffee cup to her lips. "It belonged to the old, wild life," he said simply. "The haircut is a statement of intent, in case you didn't notice," he said. "I'm showing you that things have changed." His face became somber as he searched her soft, loving eyes. "I'm almost thirty-one, Tat. I've lived hard, and I've worked in dangerous professions most of my life. But for the first time, I want a family, a home."

"With me?" she asked.

"Of course with you." He smiled gently. "I've never tried to make a woman pregnant in my life, you know," he added on a chuckle.

Her high cheekbones colored.

"What would you like to do today?" he asked when she finished the coffee.

"Anything you would," she replied. Her fingers reached up to touch his hard face, stroking down to his sensuous mouth.

"Anything?" he teased softly.

She laughed. "Well, I'm just a little...uncomfortable," she said delicately.

"I went at it hard and fast," he sighed. "I was so desperate for you, honey. I should have taken longer, both times."

"I didn't mind," she confessed.

He nuzzled his nose against hers. "Let's go shopping."

"Shopping?"

He nodded. "For a wedding gown. There are plenty of couture shops in Manaus. I want you to have a gown that we can hand down, if we have a daughter."

"An heirloom," she said huskily.

"Exactly. Like that ring." He brought her hand to his mouth and kissed it, where the ring sparkled. "My mother never took it off. It's the most precious heirloom I own."

"I'll take wonderful care of it," she promised.

"I know that." He drew in a long breath and smiled wickedly as his hand went to the buttons of his shirt that she was wearing.

She colored prettily. "Stanton..." she began nervously.

"I just want to look at you, baby," he whispered, nuzzling her nose with his. "You have to understand, this is like candy to me. I've gone without sweets for years, and now I'm in a lovely candy store with un-limited stock."

Her eyes softened even more. "I like looking at you, too," she whispered, smoothing one small hand against his bare chest.

"I noticed." He bent and brushed his mouth over her taut breasts. "It's like kissing rose petals," he whis-pered.

She arched up toward his mouth, denying him noth-ing. It felt so incredibly good, to be with him like this, to feel him wanting her, to know how he really felt about her. It was like a dream that came suddenly to life.

"You really...don't mind the scars, do you?" she asked when he lifted his head and his one good eye lingered where she'd been cut.

"I mind how it happened. I mind that I wasn't there to protect you from that animal," he confessed quietly.

Her fingers smoothed over his hard mouth, tracing the sensual curve of it. She was bereft of words, her feelings for him ran so high.

His mouth lowered to her breast and he kissed the scars, running his tongue delicately along them. She held his head to her, her fingers feeling the tension of the band that held the eye patch in place.

She started to slide it off. He caught her wrist, his good eye blazing with conflicting emotions.

"You silly man," she said softly, brushing his hand aside. "As if it matters to me. Shame on you."

With his jaw taut, his teeth clenched, he allowed her to remove the eye patch. She studied the mutilated socket, where his eye had been. There were scars there, too. He could have worn a glass eye, but he'd always refused the artificiality.

With a gentle sigh, she drew his head down and kissed the scars.

"God!" he exclaimed, torn with emotion. He caught her mouth under his and kissed her so hungrily that she gasped. It went on for a long time, as he tried to express an emotion so powerful that even words were inadequate to describe it.

He hugged her close, his mouth sliding down to her neck, to press there hungrily. "I've never let anyone look at it. Not even K.C."

"But you'll let me, my darling," she whispered against his temple, smoothing her lips over the tanned skin.

"I'd let you do anything to me," he said, his voice husky.

"That goes double for me."

He enveloped her against him, holding her, comforting her, feeling safe as he'd never felt safe in his life before. It was like coming home. His eye closed as he buried his face in her soft throat, rocked her against him, her bare breasts pressing hard into the warm muscle and thick hair of his broad chest.

"I love you so much," she whispered, almost in anguish. "If I lost you now...!"

"You won't lose me," he said gruffly. "I'll never let you go now, Tat. You belong to me."

"Yes. And you belong to me," she whispered back.

He tilted her face up to his, studying the rapt expression on it with pure wonder. He smiled tenderly as he traced the exquisite lines of her beautiful face, looked into her deep, china-blue eyes.

He looked strange, suddenly, as if he'd landed in an unfamiliar place and couldn't get his bearings. After a minute, he smiled a little remotely, and buttoned up the shirt, hiding her pretty breasts again.

"Let's go and visit the museum. You game?"

She laughed softly. His mood seemed to lighten. "Okay." She got off his lap. "I won't be a minute."

"I'll wait."

He watched her go with a terrible sense of foreboding. He didn't really have psychic abilities, but he was sensitive to mood and place and situation. It was a gift that had saved his life more than once. He didn't know exactly what he was feeling, but it frightened him. Something was going to happen, something perhaps life-threatening. He couldn't blurt that out in front of Tat, but he was going to be more watchful, at least for a while.

On the other hand, he was happier than he'd ever been in his life. Tat was going to marry him. He'd get to keep her forever. They'd have children; they'd make a home together. Odd, he thought, that freedom had been almost a religion to him until he'd known for sure that Tat wasn't related to him in any way. Once he was sure of that, he couldn't wait to put his ring on her finger. Maybe it was too soon for children, but he wanted those, too. So did she.

He smiled warmly, thinking about a little boy or a little girl in his arms, in Tat's arms. His parents had died brutally, when he was very young. He'd never known a settled family even so, because the man he thought was his father had been away with K.C. very often on missions overseas. His mother had loved him; she'd been kind to him. But after her death, and her husband's, Rourke had been left alone in the world at the age of ten. His children, he thought, were going to have both parents and a settled life.

That would mean making some changes in his own life. No more dangerous missions. He'd have to go administrative, like K.C. But he could make that sacrifice, just as he was certain that Tat wouldn't take the risk of going into combat zones as a reporter anymore.

It would be worth it, he thought, it would be worth anything to have Tat permanently in his life, in his arms. He was, he considered, the luckiest man on earth right now.

CHAPTER SIX

MANAUS WAS AN international city, with people of just about every ethnic group represented in its sophisticated interior.

Rourke had found an expensive European boutique online. He took Tat there in the rental car and smiled at her exuberance while she looked at a small selection of wedding gowns in her size.

She paused at one, fingering it delicately. Her eyes lit up. It was trimmed in exquisite Belgian lace, and there was just a hint of pastel embroidery in the skirt and the long train. The veil was a fingertip one, sheer and delicate, like the dress itself. It was white. She hesitated, her eyes troubled.

Rourke knew why. His fingers slid into hers. "We're engaged, my darling," he whispered at her ear. "Handfasting was one of the oldest customs in Scotland, where K.C.'s people came from. It permitted all sorts of delicious, forbidden intimacies, because the intent to marry was there." He turned her toward him. His face was solemn. "I'm sorry that I couldn't wait. I was honestly dying for you."

His headlong hunger for her was the one real thing in her life right now. He wasn't exaggerating. He had been starving for her.

She reached up and touched his cheek with just her fingertips. "It's all right," she said huskily.

He turned her hand and kissed the palm with muted ferocity. "I did try, you know," he whispered. His eye was tormented. "I really did."

"It's all right," she repeated. Her eyes adored him. "Honest."

He drew in a long breath. He searched her eyes and smiled. "You'll be the most beautiful bride who ever walked down the aisle. We'll have to talk to one of the local priests and see if he'll agree to marry us."

"I'd like Father Pete to do it," she said. "He was our family parish priest for years and years. He knew my mother."

His face closed up just briefly, but he averted his head so she wouldn't see it. He hated her mother. He was never going to be able to forgive her for the torment she'd put him, and Tat, through because of that one lie.

"If…if you'd rather have a civil ceremony," she began, disconcerted by his sudden coolness.

"No," he said at once, turning his gaze back to her. "I want something more permanent than that. I want you in church, Tat, with the priest, the candles, the whole works."

She smiled slowly. "You don't go to church."

He drew in a breath. "I suppose I'll have to work that out, won't I?" he teased. "A family man should encourage his kids to go to church."

She laughed. "Yes, he should."

"My mother was Methodist," he said. "My best friend in Jacobsville is a minster who preaches in a Methodist Church."

"Would you rather that he performed the ceremony?" she asked.

"Let's do it your way," he replied. "We can work out all the differences down the road," he added with a smile. "I just want to marry you, love. As soon as I possibly can."

"Are we in a rush?" she teased.

One lean hand went to her flat stomach and he looked her right in the eye. "Yes," he said. "I don't want people looking at your waistline. Because I have a feeling that if we wait a couple of months, they'll have a reason to look at it."

Her breath caught at the emotion she saw in his one brown eye.

"It might have already happened, last night," he whispered, and ruddy color filled in his high cheekbones. "You could be carrying my baby right now." He shivered. "God, that excites me, to think of that!"

She leaned against him, overcome with joy. She'd never in her wildest imaginings seen him as a man who'd want babies.

His arm tightened around her. He kissed the top of her head.

A saleslady, watching them with hidden amusement, approached from the counter. "May I help you with something?" she asked.

Rourke lifted his head and grinned at her. "Can you let her try on this gown?" he asked, indicating the one she'd paid such attention to. "We're getting married in a few days."

"Congratulations! And of course, you may try it on, my dear," she told Tat, who was beaming.

She took the dress from the rack. "Come with me, please."

Tat gave Rourke a long, soft look and a smile, and followed the saleslady to the back of the shop.

IT WAS BAD LUCK, to let the groom see the dress before the wedding. She felt it in her very bones. But she couldn't resist showing Rourke how elegant the couture garment was on her slender, pretty figure.

She walked out into the shop, with the veil down over her eyes, and Rourke looked at her and couldn't stop looking.

She went to him, fascinated by the expression on his face.

He swallowed, hard. "I don't care if I have to mortgage the farm to pay for it, you're having that," he said huskily.

She laughed. "It's not that expensive," she mused. "I asked. I can pay for it…"

He put a long forefinger over her lips. "I was teasing and you know it," he laughed. "Money will never be a problem. Both of us are rich beyond the dreams of avarice. But I'm paying for the dress."

"Okay."

"And the flowers," he added gently. "White roses, Tat?" he asked huskily.

She nodded slowly. "White roses."

He lifted the veil and looked into her wide, soft eyes. *"Myne vrou,"* he whispered in Afrikaans. *"Ek is lief vir jou."*

She flushed, because what he said was "My woman—my wife—I love you."

He bent and nuzzled her nose. "We'll have to find a mutual language for intimate whisperings," he chuckled.

"Afrikaans is beautiful," she whispered.

He smiled against her lips. "Then we'll make love in Afrikaans," he whispered. He laughed softly at her soft flush. He kissed her tenderly. "Buy the dress, my darling."

"Okay." She walked away from him, elegant and poised, and so beautiful that she took his breath away.

THEY SHOPPED FOR rings as well, but Tat only wanted a simple gold band to accompany the beautiful engagement ring he'd given her.

"I don't want a flashy diamond to show up this lovely ring," she explained as they stood together at the jewelry counter in an exclusive shop. "I want a band that will be like my dress," she explained. "An heirloom, to hand down to our daughter, if we have one."

He traced her eyebrows with a fingertip. "A daughter would be a long shot, honey," he said softly. "There hasn't been a female child born in my lineage in at least the past five decades."

Her heart jumped. She searched his eyes. "I wouldn't mind a son, as long as he looked like you. You're so handsome, Stanton."

He cleared his throat and looked vaguely embarrassed. "Gimpy eye and all?"

"You're the only person who has an issue with that eye patch. It makes you look very sexy," she murmured and peered up at him through her lashes with a secret little smile.

"Well!" he exclaimed.

Her fingers tangled with his. "I like this ring," she

said. It was a simple circle with white and yellow gold, not too wide, but with a vine-like pattern. "It's quite lovely."

He noticed that a man's ring was available in the same pattern. "I'll have the matching band," he said quietly.

Her eyes sought his. "You'd really wear it?" she faltered.

His hand contracted around hers. "After all these years," he told her. "Do you think I'll wander off with some flighty girl the minute your back is turned?" He leaned down to her ear. "Eight years of abstinence, Tat," he whispered. "Does that sound flighty to you?"

"Oh, no," she agreed breathlessly. "No, it doesn't."

He bent and brushed his mouth tenderly over her eyelids. "We'll buy the set. Then we'll go and talk to Father Pete. Okay?"

She smiled. "Okay, Stanton."

FATHER PETE WAS surprised and delighted at the news.

"Your father was quite fond of Rourke," he told Tat with a smile. "He admired and respected him. He would have been happy for you."

"My mother would have been, too," she faltered.

He didn't reply.

She frowned. "Father Pete…?"

"We'd like you to perform the ceremony, if you could, on Friday," Rourke interrupted. He knew immediately that Tat's mother had confided in Father Pete, had told him what she'd done. It unsettled him a bit.

"I'll make time," he replied. He gave them both a searching look and raised an eyebrow.

"Could I speak to you, in private?" Rourke asked him.

"Of course."

"I'll wait out here," Tat said, smiling. She inferred from the look they'd exchanged that Stanton had something to get off his chest. Men did have to have a few secrets, she pondered.

ROURKE'S FACE WAS hard as he faced the priest behind a closed door. "Clarisse's mother told a lie to me that kept me away from Tat for eight long years," he said coldly. "Ruined my life. Ruined Tat's."

"She was sorry for it, if that helps," Father Pete said gently. "She was afraid of your intentions. Clarisse was very young and, forgive me, you had a reputation as a rounder. Maria was concerned that you'd seduce her daughter and walk away."

"I loved Tat, even then," Rourke said heavily. "I would happily have married her at seventeen. In fact, that was what I had in mind. If her mother had spoken to me, given me a chance to tell her what I really felt…" He swallowed and shoved his hands into the pockets of his slacks. "You can't imagine what a burden she placed on me. Eight years of absolute hell. I couldn't touch another woman, in all that time…!"

Father Pete put a gentle hand on his shoulder. "I'm a priest, my son," he said with a faint smile. "You might not believe it, but I understand abstinence. In my profession, it's a requirement that brings its own burden."

Rourke relaxed, just a little. "I see." He hesitated. "Thanks. For not judging. Tat doesn't hide her emotions very well," he added with a faint laugh. "Things… got out of hand."

"When two people love each other that can happen.

The important thing is that you respect the tradition of marriage."

"I grew up in rural Africa," Rourke replied, "where tradition also has a place. I wouldn't dishonor Tat by offering her a relationship that didn't include marriage." He cleared his throat. "I love her very much."

"A mutual thing. She really doesn't hide her emotions well," Father Pete laughed.

Rourke drew in a breath. "I've never spoken about my work to anyone," he said. He hesitated. "Sometime, after the ceremony, I'd like to talk to you."

The priest's eyes were wise and kind. "I'll be happy to listen, to anything you want to say."

Rourke smiled. "Maybe it's time I made a few changes in my life besides wearing a wedding band," he replied. "Life is full of surprises."

"Yes."

"WHAT WERE YOU talking to Father Pete about?" Tat asked gently when they were outside again in the warm sun.

"Private things," he mused, smiling down at her. He linked his fingers with hers. "I'll tell you them, one day."

"All right. I won't pry."

He drew in a long breath. "I don't think I've ever been this happy in my life, Tat," he said. He pursed his lips. "That reminds me." He pulled out his cell phone, drew her close and took a selfie of the two of them with their heads together, smiling. He glanced at it, took another and nodded.

He put a legend under the photo: Guess who's get-

ting married?! And he sent it to K.C. in Africa, and
to Jake Blair and Micah Steele in Jacobsville, Texas.

THAT NIGHT SHE was still a little uncomfortable. But he
coaxed her out of her clothes, removed his and installed
them in her bed with the lights out.

He shifted restlessly.

"I'm sorry," she whispered, her mouth against his
shoulder. "If you…if you want to, it will be all right…"

He laughed deep in his throat and rolled onto his
side to kiss her worried eyes. "I'm sore, too," he whispered back.

She caught her breath. "Men get sore?"

"You were a virgin, my darling," he murmured
against her soft lips. "There was a barrier…?"

She cleared her throat. "Yes."

His whole body shivered. "I felt it tear. My God,
in all my life, nothing was ever as exciting as that, as
feeling your virginity, pushing past it…" He brought
his mouth down, hard, on hers. "You waited for me,"
he choked. "I could hardly believe it!"

Her arms slid around his neck and she pressed close,
loving the immediate reaction of his powerful body to
her nudity. "I couldn't bear to let another man touch
me, not after you," she confessed huskily. "Seventeen
years old and committed for life to a man whom I
thought hated me."

His arms contracted, bringing her closer. The embrace was almost painful. "I never hated you, baby,"
he whispered. "It was the other way around. But when
I thought there was blood between us…" He groaned,
and kissed her hungrily. "I walked into firefights, took
on the most dangerous assignments I could find, hoped

to die." His mouth slid onto her warm throat. "And I couldn't. The torment went on, year after year after year."

"For me, too." She drew in a shivery little breath. "I never understood why. It hurt, so much."

He smoothed her hair. One lean hand went down her back, savoring the silky skin, savoring its warm perfection. "Your body is absolutely perfect," he whispered. "I'd see you on television, at embassy balls, or at fund-raisers. Once when you were hostess at a tribute at the Kennedy Center. I fed on just the sight of you and hated myself for what I felt. I thought there had to be something unnatural in me."

She burrowed her face into his neck. "If only you could have told me."

"I should have," he confessed for the first time. "If I'd been honest, if we'd had things in the open, you might not have been so traumatized about it. Perhaps you might have found someone else to love, someone who wouldn't have hurt you so much."

Her arms tightened around his neck. "That would never have happened, Stanton," she whispered into his throat. "I could never have let another man touch me. Never."

His body vibrated. He groaned harshly as he found her mouth and kissed her until the aching finally stopped. He held her very close, in a bearish embrace, his arms tight around her. He groaned.

"I'm sorry..." she began.

"Hold on tight," he whispered. "It's a way of coping with unsatisfied desire. I read it in a book."

Her breath sighed out. "In a book?"

His hands smoothed down her back. "I've had prac-

tice at smothering my feelings," he chuckled. "I've
flirted with other women, invited them out, teased
them…even danced with them. But at the end of the
evening, I left them all at the door." His arms contracted. "It's hell, isn't it, loving just one person that
you think you can never have?"

"Yes."

He drew in a breath. "The difference is that I'd had
sex. I knew what it felt like in bed. It was worse, what
I felt for you, because I couldn't satisfy it."

Her fingers twirled around in the hair at his nape. "I
wouldn't have understood that, even a few days ago."

"And now you do," he whispered.

"Oh, yes," she said huskily. "It's like…eating potato
chips." She laughed softly when he chuckled. "Well,
you know what I mean."

"Actually, I do. I want you all the time now."

"I want you, too," she moaned. "And I can't do a
thing about it!"

"Do you think so?"

She heard the amusement in his deep voice as he
shifted her and suddenly brought his mouth down hungrily over one of her small breasts, suckling it.

She went up like a rocket. He heard her cries of ec-
stasy even before he felt her body shudder to comple-
tion under him. He was still laughing when he felt
her relax.

"Nothing excites me more than that," he whispered
rakishly at her ear. "That I can satisfy you by suckling
your pretty breast. You don't know how flattering it is."

"But…you had nothing," she whispered.

He cleared his throat. "My source of satisfaction is
in just one place," he confessed with a dry laugh. "And

that soreness does rather preclude having someone touch me, even with the best intentions."

She kissed his throat. "I'm sorry, just the same."

"No need to be, darling. In a few days, we'll both be back to normal," he said softly.

"Yes." Her fingers ran over his chest and up to smooth through his hair. She felt the strap of the eye patch and gently removed it, tossing it onto the bedside table. "Why do you wear it in bed?" she whispered. "I love to kiss you there, where the scars are." She did that, feeling the tremor that went through him.

"Why?" he managed. The kisses were powerfully affecting to a man who'd been sensitive about the loss of the eye for years.

"Because you were hurt, my darling, and when I do this—" she kissed the long scar that ran from his brow down almost to his cheekbone through the wound "—it feels like I'm kissing it better."

He groaned and held her close.

"I will love you every day for the rest of my life," she whispered drowsily. "I will never stop, no matter what happens."

"I will love you just as much," he promised. He brought her hand to his mouth and kissed his mother's engagement ring on her finger. "Where are we going to live, baby?"

She relaxed against him. "I'd like to live in Nairobi," she said simply. She smiled against his cheek. "I like your lion."

He laughed. "Lou likes you, too. He isn't friendly with most people." He smoothed over her back. "But when the kids start coming along, we might have to transfer him out of the compound where the house is. I won't take chances with our sons."

"Sons, plural?" she teased, kissing his throat.

"I want several. What do you think?"

She reached up and kissed his hard mouth. "Me, too," she murmured. "It's so much fun trying to make them," she confessed with a shy laugh.

"And just think, I was far too hungry to go through my whole repertoire with you," he whispered wickedly.

Her breath caught. "The mind boggles."

"Everything will boggle, when we're both back to normal," he promised. "I'll take an hour rousing you before I have you, next time," he whispered. "And when you come, we'll have to make sure the windows are closed. Because they'll hear you all the way in downtown Manaus."

She shivered. "You rake!"

"Count on it."

She nuzzled his shoulder. "Can you teach me, to do that to you?"

"Honey," he whispered, drawing her closer, "I'll teach you everything you need to know. And delight in the lessons. You are my treasure. My very soul."

She closed her eyes. "I love you."

He kissed her forehead. "I love you."

She sighed and smiled.

THE NEXT FEW days went by in a heated rush. Clarisse was still uncomfortable, so they'd spent that time talking, kissing, reminiscing. They got to know each other in the most intimate way. It was two days before the wedding. And then it all went to pot. Rourke answered his cell phone, cursed virulently in Afrikaans while he listened to the caller, made curt replies, hesitated and protested and, finally, agreed.

"What is it?" Clarisse asked. They were sitting at the kitchen table, sipping coffee.

His face was harder than she'd seen it recently. He poured himself another cup, warmed hers and dropped down into the chair across from hers. "I told you that we'd been setting up surveillance in an international kidnapping ring, yes?"

She nodded.

"It's my operation. I promised that I'd stay with it until the end. Things had gone quiet for months, but now the perpetrator is moving. He's in Algeria." His lips made a straight line. "I'm the only operative we have who's been involved with this case from the beginning. I have to go. It's my job."

She'd never found out what agency he worked for. He wouldn't tell her. It might have been one of K.C.'s, too. Rourke was tight-lipped about things.

"You're...leaving?" she faltered. "But the wedding is in two days...!" She felt so hurt that he was putting his job before their life together... He might be killed!

"I know." He searched her worried eyes and frowned. "Tat, believe me, if there was any other way, I wouldn't go. I've been on this case for over a year. This man..." His teeth ground together. "You saw some of the things that went on in Ngawa. Believe me when I tell you that this man is capable of worse atrocities than you'd ever dream could exist. Many of them involved small children, held hostage and tortured because of what their fathers knew." His whole face contracted when he saw her go pale. "I can't let him walk because of my personal life. I love you. I want to marry you.

But I have to go in the morning. We'll talk to Father Pete. It's just a postponement, my darling," he added, closing her fingers with his. "That's all. Just a postponement."

Tears were rolling down her cheeks. She knew the sort of work Rourke was involved in, because she'd been in Barrera when the offensive began. "You could be killed," she choked.

He got up and pulled her into his arms. "I have every reason in the world to want to live right now," he whispered into her ear. "We'll have a wedding, a real one. You can wear that gorgeous dress and walk down the aisle to me. I'll slide another ring on your finger—" he kissed the one that she wore now "—and we'll have a honeymoon somewhere exotic." He laughed softly. "I'll ravish you," he threatened with an earthy mock growl.

She pressed close, her eyes lifting to his. He was so precious to her, and she understood his dedication. She couldn't let him go without one more night to remember. "Are you still sore?" she whispered, and flushed.

"No," he whispered back. "Are you?"

She shook her head. Watching him, she drew the straps of her sundress over her shoulders and let the dress fall. She was wearing nothing under it except lacy pink briefs. Her nipples were standing up like little flags.

He shuddered at just the sight of her. "All of it," he said through his teeth, his eye dark and hungry on her body. "All of it, Tat."

She was a little embarrassed to be so blatant, but she bent and removed the briefs and then stood up, letting him look.

"Now come here," he said in voice like velvet. "Take my clothes off."

Her lips fell apart.

"You did it in Barrera the night I was drunk," he whispered. "I want to be sober and watch you do it."

She was entranced. She moved buttons out of buttonholes, his belt out of the loops and, finally, got her hand under two waistbands and pulled them down.

He was magnificent. Even more magnificent than he'd been that night in Barrera. She caught her breath, just looking at him.

He slid out of his shoes, picked her up and walked back to the bedroom, placing her down gently on the covers. He stood over her, shivering a little with desire, as his eye ate her from head to toe. She had silky, creamy pink skin all over. Her pert little breasts were beautifully shaped, the nipples pink and tight. Her body moved on the coverlet while he looked at her, savoring the desire he read on her face.

He eased down beside her. His mouth went down her body like fingers, touching, tasting. He moved her long legs apart and his lips smoothed over the inside of her thighs. She moaned harshly.

He laughed. "It gets better," he whispered.

He touched and tasted, explored her like fine china. She felt his mouth all the way up and down her spine while his hands made magic against her breasts. She arched up to give them better access while his mouth fed on her soft skin.

She felt the press of his muscular body down her back as he moved, slowly turning her so that she was on her side, facing him.

His expression was one of wonder. He touched her

face, her high cheekbones, her mouth, with just the tips of his fingers.

"I never thought...it would ever be like this," she managed, shivering from the slow seduction of his touch.

"I knew it would," he whispered as he bent to brush his mouth lovingly across her warm, soft lips. "That was why it was such a hell. Wanting, with no hope of relief," he said huskily. His jaw tautened as he moved back just enough to see the long, seductive curve of her body next to his in the bed. "I couldn't even touch you..." His voice broke. He moved closer, rolling her gently onto her back. "But I dreamed of it," he said. "Ached for it. Cursed myself for dreaming." His mouth moved hungrily against hers. "And now, the dreams are real, Tat. Real!"

His mouth ran down her body, possessive and slow, awakening even more sensitivity from her breasts, her flat belly. His hands found her again, roused her to such passion that she cried out and begged him to end it.

"Slowly," he whispered as he levered himself above her, between her long, soft legs. "Slowly, Tat. Make it last..."

Her arms went up around his neck and she watched his face as he touched her, letting him see her responses, letting him watch her moan in agony as he promised and promised, but drew back over and over again.

She was arching up toward him now, her whole body one silent plea for relief from the anguish of desire. Her face was red with it, her eyes open and wild. She was trembling.

"Yes," he whispered. His hand moved down and he positioned her. "Watch it happen," he said softly, drawing her eyes down to his slow, agonizingly slow possession of her.

She caught her breath and moaned so harshly that he shivered.

"Slowly," he whispered. He moved against her tenderly, his hips advancing, withdrawing, the fullness inside her growing and swelling until she gasped again and looked up at him with faint apprehension.

"You can take me, darling," he whispered, aware of his own potency. "I'm more aroused than I have been. But you'll fit me." He moved down slowly and shivered, his teeth grinding together. "You'll fit me. You'll fit me, Tat, you'll…fit me…like a glove…!"

With each deepening, sharp movement, he was lifting her completely out of the world and into realms that the two of them hadn't even touched.

"Stanton!" she cried out, shuddering, as the feeling grew so quickly, so urgently, that she was moving violently with him, her body pleading with him, her mouth open as the sensations mounted until she thought she might explode.

"Yes," he bit off as he saw her face, felt the sudden contractions around that part of him that was blatantly male. He bit off a curse and drove into her, his hands gripping the pillow on either side of her thrashing head, his hips going like pistons, the sound of their bodies straining the springs of the bed loud in the heated silence of the room.

"Now," he cried out. "Now, now, oh, God, now…!"

She gasped and shuddered as the heat went over her like a wave of pure, unadulterated pleasure, molten and hot and sweet. She convulsed under his half-seeing gaze. He went with her, shuddering, arching, shivering, as he endured the most explosive climax of his entire life.

She was sobbing. It was so sweet, so sweet, so sweet, and then it was…gone!

"No," she wept, clinging to him. "No, no, no…!"

He shuddered one last time, wringing the last silvery drops of pleasure from her as he began, finally, to relax on her damp, still-moving body.

"Stanton," she sobbed.

"Shhhh," he whispered, his voice breaking as he strove for breath. "Shhhh. I'll make it all right. Trust me."

He moved again, very slowly, watching her face. She was so sensitive now that he could satisfy her with just a very few tender thrusts of his body. She shuddered, her eyes wide-open, frozen with pleasure. He did it again, smiling.

"You like…watching me," she whispered.

"Yes." He moved again, very slowly, and his one good eye was on her face, seeing the pleasure take her once more. "I love watching you. I love seeing the pleasure and knowing that I'm the cause of it. You're beautiful, like this," he whispered. "My Tat, sweet and soft and shivery with fulfillment."

"I watched…you," she breathed as he brought her to fulfillment one last time.

He smiled tenderly. "I know. That was why I went up like a rocket," he chuckled softly. "It excites me."

She began to relax, with one last little shiver of sensation. "You don't feel it as much as I do," she faltered, trying to make him understand.

He kissed her eyelids shut. "I feel it once. A woman's body is capable of endless satisfaction. Some men can go all night. I wish I was one of them. I'd wear you out from dusk until dawn every night of my life."

She touched his mouth softly. "I only meant I wished you could feel it the same way, that you had more than a taste…"

He burst out laughing. "More than a taste? My God, I'm wrung out from the most explosive orgasm of my entire life, and you think it was only a taste?" he exclaimed.

CHAPTER SEVEN

"BUT YOU'VE HAD so many women," she said, flushing a little as she said it.

He was leaning over her, propped on an elbow, his body still completely joined to her own. He smiled. "A long time ago, my darling," he said softly. "Before that memorable Christmas Eve. What I did with you was relatively innocent, but I'd never felt the sensations you provoked in me."

"I didn't know a thing."

He chuckled. "That's what made it so exciting. Then, and now," he said, moving his hips sensuously.

She moaned softly and lifted toward his hips.

He bent to her soft mouth. "Want some more candy?" he whispered, and moved again.

Her nails bit into his lower back as he began to move on her. She curled her legs around his and he stiffened suddenly.

She felt why. Her eyes widened with fascination. "You said you…well, you said," she faltered, "that you could only do it once…?"

He felt himself swelling, burgeoning inside her. He shivered. "That's never happened before," he whispered, searching her eyes.

She gasped as he moved again.

"I want it deeper this time," he said huskily. "Harder.

Rougher." There was a wildness in him that she'd never seen. "Are you afraid?"

She shook her head slowly from side to side, excited by the expression on his face.

He caught a pillow in one lean hand. "Lift up, sweetheart."

She did. He placed the pillow under her hips, tilting them up into his.

"It isn't meant to hurt," he whispered. "If it does, or if I frighten you, you say so at once. Understand?"

"Yes." Her blue eyes gleamed with excitement. "What are you going to do to me?"

"I'm going to ravish you, my sweet," he whispered, and laughed like a devil.

"How?" she teased.

He pushed her back onto the bed, pinning her hands above her head, and moved violently against her. "Like...this...!"

IT DIDN'T TAKE LONG. He was very excited, and she was immediately responsive to the unfamiliar violence of his possession. But even then, he didn't hurt her. He was rough and hungry, and he laughed with pure delight when she wrapped her long legs around his hips and dared him to do it harder, deeper, quicker.

He laughed when he fell off the edge of the world with her, shuddering to a climax that shook her, shook him, shook the bed. He cried out, almost in anguish at the pleasure. Under him she was gasping, too, pleading for more, more, more...!

He satisfied her over and over again, rolling from one side of the bed to the other with his body joined intimately to hers. One last silken contraction riveted

them together in a twisted, hot contortion of satisfaction that left them wet with sweat and gasping for
breath as they shivered and shivered and, finally, relaxed.

"My God," she whispered.

"I thought it might frighten you, to be taken so
roughly," he mused, and then laughed. "Wildcat! You
clawed me!"

"I bit you, too," she said, wincing as she saw the
marks she'd left on his shoulder.

"What an experience," he said huskily, shaking
his head. "I've gone through everything I remember
from my youth and now I'm making it up as I go," he
laughed. "We're teaching each other pleasure, Tat,"
he explained when she gave him a curious appraisal.
"Men aren't born knowing what to do, and every
woman is different."

"Different, how?" she asked with real curiosity.

He lifted an eyebrow and gave her a worldly look.

"Come on," she teased. "I want to know."

He drew her beside him and wrapped her up in his
arms with a long sigh. "Okay. Women are sensitive in
different areas of their bodies. I even knew a woman
once whose erotic zone was her neck."

"Really?"

He saw the faint jealousy she couldn't hide. "It was
before I touched you," he said softly. "Try to keep that
in mind, okay?"

"Sorry."

He kissed her nose. "Other women are sensitive
here, like you are." He touched her breast and watched
the nipple peak instantly, despite the fact that she was
drowsy with fulfillment.

She caught her breath.

"Nice to know that I can make an impression even when you're sated, my love," he whispered, rubbing his forefinger over the small hardness.

She cocked her head at him. "I don't understand."

His eyebrows arched. "Don't you know why your nipples get so hard?"

She shifted. "Well… I guess I don't, really."

"A woman's body shows desire in a different way than a man's does," he explained gently. "Yours is visible here." He touched her breast lightly. "That's what happened that long-ago Christmas Eve. I looked at you and your nipples went hard under that slinky dress. I knew you wanted me before I ever touched you."

"Oh!"

He laughed softly. "You have beautiful breasts, Tat," he said, gazing at them with quiet delight. "I love kissing them." He traced around one and his face grew thoughtful, almost somber.

"What are you thinking?" she asked.

"I was thinking about the baby you had in your arms in Ngawa," he said quietly. "And wondering how it would be to watch you breast-feed ours."

Her breath caught.

He looked up into her eyes. "Would you breast-feed him?"

She was so choked with feeling that she could only nod.

He smoothed back the disheveled blond hair from her face. "I hope we made a baby, Tat," he said gently. "I want one with all my heart."

"So…do I." Tears ran down her cheeks.

He kissed them all away. "Everything is going to

be all right," he promised her. "I'll only be away for a few days, a week or two at the most. When I get back, we'll be married immediately."

She pressed close to him, shivering. "I'll die if something happens to you. I mean it."

He hugged her close, his eye closing as he kissed her soft throat. "Nothing is going to happen. Not now. We have a long and happy life ahead of us." He lifted his head. "I'll have to make some changes," he added, seeing the quiet terror in her face. "I won't have you worried like this again. I swear it."

She traced the hard, beloved lines of his face. "You're my whole life, Stanton," she whispered, her lips trembling. "I can't lose you again...!"

His mouth ground down into hers. "You won't," he said huskily. "You'll never lose me. Never!"

He wrapped her up tight and held her until the fear subsided. But it was still there, coiled up in her heart like a serpent hatching, waiting to break loose. She'd never had premonitions before, but she was afraid for him to go. And she couldn't do a thing to stop him.

HE WAS PACKED and dressed when she woke the next morning, her sleep disturbed by sounds of movement.

She looked up. He had his suitcase ready and he was standing over her, wearing khakis, looking so sexy that her breath caught at just the sight of him.

"You're bad for my ego," he mused, sitting down beside her to strip away the covers so that he could look at her beautiful, nude body. "You'll make me strut, looking at me like that."

"You're so gorgeous," she laughed, but it had a hollow sound.

"Not like you, sweet," he whispered. He bent and put his mouth over her soft breast, his tongue working tenderly at the nipple. He raised his head and smiled at her rapt expression.

"Don't you make eyes at other women," she said firmly, and her eyes twinkled. "You belong to somebody."

"I belong to you, my darling," he said huskily. His fingers touched her lovely face as if they wanted to memorize it. "And you belong to me. When Carvajal comes back, you tell him that," he added with a flash of jealousy in his pale brown eye.

She smiled lazily. "He'll know it just by looking at me. I can't hide what I feel. I never could."

He bent and brushed his mouth tenderly over hers, and then not so tenderly, with passion and hunger and remorse.

He got up at once, before she could tempt him back into the bed. "I have to go. This isn't my decision, or my choice. If it was, I couldn't be got out of here with ropes."

"I know."

His eye swept down the length of her and he shivered. "I won't be long. Not if I have to get them to bring in somebody else for me to train. This is the last job of this kind that I'll ever take."

"Can you call me?" she asked. "Can I call you?"

He smiled. "I can call you. I'll have to do it covertly, so we won't be able to chat much. But I will keep in touch."

"All right."

He drew in a long breath. "Best I go, now, while I

still can. I love you," he added curtly. "Don't ever forget that, no matter what happens—you hear me, Tat?"

"I hear you. I love you, too."

His eyes swept over her one last time. He had a feeling of such sadness that it almost knocked him to his knees, as if he knew something tragic lay ahead, but not what.

"So long, Tat."

He picked up his kit and walked out the door, closing it behind him. He didn't look back. Clarisse waited until she heard the rental car start up and drive away before she let the hot tears run down her face.

THE FIRST DAY without him was like hitting a stone wall headfirst. She couldn't settle anywhere. She tried to watch television, but she couldn't bear to sit still. She cooked, but she couldn't eat. She walked near the house, her arms wrapped tight around herself, drowning in memories so sweet that they made her ache.

Just when she thought loneliness might actually kill her, a car drove up out front. She knew it wasn't Rourke, but she ran to the door just the same.

Peg Grange got out of her limousine and ran to meet Clarisse, her arms open. "Hi!" she exclaimed. "Did you think I'd forgotten you?"

Clarisse hugged her and hugged her. "Oh, I'm so glad to see you!" she exclaimed. "Rourke's gone off on a mission and I'm scared to death for him…"

Peg's eyes widened. "Rourke…?"

Clarisse held out her left hand and flushed. "It was his mother's. We're engaged. We were supposed to be married tomorrow, but then he got a phone call and he was asked to go somewhere to help. He was the only person who could go."

"You're engaged. To Rourke." Peg was still trying to digest it. "But he hates you...!"

Clarisse's eyes were full of wonder. "He thought we were related," she said. "Somebody told him we were. But he found out the truth and came looking for me." She flushed. "I still can't believe it. He loves me. He wants children with me."

"Now a lot of things become clear," Peg laughed softly. "I couldn't understand the way he was with you when they were invading Barrera. He looked at you as if you were his greatest treasure. He was wild when he knew you'd been hurt. I remember, he didn't even glance at anyone else when he came into the camp—he headed straight for you." She sighed. "Winslow was there when the man who tortured you came rolling down the steps at the general's headquarters. He said he'd never seen Rourke like that. He was hell-bent on avenging you." She smiled. "Now it makes sense. He loved you."

"I can't imagine who could have told him such a thing," she confessed. "At first I thought perhaps K.C. did, but K.C. likes me..."

"The important thing is that it's settled now," Peg said.

Clarisse was staring pointedly at the other woman's stomach.

"Yes," Peg laughed. "I'm pregnant. We're both over the moon! I don't care what gender the baby is, I'm just so happy!"

"I'm happy for you. I hope very much to be in a

similar condition soon. Want some decaf?" she added with a grin.

"I'd love some!"

CLARISSE LED HER into the house and they sat talking for a long time, going over the amazing path they'd both taken from misery to joy.

"He actually followed me here from Barrera," Clarisse sighed, smiling. "I was sure that he was only bent on conquest. You know, the one woman he wanted and couldn't have. But it wasn't like that at all." She flushed and lowered her eyes. "Things...sort of got out of control."

"You're getting married," Peg replied warmly. "It doesn't really matter, does it? You'll both love a child."

"I want one more than anything. I just wish they'd waited a few more days to call him back to work."

"Who does he work for?" Peg asked.

Clarisse shook her head. "I've never known. He did some intelligence work for K.C. in the past, but I think he's working for somebody else now. He never talks about it."

"It's classified stuff, I imagine," Peg said. "General Machado's son, Rick Marquez, is married to the daughter of the head of the CIA. We know about classified." She grinned.

"How's your dad?" Clarisse asked. "We heard that you and Winslow were in the States..."

"He's going to be fine," she said. "It was his gallbladder. They had to take it out. He had some really bad attacks until they found out what was causing them. I didn't realize how serious it could be."

"I'm glad that he's going to be okay. The awards ceremony was very nice. We all got medals."

"The general sent ours to us, express," she laughed. "We're having them framed. Something to brag about to our children when they're old enough."

"Life is funny," Clarisse said warmly.

"Indeed it is."

THE DAYS PASSED slowly after that. Clarisse went shopping, did the housework, worked in her flower garden. But mostly she missed Rourke.

He did phone every other night, although the conversations were necessarily brief.

"Miss me?" he teased during the last call.

"So much that I'm breaking out in hives," she laughed. "When are you coming home?"

"Home." There was a smile in his deep voice. "Wherever you are will be home, Tat. I miss you so much."

"I miss you, too."

"So, are you pregnant yet?" he asked wickedly.

"I don't know," she laughed.

"If you aren't, it's not my fault," he murmured drily. "I'm looking forward to having a child of my own."

"So am I."

"We'll spoil him rotten."

"I know."

"I wish we could... Wait a sec." He covered the microphone with a big hand, and there was mumbled conversation. "Damn! He's skipped the country. Headed out to a certain Middle Eastern country that I don't dare name, and we have to get packed and go after him. Listen, sweetheart, I'll call you the minute I can, okay?"

"Okay. Please be careful!"

"I will. I promise. I love you."

"I love you, too."

The line went dead.

She hung up and glared at the telephone. "Damn!" she said fervently.

THE WEEK TURNED into weeks. She heard from Rourke one more time, a terse conversation that had undertones of anger and exasperation at the time the project was taking. He promised to phone her again as soon as he could, but they were required to maintain radio silence for the next few days. It would be all right, he promised. He was safe and he wasn't taking chances. He'd be home, very soon.

She wanted to believe him, but his quick job seemed to be turning into a career. She'd wanted to tell him during their last conversation that he needed to hurry up. She was losing her breakfast daily and her waistline was increasing. She was almost certain that she was pregnant.

IN THE MIDDLE of her worry, Ruy Carvajal came home from Argentina. The minute he saw her, he was worried.

"You've lost weight," he exclaimed. "And you look…terrible. Forgive me…"

She managed a smile. "I'm just pregnant, Ruy, that's all." She held up her engagement ring. "We were supposed to be married just before Rourke left on a job overseas. He's trying to get back, but the job seems to be growing more complicated by the minute."

He frowned. "You're certain that he does intend marriage?" he asked suspiciously.

She was less certain than ever. She grimaced. "This was his mother's engagement ring," she said softly, touching it. "It's the most precious thing he owns."

He sighed. "Then perhaps I misjudge him." He cocked his head and studied her, smiling softly. "Well, if things don't work out, I will marry you and help you raise your child," he said gently. "It is the closest I would ever be to having one of my own." His voice was sad.

"If things don't work out," she said gently, "I'll take you up on that."

He smiled.

"How was your trip?" she asked, to divert him. "I'll make coffee and you can tell me all about it."

ANOTHER TWO WEEKS went by with no word from Rourke. Clarisse didn't even know how to contact him. She'd tried using his cell phone number, the one she had, but it was never answered. In desperation, she contacted K.C. in Nairobi.

"No, I haven't heard from him, either," K.C. replied solemnly. "I have to confess that I'm concerned. It isn't like Rourke to keep me in the dark. I have top secret clearance. Even if he couldn't tell you what's going on, he could talk to me. I haven't heard from him in two weeks."

"Oh, dear."

"He said you were getting married."

She laughed. "Yes. I'm wearing his mother's engagement ring. I can't even tell you how happy I am. It's like every dream I've ever had in my life came true. I love him so!"

"No news there," he replied. "He feels exactly the same. All he talked about was getting to you in Barrera, making you listen, getting you back in his life. He was like a poor man who'd just won the lottery."

She smiled at the words. "Now I do feel better. I wondered, you see, if maybe he'd had second thoughts..."

"The man who left here for Barrera several weeks ago wasn't looking for ways out of a relationship, Clarisse," he chuckled.

"I suppose not."

"Where are you two going to live?"

"I suggested Nairobi," she said. "When the kids come along, it would be nice for them to have at least a grandparent around. There's nobody left on my side of the family, you know."

There was a pause. "That's nice of you. I'd love being a grandfather. I'm still in the early stages of fatherhood. I love it," he laughed. "I always suspected Rourke was mine, but I never had the guts to get the tests done. I wanted it too much."

"So did he. You're all he ever talked about."

"Sometimes," he said, "life is good."

"Sometimes it is. If you hear anything, anything at all...?"

"I'll certainly phone you," he replied. "And the minute he comes home, I'll send a plane for you."

"That would be so kind," she said.

"We'll have one hell of a celebration," he said. "A

welcome home and engagement party, all rolled into one."

"I can't wait!"

He chuckled. "Neither can I. It shouldn't be much longer, surely."

"That's what I'm hoping."

BUT ROURKE DIDN'T CALL. Clarisse felt a sense of foreboding that wouldn't go away. A man as passionately involved with a woman as Rourke was with her didn't just stop communicating all at once. She didn't even consider that there might be another woman. She was as certain of Rourke's feelings as she was of her own. But why didn't he call? Had something gone wrong? Was he hurt, injured, maybe dying?

She was pacing. Ruy had cooked a nice stew for them and coaxed her to eat some of it. "You have to stop this," he said, concerned. "If not for your own sake, for the child's."

She grimaced. He'd done the blood test himself, without revealing to anyone who the patient was. She was very definitely pregnant. There was that worry along with the concern for Rourke. Even in a city the size of Manaus, there were many people who knew Clarisse's family and would remember her saintly mother. It would be unspeakable for her to fall pregnant out of wedlock. She would never get over the disgrace.

"Listen to me," Ruy said quietly, "if he doesn't come back, we'll get married in a civil service," he added. "It won't be binding as it would if we married in the holy church. If he does come back, I'll step aside. But we must not wait too much longer."

She was wan and depressed, but she smiled at him.

"Dear Ruy," she said gently. "I wish I could care for you the way you want me to."

He shrugged. "It is as well," he replied with resignation. "I could only give you a half life, never a child or a full relationship." He smiled sadly. "But it would honor me to have people think I was the father of your child, even if it is a fiction. It is difficult to reach my age among the people I treat, to have them wonder why I do not marry and have a family of my own. We would be helping each other. A marriage of friends."

She reached out and touched his dark hand gently. "If worse comes to worse, I would be honored to marry you. And grateful for the kindness."

His hand curled over hers. "But perhaps it will not even be necessary," he said, trying to comfort her. "Surely you will hear from him soon."

"I pray that I will," she said. "If he's just alive," she added, her eyes dark blue with worry. "That's all I ask. Just for him to live, even if I lose him…!"

Almost as if in answer to the prayer, the telephone rang, making her jump.

She ran to pick it up. "Yes?"

There was a pause. "Clarisse, it's K.C.…."

"How is he? Is he alive?" she burst out.

He drew in a breath. "Yes. He's alive. They're air-lifting him home to Nairobi. It was touch and go for a few days. I didn't know, or we'd both have gone to see him in Germany. You see, they didn't know he had family," he ground out. "I haven't made it public yet that I'm his father, so nobody was even notified."

He sounded anguished. Her hands were cold around the phone. "Is he…conscious?"

"He's conscious. But…there's a complication."

"What?" she asked, her mind wrapping around all sorts of horrible complications. Had he lost a limb, lost the sight in his other eye...?

"He's lost his memory," K.C. said curtly. "God, I hate to tell you this! He doesn't remember anything about the past few months. The last thing he remembers is the incursion into Barrera. Nothing since."

She sat down hard in a chair. "Oh, my God," she whispered brokenly. Tears ran down her cheeks. "Is it...permanent?"

"The neurosurgeon doesn't know. It's possible that he may regain some memories, but it may take a long time. How much of the memory will come back is anybody's guess. There's no permanent brain damage, at least."

She drew in a breath. "Can I come and see him?"

There was another pause. "I'll send the Learjet to pick you up. Clarisse, if he remembers you, it won't be as a fiancée. Do you understand? He'll be back in the past, before he knew the truth, before he understood that you weren't related to him. Damn it all!" he burst out.

She felt the blood draining out of her face. She was engaged. She was pregnant. And Rourke didn't remember.

"Clarisse?"

She swallowed. Hard. "Yes, I'm still here."

"I'm so sorry, honey," he said softly.

"Thanks, K.C."

"I'll call you back when I've alerted my pilot. If he has to...he'll fly you back to Manaus. Okay?"

She understood what he was saying. "Okay," she said. She hung up and went to get her things together.

"What?" Ruy asked, lounging against the doorway while she packed.

"He's alive but he doesn't have any recent memory," she said.

He nodded. "Focal retrograde amnesia." He understood.

She turned. "Prognosis?"

He grimaced.

She drew in a breath. "That's what I thought." She continued packing. As she opened her closet door, some of the lace of the beautiful wedding gown spilled out onto the clean wood floor. She looked at it with anguish.

Ruy moved closer. He turned her into his arms and held her while she cried as if her heart would break.

"You will have your own memories, Clarisse," he said at her ear. "And the baby. Even if you lose every other thing, you will still have those."

She nodded. "Yes."

"Go to Africa. See him. But if you have to come home, we'll arrange the wedding as soon as you're back."

She dried her eyes and looked up at him. "You're the nicest man I know, Ruy," she whispered.

He smiled and bent to kiss her forehead. "That's something, at least. Finish packing. When K.C. calls you back, I'll drive you to the airport."

HE DID, PUTTING her on the small aircraft with a sad smile. He knew, as she did, that the trip was likely to end in more misery.

Clarisse thanked the pilot for coming the long way to get her. He was personable and friendly, and very good at the controls. His copilot was also a certified pilot. They made sure that one of them was always feeling fresh. Pilot error accounted for most fatal crashes.

She settled into her seat and closed her eyes. At least she could see Stanton one more time, feed her heart on the sight of him, even if he wasn't welcoming, even if he threw her out on her ear.

He wouldn't remember how sweetly they'd loved. He wouldn't remember the tenuous new relationship that had given them pleasure beyond words, companionship and friendship that they'd never enjoyed. He'd loved her. Could he have forgotten? Such a memory, so ardent, so consuming, how could anyone forget something so poignant?

Of course, amnesia would shroud all the memories, good and bad. She wondered during the long way to Nairobi what she was going to find when she got there.

There was one tiny spark of hope that the sight of her alone might work a miracle, might bring back those memories that they shared of the magical days in Manaus. That hope kept her going.

CHAPTER EIGHT

It was late afternoon when the pilot set down at the Nairobi airport. K.C. had a car waiting to take Clarisse to the compound.

"I'm calling in my relief pilot, just in case," the pilot told her with a gentle smile. "I don't think you'll be going back to Manaus today. But…"

"But it's best to cover all your bases," Clarisse agreed sadly. "Thanks very much."

He nodded. "Good luck. I hope everything turns out well."

"So do I," she agreed.

The driver took her out of Nairobi and down long roads to the game park that Rourke owned. K.C. had already said that was where they were taking him. All the way, she worried about her reception. She remembered how it had been in the past, how Rourke had hated her, how he'd spoken to her. It would be so much worse now, after the happiness he'd given her in Manaus, to go back to those sad days. But, after all, he was still alive. She had to remember how it had been when she didn't know. He was alive. That was what really mattered.

She laid a gentle hand on the small bump under her dress where her child lay. She'd already decided that she would tell no one, not even K.C., about the baby.

If things didn't work out, if she had to leave, it would be just as well if everyone thought Ruy was the father of her child. She couldn't risk having K.C. let something slip. The old Rourke, if he knew it was his child, wouldn't have been above a court battle to take the child from her. He could be ruthless. She simply didn't dare take the chance. The baby was all she would have of him, for the rest of her life. And she wasn't going to let Rourke take him away from her.

Just the same, she hoped all the way down the dusty road to the game park that her fears were going to be needless. Surely he'd recognize her. He had to!

THE DRIVER PARKED at the front door. Rourke's house was huge. It had porches all the way around with luxurious furniture, just meant for lounging. The roof was tin, red and shiny. The fences around the property were sturdy and high. Behind one, Rourke's lion, Lou, sat chewing on a big beef bone. He looked up briefly into Clarisse's eyes before he went back to his bone.

K.C. met her on the porch. He looked devastated.

She joined him on the top step.

"He doesn't remember that I'm his father," K.C. said quietly. "Dear God…!"

She hugged him gently. He looked as if he needed comforting. "Give it time," she said softly. "It's early days yet."

He managed a smile. "You look terrible," he remarked.

She sighed. "It hasn't been the best few weeks of my life, either. At least he's alive, K.C.," she reminded him. "At least, there's that."

"Yes."

Voices came from inside the house. A woman's voice, laughing.

Clarisse's face went pale.

K.C. drew in a breath. "Charlene," he said under his breath. "She was here with her father, a business associate of mine, when Rourke came home. They've... become close. God, I'm sorry!"

"What could you have done about that?" she asked with a sad smile. "It will be all right." She grimaced. "I guess it's time to face the music."

"I'll go with you. Moral support, at least."

"Thanks."

They walked inside, into Rourke's room. He was lying on the bed, under the covers. His broad chest was bare. A bandage was wrapped around it, under his arms, with heavy padding over the left side. There were stitches high on his head, just below his hairline. She winced.

Rourke looked up and saw her as she approached the bed.

For a few precious seconds, she hoped against hope that the sight of her might trigger the memories, might help to bring them back, bring him back. But so quickly, those seconds passed.

His one pale brown eye narrowed, but not with pleasure. A sarcastic smile tugged at his hard mouth. "And just what the hell are you doing here, Tat?" he drawled. "Were you thinking you'd come running and do a spot of nursing, like the time in Nairobi when I lost my eye? Sorry, I don't need help from you. Charlene's looking after me, aren't you, love?" he asked the other woman, who was very young and obviously smitten.

"Sure," Charlene said shyly. She smiled at Clarisse.

Clarisse was beyond smiles. She moved a little closer. She felt wobbly. "I'm glad you're all right, Stanton," she said.

"Are you? Why?" He looked at the hand she raised to her short hair and he sat straight up in bed. His eyes glittered with fury. "Where the bloody hell did you get that ring? Give it here!"

Shocked, she felt him grab her wrist and turn it, forcing her to sit beside him on the bed as he tore the engagement ring from her slender finger.

"How did you get it?" he demanded hotly. "You stole it, did you? There's no way in hell I'd have given my mother's engagement ring to a tramp like you!"

It was far worse than Clarisse had expected it might be. She got to her feet and moved away from the bed, back toward K.C., who was livid.

"Your manners need a little work," K.C. said curtly.

"You're one to talk about manners, mate," Rourke told the older man. "Did you invite her here?"

K.C. ground his teeth together.

"Get her out of my house," Rourke said in a voice that was soft in rage. His one pale brown eye glittered. "Right now!"

Clarisse swallowed down her anguish and managed a smile.

"I'm sorry," Charlene mouthed and grimaced.

Sympathy from her replacement hurt as much as Rourke's rage.

"Get out!" Rourke shouted at Clarisse. "And don't you ever come near me again, you harlot! Go pile into bed with one of your conquests...!"

K.C. had Clarisse out the door and onto the porch before Rourke could add to what he'd already said.

"Here, now, it's all right." K.C. comforted her. "I should never have let you come. I was afraid he wouldn't know you. But I had hoped…"

"Yes. Me, too."

"I'm sorry," he said. "Head injuries are tricky—you know that."

"I do know. I had one of my own, in Barrera. I still don't remember some things about what happened there." She drew away, pale but composed. "I'm going home, K.C."

"I had my pilot bring in a new crew, a fresh one," he said, confirming what the pilot had already told her. "Want to stay at my place overnight and fly out in the morning?"

She shook her head. "I can't. I want to go home."

"I understand. God, I'm so sorry!"

She took a long, shaky breath. "I'm sorry for you, as well," she said gently. "You and I both had started down a new path with him." She smiled sadly. "Well, at least I know how things are now. I'll stop living in dreams. But he's alive, K.C.," she added solemnly. "That's the only really important thing. I never really believed it would work out, not even when he proposed." She sighed wistfully. "It's a way of life, having him hate me. I suppose I'm used to it. Keep well, K.C."

"You, too. If you ever need help…" he added awkwardly.

She just smiled. She turned and walked away. She didn't even look back.

SHE AND RUY CARVAJAL were married in a civil service in Manaus two days later. She was almost angry enough to send a news clipping of the ceremony to

Rourke. But it would have accomplished nothing. It was just as well to leave things the way they were. After all, she couldn't force him to love her, no matter what she did.

She settled comfortably into marriage with Ruy. But she moved into his house. The memories in her own were killing her.

Peg came to see her soon after the ceremony, to be told about Rourke's injury and the subsequent estrangement. She was obviously curious about why Clarisse had rushed into marriage with a man she'd known for years, but she didn't say anything. And if she had suspicions, she didn't voice them.

"It would never have worked out, despite my pipe dreams," Clarisse told her friend quietly. "Rourke and I have known each other...oh, so long," she laughed. "I was eight when my parents moved next door to K.C.'s house. That was in the days when K.C. still made his living as a mercenary, and he was gone a lot. He had houses all over the world. I believe he still maintains one in Mexico. But his main house is just outside Nairobi. Rourke was always hanging around the little village, trying to sneak back into a commando group."

"How old was he?" Peg exclaimed.

"He was thirteen." Clarisse laughed and shook her head at the other woman's surprise. "Rourke was... mostly orphaned at the age of ten. His father was killed during a mission with K.C. Rourke's mother was still alive until about a month after my father was stationed at Nairobi, at the embassy. She couldn't do anything with Rourke, so when he was ten, he signed on with a rebel group and learned the lifestyle. By the time K.C. got back from endless missions, Rourke was leading a band of insurgents. K.C. grabbed him up, forcibly carried him back to his mother and dared him to leave home."

"I've never met Mr. Kantor, but I've certainly heard of him," Peg said.

"Most of what you've heard is true," she said ruefully. "Although he's mellowed a bit since those days." She sat forward with a sigh. "Rourke's mother was a sweet woman, but she was very ill. My family lived next to K.C.'s place in a house the embassy rented for us. I was with Rourke when his mother…died," she added, hesitating. It was just as well to let her friend think that Mrs. Rourke had died of natural causes. "I sat with Stanton all night. He wouldn't let anyone else near him."

"You go back a long way."

"A very long way. I was just eight years old, but I'd already attached myself to Stanton." She laughed. "I was fascinated with him. He was very mature for a thirteen-year-old and I adored him. He never seemed to mind that I tagged along behind him wherever he went. K.C. said once that the only reason Stanton didn't fall back in with the militia was that he knew I'd go right along with him, despite any interference from grown-ups."

"Had he lost his eye at that age?"

She shook her head. "He lost it when I was eighteen, just after Christmas…" Her face was drawn with pain at the memory. "I raised Cain until my father put me on a plane for Nairobi. I sat and nursed Stanton while they fought to save his eye and his life. He was badly wounded. I never knew why. He was good at what he did, and he was usually careful. One of his comrades said he'd been drinking." She shook her head. "Until then, I never thought he took a drink of hard liquor."

"Anyone can be pushed beyond his or her limits," Peg said quietly.

"I suppose so. Anyway, I sat with him in the hospital. K.C. wanted to, but there had been a lot of gossip just after Stanton's mother died, about K.C. being his father, and K.C. didn't want to start it all up again by staying with Stanton in the hospital. I even asked Stanton about it once and he didn't speak to me for ages afterward. He was touchy about it until just recently, when K.C. had a DNA profile done and found out that Rourke really is his son. It's a long and sad story," she added, when Peg looked shocked. "K.C. lost the only woman he ever loved to the church. She's a nun. He wanted to marry her. He got drunk and Stanton's mother felt sorry for him. She loved him very much." She lowered her eyes. "So many people loving the wrong people. You and Winslow got lucky," she added with a sad smile.

"We did," Peg agreed. She studied Clarisse's pale face quietly. "Your husband is very kind. But he's a great deal older than you."

"Yes." Clarisse's eyes were haunted. "He married me to give my child a name, Peg," she said in a husky whisper. "And you must never, never tell anyone."

"Dear God," Peg ground out, and tears wet her eyes. "I'm so sorry!"

Clarisse drew in a harsh breath. "Yes. I'm sorry, too, but Stanton remembers nothing about being here with me. Nothing at all. My mother's reputation would suffer if I had a child out of wedlock. People remember her here with reverence, even though she's long dead.

I can't…compromise her memory in such a way. And I am very fond of Ruy."

"He must be an extraordinary person," Peg replied with a smile.

"He is. He can't have a child of his own. So this one will be precious to him."

"And to you."

Clarisse's hand went protectively to her stomach. "I'm going to be so very careful," she said in a breathless whisper. "I've never wanted anything in my life as much as I want this baby."

"Will you tell Rourke, one day?" Peg asked.

Clarisse smiled wistfully. "He'd never believe it was his. He's back in the old days, accusing me of having affairs with endless men." She drew in a breath. "Hurting me was a habit he got into. It was to protect me, at the time, from a relationship he thought was forbidden. He may still believe it. Or he might just remember that he hates me, but not why."

"Will he ever remember?" Peg asked.

"There are some cases of spontaneous remission," Clarisse said. "Sometimes partial memory returns. Usually there will be some missing spots. He'll remember his childhood, he'll be able to memorize things and remember things that happen to him now. But that period of time just before he was injured may be lost forever. Nobody really knows. There are no magical cures."

Peg touched her hand gently. "I'll keep you in my prayers."

Clarisse's hand returned the gentle pressure. "And I'll keep you in mine. When is your baby due?"

"Four months," Peg said gleefully. "Winslow and I are over the moon. So is my dad."

Clarisse wished that she had family to be excited about her child. But there was nobody left. "I know you are."

"How about yours?" Peg asked gently.

"Six months," she laughed. "I can hardly wait!"

"I know exactly how you feel," Peg said with a grin.

RUY WAS A good husband. He took her sightseeing on the weekends, when his work permitted. He was an artist, as a hobby, and his portraits were unbelievably good. He painted Clarisse when she was six months pregnant, and her face was radiant and soft, her eyes a clear blue in her beautiful face. He painted her in a green silk dress, like the one she'd worn that long-ago Christmas Eve when Rourke had kissed her with un-believable passion.

She loved the portrait. For Ruy it was a true labor of love. He tried to hide it, but he was fascinated with his pretty wife. He enjoyed showing her off to his friends and distant relatives. Everyone thought the child was his, of course, which saved his reputation among the people he knew. Clarisse had his name and a safe place to wait for her child.

She'd had just one phone call from K.C.

"I thought you'd like to know that he's back on his feet and recovering well," he told her quietly. "His memory is still gone, but today he came out with some-thing unexpected and spoke of the job he'd been on, searching for a kidnapper. They did get the guy, even if the shoot-out cost them two agents and almost killed my...son."

"He still doesn't know about you, either?" Clarisse asked gently.

"No." He sighed heavily. "I want so badly to tell him. But the doctor is uncertain. He says the fact that Stanton remembers anything from that period of time is encouraging. He says other memories may follow, even if it takes time."

"He might remember one day, then?"

"He might." There was a pause. "How are you? I heard about the marriage through the general."

She smiled. "Yes, I married Ruy Carvajal. I've known him for many years. He's a good and kind man. He'll be a wonderful father."

"I was…going to ask you. There were rumors of a child…"

"Yes," she said.

There was a hesitation.

She knew what K.C. wanted to know, but it was a risk she couldn't take. "Ruy is over the moon. So am I. We're arguing over names," she added with a forced laugh. "And wondering if he'll favor me or Ruy."

"I see." His voice was resigned. It sounded hollow, devoid of hope.

"How about Charlene?" she asked with deliberate indifference.

"Stanton got engaged to her a couple of weeks ago," he said stiffly. "About the time I was talking to Machado. He mentioned that you'd been ill."

Her heart jumped. "Did you tell Stanton anything? About the marriage, the baby…?"

"Nothing. He won't have your name mentioned," he confessed heavily. "I did manage to tell him that Peg Grange had gone to see you and said you and Ruy

Carvajal were very close. I didn't say you were married. He went deathly quiet. The next day he proposed to Charlene." He let out a breath. "He doesn't love her. She's terrified of him up close. She spends her life traveling with her father and his very attractive business partner. I think Stanton bulldozed her into the engagement, but he won't speak of setting a wedding date any more than she will. I think it's...well, payback."

She felt the words to the soles of her feet. "I got involved with Ruy. He's getting even."

"In a nutshell," he said curtly. "It's the sort of thing he does. He's my son and I love him, but he's no angel."

"Yes. I know that."

"I'm so damned sorry, Clarisse," he said through his teeth.

"So am I, more for you than for myself," she replied softly. "At least my son will know who I am...sorry."

"Don't be. He'll be a fine youngster. I would...like to know when he's born," he said a little hesitantly. "I've known you for so many years. I could be his godfather...what do you think?"

She laughed through tears. "I'd be honored."

He swallowed. Hard. "Thanks."

"I'll let you know."

"That's very kind of you."

"Take care of yourself, K.C."

"You, too. Good night."

She hung up, fighting tears. K.C. was nobody's fool. He knew Rourke from the ground up, and he'd have at least a suspicion about who the father of her child really was. She couldn't admit it, and he wouldn't ask her to. But she wanted K.C. to be in the child's life, even if Rourke could never be.

SHE AND RUY lived quietly together, looking forward to the child's birth. Peg had already had her little boy, John, and stopped by to show him to Clarisse and Ruy. They were delighted to get to hold him. Clarisse was on pins and needles anticipating the arrival of her own child. There were tests that could determine sex, but she and Ruy didn't have them done. She wanted it to be a surprise.

But in the eighth month of her pregnancy, something unforeseen happened. Peg phoned her and sounded apprehensive.

"Something going on?" Clarisse asked gently, because Peg sounded really upset.

"You know that we had Arturo Sapara on ice here in the Medina prison for treason, a life sentence without hope of parole?" Peg asked.

"Yes. It was a dream come true for many people, including me."

"Well, he had a group of mercs come into Medina this morning and take him right out of the prison courtyard with a helicopter in broad daylight."

Clarisse sat down, hard. "He vowed bloody vengeance on anybody who had a part in his arrest, including me," she said.

"You, your husband, me and my family, the general's, even the poor old jailer who let you go."

"I guess we'll all be wearing bulletproof vests and sleeping with firearms under our pillows." Clarisse tried to joke.

"Coming at people head-on is not Sapara's style at all," Peg said coldly. "He's a coward. He'll hire people to do his dirty work for him. You keep your doors and windows locked and be very suspicious of any visitors you don't know."

"I will." Clarisse's blood ran cold. "What about Stanton?" she asked worriedly.

"General Machado talked to K. C. Kantor," she replied. "K.C. said if the ex-dictator wanted to come after Rourke, he'd better bring a full battalion, because he'd call in markers from all over the world and Sapara would be carried back to the Barrera prison in a shoe box."

She laughed involuntarily. "That sounds like K.C. all right."

"He wasn't going to mention Sapara's escape to Rourke, however. He was afraid it might be too much information, if he had to explain it all to him. It won't matter anyway because K.C. will have him covered like tar paper. Listen, you need to get out of Manaus," Peg said. "You can stay with my dad in Jacobsville... and Cash Grier and his wife Tippy offered you their spare bedroom."

"If I came, I'd put your poor father right in the line of fire, sweet girl," Clarisse said gently. "I'd take the Griers up on that offer in a heartbeat. Nobody frightens Cash Grier, from what I've heard. But I can't leave. It's too close to my time, and my obstetrician already has me coming in every week..."

"Oh, Clarisse," Peg moaned. "What's wrong?"

She drew in a breath. "Nothing, I hope. He and Ruy consulted and wouldn't tell me a thing. But Ruy watches me like a hawk and won't let me even exercise."

All sorts of things ran through Peg's worried mind. "If you need us..."

"I know that," Clarisse said softly. "You're the only friend I have. I'd do anything for you, too."

"I know." Peg hesitated. "Winslow has a friend who's on vacation down here. Suppose we send him over to see you?"

Clarisse laughed. "Ruy would have a fit. It would reflect on his manhood if I thought he couldn't protect me."

"I suppose it might sound that way," Peg said, miserable. "But what if he didn't know?"

"If he didn't know… I suppose he couldn't say anything," Clarisse agreed with a faint laugh.

"You won't know him, but he'll be around."

"What does he look like?"

"Tall, dark and handsome," Peg teased.

"I'm married to one of those," Clarisse laughed.

"So you are! Anyway, he'll keep an eye on both of you. But be careful. Nobody even knows where Sapara is right now."

"You'd better believe that Interpol and a handful of letter agencies from the States will be on his tail today," Clarisse replied, "including the general's best spy network."

"That's true. Listen, when the baby comes, I really want you to consider going to Texas."

Clarisse thought of her child. Ruy would never agree to leave Manaus and she couldn't very well go without him. She was afraid that Sapara might want revenge even on the newest member of her family when he was born.

"I'll think about it." Clarisse put her off. "Thanks for being so concerned about me."

"It's what friends do," came the warm reply. "I'll talk to you soon."

"You be careful, too."

"Always."

CLARISSE TOLD RUY about Sapara's escape, although not about the man Winslow Grange was going to send over to watch them.

He drew her against him gently and held her. "I am so deeply sorry for the way things have worked out for you," he said quietly. "I had hoped that perhaps Rourke would regain his memory, even if it meant I would lose you in the process." He drew back and smiled down at her. "You are so sad, my darling. It should be the happiest time of your life."

She reached up and touched his cheek, smiling at him with real affection. "It is the happiest time of my life. I have a baby on the way and a handsome, kind husband who cares for me."

He brought the soft hand to his lips and kissed it. "Fate has been unkind to us both."

"The baby will make a difference," she replied, and smiled with pure joy. "I can't wait to see if it's a boy or a girl," she laughed.

He grinned. "Neither can I. I must make a house call or two. Then we might have a very small glass of wine and watch television."

She pressed close to him with a sigh. "I'd like that."

He smoothed her hair and kissed it. "I won't be long."

"All right."

CLARISSE SAW A shadowy figure on the porch just before Ruy came home. It seemed to hesitate at Ruy's bedroom window for a minute or two, after which it faded back into the shadows. There had been an odd sound, too, like a jar being unscrewed.

She was certain it was the man Grange had sent to watch out for her and her husband, so she didn't mention it to Ruy. Not for anything would she upset him or make him feel incapable of taking care of her.

HE WAS SLUGGISH at breakfast a few mornings later.

"You don't look well, Ruy," she said, with some concern.

He laughed. "I had to put up mosquito netting, for the first time in ages. I think I got bitten several times over the weekend in my bedroom."

"Oh, dear," she said worriedly.

"I can take quinine if it looks like malaria coming on," he assured her with a smile. "Don't worry. I'm a doctor. I know how to take care of myself." He frowned. "Clarisse, we haven't had mosquitoes in the house, ever."

"I know." She was going to call Peg and ask her about their bodyguard as soon as she had a minute. Surely, there was no connection…

"I feel…unwell…" Ruy fell out of the chair.

THE NEXT FEW hours went by in a dizzy haze. Clarisse phoned a mutual friend, also a physician, who came right over and did tests. Ruy had to be moved to the hospital. The fever came on rapidly. It was high. He had the other symptoms of malaria, as well—shaking chills, delirium, nausea.

"You should not be here with him," the doctor said

worriedly. "The baby is due soon, Clarisse, you can't put him at risk."

"I can't leave Ruy," she protested, torn between two human beings she adored with all her heart. "I won't leave him. He wouldn't leave me, no matter what the risk," she added on a sob. She was clinging to his hand while technicians moved around him, doing necessary things. "He's had malaria before," she said. "But it was never like this...!"

"I have rarely seen a case like this," the other doctor replied quietly. He didn't add that the cases he had seen were invariably fatal. The blood test had revealed a plasmodium that was rarely seen in Manaus, a particularly dangerous strain. "Has Ruy been out of the Amazon recently?" he added.

She shook her head. "He went to Argentina, but that was five months ago. He hasn't been out of Manaus since then."

"Not to Asia or Africa or any known mosquito-infested areas?"

"Goodness, no," she said uneasily. "Why do you ask?"

He only smiled. "I'm grasping at straws, perhaps. If you won't leave him, I'll have them roll a bed in for you."

"I'm not leaving him," she said firmly.

"Very well." He smiled. "You are very like your mother, Senhora Carvajal," he said gently. "She was like that also, a kind and compassionate woman."

She bit her lower lip. "Thanks."

He put a gentle hand on her shoulder. "If you develop a fever..."

"I'll be the first to tell you. Honest."

He nodded.

SHE HOPED THAT Ruy would recover. But he only wors-
ened. She held his hand, talked to him, thanked him for
the kindness he'd shown her. She begged him to live.
But he lost ground. The next morning, while she slept,
he slipped quietly away into the unknown darkness.

SHE SOBBED BROKENLY when they told her. "But he can't
be dead," she whispered, shivering. "He can't be…!"

The physician felt her forehead and ground his teeth
together. He called for an orderly. By the time the gur-
ney came, Clarisse had fainted dead away.

PEG GRANGE AND her husband, Winslow, sat in the waiting room, hoping for news of Clarisse. Finally, Grange
got up and went looking for the doctor. He came back,
grim-faced.

"Whatever killed her husband is about to take her
out, too," he said curtly. "They're going to go ahead
and take the baby. If they wait, they may lose them
both. The physician said that what killed Ruy was a
strain of malaria that was usually fatal when it causes
cerebral malaria. He doesn't understand how Ruy got
it. Clarisse said he was a fanatic about keeping the
property sprayed for mosquitoes."

Peg looked at him with horror.

He drew in a breath. "It would be a vicious, cowardly way to kill someone. Just like Sapara."

She nodded. "Don't you know someone in tropical
medicine in London?" she asked suddenly.

His eyebrows arched. "Radley Blackstone," he said.
"Yes, I do." He pulled out his cell phone and got busy.

A day later, Blackstone flew in to Manaus and went
straight to the hospital. He barely took time to shake

hands with Peg and Winslow before he and the physician on Clarisse's case went back through the swinging doors where critically ill patients were kept.

"Should we call Rourke?" Winslow asked quietly.

Peg bit her lower lip. She shook her head. "He doesn't remember anything," she said. "And Clarisse has never admitted that the child is his. She's told everyone it was her husband's." She looked up at him. "They might both die, in spite of everything."

Winslow looked at her with his heart in his eyes. "If it was me, and I was Rourke, I'd never get over it if you died and I never knew you had my child under your heart."

She touched his cheek with her small hand. "I know. But he doesn't remember anything. He hates Clarisse. K.C. said he won't even mention her name or let anyone talk to him about her."

"What a hell of a mess," he said shortly.

"Yes." She hesitated. "Perhaps you should call K.C. anyway."

He nodded slowly. "Perhaps I should."

CHAPTER NINE

K.C. KNEW IMMEDIATELY why Winslow Grange would be calling him. "Something's happened to Clarisse," he said at once. "What? Did something go wrong with the baby?" he added, his voice taut with concern.

"No," Grange said heavily. "At least, we don't think so. Ruy Carvajal died two days ago," he said. "Of a deadly cerebral malaria, a complication of an often-fatal strain of malaria. *Plasmodium falciparum.* Odd thing, too, there were no mosquitoes anywhere on the property. Ruy was a fanatic about prevention. He'd had the place sprayed just recently."

"Then how did he get it? Had he been overseas…?"

"No." He hesitated. "Clarisse said she heard a noise on the patio last week, something like a jar unscrewing outside Ruy's bedroom. She thought she was dreaming. It seems very likely that someone transported anopheles mosquitos and released them in the house." He sighed. "Ruy thought he had flu, so he didn't go to the hospital and have it checked."

"Sapara," K.C. said through his teeth. "What a damned cowardly, underhanded…!"

"All of the above," Grange agreed. "Clarisse was nursing Ruy in his room when she developed it, too, probably from a mosquito bite there. They're debating how to proceed. I have a friend who's an expert in tropical diseases. I had him flown here from London. He's conferring with Clarisse's physician. They're trying a combination of drugs, some of them fairly new. I thought someone should know how serious it is," he added slowly. "Just in case…"

There was a long, heavy pause. "When will you know something?"

"That's anybody's guess. She's very ill."

"I'm coming over," K.C. said shortly.

"It could be dangerous…"

"God in heaven, I've been living on borrowed time since I was twenty-four years old," K.C. exploded. "I've known Clarisse since she was eight. I'm coming over."

"All right. I'll put on extra security," Grange replied quietly. "Damn it, I had a man watching them, right outside the house. I don't even know where the hell he is. He hasn't reported in. I told him to keep a low profile, but this is ridiculous!"

K.C. was very still. "Perhaps you should check the morgue, Winslow."

Grange felt the words to the soles of his feet. "I'll do that. You have the jet checked out before you put a foot on it, and bring a couple of your guys with you. Just in case."

"I will."

"What about Rourke?" he asked, having put off the question as long as he could.

"I don't know where he is," K.C. said through his teeth. "He took a job and it's classified. He put his fiancée on a plane to Paris with her father and her father's good-looking business associate, and lit a shuck out of here. He's barely speaking to me."

"Why?"

"I brought Clarisse to see him several months ago," he said with a hollow laugh. "He's so eaten up with hatred for her that I can't get a civil word out of him. I don't know why. Even when he seemed to hate her the most, he was always first on the line if anything happened to her."

"Head injuries are tricky," Grange reminded him. "His was pretty bad."

"Yes." He hesitated. "When he's himself again, if he ever is, I'm going to beat the ever-loving hell out of him!"

Grange laughed. That sounded like the old K.C. "I think Clarisse may help you."

If she lives. They were both thinking it. Neither of them spoke.

"I'll see you in a few hours," K.C. said, and hung up.

CLARISSE WAS FIGHTING for her life. The fever brought on premature labor. She never dilated even a centimeter. They had to do an emergency C-section to save her and the baby. The baby was diagnosed also with the plasmodium, but by the next day it had begun to clear, to Peg and Winslow's delight. The physicians attributed this to the antibodies produced by Clarisse's own body, and noted that it was not an uncommon outcome.

Meanwhile, the British physician had isolated the strain of malaria infecting Clarisse—*Plasmodium falciparum*, the same as Ruy's—and he and Clarisse's doctor prescribed a series of drugs in combination, hoping to help her fight off the malaria and prevent the cerebral malaria that had killed Ruy. The drugs were dangerous, but the malaria itself was potentially fatal. They had nothing to lose.

K.C. arrived the day after Clarisse's little boy was born after an exhaustive journey made longer by delays at the Nairobi airport because of a terrorist threat that proved untrue.

"It's a boy," Peg said softly, when K.C. joined them.

K.C.'s breath caught. "A boy. A son." He turned away. His eyes were wet. Despite Clarisse's best efforts, he knew the child was Rourke's. It was his grandson. His only grandson—and he didn't dare let on or tell a soul.

Peg got up and hugged K.C. She didn't know him well, and she was usually shy with men, but she had an overdose of compassion and she knew pain when she saw it.

He didn't even resist. He let her comfort him, while he fought the wetness in his eyes and tried to keep it from showing. After a minute he drew back with an odd little smile. "Thanks," he said huskily.

"Is the baby all right?" he asked after a minute.

Peg nodded. "It was touch and go at first. He was born with congenital malaria. But it cleared on its own." She smiled. "Want to see the baby?" she asked. "They have him in the nursery."

"I would...love to see him," he said huskily.

Grange slid his hands into his pockets and smiled. "He's a good-looking kid," he said. "Not quite as handsome as ours, but then, nobody's perfect," he teased.

"I heard about yours. John, was it?"

Grange nodded, smiling from ear to ear as the three of them strolled down the long hall to the nursery and stood in front of the viewing window.

"That's Clarisse's little boy," Grange said. It was the only blue blanket in the nursery. He grinned at the nurse and indicated the baby. She smiled, picked up the little boy and brought him right up to the glass.

K.C. was speechless. He'd seen Rourke soon after he was born, and pretended to be happy for Rourke's mother and father, even though he suspected the child was his.

He couldn't hide his pleasure now. He smiled from ear to ear, his eyes misting as he searched out all the little similarities between the baby and Rourke. The little boy's eyes were already open, blue and soft. His ears had the shape of Rourke's, although his eyes had the shape and spacing of Clarisse's. He saw generations of Kantors in that tiny face.

"God, he's so beautiful!" K.C. managed in a hoarse, husky whisper.

"Yes, he is," Peg said gently. She drew in a shaky breath. "Clarisse has to live. She just has to!"

"I'll do everything I can to help," K.C. said. "But if worse comes to worse, I'll take him and raise him and love him. He'll never want for a thing!"

Peg looked at Grange and they both winced. How he'd do that without telling Rourke was something nobody mentioned.

The joy K.C. felt, looking at the tiny little boy, was overwhelming. "Did she mention names?" he asked.

"Yes. It was going to be Katrianne Desiree for a girl. Joshua Stanton for a boy. Although," Peg added quickly, "she wasn't planning to advertise his middle name…"

"Neither will I," K.C. promised. He shoved his

hands into the pockets of his khaki slacks. "What a hell of a mess!" he said angrily.

"Yes," Grange said. His face set in hard lines. "Machado has teams of men out looking for Sapara, with orders to terminate with extreme prejudice. They won't bring him back, I promise you. He'll never make it to prison again."

K.C. looked at the other man. His glittery light brown eyes held traces of the cold-eyed mercenary he'd been for most of his life. "I'll contribute a couple of my men to that effort."

"I'm sure President Machado would be grateful. He's fond of Clarisse."

K.C. looked back at the child, smiled sadly and turned away. His face was rigid with misery.

"Rourke doesn't remember that he's related to you, either, does he?" Peg asked softly.

He shook his head. "We don't speak much," he replied. "His behavior was a little erratic just after he got back home. It's improving, but his temper keeps most people at bay. Especially his fiancée, who's terrified of him," he added on a chuckle. "I think she'd break off the engagement, given the slightest opportunity."

Peg sighed. "Did he give her his mother's engagement ring?" She had to know.

He shook his head. "He locked it back in the safe. Asked me if I had the combination, and seemed to think I might have given it to Clarisse. I didn't know the combination. That started him thinking, but he said he'd probably just left it lying around and Clarisse had picked it up. You can't argue with him," he added heavily. "God knows, I've tried."

"I've seen men in combat with amnesia due to traumatic injuries," Grange said. "So have you. There are cases on record of spontaneous remission."

"It's been months," K.C. said quietly.

"Sometimes it can take years," Grange added. "Hope is the last thing we lose," he reminded the older man.

K.C. managed a smile. "So they say."

"I just pray that Clarisse will live," Peg said quietly.

Grange put his arm around her and drew her close. "Faith moves mountains," he reminded her.

K.C. chuckled. "I have a goddaughter," he said. "She's the niece of the woman I once wanted to marry, the only woman I ever would have married. Her name is Kasie. She's married to Gil Callister, of the Callister ranch properties in Montana," he added.

"I know about them," Grange said, surprised.

"Most ranchers do," K.C. chuckled. "They're richer than pirates. Kasie has had a hard life, but she landed well when she married Gil. He was a widower with two small daughters. He says Kasie brought the sun back into his life."

"Kasie?" Peg asked.

He nodded. "I saved their mother after a rebel incursion that almost took my life. She and her husband sheltered me, hid me from the insurgents. I got her to safety just before she gave birth to twins. They were named for me. Kasie and Kantor. Kantor died in Africa. He and his family were in a small plane. A rebel with a rocket launcher took it out."

"Poor girl," Peg said softly.

K.C. nodded. "I gave Kasie a pendant for a wedding gift. A mustard seed necklace."

"Faith as a grain of mustard seed can move mountains," Peg said, getting the connection at once.

He smiled. "Yes." He drew in a long breath. "I hope your British physician has a miracle or two in his pocket, Winslow."

"So do I," the other man replied.

TWO DAYS AFTER Clarisse developed the fever, the course of treatment started to show results. They were slow ones at first, but as the fever came down, and the chills lessened, and she became conscious again, it did seem as if a miracle had occurred.

Clarisse opened her eyes on the fourth day of her hospital stay and saw three worried people standing by her bedside.

She managed a weak smile. She was nauseated, and her stomach hurt. She grimaced as she moved. "The baby...!" she exclaimed, terrified.

"A little boy, Clarisse," K.C. said softly. "He's fine. He's in the nursery."

"Oh." She let out the breath she'd been holding. "Oh. A son." Her face softened. Then it contorted. "Ruy. He died...!" Tears burst from her eyes. "He died!"

There was a grim silence in the room.

Clarisse wiped at the tears. "Peg, you said...there was a man watching us. I saw him on the porch. I thought he was protecting us so I didn't say anything. I thought it might upset Ruy, reflect on his ability to protect us. Ruy said he was bitten by mosquitoes in his bedroom. You know, he had the whole area around the house sprayed constantly so we didn't have any mosquito infestation. That's why he waited to go to the doctor. He thought he'd caught a virus from one of his patients. He was so tired. He'd worked fourteen-hour days because of the outbreak. So neither of us connected the bite with his illness... I didn't realize, until his fever shot up a few days later and I called for an ambulance..." She started crying again.

Grange ground his teeth together. He didn't want to tell her. But he had to. "Clarisse, the man I sent to keep watch on your house was murdered," he said quietly. "The man you saw outside Ruy's window wasn't mine. God, I'm sorry!"

"Not...your fault," she managed. She swallowed. Her stomach was very painful. "I remember, I heard a sound that night, like a Mason jar lid unscrewing." Her eyes were closed. She didn't see the solemn looks exchanged between a furious K.C. and a guilt-ridden Grange.

K.C.'s pale brown eyes glittered. "We'll find Sapara. Whatever it takes."

"I've got a good intelligence network," Grange said. He grimaced at K.C.'s expression. "Well, not good enough, apparently," he added curtly. "A helicopter took Sapara out of the prison yard in broad daylight."

"Money changed hands," K.C. said. "Track the money. Find the person who was bribed."

"That's going to be my first priority when I get home," Grange agreed.

"Lay on more security for your family, as well," K.C. advised. "This is only the beginning. You know that. He's out for revenge and he has nothing to lose. He knows he won't be taken alive."

Grange nodded. "I've been careless. I won't get caught twice."

K.C. laid a big hand on his shoulder. "I've made

similar mistakes. But only once," he added with a smile. "You're okay."

Grange chuckled. "Not in your class, though. Not yet."

K.C. shrugged. "I've got a few years on you," he said kindly.

"My baby," Clarisse said drowsily. "Does he look like me?"

"Yes," K.C. said, smiling. "Exactly like you."

She let out a sigh of relief.

"He's quite beautiful, Clarisse," K.C. said softly.

She opened her blue eyes and looked up into his, with pain and sorrow and grief all making shadows in them. Tears rolled down from the corners of her eyes.

K.C. knew exactly what she was feeling. He brushed the tears away with his thumb. "He doesn't know I'm his father," he said in a tender tone. "He may never know."

She understood what he was saying. She just nodded. She swallowed, hard. "Why am I still alive?" she asked after a minute. "The doctor said that I'd probably develop the same cerebral malaria that killed Ruy..."

"I have a friend," Grange said, smiling. "Dr. Blackstone. I had him flown here from London. He's a magician when it comes to tropical diseases. I don't know exactly what he did," he added. "But it was obviously the very thing to do."

She smiled. "Yes."

"We have to get you out of the country, Clarisse," K.C. said. "He won't stop."

"I know." She bit her lower lip. "I don't care about me. I want Joshua where they can't find him, or hurt him."

"Cash Grier says you can stay with them," Peg reminded her. "There's no safer place on earth. Cash has all sorts of evil friends, too," she laughed.

Clarisse managed a smile. "It would be such an imposition…"

"Are you kidding?" Peg laughed. "Tippy's bought all sorts of things for the baby. She can't wait! Tris is almost three now, and Tippy's got baby fever."

"She and the police chief should have another one of their own," Clarisse said.

"I think they've tried, but with no results. Meanwhile, there's you and your brand-new baby, and Tippy's over the moon that you'll stay with them."

"In that case," she said, "I'll be very happy to go." She hesitated. "K.C., there's no chance that Stanton might show up in Jacobsville?" she asked worriedly.

He drew in a long breath. "He told me that he had no plans to go back to America," he said honestly. "Not for a long time. Maybe never. The cases he's working now are all European."

"I see."

"Classified stuff," K.C. added. "I don't even know who he works for or what he does. I'm not privileged."

She grimaced. "I'm so sorry."

He sighed. "Me, too, but unless he recovers his memory, I suppose we're both just out here in the ozone layer together," he added with a twinkle in his eyes. "Don't you worry. That baby will want for nothing. I'll be the best…godfather…a child ever had." He forced the word out. It wasn't the word he wanted to use.

Clarisse understood that. Her gratitude was in her eyes. She couldn't risk letting Rourke know about the child. Ever. He'd go after her in court with no provocation at all to get his child away from her. The thought of Rourke and little Charlene raising her son made her neck hair rise up.

"Don't worry so much," K.C. told her. "Things usually work out eventually."

"Think so?" she asked with a smile. "I wonder."

Dr. Blackstone walked into the room with the physician on Clarisse's case. Both men were smiling from ear to ear.

"My greatest success story," Blackstone chuckled, looking at Clarisse. "I believe you may be the first of many to survive this deadly form of malaria in the final stage. If so, we may be looking at a breakthrough of epic proportions with the new treatment we used."

She smiled wearily. "I hope it saves many more lives. Thank you for mine," she said softly.

"I'm only sorry that I wasn't here in time to save your husband," he replied. "They speak of him with great respect here."

"Ruy was a fine physician." Tears stung her eyes. "Sorry. I'm still not used to it. And I must arrange the funeral…!"

"I'll take care of that," K.C. said quietly. "We'll plan a memorial service when you're better. No chance of your getting up this soon."

"None at all," Blackstone agreed. "But you're on a good path to a complete recovery. And you have a fine son to show for your labors," he chuckled.

K.C. STAYED UNTIL Clarisse was released from the hospital and she and the baby were back home again. He had two men in the house with her, both veterans of many foreign wars.

"This is very kind of you, K.C.," she said gently.

His hands were deep in the pockets of his khakis. "Nothing will harm you or the child as long as I live," he promised solemnly. He moved closer, his eyes tender on the baby in her arms. She was still weak, but she got around well. She was sitting in a wicker chair with little Joshua, in a light blanket, in her arms. She winced. Then she laughed. "The stitches are still sore," she laughed.

"You aren't supposed to be lifting weights," he chided.

"I'm not supposed to lift heavy things. Joshua only weighs seven pounds," she teased. She saw the hunger in his pale brown eyes as he looked at the child. "Would you like to hold him?"

"Would I!"

He bent and took the baby up in his big arms, smiling and then laughing as he looked into dark blue eyes. "I wonder if he'll have your eyes or…his father's," he had to hesitate, because he'd almost said the name.

She sighed. "You know, don't you?" she asked.

He looked down at her. "I know. But he never will. I give you my word."

She swallowed. "Thanks." Her eyes fell. "He hates me more now than he used to. He'd go to court…"

"He won't know," he said quietly. He drew in a breath. "But I know. That's enough." He looked into the baby's eyes and smiled, jostling him gently. "He'll never want for anything."

"No, he won't. I'm filthy rich myself, if you recall," she laughed.

"So you are." His lips pursed. "I was thinking about bodyguards, however."

"That sort of help I'll take, with gratitude." She moved restlessly and winced as the stitches pulled. "I think Peg's right about leaving the country. Sapara would have a hard time getting to me in Texas. Especially in a small town like Jacobsville, where everybody knows everybody."

"And where half the decent mercs in the country call home," he laughed. He walked around the room with Joshua, his eyes soft and affectionate. "Joshua will have plenty of attention there. Cash Grier will guarantee that nobody hurts him, or you."

She looked up at him. "Sapara has some of the bloodthirstiest operatives of anyone I've ever known, like that crazy man who tortured me when I was imprisoned in Barrera. It was diabolical, to kill my husband with an insect parasite."

"Risky, too," he added. "Ruy was a physician."

"He was a very tired physician. I'd had some episodes of bleeding and he was worried about me. He didn't sleep much, at any rate, and he'd worked himself sick taking care of people from the latest virus outbreak. That's why he didn't realize it was malaria. I should have noticed. I even know the symptoms. I nursed Rourke through it once, when I was about ten."

K.C. stopped and smiled. "He's been part of your life for a long time."

She nodded. She bit her lower lip. "You don't know how it was, those weeks we were together here." She had to stop. It choked her up to remember the savage joy she'd felt with Rourke, basking in the love he couldn't hide from her.

"It was that way for him, too, Clarisse," he said softly. "I talked to him several times before the assault that left him injured. All he talked about was you and the future."

She managed a watery smile. "That makes it so much worse, you know," she said. "They said the gods used to punish men by taking them to paradise and then releasing them back on earth. The contrast drove them insane." She lowered her eyes. "It's like that."

"There's always hope that he'll regain his memories. Sometimes it happens spontaneously."

"Have you spoken to that neurosurgeon?"

He nodded, jostling Joshua, who was watching him intently as he walked the baby around the room in his arms. "He said that we could tell Rourke about things that happened in the past, but that it wouldn't make any difference. It wouldn't prompt his own memory. It would be like reading him a story."

"That's so discouraging."

"Yes." He grimaced. "He said that the mind can create new pathways to portions of the brain associated with past memories. It's a time-consuming process. Sometimes it doesn't happen. Sometimes it does, but it can take time. A lot of time."

"It's been so long," she said heavily.

"A very long time, for me, too. I'd only just found out that he was my son. I've lost him…"

"You have to have hope, too," she said, interrupting the painful statement. "He's still your child."

He smiled. "So he is." He drew in a breath. "And I'm a grandfather." He grinned from ear to ear. "I want to shout that from the rooftops. I'm so proud of him. And I can't tell a soul."

"You can be his godfather in public," she pointed out. "You need a fedora and a machine gun, though…"

He chuckled. "How about a Ka-Bar and an Uzi?"

"Sounds just fine to me."

He handed Joshua back to her reluctantly. "I have to go home. I don't want to, but I left projects hanging."

"Thanks for arranging the service for Ruy," she said quietly. "It was very nice. He would have approved. I buried him next to his mother. He loved her very much."

"He was a good man."

"Yes." She glanced up at him and frowned. "Something's worrying you."

He nodded, sliding his hands into his pockets. "Sapara had an enforcer whose face wasn't known to most of his enemies. Rourke was the only man I know who would have recognized him on sight. His chief skill was to be able to blend in anywhere. He was ordinary-looking. He acted as Sapara's hit man."

"Do you think he's the one who planted the mosquitoes in Ruy's bedroom?"

"No. That was donkey work. Any of his minions could have accomplished that. His enforcer was always used in covert assassination, and he was inventive. Something like that scoundrel who tried to murder a woman in Wyoming who was involved with one of the Kirk brothers. He used malathion in migraine capsules. That's the sort of thing Sapara's assassin excels in—unusual, extreme, vicious murder. They say he learned his trade in the Middle East, under one of the more bloody dictators."

She felt chills all over. "You think I'm more a target than Peg or Winslow, don't you?"

"I do. Because you're vulnerable. Or Sapara will think you are. It was your escape that led to his downfall. That's the way he'll see it. He's waited a long time to plan his break from prison. I don't imagine he's wasted his time behind bars, either. He'll have a plan and he'll be putting it into effect soon. That's why you're leaving tonight for Texas."

"Tonight...!"

He nodded. He looked toward her bedroom, where two tall, dark-eyed men were bringing out suitcases. "Tonight. I'm flying you over myself," he added.

"K.C.—you've done so much already," she began.

"You saved a whole country from Sapara," he mused. "We're even. Besides, I'm not having my godson on any commercial flight."

She smiled. "Okay. Thanks."

He shrugged. "We go back, Clarisse," he said, smiling. "I still remember you with pigtails and Band-Aids on your knees, following Stanton through the bush looking for fossils."

"We found lots of things besides fossils," she pointed out.

"Yes. Including a very vicious viper, as I recall," he mused.

She laughed. "Stanton picked me up and ran with me all the way to the clinic," she recalled. "He never left me, until I was almost completely recovered. I remember my mother thought it was scandalous."

"Your mother, God rest her soul, thought everything was scandalous."

"I suppose so. She was a good person, though."

Oddly, K.C. didn't comment. He knew, as Rourke did, what had caused the traumatic separation between his son and Clarisse all those long years. Maria Carrington had been the serpent in paradise, where Rourke was concerned.

"Check behind the men and make sure they've packed you properly," he instructed. He held out his arms. "I'll hold Josh while you do that."

She handed him over. "He's such a good baby," she said.

"Not surprising. Not surprising at all," he teased, looking at her.

She laughed and went to make sure the packing had been done properly. She went into Ruy's bedroom, hesitating. He'd collected things sparsely over the years of his life. But one thing he prized was an award he'd been given by an international coalition of physicians, for his work in war-torn areas of the world. She took it off the wall. She also took the rosary he always kept in the bedside table next to his bed. Her eyes teared up as she looked down at it. He'd been kind to her. He'd loved her, in his way. She felt great affection for him, but she could never love him the way she'd loved Rourke. He knew that, accepted it, was grateful for her company and the protection of the marriage.

"I won't forget you," she whispered to the room.

She clutched the rosary tight in her hand, bit back the tears and walked out, closing the door behind her.

IT WAS A long flight to Texas. K.C. stopped along the way several times to let her stretch her legs and to refuel the small jet when necessary. When they landed at the Jacobsville airport, a police car was waiting on the apron, near the trailer that served as the fixed base operator's office.

Cash Grier came forward when they got off the plane.

Clarisse was a little intimidated by him; he seemed the sort of man whom criminals would really fear. But he smiled at her and the child in her arms and she relaxed.

He shook hands with K.C. "Long time no see," he teased the older man. "You can still fly? My God!"

"I'm not that old, Grier," K.C. chuckled.

"You'd be Clarisse," Cash said.

"Yes. And you'd be Chief Grier," she said, nodding. She looked at his head intently.

"What are you looking for?" Cash asked.

"Horns," she said with a straight face.

He burst out laughing. "Who's been telling tales?" he chided, glancing past her at K.C.

"I didn't say you had horns," K.C. denied.

"Lies," Cash mused.

He went to help K.C. unload the luggage. "You staying overnight?" he asked K.C.

"I think I'd better," K.C. sighed. "I don't fancy flying straight back to Africa. I didn't bring a relief pilot for the trip. I hear there's a hotel with a Jacuzzi here in town…"

"You won't need it," Cash said. "We live in a huge Victorian house right downtown. Plenty of guest rooms," he added with a grin. "Tippy's worn herself out working on the guest room for Clarisse and the baby." He put the bags in the trunk of the car and went back to Clarisse. "May I?" he asked.

She handed him the baby. The change it made in that hard face was miraculous. He seemed like a different person. He smiled and let the baby hold his big finger. "He's beautiful," he said softly.

"You have a daughter, don't you?" Clarisse asked.

He nodded. "Tris. She's almost three. We want another baby, but it's taking more time than we expected," he chuckled.

K.C. clapped him on the back. "Good things do," he pointed out.

"Absolutely. Meanwhile, my daughter is the light of my life. Next to her gorgeous mother," he added with a sigh. He shook his head as he handed Joshua back to Clarisse. "I never saw myself as a family man. Now it's hard to remember that I wasn't one."

"I've seen photos of your wife," K.C. mused. "She's a knockout."

"And I know things about you," Cash retorted. "She's married. You keep that charm to yourself."

"Spoilsport. Tough luck that I wasn't around when she was shopping for a husband," K.C. joked.

"Good luck for me," Cash laughed. "Let's get going. Tippy will be standing on the porch with binoculars. She's that excited about our houseguest."

"I do so appreciate the offer of a place to stay," Clarisse began. "It's been a rough few days."

"I'm sorry about your husband," Cash said with genuine feeling. "But the thing now is to keep you and the child out of Sapara's reach. Believe me, he'll find no refuge here. You'll be more secure than Fort Knox."

"Thanks," Clarisse said.

"All in a day's work," Cash replied. "Shall we go?"

CHAPTER TEN

Tippy was standing on the top step when Cash pulled up to the porch. The sun was setting behind the house, catching Tippy's glorious red-gold hair and making a halo of it as she ran down the steps to meet their guests.

"I'm Tippy," she said, hugging Clarisse. "Welcome to Jacobsville!"

"Thanks," Clarisse said. "And thank you for letting us stay with you."

"No thanks necessary. I'm so excited. It's been almost three years since we had a baby in the house. Could I...?" She held out her arms, as Cash had at the airport.

Clarisse laughed. "Yes, you may. He isn't heavy, but the stitches pull and I'm still very sore..."

"Sore?"

"C-section," K.C. answered for her. He smiled at Tippy. "I'm..."

"K. C. Kantor," Tippy said at once, laughing. "Sorry. I know Rourke. You're the image of him... Oops," she added when K.C.'s face tautened.

"I'm not angry," K.C. replied, and smiled sadly. "I really am his father. We had a DNA test done. But Rourke doesn't remember that I'm his father," he added. "It's...difficult."

Tippy winced. "I'm so sorry."

"So am I. He's lost a good deal of his short-term memory."

"He called Jake Blair from the last place he was stationed," Cash remarked as he started bringing in suitcases. "Jake said he remembered most of what happened the last time he was here. So he does have some memories."

"Jake?" Clarisse asked.

"He's minister of the local Methodist Church."

Clarisse smiled. "Rourke mentioned that he was friends with a minister."

"He's not exactly your ordinary minister," Cash remarked, chuckling. "And that's all I'll say. Come on inside and meet the rest of the family."

She and K.C. and the baby were introduced to little Tris, a mirror image of her gorgeous mother, who was sitting in her uncle Rory's lap watching a cartoon movie. She ran to Clarisse to be picked up. It made Clarisse feel so warm inside, the child's immediate, affectionate response to her, a stranger.

Clarisse laughed and knelt down. "Hi, Tris!" she said, and hugged the little girl warmly. "I'm sorry, I can't pick you up. I was very ill…"

"I'm sorry, too," Tris said. She smiled shyly. "You're pretty, like Mommy."

"Thank you!"

"Is that your baby?" Tris asked. "Is it a girl or a boy?"

"It's a little boy. His name is Joshua."

"That's a nice name."

"It is. The Coltrains have a son. His name is Joshua, too, but they call him Tip."

"Tip?" Clarisse asked, rising.

"He likes to turn stuff over," Cash said with a grin. "Mostly model trains. His parents have a whole room devoted to Lionel trains. His first word, I understand, was *derail*. Hence the nickname."

Clarisse laughed out loud. "I love trains."

"At Christmas they have open house," Tippy said. She was walking around with Joshua, smiling and kissing his little nose and hugging him. "He's precious, Clarisse!"

"Thanks. I think so," Clarisse said. "Your Tris is precious, too," she added, smiling at the child, who beamed.

Rory approached them. He had dark hair and green eyes and a big smile. "Could I hold him? He's so cute!"

Clarisse was surprised, but she nodded.

"He loves children," Tippy said as she lowered the little boy into Rory's arms. "But this is going to be a little awkward..." She grimaced when Tris glowered at her uncle.

"Rory!" Tris protested, sticking out her lower lip. "You should carry me!"

Rory laughed, kissed the baby, handed him back and picked up Tris. "You are spoiled," he told her.

"Want Rory." She snuggled close. "My Rory."

"My goodness," Clarisse laughed when Rory and Tris were back on the sofa, engrossed in the movie.

"It's been like that since she was born," Tippy said, shaking her head. "Cash and I have to fight to get to hold her. She loves her uncle."

"He's a nice boy," Clarisse said. She sighed. "I'm not used to children, but I seem to have taken to it like a duck to water. I love my son."

"He's such a quiet child," Tippy said, handing him

back to Clarisse reluctantly. "Tris bawled for the first two weeks."

"I think perhaps it's the circumstances of Joshua's birth," Clarisse said quietly. "He was born while I was fighting for my life…"

Tippy took her arm. "Come in here and I'll make coffee. I'd like to hear about it."

Clarisse fought tears. "It's hard…"

Tippy hugged her. "Life is hard. We'll share horror stories while you're here."

Clarisse smiled unsteadily. "Thanks."

"I'll enjoy the company. Cash is away so much these days," she sighed, shaking her head as she glanced back toward her husband, who was talking to K.C. "It's one thing after another. They're working on several cases that have federal connections and he's in the thick of it. I worry. But he's good at taking care of himself, and all of us. If you'd known him before…" she added with a secretive laugh. She just shook her head.

THEY SAT OVER coffee while Clarisse nursed Joshua.

"I nursed Tris when she was born," Tippy said with sad nostalgia. "I had hoped that we could have a second child…" She laughed self-consciously. "But even one is more than I ever expected. We're so proud of our little girl."

Clarisse smiled at her. "You shouldn't give up," she said softly. "My parents had the same problem. Well, not really a problem, but they wanted more children than just me. My sister, Matilda…" She stopped and swallowed, hard. "My sister was born sometime after I was. There were several years between us."

Tippy laid a gentle hand on Clarisse's shoulder. "You lost her," she guessed.

Clarisse's eyes teared. "Her and my father. They were in a native boat, touring villages, when the boat capsized. There were piranha in the water. Matilda made it to shore safely, but she went back to try and save my father. I lost both of them. I was too far away to do a thing." She closed her eyes and shuddered.

"It must have been very hard. I'm sorry."

Clarisse drew in a breath. "Rourke managed everything, even the funeral services. I was too torn to cope." She smiled sadly. "He was always there, at every traumatic event in my life. But he hates me, passionately. He had for years, until the awards ceremony in Barrera. He followed me home to Manaus." Her eyes closed. "We were so close for a couple of weeks, so very close. Then he had to leave for an assignment. He'd be back in a few days, he said, and we'd be married. We had the rings, my wedding gown, everything, including a priest to perform the ceremony. Well, he did leave. But he suffered a traumatic head injury and lost his short-term memory. All that came back to him was that he hated me. I'm not sure he even remembers why."

"Retrograde amnesia?" Tippy asked gently. She remembered that because a friend of Cash's, a former mobster named Marcus Carrera, had suffered a similar episode.

Clarisse nodded. "It's been almost a year, and he's remembered nothing." She smiled sadly. "I would think those memories are gone forever."

Tippy didn't say a word, but her eyes went from Clarisse to the baby in her arms. Clarisse didn't mutter a single word. She couldn't share that secret, even with her kindly new friend.

K.C. WAS GETTING ready to fly back to Nairobi the next morning when he had a phone call. His face went white.

"K.C., what's wrong?" Clarisse asked, because she knew it was something catastrophic. "Rourke...?" she exclaimed, horrified at his frozen features.

"No," he managed in a curt, wounded tone. He was breathing like a runner. "Mary Luke Bernadette," he said, almost in a daze. "Her neighbor found her this morning, lying beside her little goldfish pond. She'd been...dead...for several hours. Kasie, my goddaughter, thinks it was a massive stroke. She's devastated." He drew in a breath. "I have to fly to Montana. Right now!"

"No," Clarisse said shortly, getting in front of him. Mary Luke had been the love of his life, the reason he never married. For her, it would be the same as losing Rourke. K.C. must be absolutely sick at heart. "You call someone to fly you there and back, and to Africa. If you even try to fly yourself out of here, I'll call the FAA myself and have you taken out of the plane!" she said shortly.

Tippy and Cash were listening, frowning. K.C. didn't seem the sort to take orders from anyone, much less a woman.

But he did. He swallowed and a faint smile touched his hard mouth. "You sound just like...her," he said roughly. He turned away. "I'll leave the Learjet here and call a service to provide me with private transport." He pulled out his cell phone and started thumbing through names.

While he was on the phone, Clarisse drew Cash and Tippy into the kitchen, away from the kids, who were watching television. Clarisse still had Joshua in her arms.

"K.C. was in love with her," she told them in a voice that didn't carry. "She was a nun."

"I see," Cash said heavily. "God bless her."

"What can we do?" Tippy asked. "Here, let me have him, Clarisse, you're going to pull those stitches. You aren't even supposed to be lifting yet."

Clarisse smiled gently and handed her the baby. "Thanks. He's quite heavy for such a small child," she laughed. "I think he's going to be tall."

"I'm sorry for K.C.," Cash said quietly.

"So am I," Clarisse said. "But there's no way I'm letting him fly himself." She winced. "If only Rourke was himself. He'd be with his father like a shot!"

"Could you call him?" Tippy ventured.

"I don't know how," she said simply. She didn't add that Rourke would probably hang up the second he heard her voice. "K.C. said the assignment he's on is top secret. Even he can't contact him."

"Poor man," Tippy groaned.

K.C. came through the door a minute later. "I have to get to the airport. They're sending a Learjet for me." He grimaced. "Sorry…"

Cash dug out his car keys. "Sorry, nothing. Got your bag?"

"It's still on the porch," K.C. said. He moved to Clarisse and took her hands in his. "Thanks, kid," he said softly.

She hugged him, hard. He resisted for a few seconds. Then he hugged her back, giving in to the need for comfort. His face contorted as he tried to even imagine a world without Mary Luke in it.

Finally, he drew away, his eyes faintly wet. He shook his head, to keep the moisture from showing. He cleared his throat. "I'd better get going." He looked down at Clarisse. "You going to be okay?" he asked. "I'll call Eb Scott on the way to Montana. Just in case."

Clarisse frowned. She looked into the living room, where Tris was sitting with Rory. "I may be putting you all in danger, just by being here," she worried.

Cash shook his head. "I'm chief of police," he chuckled. "Danger is my business. Eb can provide outside support, I'll take care of things inside." He jerked his head toward Tippy. "She's still got that iron skillet, too," he mused, grinning at his laughing wife.

"It's a really remarkable weapon," Tippy agreed. She smiled at Clarisse. "Don't worry. It will be all right." She went to K.C. "I'm so sorry," she told him.

"Me, too." He managed a smile for her. He glanced at Clarisse. "If you need anything, anything at all…"

"I'm fine, K.C. You do what you have to do." She winced. "I'm so sorry!"

"Yes. So am I." His eyes were haunted. He turned and followed Cash out the door.

"IT'S SO HORRIBLE," Clarisse said when he'd gone. "To love a woman like that, so much, and have to give her up. Surely, he still hoped that one day, maybe…" She laughed self-consciously. "That's me, too. Hoping. That one day, maybe, Rourke might remember what happened in Manaus." She drew in a breath and touched Joshua's blond hair as he lay in Tippy's arms. "But even so, I can live on those few days for the rest of my life."

"I could have done that, with a few days in New York, just before Christmas, a few years back. He didn't want to get married. He hated me at first, for making him weak. Then I got kidnapped, and he came rushing up to the city to save me. He brought me here, took care of me, worried about me." She laughed self-consciously. "I never thought of him as a family man. Now look!" she added, nodding toward her daughter, Tris, as she cradled Joshua in her arms.

"I would never have believed that he could really settle down, from what I heard about him," Clarisse agreed.

"You've known K.C. a long time, haven't you?" she asked.

"Yes, I have," Clarisse replied, dropping gingerly down into a chair at the kitchen table. "Since I was about eight years old. He was heavily into mercenary work in those days. My father rather idolized him," she laughed. "Dad was a diplomat, very practiced with people, very correct. I think he saw a wildness, a masculinity in K.C. that he envied." She drew in a wistful breath. "My mother hated him," she added with a grin. "She thought he was a bad influence not only on Dad, but on me, as well. I got into some scrapes when I was a child in Africa."

"You were a landmark in Washington society for a number of years," Tippy said. "I remember seeing photos of you in magazines and newspapers. You were escorted around by movie stars and famous athletes and even royalty."

"Window dressing," Clarisse replied with sad eyes. She looked at Tippy wistfully. "When I was seventeen, Rourke came to a party my parents gave in Manaus." She colored a little with the memory and cleared her throat. "After that, I couldn't feel anything for other men. Rourke accused me of being a rounder, of sleeping with any man I saw." She winced. "It's been a hard few years."

"I'm sorry. I've had a bad time myself, with men." Tippy lowered her eyes and told Clarisse about her mother's boyfriend.

"He should have been shot!" Clarisse said at once, her blue eyes flashing.

"He's in federal prison. He was badly beaten a few weeks ago. It got around, what he did to me." Tippy sighed. "Men who abuse children have a hard time in prison. Usually, they don't survive very long. Many of the people serving time for various violent crimes were victims of child abuse themselves, you see."

"It's a hard world, isn't it?" Clarisse asked.

"Harder for you than me, from what Cash says about you," she added. "You were tortured in Manaus for information they thought you had about General Machado's invasion. Cash said you didn't tell them a word. He was impressed. You see, he was captured and tortured in Iraq, during a top secret incursion."

"I didn't know," Clarisse said. "He's a very...masculine sort of man."

Tippy laughed. "Very." She cocked her head. "Why does Rourke hate you so much?"

"Actually, someone told him that we were related by blood, that my mother had a one-nighter with K.C. and I was the result."

"Oh, good heavens," Tippy exclaimed.

"It wasn't true," Clarisse went on. "He found it out." She laughed. "K.C. knocked him over a sofa when he accused his father of being intimate with my mother. They had a DNA test done that proved Rourke was K.C.'s son. Rourke had one done, God knows how, that also proved he and I weren't related at all by blood." She sighed. "They can rule parentage out with a blood test as well, or so Ruy told me. He was my husband," she added quietly. "A good and kind man. The doctors saved me. But they couldn't save him." Her eyes teared. She brushed at them. "I'll always be grateful to him for taking such good care of me, and for being a friend when I needed one desperately."

"What blood type does your son have?" Tippy asked.

Clarisse hesitated. Cash came back in the door and saved her a reply. Tippy went to meet him, still holding Joshua.

Cash touched the little boy's cheek gently and smiled wistfully.

"I wish we could have one of these," Tippy said quietly. "Boys are nice. Not that I don't love our girl," she added, casting a loving gaze toward her daughter, still watching television beside Rory.

Cash's eyes touched his wife's. "Maybe someday," he said with a grin.

She laughed. "Yes."

Clarisse got up from the table and joined them. "Did K.C. get off all right?"

Cash nodded. "I talked to the pilot and the copilot. They're both licensed to fly the little jet, so they'll be transporting K.C. where he needs to go. After the funeral, they'll bring him back here and make sure he has a relief pilot at the controls when he goes back to Africa."

"Thanks, Cash," Clarisse said solemnly. "I worry about him. He's a good man."

Cash chuckled. "Yes, he is, but if you say that to most people who know him, you'll get stares and shocked expressions. You knew K.C. when he was still doing merc work, didn't you?" he added.

"Yes. Rourke idolized him. It's why he did some of the crazy things he did, as a boy." She looked up at Cash sadly. "I'm so sorry for K.C. I worry about what he might do, after the funeral. I do so wish that Rourke remembered that K.C. was his dad. K.C. is going to go wild when the first shock wears off."

Cash grimaced. "I'm afraid you may be right." He looked at Tippy with the baby in her arms. "I know I would," he said softly, and the look he exchanged with his wife was so expressive that Clarisse felt like an intruder.

"I need to put Joshua down for the night," Clarisse interrupted. "Sorry, but I have him on a strict schedule." She laughed. "I pretend we're in the military. They say a child needs a structured life. I never really had one. My father was rather flighty, and my mother was forever nursing people or taking care of elderly neighbors. She was a saint."

"I've heard about her," Cash agreed. He didn't impart what he'd heard from Jake about her. No need to shatter her illusions.

"You're sure that Rourke won't come back to Jacobsville again?" Clarisse asked worriedly.

"I'm absolutely positive," he replied. And he smiled.

K.C. WAS BACK that weekend. His expression was bland. His eyes were tormented. Blazing. Wounded.

"I'm so sorry," Clarisse told him, and winced as she felt his pain. "I know how I'd feel, if it was Rourke…"

"Yes, I know you do," he agreed quietly. "You were going to be married, before he turned on you. It must feel almost as bad as giving him up to death."

She swallowed. "Yes."

He drew in a breath and pulled her to him, hugged her warmly. "I'll get over it. I'll have to. Kasie is taking it hard. Mary Luke was her last living relative. Her parents died in Africa. Her brother Kantor and his whole family died in an airplane when some idiot revolutionary sent a rocket into it. She's had a hard life."

"She's married to Gil Callister, isn't she?" Clarisse asked. "I know his parents. They socialize in Washington quite a bit."

"They've become much closer to Gil and his brother, John, since Kasie came into their lives," he said quietly. "She's changed both of them, although John's living in Hollister, Montana, with his new wife, Sassy." He hesitated. "Rourke was there a few months ago, providing security for Sassy and her friend when the friend was being stalked by a former employee of her uncle."

"Poor woman," she said.

K.C. pulled back and looked down at Clarisse, sharing the pain of Rourke's lost memory. "I'm going home, but I may be away for a while, maybe down to my villa in Cancún for a rest," he lied, and Clarisse was relieved. She thought that a vacation might be just the thing to ease his agony. "But if you need me, you can call the compound outside Nairobi. I'll give you the number of my houseman," he added, and moved to write it down for her on a pad with a pen that Tippy kept by the telephone. He gave it to her.

"But I have your cell phone number," Clarisse said, confused.

"I may be away from a phone."

She looked up at him with horror. "No! No, don't you dare commit suicide!" she burst out, lowering her voice so that nobody would hear them. She took K.C. by both arms and shook him. "Joshua only has one grandfather…!"

K.C. touched her hair gently. "It's okay," he said softly. "I would never do something like that. I loved him the moment I saw him, in the nursery in the hospital in Manaus. He's…the absolute image of Rourke as a baby."

"You can't tell him," she said miserably. "He hates me, even if he doesn't quite remember why. He'd want the baby. He'd tie me up in court for years…!"

"That won't happen. I'm still keeping secrets from years ago." He withdrew his hand. "I don't do down and dirty with freelance work anymore," he added. "I plan and take care of logistics for my men. I'm too old, and too slow, for forward units. Okay?"

She smiled. "Okay."

"Nice, to have someone care if I live or die," he said after a minute, and he smiled.

"You have two people who do," she replied. "Me and Joshua."

He kissed her forehead. "You're a nice woman. Pity I'm a fossil. I'd hang my son out to dry and marry you myself." He grinned.

She laughed. "Thanks. You take care of yourself. Please keep in touch," she added.

"I will." He stuck his hands in his pockets. He looked every year of his age. "Perhaps, one day, he'll remember. In the meantime, I have to keep busy, so that I don't go completely mad."

"That's not a bad idea. Just please don't take it to extremes."

He gave her a lopsided smile. "I won't." He went to say goodbye to the other occupants of the house and got in the car with Cash, en route to the airport.

"I wish there was something I could do," Clarisse said solemnly.

Tippy put an arm around her as they stood, looking through the window as Cash and K.C. drove away. "Me, too."

K.C. ARRIVED BACK in Nairobi cold-eyed and remote. He was no longer the affable man of recent years. He got out his old kit and started cleaning automatic weapons.

When Rourke knocked absently at the door and walked in, he stopped short at the array of weapons, newly cleaned, laid out in a pack on the dining room table.

K.C. came back into the room carrying a suitcase. He was dressed in khakis, and his eyes were like ice.

"What the hell is wrong?" Rourke asked at once, because he didn't recognize the man he was seeing.

"We've got a job," he replied without looking closely at his son. He started dismantling the weapons in preparation for a commercial flight to an African nation under siege by insurgents. "I'm going along. I've put all the important papers in the safe. This is the combination, just in case." He handed Rourke a folded piece of paper. "There are instructions, as well. My attorney has everything else you might need, legally."

Rourke felt his heart stop. He remembered K.C. dressed like this when he was a child. He remembered that cold, dangerous expression on his face. Something was terribly wrong.

"What happened?" Rourke asked, his tone softening.

K.C. lifted his head and looked at his son evenly. "You wouldn't understand."

"Try me."

"Mary Luke Bernadette died a few days ago," he said, barely able to get the words out past his tight throat. He turned his attention deliberately back to the guns, focusing on them, to ward off strong emotion.

Mary Luke Bernadette. Rourke frowned. The name was familiar. It was on the tip of his tongue. He concentrated, very hard. "She was...a nun." He looked up at K.C. "You loved her," he said softly, wincing at the older man's expression, although it was quickly hidden.

"Yes," K.C. replied. "She was the only woman I ever loved in my whole damned life."

Rourke moved closer. "You're not going out to get yourself killed because of it," he said firmly. "I won't let you."

K.C. fell into a fighting stance. His eyes were colder than ice. "Try to stop me."

Rourke frowned. Amazing, how similar they were. The older man looked just like him! The frown deepened. "You...look like me," he faltered.

"Yes. What a strange coincidence, isn't it?" K.C. drawled. Rourke didn't come any closer, so K.C. went back to his packing, his movements starkly efficient.

"Why? You never go on missions. You stay here and do intel for your men."

K.C. wasn't looking at him. "I have nothing left in the world that matters," he said. "No family, no... Mary Luke, no nothing. Money and power are wind. Air." He closed the suitcase. "I've lost everything I loved." He turned to Rourke. "You remember what I told you, about the safe." He picked up the suitcase.

"No!" Rourke moved right up to him. There was something, deep in his mind. He'd had flashes of insight in recent weeks, confusing images, night terror about something that had happened in Barrera. There was another faint memory, connected with this man. "You have AB Negative blood," he said, blinking.

K.C.'s chin lifted. "Yes."

Rourke scowled. "So do I."

"Coincidences happen," K.C. said shortly.

"It's not...a coincidence." Rourke put a hand to his head. "We had tests done. Neither of us knew for sure." He looked up. "You knocked me over a damned sofa!"

"You had it coming," K.C. said angrily. "You accused me of sleeping with Clarisse's mother!"

Rourke kept staring at him. The remark about Clarisse made no sense. "You're my father. My real father."

K.C.'s heart jumped. He didn't say a word. There was a faint flush high on his cheekbones as he stared at the younger man.

"You're my father," Rourke said roughly, fighting emotion.

K.C. drew in a long breath. He seemed to slump. "Yes," he bit off, averting his head.

"How? Why?"

"Mary Luke took the veil and became a nun," he replied in a tired, wounded voice. "I tried to stop her, tried to make her understand how I felt, what we could have together. She was sorry. She was very fond of me, but she loved the church more. I drank myself into a stupor. Your mother was married to my best friend. He was away on a mission. She came to see about me. She'd heard from one of the girls who worked for me. I was drinking and she had a drink with me. One drink led to more drinks and then…" He stared out the window. "She loved me. That made it worse, somehow. Both of us had to live with it, to pretend that nothing happened, that you were your father's child." His eyes closed. "I betrayed my best friend. I've carried the guilt for thirty-one years." He turned to Rourke. "But I can't regret you," he added in a husky, soft tone, his eyes seeking out all the similarities, all the things they shared. "You're the only damned thing I ever did in my life that was good. I'm…so proud of you." His voice broke and he turned away.

Rourke moved closer. He reached out, hesitantly, and embraced his father.

K.C. lost it. He broke down. At least he had something. He had his son. Rourke had remembered.

"I'm so sorry, Dad," Rourke said huskily. "I'm so damned sorry!"

K.C. felt the wetness in his eyes, on his cheeks. Mary Luke was gone forever. He'd never have another letter from her about the exciting things in Kasie's life, the amusing notes about her neighbors and her efforts to improve her small house. He'd never see her eyes,

her beautiful eyes, laughing up at him. He'd never see
her again, in this life.

He let out a curse so violent that Rourke felt the heat
of it. He held his father closer. "It will be all right," he
said heavily. "It will. You just need time, to get over
it. You can get over anything. Even this."

"I can't…bear it!" K.C. choked.

Rourke held him tighter. "You can. You're strong.
You'll have all the strength you need. I'm right here.
I'm not leaving you in this condition. And you're not
taking that damned bag out of the house. Get me?"

K.C. felt the weakness. It was new, to want to be
protected. It was new, to have Rourke remember. He
drew in a long, shuddering breath. "Maybe I can do it
over the phone," he said after a minute.

Rourke chuckled. He felt as if some light, some
warmth, had finally come back into the cold empti-
ness he'd been fighting lately. "Maybe you can, Dad,"
he said gently.

K.C. drew back after a minute and turned away,
dashing at the wetness in his eyes. "Where were you?"

"I could tell you, but I'd have to…" He laughed out
loud. "Well, you know."

K.C. turned, his expression whimsical. "Listen, kid,
I've got better top secret clearances than you have."

"Yes, but you don't have clearance from the agency
I'm working for." Rourke grinned.

K.C. smiled. "Maybe not."

"How about something to eat? Can we get Brady to
work in the kitchen? I've just got in from the airport
and I'm starved. I had enough peanuts to qualify me
for a cage in the zoo beside the elephants!"

K.C. threw an affectionate arm over his shoulders.
"Let's go see."

LATER, HE WONDERED if he should tell Rourke anything about Clarisse. When Charlene showed up with her dad and his handsome business partner, he decided against it. Rourke was affectionate with Charlene and he mentioned setting a wedding date. Amazing, K.C. pondered, how reluctant the young girl was to do that. She had more traveling to do, she told Rourke. She was sorry, but she just didn't see herself settling down to dishwashers and washing machines and kids. Not for a long time.

Rourke went over to his own house, let his pet lion out of the cage and walked into his house with the affectionate cat. They got inside and the lion jumped up on the sofa and rested his chin on the arm of it.

Rourke laughed. "I've missed you, too, you great yellow nuisance," he said, bending to smooth his lean hand over the cat's pelt and kiss him on the head. "Want to watch the telly, do you? Okay. I'll find you a nice nature special if you promise not to attack the wildebeest on the screen. How's that, Lou?"

The lion just yawned.

CHAPTER ELEVEN

CLARISSE SETTLED DOWN into life with the Griers. She found a nice house that she liked inside the city limits, near a grocery store, the post office and the Methodist Church. There was a grammar school a few blocks away. The house was Victorian, with a long porch, high gables with gingerbread scrolling and even a turret room. She bought it at once and called in carpenters and decorators, some from San Antonio, to make it livable. One of the perks of being rich, she thought to herself, was that she could buy most anything she liked without having to check the balance in her bank accounts. Her parents came from great wealth, and all their valuables, including stocks, went to Clarisse, as the only surviving member of her family.

"I'll miss you," Tippy said when the house was ready to be occupied, and Clarisse had hired a sweet young Hispanic woman, Mariel, to take care of it and help with Joshua.

"I'll miss all of you, too," Clarisse said softly. "But I'm right nearby," she added with a grin. "You can come and visit whenever you like."

"I'll do that," Tippy agreed. Her eyes were on the baby in Clarisse's arms. "He's such a sweet boy."

"Yes, he is," Clarisse agreed. "Your Tris is a little doll. And I think Rory's the greatest," she added. She laughed. "He tried to teach me how to play those video games he has. I died so much he said they should dedicate a street to me in-game."

Tippy laughed. "He's crazy about those online games, and he's drawn Cash into them, too." She shook her head. "I can't manage the controls."

"Neither can I!"

"Talking about me, huh?" Cash said as he came into the room.

"And why would we be discussing you?" Tippy teased, resting her body against his to look up at him with soft, loving green eyes. "I mean, just because you're devastating is no reason to talk about you."

"I'm sweet, too," he mused, bending to kiss her softly. "You say it all the time."

"It's absolutely true," Tippy sighed.

Cash grinned and kissed her once more before he let her go. His eyes went worriedly to Clarisse. "I'm still not sure this is a good idea."

"Eb Scott phoned me last night," she told him. "He says he's got two of his top new trainees on my case. They'll follow me night and day and keep me safe." She bit her lower lip. "Sapara has killed two men who were instrumental in helping General Machado set up the new government. The Granges had to hire extra security. He sent a man after them, as well. But he didn't try to do it with a jar of deadly mosquitoes," Clarisse added angrily, remembering what had been done to Ruy, and what was meant for her.

"No, he used a knife," Cash replied, revealing that he'd been discussing things with Eb, too. His black eyes met hers. "You'll have more people watching than just Eb's men," he added. "Nobody is going to hurt you or the child in my town. I promise you that."

She smiled warmly. "Thanks, Cash. Thanks to both of you for giving us a place to stay until we could find one of our own."

"Oh, we had ulterior motives," Cash murmured. He held out his arms. "May I?"

She placed Joshua in them and watched the expression on his face, and on Tippy's, as she moved closer to touch the baby's little hand.

Clarisse, watching, felt the hunger in them for another child. Maybe that would happen. She hoped so.

"I'm driving you to your new house," Tippy said after a minute, smiling up at Cash.

"I would offer, but I've got a meeting in... Damn, I'm already late. Have to go." He kissed Tippy softly, handed Joshua back to Clarisse and went in to kiss the rest of the family.

"We always do that when he leaves," Tippy explained as she drove Clarisse in the Jaguar to her new home. "We kiss each other and say we love them. You never know," she added quietly. "Cash can't live without a little danger. I worry, but I don't obsess."

"I worried myself sick when Rourke left on that mission," she replied. "I know that he does dangerous work. I had hoped, so much..." She drew in a breath and changed the subject. "I think I'll like Jacobsville," she said warmly. "It's very special."

"We think so, too," Tippy agreed. "You'll need a car."

"That's my next priority. Where did you get the Jag, and does the dealer have a good inventory?"

Tippy laughed. "Yes. They're in San Antonio. I'll

give you the website address and you can see for yourself! When you want to go looking for it, I'll drive you."

"Thanks."

"Oh, I have ulterior motives," Tippy mused. "I get to hold Joshua while you deal with the salesman," she added, tongue in cheek, and both women laughed.

MARIEL WAS IN her late twenties, quiet and respectful. Clarisse had found her through a nice-looking cowboy, Jack Lopez, who worked for Luke Craig. She'd met him in Barbara's Café and they lunched together from time to time when she took Joshua into town. The cowboy said she was a cousin and she had excellent references.

She was a treasure. Mariel fell in love with the baby on sight. She took him, cooing, and invited the older adults to follow her. She'd prepared two rooms on the ground floor, because Clarisse's incision was still painful and it was hard for her to climb stairs. Next to Clarisse's room was an adjoining one with sliding wooden doors. There was a nursery behind them, beautifully decorated and painted in eggshell blue, with a complementing blue carpet. The baby furniture was white. There were mobiles over the crib.

"This is wonderful," Tippy exclaimed.

"Yes, it is. I found them on the internet," Clarisse chuckled, pulling out her iPod. "And next on the list is a car!"

She pulled up the website, checked out the inventory and called the number listed to speak to a salesman. He had several new Jaguars in inventory and invited her up to see them. She promised to come the next morn-

ing after glancing at Tippy to make sure she was free
to drive with her.

Mariel took the baby into the nursery to change a
dirty diaper. "I will take wonderful care of him," she
promised Clarisse. "You need not fear for him."

"I know that. Thanks."

"Now," Clarisse said when she and Tippy were
alone, "I have to do what I promised Eb." She called
him and told him her itinerary. "And thanks, Eb. I don't
mind paying the salaries of the men you've hired..."
She paused and laughed. "Okay, but you have to promise that you'll let me reciprocate. Deal. Thanks."

"Eb's in a class of his own, isn't he?" Tippy asked
gently.

"A truly good man." Clarisse led the way into the
remodeled kitchen. It was a gourmet cook's delight,
containing every single appliance that would be needed
for a grand meal.

"You love to cook, don't you?" Tippy asked.

"Oh, yes." Clarisse didn't add that she'd learned because it was something Rourke was quite good at. He'd
actually been a chef in a restaurant in Johannesburg for
a time during his younger days. During their blissful
few weeks in Manaus, they'd shared cooking chores.

Mariel was back with the baby just as Clarisse
served coffee. Tippy took Joshua and cuddled him
when he began to fuss.

"He's hungry," Clarisse laughed. She called to
Mariel in Spanish and asked her to bring a diaper as
she took the baby and unfastened her blouse and her
nursing bra. She shivered and laughed again as the
baby started to nurse.

"I nursed Tris," Tippy said, sighing. "There are so many benefits. But it must hurt you."

"The incision pulls. And a weird thing—it feels like labor pains when he starts suckling," she added.

"I know what you mean! I had the same experience." Her eyes were dreamy. "I would love another baby."

"I'll cross all my fingers and toes for you," she promised, and grinned.

Tippy just laughed.

CLARISSE WAS OFFERED an XK, one of the top-of-the-line sports cars that Jaguar produced, but she shook her head. A sedan was far more sensible. But she did opt for a supercharged V8, in white with beige upholstery.

"Cash had a red XK when we started dating, in New York," Tippy recalled when they were finally back home and she was getting ready to go home. "He loved it, but he traded for a sedan when we knew Tris was on the way. The convertibles do have a bench seat in back, but it was barely big enough for Rory to stretch out in when Cash drove us around."

"Two-seaters are for young people with no children, or older people whose children are grown," Clarisse said with a grin.

"I know. But it was a honey of a car," Tippy said with a wistful sigh.

"So is my new sedan. We can go shopping up to San Antonio when you have another free day."

"Translated, when I have another free day that Rory also has a teacher workday, like today," came the amused reply. "He's just the greatest babysitter."

"He's really sweet," Clarisse added.

"I've always thought so." She glanced at Mariel, who came smiling to take the baby from Clarisse, who was looking worn. "You need to have an early night," she added, concerned. "You've had a rough few weeks."

"I know. I'm low on the malarial pills, too. I'll run by the pharmacy first thing tomorrow and pick up the refill. I called it in yesterday, but I was just too tired to go there today."

"I could go for you," Tippy offered.

"I'll go. Would you like to have lunch at Barbara's tomorrow? If you would, I'll pick you and Tris up after I stop at the pharmacy."

"Cash is off tomorrow, so I'll be on my own. You can pick me up before you go to the pharmacy and I'll hold Joshua while you pay for the pills."

"Ooooh, do I sense an underlying motive here?" Clarisse asked with almost the first flash of her sense of humor since her ordeal had begun.

"You certainly do!"

"In that case, I'll see you about fifteen until eleven in the morning."

"Okay!"

"BUT I COULD keep him for you," Mariel fussed when Clarisse, dressed in jeans and a long-sleeved beige sweater and loafers started for the front door, with Joshua in a blue footed fleece suit wrapped in a blanket in his car seat.

Clarisse just smiled. "I'll get used to leaving him, but right now, it's too soon after Manaus," she explained. "I'm...what's the word? I'm twitchy."

"Ah," the other woman said, and smiled sadly. "You

have had a very hard time. But it will be better. It takes time."

"Yes. Thanks for offering, though."

"That is what you pay for me for, yes?" she replied and laughed as she went in to start work on cleaning the bedrooms.

TIPPY WENT TO look for a new lipstick, carrying Joshua, while Clarisse stood in line at the pharmacy counter. Tippy had just come back when Clarisse turned her head, and her heart stopped cold in her chest. She couldn't even manage words.

"Son of a...!" Rourke burst out. He moved closer, wearing jeans and a knit shirt and a shepherd's coat. His one pale brown eye flashed murder as he saw Clarisse. "And just what the bloody hell are you doing here, then?" he demanded hotly. "Found out I was working here and came over to see the sights, did you?" he accused. His eye looked up and down her with pure hatred. "Sorry, but I don't see myself taking a number to take my place in your bed!"

Aware of murmurs around her, because the pharmacy was crowded, Clarisse handed her credit card to Bonnie, who was glaring at the blond man. Bonnie rang up the purchase, handed back her credit card, waited while she signed the slip and handed her the prescription medication for the malaria.

"Here's your son, Clarisse," Tippy said, coming forward with a taut face to hand the baby to her friend.

"Your son?" Rourke felt his whole body explode. He'd never known such grief in his life, and he didn't know why. He looked at the child in her arms with blazing rage. "You had a child? Got careless, I see.

Do you even know who the father is, Tat?" he added with pure venom.

Tippy moved forward. "If you say one more word to her," she said in a voice thick with anger, "I will have my husband arrest you and prosecute you for harassment, and I'll testify in court if I have to! I don't imagine it would be difficult to find a few other willing witnesses, either!"

"Damned straight," Jack Lopez, one of Luke Craig's new cowboys, agreed. He was tall and good-looking, with black hair and a faint Hispanic look. He'd had lunch with Clarisse at Barbara's and he'd helped her find Mariel to keep the baby. He smiled at Clarisse. "It would be my pleasure, Miss Clarisse." He gave Rourke an odd look, but Rourke paid him no attention at all. He was glaring at Clarisse for all he was worth.

"Let's go, Clarisse," Tippy said, shooting a venomous look at Rourke, who met it with studied amusement.

She herded a shell-shocked Clarisse out of the pharmacy and back into the new Jaguar. "You get in," she said. "I'm driving. I'll put Joshua in the backseat."

Rourke had picked up the prescription Jake Blair had asked him to get, amid icy-cold looks, and walked out just in time to see Tippy put the baby in its carrier into the backseat. She climbed into the driver's seat beside Clarisse, slammed the door. Seconds later, they drove away. Neither woman had looked at him again.

He stared after Tat with his heartbeat almost smothering him. He felt betrayed. It was the most incredible feeling, because he knew he hated her. He'd hated her for years. He couldn't remember why. But there was something, an anguish, a sensation of utter loss, that overlaid the resentment. It hurt him to look at the child. Why?

He put a hand to his head. There was a memory there, somewhere, but he couldn't reach it. He didn't understand why he'd gone after her so savagely. But it irritated him that she'd followed him to America. Well, she did live in America, most of the time. Or he thought she did. He remembered her in a political background, at cocktail parties. Washington, DC, perhaps? But she'd never been to Texas. Had she? And why did she turn up here just as he was back in the country on a new assignment, one that would keep him here for several weeks.

He went back to Jake Blair's house and put the prescription in its bag on the dining room table. He was so quiet and subdued that Jake scowled.

"What's wrong?"

"Tat's here."

Jake winced. "I'm sorry. I should have told you that she was living here…"

"Living here?! What in hell for?" Rourke burst out.

Jake let out a long sigh. "It's complicated. I can't tell you much. She was living with the Griers until she bought a house of her own and had it furnished."

"That was Tippy Grier in the pharmacy, then," he said after a minute. "I thought she looked familiar."

"In the pharmacy?" Jake was feeling uneasy.

"Tat had a baby with her. Her son, Tippy called him." His face was harder than stone. "She had a kid with some poor sucker. I asked if she knew who the father was… Why are you looking at me like that?"

"Sit down, Rourke," his friend said gently.

Rourke scowled, but he did as he was asked.

Jake went into the kitchen and came back with cups of black coffee. He gave Rourke one, took the other and sat down at the table with him.

"I don't know if K.C. told you anything about what's happened to her recently."

"I wouldn't have her name mentioned around me," Rourke said bitterly. "She came to the damned compound, right into my own bedroom when I got home after I was wounded. She was wearing my mother's engagement ring! She had to have stolen the damned thing. I jerked it off and kicked her out. I didn't even speak to K.C. for months afterward. He actually had her flown there…!"

Jake closed his eyes. It was even worse than he thought.

"Okay, what's that look about?"

Jake sipped coffee. "She was married, Rourke," he said quietly. "To a friend of hers in Manaus, a doctor named Ruy Carvajal."

"Married…" He felt his breath catch deep in his throat. He lifted the cup to his mouth. The coffee was hot and it burned his lips, but it helped disguise the anguish he felt. "She married Carvajal? My God, he was twenty years older than her, at the least!"

"They had a child," he said, and he didn't look at Rourke as he said it.

"The one she was carrying. A boy. A son." His face tautened. "I see." He drew in a long breath. "So, is he living here with her?"

Jake shook his head. "He died. Of cerebral malaria. A few weeks ago. In Manaus."

Manaus. There was something about Manaus. Why did the place seem so familiar to him? He'd only been there a handful of times, mostly because of Tat. When her mother died. When her father and sister were killed on the river...where the hell did that memory come from? He held his head. It throbbed.

"You okay?" Jake asked, worried.

Rourke lifted his eyes to the other man's. "Ya," he said after a minute. "So she came over here. Why?"

"She has nobody left in the world," Jake said. "She had the same strain of malaria that her husband did. Peg and Winslow Grange contacted a tropical disease specialist in Great Britain and had him flown to Manaus to treat her. It was touch and go. They did a C-section because they thought she couldn't live..."

"Dear God!" Rourke got to his feet and turned away, his heart shaking him. The reaction he felt to the news devastated him. Why? He hated Tat. He didn't care if she died...if she died...she could have died. He didn't know about the marriage, about the baby, about the fever...

"She lived, against the odds," Jake continued solemnly. "But she was afraid for the baby. She wanted to be somewhere that he could be cared for, if...something happened to her."

He turned back. "She's all right now?" he asked worriedly. "The fever won't recur?"

Jake sipped coffee. "You've had malaria. You know what it's like."

"I had several kinds, none of which recurred."

"This one does," Jake replied. "We saw it when we were in Asia, and Africa, and even far back in the Amazon, if you recall. It was almost endemic in certain areas. *Plasmodium falciparum.*"

"From the anopheles mosquito," Rourke replied

heavily. He'd seen cases of it. Cerebral malaria was invariably fatal. He bit his lower lip. "How in hell did they get infected from that one?" he burst out. "You live in a country where it occurs, you take precautions!"

"He did," Jake replied. "He had the grounds sprayed constantly."

"Well, not good enough, obviously," he shot back, "and why the hell didn't he recognize the symptoms? He was a doctor, for God's sake!"

"There had been an outbreak of virus in the community. He was working eighteen-hour days, and he was exhausted. He thought he'd caught the virus. It had much the same symptoms. He waited until it was too late to do anything. Clarisse nursed him. She caught the fever. She was burning up with it when he died."

Rourke looked away. Clarisse, all alone, with nobody who cared for her when the baby came, when her husband died.

"She didn't want to move here," Jake added. "They—" he almost said K.C. and had to catch himself "—had to browbeat her into it."

"Why?"

"She thought you might come over again," Jake said shortly. "Everyone said you'd mentioned that you were getting married and you'd be taking cases in Europe from now on."

"She didn't want to risk running into me," Rourke said aloud. It hurt to put it into words. His hands, in the pockets of his khaki slacks, balled into fists.

"Would you look forward to seeing someone who did nothing but belittle you, torment you?" Jake asked softly.

"No. Of course not." He stared at his feet. "She nursed him."

"Yes. She had the infection, too, but sometimes it takes a week or two to present symptoms—you know that. By the time it did, she was in labor. Her fever was over a hundred and five and climbing. The doctors did what they thought they had to. She fought so hard to live," he added, having had the story from K.C. "She was worried about the baby."

The baby. Carvajal's baby. He felt bile in the back of his throat. He hated the idea of Clarisse with another man. Although why he should, when he hated her…

He drew in a long breath. "I said some harsh things to her," he said after a minute. "It was the shock, of seeing her unexpectedly. I've avoided her for months. Ever since…" He hesitated. He scowled. "I don't understand how she got my mother's ring, you know? It was in the safe, and I had the only combination. I never left it lying around. Never!" He turned, his face flushed with feeling. "The only time she was even in the compound was when she came to see about me, when I was wounded, and the only room she was in was my bedroom. There was no way…!"

"You've spent years hating her," Jake replied. "Some habits are hard to break."

Rourke stared at the wall. "I don't know why I hate her so much," he confessed. "She was always tagging after me in Africa, when she was little." A faint, tender smile bloomed on his hard mouth. "She wasn't afraid of anything. I was part of a merc group when I was ten. I wanted to go back, the year after K.C. became my guardian, but I hesitated because I knew Tat would follow me. Even then, she was my shadow." His head hurt suddenly, violently. He put a hand to it. "Why can't I remember?"

"Stop forcing it." Jake got up and clapped him on the shoulder. "You're remembering a few things, aren't you? Things that had gotten lost over the past few months."

"I remembered that K.C. was my father," he returned. "He was packing his guns when I got home. Mary Luke died." He winced. "He loved her desperately. He'd have married her, but she became a nun. He was going to go with his men on a mission. I remembered then, remembered who he was, what he was to me. I got in front of him and dared him to try and commit suicide." He chuckled. "That took guts, let me tell you. He knocked me over a sofa..." He stopped, frowning. "He hit me. I'd said something to him, something about Tat." He ground his teeth together. "I can't... remember what."

"The neurologist said that you might regain some of those memories," Jake told him. "But it's going to be slow. Just relax. Take it one day at a time, the way you've been taking it. Don't try to force it."

"I asked him about letting people tell me what happened." He laughed shortly. "He said it wouldn't matter—it wouldn't make sense to me. It would be like listening to a story." He shook his head. "It's driving me mad."

"You'll get through it."

"I guess." He drew in a breath. "I'll apologize to Tat, when I see her," he said slowly. "That was a hell of a way to treat someone who's been through what she's been through. That cold-blooded so-and-so tortured her in Barrera for information on the offensive, but I put a knife in him…" He gasped, staring at Jake.

"Yes," Jake said, nodding.

"Why didn't K.C. tell me she'd married?" he wondered aloud.

"You wouldn't let anyone talk to you about her," Jake replied.

Rourke sighed. "I guess not." He shook his head. "So much pain. I wouldn't have hurt her like that deliberately. Or would I? I've spent years making her pay…making her pay…for what?" he added, almost to himself. "Damn it!"

"One day at a time," Jake interrupted. "I think it may come back."

"Do you?" Rourke sat back down. "Well, I can hope, I guess."

Jake didn't reply. He knew something that he didn't dare impart to Rourke, not yet. Sapara had sent a cleaner after Clarisse, and nobody knew what the man looked like. Nobody except Rourke. He'd seen Sapara's chief assassin long before the assault on Barrera. He knew what the man looked like. And he might be the only chance Clarisse had, if his memory returned in time.

But that was unlikely. In any case, Cash and Eb Scott had things in hand. Anybody who made a step toward Clarisse would find himself on the business end of whatever weapon several covert operatives could produce. She was safe enough. For now.

CLARISSE HAD TAKEN Joshua to the city park. It was mid-March, a beautiful day in the beginning of spring, and there was a performance by the local high school band for the community. It was one of many cultural events sponsored by local merchants in cooperation with the Jacobs County Chamber of Commerce.

She had a thick quilt lying on the dry grass, with Joshua lying on it in his little blue fleece footie suit. She was wearing jeans and a sweatshirt, without even a trace of makeup. She loved being Joshua's mother. She didn't want to pick up men, so she did nothing to make herself more attractive.

She couldn't know that, to the man watching her covertly, she was beautiful without artifice. Rourke stared at her from a few yards away, taking in the tenderness with which she handled the little boy, the freshness of her complexion, the quiet grace of her movements.

He'd started over badly with her, and he felt guilty. She'd been through hell. He was sorry for the things he'd said to her in the pharmacy. She'd probably snub him, but he didn't care. He wanted to apologize.

She felt him. It was uncanny, how she always knew when he was close by. Even in the pharmacy, she'd felt a tingling just before he confronted her. She looked up with faint fear in her eyes. She started to reach for Joshua, to run away.

"Don't go," Rourke said gently. He went down on one knee, his eyes on the little boy. Odd coloring, he thought, for the child of a man who was visibly Hispanic. He recalled Carvajal, who had black hair and eyes and a dark olive complexion. But the child resembled Clarisse, and he did have her coloring.

"What do you want?" Clarisse asked tautly.

He shrugged. "To apologize. I didn't know about your husband."

She didn't look directly at him. It hurt too much. She didn't speak, either.

"He's a good child, isn't he?" he asked after a minute. The sight of the child was painful. He didn't understand why.

"Yes," she said.

"Jake said you were staying with the Griers."

She nodded. "They were a lot of help. The stitches still pull..." She broke off.

"Jake told me about that, too," he said. He studied her. She looked older, worn, thinner. "You've had a hell of a time, haven't you, Tat? I'm sorry I made things worse."

She didn't answer him. She was hoping he'd just leave. He was upsetting her.

He felt that discomfort. He didn't blame her. He got to his feet. "I won't be around long," he said after a minute. "This will probably be my last assignment in the States for a while."

She nodded. She didn't look up.

He clenched his jaw. There was something between them. Something that his remembered hatred of her didn't explain. "Why is it like this?" he asked suddenly.

"Excuse me?" she faltered.

"Why am I...this way with you?" he added. "You tagged after me like my own shadow when you were a kid. You went everywhere with me...!"

"That was years ago, Rourke," she said, unconsciously using the name everyone else did, not calling him by the name that was familiar, that made her feel unique in his life.

He registered it, but not consciously. "We were together in Barrera," he began.

"Yes, at the awards ceremony."

He felt as if someone had hit him in the gut. "What awards ceremony?"

"You said…"

"At the camp," he emphasized. "After that cold-blooded minion of Sapara's tortured you," he added.

"Oh. Yes." She could have bitten her tongue through for that stupid slip.

"He paid for what he did to you," he said coldly.

She nodded.

His mind was working. He was getting flashes of color. The camp. The assault on Sapara's position. The little dictator who'd killed so many innocent people, flustered, cowardly without his minions, trying to escape Machado, trying to explain his treachery.

What had he overheard K.C. say about Sapara, just recently? Something about a helicopter. He couldn't remember. Funny memory, that.

"You shouldn't be trying to lift the baby by yourself," he said suddenly, frowning. "He isn't six weeks yet, is he?"

"Almost."

He hesitated. His face softened. "You had a baby in your arms in the refugee camp in Ngawa," he said abruptly. "You looked beautiful to me, even with your clothes stained and your hair unwashed. I thought I'd bury you that time, Tat. You'd been captured and threatened with execution. My God, you've got more lives than a cat!"

The comment shocked her into looking up. What was that expression on her lovely, sweet face? Hope?

"I'd forgotten, hadn't I?" he asked. "I got you out, just before the offensive." He scowled. "I'm always getting you out of trouble, always there when you're traumatized. I always have been. So why is it like that, if I hate you so much?"

For a few seconds, hope had washed over her like liquid joy. And now it was gone. Gone again.

She managed a faint smile. "I've never known," she replied.

Her eyes were soft, china blue and beautiful, warm with feeling. "So beautiful," he said without thinking. His jaw tautened. His one pale brown eye flashed.

"Truce over," she said at once, getting up with obvious effort. "And I have to go. Mariel will have lunch."

"Oh, now, Mrs. Carvajal, don't you dare try to lift that baby!"

A tall, handsome man came closer, grinning. "I'll be happy to carry him for you. I'm going that way, anyhow. Mr. Craig sent me into town to the hardware store to get some more butane for branding."

"That's very kind of you, Mr. Lopez." She glanced at Rourke, whose expression was unreadable. "Stanton Rourke, this is Jack Lopez." She introduced him. "He's been helping me with groceries just lately. I have a hard time lifting things. We met at Barbara's Café and he volunteered." She smiled up at the man, relieved that she didn't have to bear the explosion that she'd expected from Rourke when his eye had flashed at her.

"No problem to help a new mother," the cowboy said, with a faint accent. He tipped his hat at Rourke. He stared at him intently for a minute, but Rourke's expression didn't change. "Nice to meet you." He bent over and picked up the little boy, holding him gingerly in one arm while Tat struggled to pick up and fold the blanket.

"Here, I'll do that," Jack said quickly. He picked up the bag with diapers and wipes, and the blanket while holding Joshua easily in one arm. "Ready?" he asked.

Clarisse nodded.

"See you," Rourke said, and it was almost a threat as he glared at the other man.

She managed a faint smile. But she didn't answer him as they walked away.

CHAPTER TWELVE

ROURKE WAS WORKING surveillance on a small business that was suspected of involvement in an international kidnapping ring. Young women would be lured in with prospects of exciting work and travel, and then sold into prostitution all over the world. It was a sordid business, especially when some of the women they handled were barely fourteen years old. There was a tie to drug trafficking, as well, because the women were usually heavily medicated before they were put to work in brothels, to make sure they didn't protest.

He was in San Antonio, taking a lunch break, when he spotted Clarisse walking out of a high-end baby boutique. She was alone, he noted, as she went toward the new Jaguar sedan she'd bought. Odd, how he felt when he looked at her.

He hated the idea of other men watching her, touching her. He'd accused her for years of being promiscuous. It was why he'd asked her, sarcastically, if she knew who had fathered her child. But she didn't dress like a siren. She didn't act like one. Why did he class her in that company?

So many questions, he thought miserably, and no answers. He'd avoided K.C., avoided the States, even avoided his friend Jake Blair in recent months until he'd come over for this assignment. Perhaps he didn't really want to remember the recent past. Which provoked another question. Why?

Tat's marriage was still a puzzle. He remembered Ruy Carvajal from years past. The Manaus physician had attended Tat's mother when she died. He'd taken care of Tat when her father and sister were killed on the river. He was always around, a kindly sort of man with no real fire or spark. And he was well over twenty years older than Tat. So why had she married him? It had to have been after she went rushing to Nairobi to see Rourke when he was shot.

That was a very unpleasant memory, one which did him no credit. He'd raged at her, accused her of stealing his mother's ring, thrown her out of the house. He grimaced. Her child was only a few weeks old, and it had been months ago that he'd been shot. He did the math. Tat had been pregnant. She'd been pregnant when he'd made her feel small for caring about him, for worrying. His eye closed on a wave of shame. He could have caused her to lose her child.

Had she been married to Carvajal at the time? But if she had, why had she been wearing that engagement ring, the one Rourke's father—rather, the man he'd thought was his father—had given his mother before they were married?

He drew in a breath. It hurt, trying to remember. It hurt more, looking at Tat as she paused to smile at a young child on the street, holding its mother's hand. She'd loved kids. He remembered her in a refugee camp, holding a baby. He scowled. Ngawa. Yes. She'd been in Ngawa and he'd gone to get her out. Since she was eight, he'd been her protector, her hero.

Any tragedy in her life drew him, immediately. But if he hated her—why had he always gone?

He kept getting flashes of memory. A Latin dance club. He and Tat were dancing together. He only remembered doing the tango at one such club, and it was in Japan, years before. He hadn't danced with Tat then, either. There was another memory, of a wedding gown and a shadowy priest.

He laughed. He was getting fanciful. His mind, the neurologist had told him, would most likely create new pathways to memories he'd lost, in time. Well, perhaps it was creating false ones. He was certain that he'd never contemplated marriage until now, with Charlene. He grimaced. The girl was juvenile. Worse, she was obviously attracted to her father's young business partner. Not that Rourke really wanted to marry her. He'd made sure all his friends knew he planned to marry her, though, so it would get back to Tat. He scowled. Why did he want to hurt her?

She was on the move again, opening the door of her Jaguar. Just as she got in, he noticed a movement behind her. A man in a dark sedan pulled in behind her. Rourke had spent his life following people, on the job. He knew surveillance when he saw it.

He told his team leader he had to go out for a bit. He radioed another operative and gave him a description of the Jaguar and its direction of travel. Then he went looking.

TAT WENT INTO a small bed-and-bath boutique and found a shower curtain she liked. She smiled at the young clerk as she paid for it and carried it outside in a bag. She'd had to park almost half a block away. As she walked, a man fell into step behind her.

She must have left the baby with her housekeeper, or with Tippy Grier, Rourke reasoned. He followed along behind her unknown shadow, his pale brown eye narrow with subdued anger. Nobody was hurting Tat on his watch.

He rounded a corner. She was going into another shop, this one an exclusive coffee shop. The tall man surveilling her was paused in an alley, quietly watching, not drawing attention. He didn't even hear Rourke come up behind him until he felt the cold metal of the .45 Colt ACP shoved into his spinal column.

Rourke felt the man tense and moved back. "You try it, and you'll be a few grams heavier, mate," he said curtly, because he knew the counterattack the man was pondering.

"Rourke!"

His surprise was visible as the man turned. "Who the hell are you?" he demanded.

"I'm Kilpatrick. I work for Eb Scott."

Rourke made a face and lowered the pistol. "Then what in the seven hells are you doing shadowing Clarisse Carrington?" he demanded.

"Mrs. Carvajal, you mean?"

"Ya." He hated her married name.

Kilpatrick shrugged. "I can't tell you," he said. "Eb just said to keep her under constant surveillance or he'd stick lighted matches under my fingernails."

"Who ordered the surveillance?" Rourke persisted.

"Cash Grier. Go figure." He chuckled. "I guess he and Tippy are worried about her settling in here."

Sure. That was why men were watching her, he thought sarcastically. But he didn't say it out loud.

"Thanks, mate. Sorry about the…well, you know," he added sheepishly as he shoved the pistol back into the holster under his jacket.

"No problem. I'll just go change my trousers now," Kilpatrick said with a wicked grin.

Rourke clapped him on the shoulder and walked off.

HE WORMED HIS way into Cash's office during the lunch hour. Carlie Farwalker was eating a sandwich at her desk, as she did when her husband, Carson, was doing overtime at the local hospital as an intern. She was obviously pregnant and beaming.

"Is he about?" Rourke asked with a smile, nodding toward Cash's office.

"Yes. You can knock and go in, he's just doing paperwork," she said.

"Thanks. You look blooming," he added.

She laughed. "We're so, so happy."

"So your dad told me. Nice of him to give me a room," he added. "I'm so sick of hotels."

"He likes the company. He's lonely since I moved out."

"He told me that, too. Give your husband my regards. I'll try to make time to see him before I leave town."

"Do that. He'd love to see you."

Rourke remembered Carson as he had been. Amazing, the change in that lobo wolf, to end up married with a child on the way, working his way through an internship at Jacobsville General Hospital. But then, life was surprising.

He smiled at Carlie, knocked on Cash's office door and went in.

CASH WASN'T AS friendly as Carlie. In fact, he glared at Rourke with pure venom.

"Did you teach your wife that expression, then?" Rourke mused as he closed the door behind him. "Because I can feel a rash breaking out all over my backside already!"

"Embarrassing Clarisse will land you in trouble if you try it again," Cash promised him. "And if you think you've seen the extent of my wife's temper, you're badly mistaken."

Rourke sighed. He sat down in front of Cash's desk and crossed his legs. "I don't know why I hit out at her," he confessed.

"Neither do I," the other man replied. He put aside a stack of reports. "I thought you were getting married."

Rourke looked uncomfortable. "She's very young and infatuated with her father's business partner," he said. "I sort of pushed her into the engagement."

"Why?"

He shrugged. "I knew it would get back to Tat," he said solemnly.

"Good God," Cash said softly, because he knew how Clarisse felt about Rourke. Surely, Rourke did, too. "Is that your idea of entertainment? Torturing a woman who's just lost her husband, and almost her life?"

Rourke felt the flush high on his cheekbones. "Tat and I go back a long way," he said without answering the question. It made him sick to contemplate how far he'd gone in his attempts to push Tat out of his life.

"Don't make it hard for her," the older man said, and his eyes were like ice. "Or you'll have more trouble than you can handle. Finish your project and go home."

"How would you know what my project is?" Rourke mused.

"Get real. I may not do covert jobs anymore, but I know people who do."

Rourke shrugged.

"What do you want?"

Rourke leaned forward, his one pale brown eye narrow and intent. "I want to know why you're having one of Eb Scott's men shadow Tat."

Cash hesitated. "And how would you know that I am?"

"I walked up behind him and stuck a .45 in his ribs," he replied. The eye narrowed. "Why?"

Cash didn't dare tell him the truth. There was always the chance that Rourke might let something slip because of that traumatic injury and put Clarisse in greater danger. He lifted his chin. "She's had a problem with a persistent admirer," he said finally.

Rourke drew in a breath. That he could believe. She was beautiful enough to cause men to obsess. "I see." His eye narrowed. "Would it be that Jack Lopez character who works for Luke Craig?" he added. "Because he seems to be everywhere she is lately."

Cash frowned. "No. It's not him. He looks out for her."

Rourke didn't add that he was uncomfortable with the idea of another man signing on as Tat's protector. That was his job. It always had been.

"Who told you I was behind it?" Cash asked abruptly.

"Birds," Rourke said easily, nodding. "They speak to me. Usually, it's crows, but I have had the odd piece of intel from grackles… Why are you laughing?"

Cash waved a hand at him. "Go back to work, and let me finish these damned reports before I'm buried in them."

Rourke got up. "I did apologize, you know," he said after a minute. "I had no idea that Tat was married. Certainly I didn't know what she'd been through."

"An amazing young woman," Cash said. "To survive the death of her entire family, kidnapping, torture…and still be able to smile."

"She was always like that," Rourke said, an odd softness in his voice. "She looks like a cream puff, but she's got grit."

"Yes."

Rourke paused at the door. "Who's after her?" he asked.

"Someone local," Cash said. "Not anyone dangerous," he added, lying with a smile, "just a boy who's overly infatuated. We don't think he'd harm her. We're just being careful."

Rourke nodded. He went out the door, closing it behind him.

IT WAS A long week. He was sick of black coffee and darkened rooms and spotting scopes and listening to endless rounds of audio tape as they tried to get enough evidence to arrest the suspect in the trafficking ring.

On Saturday, there was a dance in Jacobsville in the park. A local band played for it. There were concession stands and a wooden platform had been constructed to double as a dance floor. Whole families came, enjoying the warm spring weekend. Tat was there, with the woman who kept the baby for her. She was dancing with a tall, good-looking cowboy when Rourke leaned against a tree to watch. That Lopez man again, he thought disgustedly.

He was wearing khakis. He looked, and felt, out of place in a town where most men wore jeans and boots and big hats. But he was right at home in the small-town atmosphere.

He didn't like that man dancing with Tat. He didn't know why. He had no reason to feel jealous of her. The man didn't seem dangerous. He was pretty sure he wasn't a stalker. Still, there was something oddly familiar about him. Disturbing.

Tat was wearing a long denim skirt with a short-sleeved blue-checked blouse and flat shoes. She looked young and beautiful in the fading sunlight as lights came on automatically in the park and the dancing platform lit up with fairy lights.

Tat, dancing. Why did that disturb him?

The dance ended. She and the cowboy went back to the table where Mariel was holding the baby.

On an impulse he didn't even understand, Rourke went to the bandleader and had a brief conversation with him.

The rhythm changed. Rourke went to the table where Tat was sitting with her cowboy friend and the woman who was holding the baby.

He didn't ask. He caught her hand in his and tugged her along with him to the wooden platform.

The song was a tango. Cash Grier and Tippy were on the dance platform turning heads. Cash's eyebrows raised as Rourke drew Tat against him, and an amused smile touched his mouth.

Rourke didn't see the look. His pale eye was riveted to Tat's soft blue ones.

"This isn't a good idea," she began.

He only smiled. He drew her slowly into the soft, sensuous rhythm. And it became clear, all at once, that even Cash Grier was not in Rourke's class. He moved Tat along with him, expertly, through intricate twists and turns, with quick, graceful steps that brought a sudden silence to the people around the platform.

Oblivious, Rourke smiled down at Tat while they set a new standard for the elegant, exquisite dance in Jacobsville.

"You still dance well," he said softly.

"So do you," she replied, but she felt uneasy. She didn't understand why he was dancing with her at all. He'd been so antagonistic that she hadn't expected him to even speak to her again.

He made a quick turn. She followed him effortlessly. It was like being back in Manaus, when they'd danced into the wee hours of the morning at the Latin dance club. Except that here, they were drawing attention. Very few local citizens could manage this intricate dance. Matt Caldwell and his Leslie could, but they were out of town. Cash and Tippy certainly could, but even they were standing on the sidelines, entranced as Rourke and Tat swept across the wooden platform to the passionate rhythm of the dance.

Clarisse kept her eyes on Rourke's broad chest. She'd tried so hard not to look back. But it was impossible not to, as they moved together like one person. The feel of his powerful body against her was intoxicating. She loved the thrill it gave her to hold his hand, to have his arm around her, drawing her gently close to him. She loved his skill at this most difficult of dancing styles. She loved everything about him, and fought to keep it hidden.

"We were at a Latin club in Japan," he said suddenly, scowling. "We were both doing the tango. But we weren't dancing together..."

Her indrawn breath was audible.

He looked down into her eyes as he made another quick turn. "It's like strobe lights," he faltered. "Memories that flash, places, people. It's like pieces of a puzzle, but scattered."

She bit her lip.

"Why do I hurt you?" he asked in a husky whisper. "I don't mean to. I don't want to..."

She averted her gaze to his chest. "Don't be silly. You haven't hurt me," she lied with a smile. "We've known each other since I was a child, that's all. I'm familiar to you."

His hand contracted around hers as the dance wound to a close. "Familiar..."

Her heart was racing when he turned her across his tall, powerful body and leaned her down against his arm for a finish. He drew her back up, very gently, so that he didn't cause her any pain with the stitches she was still carrying from the C-section.

Applause shocked them apart. Rourke chuckled. "Sorry," he murmured. "I didn't realize we were on show."

"It's all right."

Cash and Tippy came up to them as the music started again, a modern rhythm this time that the younger set danced to.

"I thought I knew how to dance, until I watched you do it," Cash chuckled.

Rourke shrugged. "I used to teach the tango," he said simply. "I lived in Buenos Aires for a few years, doing covert work. I needed a cover. That was it."

"You dance very well," Tippy said with reluctant admiration.

He pursed his lips and his pale eye twinkled at her. "Thanks."

"You never told me you could do the tango," Tippy said, smiling at Clarisse.

"My father was an ambassador. He thought I should have all the usual social graces, so he hired a dance instructor to tutor me."

"There was a club in Manaus," Rourke said suddenly, frowning. "A Latin club. They had waitresses wearing red flamenco dresses…" He put a hand to his head and grimaced.

Clarisse winced. "Are you all right?"

He drew in an uneasy breath. "Strobe lights," he murmured. "I don't know where that memory came from. I was only in Manaus once or twice. When your mother died. When your father and sister were buried…"

"Yes." She averted her gaze. She'd hoped for an instant, just for an instant, that he might remember another time he'd been there.

The tall cowboy, Jack Lopez, came up to them. "You sure can dance, Mrs. Carvajal," he said, grinning. "How about letting me stomp on your feet again? If you'll excuse us?" He drew Clarisse onto the dance floor.

Rourke's eye flashed murder.

Tippy and Cash saw it and Cash ground his teeth together.

The housekeeper, Mariel, was cuddling the baby at the table. He was fussing.

Rourke paused beside Mariel with Cash and Tippy.

"What's wrong with the little fellow?" he asked.

"The colic," she said, smiling. "Something that babies get."

"Oh, yes," Tippy agreed. "We had our sleepless nights with Tris when she was that age."

Rourke stuck his hands in his pockets and stared at the child intently. There was something about kids. He wished he could remember why he had a sudden hunger for one of his own. That child was the product of Tat's passion for a man old enough to be her father. He grimaced, excused himself and left the dance.

ROURKE AND JAKE BLAIR were playing chess Friday evening a week later. It was an old pastime for the two men, who used it to work out strategies in the old days. Now it was just fun.

In the middle of the game, the phone rang. Jake picked it up and grinned. It was his daughter.

"Yes, I thought you might call. How did the exam go? Really?" He chuckled. "You're sure you don't want to know if it's a boy or a girl? No. I don't blame you." He paused. He glanced at his companion. "Rourke and I are playing chess. I'm beating him."

"Like hell you are," Rourke said with a grin.

"You wash your mouth out with soap," Jake said, pointing a finger at him. "What was that?" he said into the phone. "No, I don't have the radio on." He frowned. "AB Negative? No, I don't remember anyone in our congregation mentioning that they have it.

They'll have a time finding that. They'll probably have to relay some down from San Antonio…"

"AB Negative blood?" Rourke interrupted, frowning.

"Yes. There's a patient who needs emergency surgery at the hospital. Carson says they don't have any blood on hand and the patient's AB Negative."

Rourke got up. "My blood type is AB Negative. I'll drive over to the hospital and donate some."

Jake told Carlie. He smiled. "She says to tell you that they'll be very grateful. It's Micah Steele's case. He's operating."

"Tell her I'll be right there. And don't move those chess pieces until I get back," Rourke cautioned facetiously.

Jake just made a face at him.

ROURKE WAS USHERED back into a treatment room where blood was drawn for a transfusion. He waved at Micah Steele as they asked questions and filled out paperwork. He and Micah had often done covert work together in the old days.

Fortunately for the patient, whoever it was, Rourke hadn't had malaria in the past three years or they wouldn't have allowed him to donate blood at all. It had been longer than that since he'd had a bout of it. He didn't have the recurring sort, and that was pure luck.

"Damned decent of you to do this," Micah Steele told him when they'd taken the blood and he was sitting up and drinking orange juice. "I can operate at once."

"No problem," Rourke said. "It really is a rare blood type. K.C. and I share it," he added with a grin.

"I heard."

Rourke clapped him on the shoulder. "Go to work. I have to finish beating Jake at chess."

"You'll have your work cut out for you," Micah chuckled as he left the cubicle.

ROURKE WAS ON his way out of the hospital past the emergency room waiting area when he spotted Tat sitting with Tippy Grier.

"What are you two doing in here?" he asked. "Somebody hurt?"

"It's the baby," Tippy said, glancing worriedly at Clarisse, whose face was contorted. "A hernia. They have to operate, but they don't have any AB Negative blood..."

"I just donated it," Rourke said. "Micah's getting ready to operate. It's the boy?" he asked Tat, scowling.

She looked up with red, wet eyes. "Yes. Thank you...!" Her voice broke.

"God!" He scooped Tat up and sat down in the chair with her in his lap, cradling her against his chest. He kissed her disheveled blond hair. "Now, now, it's all right. Micah's damned good at what he does. The baby will be fine."

A sob shook her. "Oh, damn," she choked. "Damn! Why this? Why now? There's been so much...!" She collapsed in tears.

Rourke's face contorted as he held her closer, rocking her in his arms, his face in her throat. "I don't know, baby," he whispered. "I don't know why."

Tippy was fascinated by the look on his face. The man who'd verbally flayed Clarisse in the pharmacy bore no resemblance to this man, whose expression told her things he never would have.

"He can't die," she choked. "He just can't! I've lost everything else, my family, my husband, I can't lose my child, too!"

Rourke's arms contracted. The mention of her husband was like a knife in his ribs, but he didn't let it show. He just comforted her, his big hand lying against her wet cheek, his lips on her forehead, her eyelids, her nose.

"You'll get through it," he said quietly. "We all have storms, Tat. They pass."

Her hands clung to him. She hadn't had comfort, real comfort, in so long. The feel of his powerful body, the scent of him, were so familiar. She'd loved him most of her life. And he'd always been there, during the most traumatic times she'd experienced.

"That's what you said when my father and sister died," she managed weakly.

He drew in a breath. "Ya. I guess I did."

"I got through it. I always seem to live in spite of the odds. Like when the viper got me…"

He drew in a breath. "My God, I thought you were a goner that time. I ran with you in my arms to the clinic. It must have been half a mile. I never thought I'd get you to a doctor in time. And you were busy comforting me," he added, lifting his head to smile at her. "Me, a tough kid of fifteen, being comforted by a little tomboy ten years old."

"You've known each other a long time," Tippy said.

"A very long time," Rourke said. He dug in his pocket for a handkerchief and dabbed at Tat's eyes with it. "She was eight and I was thirteen when her parents moved next door to K.C." He chuckled. "I'd been fighting in militias since I was orphaned at ten.

K.C. had himself appointed my legal guardian, but he was off on missions all over the world, so I did pretty much what I pleased. Then he came home and Tat here told him that I'd gone out with a group of mercs to liberate prisoners from an enemy camp in the bush." He glared down at her.

"After that, he had you watched," Clarisse agreed, nodding. "You'd have been blown to pieces on one of those wild-eyed exploits if I hadn't."

"Landed you with a nickname, too, didn't it, little Tattletale?" he teased softly. He glanced at Tippy. "She's been 'Tat' ever since."

Tippy was watching them curiously. "Eighteen years," she said quietly. "That's quite a history."

"It is, isn't it?" Rourke replied.

Micah Steele came out to the waiting room. "We've got Joshua prepped. We're going to fix that hernia. He'll be fine." He smiled at Clarisse. "Don't worry. I know what I'm doing."

"Saved Colby Lane's life," Rourke added with a smile for the big blond man. "Did an amputation under fire, in Africa, after we walked into an ambush."

"Lucky for us that Colby was garden variety type O Positive," he chuckled. "And very lucky for us tonight that you and the baby share a blood type," he added.

"Jake would call that an act of God," Rourke said with a grin.

"How long will it take?" Clarisse asked.

"Not long. I'll come out and talk to you when it's done."

"Thanks," she said softly.

He nodded, faintly amused at the easy way Clarisse was lying in Rourke's arms without a single protest.

In fact, Rourke showed no sign of being willing to let her go. Micah went back though the swinging doors.

ENDLESS CUPS OF coffee later, Micah came out smiling. "He'll be fine," he assured Clarisse. "We'll keep him for a few days, just to make sure, and we'll have a rollaway bed put in the room for you, so you can stay with him."

"Thank you so much!" Clarisse said huskily.

"I love my job," he replied, grinning.

Rourke touched Clarisse's cheek gently. "If you need me, call Jake's number. If I'm not there, he'll know where to find me. For a few more days at least." He sighed. "Then I have to go back to Nairobi. My case is almost wrapped up."

Clarisse was good at hiding her feelings. She smiled at him. "Thanks for everything," she said.

He searched her blue eyes quietly. It hurt him to look at her, to see the pain in her face. "He's a sweet child," he said.

"Yes. He's my whole life."

"Take care of yourself."

"You, too, Stanton," she replied. "Tell K.C. I said hello. Is he all right?"

"He's dealing with it," he replied. "Not very well, I'm afraid. He keeps trying to sneak off with his men, but so far I've managed to talk him out of it with veiled threats."

"He loved her."

"Yes." Love, he was thinking, seemed very painful, if K.C.'s response to his loss was any indication.

He was certain that he'd never felt that sort of obsessive love. Except sometimes at night, when he was alone, and he had flashes of memory accompanied by excruciating emotional pain. A shadowy woman, anguish at leaving her, almost a physical pain, loss, because he couldn't find his way back to her.

When he looked at Tat, he felt something tugging at him, some violent emotion that made him want to run. How very odd.

He managed a smile. "Get some rest. You've had a hard night."

"Thanks for staying with me," Clarisse said quietly.

"I've always been around when you needed me," he returned without realizing what he'd said. He drew in a breath. "Well, I'd better go. Jake is probably hiding my chess pieces as we speak. He hates to lose."

Clarisse smiled sadly. Tippy was watching him with curiosity and a lack of antagonism. She smiled, too, as she followed Clarisse back toward the intensive care unit.

Rourke climbed into his rented car and drove back to Jake's house.

CHAPTER THIRTEEN

ROURKE GOT OFF the airplane at the Nairobi airport with a feeling of utter loss. He couldn't imagine why it had hurt so much to leave Texas. Tat was fine. She had friends and her child. She didn't need him. In fact, nobody needed him.

He thought of Charlene with vague distaste. He didn't understand why he'd decided to get engaged to her. Then he remembered. K.C. had told him that Tat was coming over to see him when he was wounded. He'd got engaged to show Tat that he didn't want her.

His eye closed in torment as he recalled what Cash Grier had said to him, about the miserable sort of life that could see tormenting a young woman as a form of entertainment. He'd hurt Tat deliberately. And it hadn't been for the first time. He couldn't remember everything, but he certainly remembered enough to put his conscience on the rack.

Charlene was the last person on earth he'd marry if he was in his right mind. She was flighty and unsettled and all she thought about was clothes and more clothes. Well, that and her father's attractive business partner.

K.C. MET HIM at the airport. The other man seemed older, but less anguished than he had been when Rourke left for Texas.

"Pain getting better?" Rourke asked when they were on their way back to the compound.

"A little." K.C. sighed. "It's just…you know, we live on hope. It's the last thing we ever give up. I had thought that one day, maybe, Mary Luke would throw it all up and marry me." He smiled wistfully. "That wasn't realistic. She did a job that made her feel useful, that gave her life purpose. I've spent my life taking other lives—she spent hers saving them. It was never a good match, but I was obsessed with her." His face tautened. "It's hard to adjust to a world without her, just the same."

"I've never been obsessed with a woman," Rourke said involuntarily.

There was a quick glance from K.C., and stark silence from the other side of the Land Rover.

Rourke was quick. He scowled, glancing at his father. "Okay, what was that look about?"

"What look?" K.C. asked innocently.

Rourke glared at him. "You know things that you aren't telling me."

"Things you don't remember. Reciting them does no good—the neurologist said so."

"It's so damned frustrating!" Rourke ran a hand through his blond hair. "I was dancing a tango with Tat, in Jacobsville. And I remembered a Latin club in Manaus, of all the places. I've never gone dancing in Manaus!"

The silence grew.

"Or have I?" Rourke's eye narrowed.

"How is Clarisse?" K.C. asked.

"She's a survivor. She's doing fine. Well, there was

an emergency with the baby...watch it, mate!" he exclaimed when K.C. jerked the wheel.

K.C. stopped the vehicle in the middle of the road. "What emergency? Is he all right?"

Odd bit of concern there, Rourke thought absently. "It was a hernia. Micah Steele operated. He's going to be fine. They were lucky I was close by, though, I had to donate blood. Amazing, how hard it is to get our blood type, isn't it?" he added with a smile.

"Yes. Acts of fate," K.C. replied, relieved. "God, poor Clarisse! It's one thing after another!"

Rourke nodded. Something was nudging his mind. He didn't know why.

"Heard from Charlene?" Rourke asked.

K.C. made a face. "She flew back in this morning."

Rourke let out a breath. "I'm going to break the engagement," he said absently. "She's not ready to get married and neither am I."

"She might be relieved," K.C. mused. "She's crazy about her father's business partner."

"I noticed."

CHARLENE WAS OVERJOYED when Rourke told her. It was hardly flattering.

"I'm sorry," she said, and smiled at him. "But you're just too much for me, Rourke. I can't live with the work you do. If I cared at all, I'd be a basket case!"

He'd never considered that his job might be a point of contention in a relationship. He did seem to enjoy it a little too much for comfort.

"I suppose so. Well, I hope you'll find someone good enough for you, kid," Rourke added with a grin.

Charlene's eyes went covertly to the tall, handsome

man talking to her father and K.C. near the patio doors. "Oh, I might have done that already."

"So that's how the land lies, hmm?" Rourke chuckled. "Good luck, then."

Charlene hesitated. "That poor woman who was here when you got wounded, is she all right?" she asked. "I've never seen anyone so tormented..." She bit her lip because Rourke's one good eye started flashing fire at her. "Sorry."

He forced the anger away. No need to frighten the kid. "No sweat. I think I'll get some coffee."

Charlene just nodded. She wasn't eager to prod Rourke's temper again. He was frightening like that.

HE SAT IN the kitchen sipping black coffee, his mind racing as he recalled Tat's poor shocked face when he'd raged at her in his bedroom. Charlene had brought it all back with her comment. Tat had been miserable. It hurt him to recall the things he'd said, the way he'd ordered her out of the house.

She'd been carrying Joshua at the time, although he hadn't known. The little boy was precious. What if he'd caused her to miscarry? The thought haunted him.

He still didn't understand why he hated her so much. What had she ever done to him to provoke such a response? She was a kind, gentle woman. She never went out of her way to hurt people. So why did he torment her?

He finished the coffee, got up and walked out into the compound. His lion was in the fenced enclosure, where he'd been since Rourke had gone to Texas.

"Sorry, old man," he told the big cat. "When company leaves, I'll let you back in the house, okay?"

The lion just yawned.

"Boring you, am I?" he teased.

K.C. joined him at the fence. "Does he answer you?" he asked.

"Not yet," the younger man chuckled. "But if he ever does, I'm having a CAT scan." He paused and grinned. "I made a funny!"

"I hear you've broken the engagement."

"Ya. I told her to keep the ring," Rourke said easily. "If I ever get married, and don't hold your breath, I'll give her my mom's ring." His mother's ring. His mother's ring. He would only have given it to a woman he loved. Loved desperately, at that. A woman he wanted to have his kids, to live with him, to love him.

K.C. didn't take him up on it. "How did the job go?"

"I thought we'd wrapped it up," he replied. "But one of the key men got away. I may have to go back." He didn't add that the thought appealed. He could see Tat again.

"Tough luck."

"Well, I'm going to have an early night. It was a damned long flight. Thanks for sending the jet."

"No problem."

He walked back to his own house in the compound and stripped off for bed. He started to put his wallet and his keys and spare change into the drawer by his bed when something caught his eye. A letter. Opened.

He pulled it out and read it. His heart ran wild. It was an invitation to an awards ceremony in Barrera. Ten months ago. Beside it was a stub from a trip to Manaus, dated a day after the awards ceremony. Tat's name was on the list of recipients of the awards.

He sat down, hard. He'd been in Manaus, with Tat. It had to have been with her, because she lived there most of the time. He would have had no other reason to go there, unless it was to see her. His heart began to race. He'd been in Manaus ten and a half months ago. Tat's baby was six weeks old. She'd been pregnant when she came to see Rourke after he was shot. The baby had AB Negative blood. Like he did. Like his father did.

He threw on a pair of slacks and ran barefoot to his father's house. K.C. was sitting on the sofa drinking straight whiskey.

Rourke didn't say anything. He picked up a tumbler and filled it halfway. He took several sips before he sat down on the sofa across from his father's armchair.

"You've remembered something," K.C. ventured.

"I was in Manaus ten and a half months ago," Rourke said. "I found a ticket stub. Tat lived there. Her baby is six weeks old. She was pregnant when she came here to see about me. Her baby has type AB Negative blood…" His face was white. Stark white.

K.C. drew in a long breath. He pulled out his cell phone. He turned to the photographs app and handed the phone to Rourke.

It was all there. Tat and Rourke, beaming, with the news that they were engaged. Then there was the nursery. There was Joshua, being shown through a glass window, wrapped in a blue blanket. There was Tat, white as a sheet and thin and worn, trying to smile as she held the baby. There was a beaming K.C. holding the baby. Several of that one.

Rourke closed his eyes and shuddered. Now, when he least wanted to remember, he remembered. He and Tat had been lovers. They'd been inseparable. He took his mother's engagement ring out of the safe to take with him to Barrera because he was going to propose to Tat. He'd only just found out that they weren't related, that he could have a life with her. She'd been reluctant to trust him, because he'd hurt her so badly in the past. But she'd loved him enough to trust him. His eye closed. If he thought about that, he'd go mad.

He'd bought her a wedding gown. They'd gone together to see the priest. Then he'd accepted a job out of the country, two days before the wedding. He'd left her to finalize one last mission.

All of it, her marriage, her husband's death, her close call with death, all of it had the same, terrible foundation. He'd made her pregnant and he'd left her. His injury had taken his memory away and he'd thrown her out of his life all over again.

"Damn me," Rourke choked. He handed the phone back to his father. "Damn me!"

K.C. sat beside him and pulled him roughly into his arms.

"Dear God, she'll hate me for the rest of her life, and she should," Rourke bit off, shivering. "I threw her out of the house. She was pregnant, with my child…!"

K.C. patted his back awkwardly. "Yes."

"Joshua is my son. I have a little boy. I have a child!" He pulled back. The look in his good eye was wild. "I have to go back…!"

"No," K.C. said firmly.

"No?" Rourke was puzzled.

"If you tell her that you know about Joshua, she'll

run," K.C. said quietly. "She didn't even want to tell me. She's afraid of you. She thinks you're marrying Charlene, that you'll try to take Joshua away from her if you know the truth."

"But, I wouldn't…!"

"She won't know that." K.C.'s face was hard. "We can't afford for her to run. Not now."

The way K.C. said it chilled him to the bone. "Why?" he asked, and he was certain he wasn't going to like the answer.

K.C. took another sip of his drink. "Do you remember me telling you that Barrera's former dictator, Arturo Sapara, was liberated by a few of his minions from a prison in Barrera? That he swore bloody vengeance against everyone who helped him lose power?"

Rourke was very quick. "Tat's husband didn't die a natural death, did he?"

K.C. shook his head. "We don't think so. Ruy was meticulous about malaria prevention. A few days before he contracted the malaria, Tat heard someone on the porch outside his bedroom and a sound like someone opening a jar. Grange had sent a man to watch them, once we knew Sapara was loose. We knew he might try to kill her. She thought it was Grange's man outside the house, so she didn't say anything."

Rourke felt sick to his stomach. "You think the anopheles mosquitoes were in a jar, and they were deliberately placed in Ruy's room."

"Exactly. Tat was bitten, too. She didn't suspect a mosquito bite because she knew they didn't have mosquitoes. Certainly she wouldn't have expected to find them in the house. Even so, nobody had sprayed inside for some time."

"She could have died." Rourke felt the words to the soles of his feet. He closed his eye on a wave of pain. "He meant her to, didn't he? He meant to kill them both!"

"That's what we think," K.C. replied. "When you were wounded, I was afraid he'd gotten to you first. But I did some checking. It was an accident. Terrible, but not deliberate."

"I never considered that he'd come after me. But I should have known he'd blame Tat. She wrote a dozen stories about the experience, none of them flattering to Sapara."

"Besides that, she was instrumental in helping you to assault the governmental complex," K.C. added. "Brave woman."

"Very brave." Rourke took another long swallow of whiskey. "She's had so much in the past year. Most of it my own damned fault!"

"She didn't blame you," K.C. said sadly. "She knew that you didn't remember. She was only grateful that you lived, even if you married someone else."

A stinging hot mist worried his eye. He averted it to hide the wetness. He sipped more whiskey. "Sapara won't stop," he said. "He's got a professional assassin on staff. I know the man. He trained with me years ago…"

"Yes, and you're the only person I know who could identify him on sight," K.C. said.

"That's why Eb Scott has men shadowing Tat," Rourke said with sudden realization. "They think Sapara is still after her! That's why she went to Texas in the first place!"

K.C. nodded. "Yes. It's been a concern. I talked it

over with the Granges and Cash Grier. We all agreed that she'd be safer in Jacobsville, where Sapara would have a harder time getting to her. I flew her over to Jacobsville with the baby. I was going to spend a few days with Cash, too, but the call about Mary Luke came and I had to leave."

"I'm going back," Rourke said, rising. "I won't tell her that I remember anything," he said to reassure his father. "But I have a team on-site already, and a mission still ongoing, which gives me a good excuse to return. I'll know the man if he shows up in Jacobsville. I'll get a flight out in the morning…"

"Flight, nothing. I'll get my pilot up here."

Rourke stared at the face that was so much like his. "Thanks."

"Take care of them," K.C. said. "But don't let Clarisse catch on that you know. Not yet."

"I understand." Rourke drew in a breath. "At least I can protect her and the baby, even if she doesn't know I'm doing it." He winced. "I could kick myself for leaving the day before our wedding!"

"You've spent your life trying to save other people, keep them safe. It's hard to break old habits."

"I thought it would be just one last job. I'd been working on it for months. Children were involved." Rourke groaned. "But I had to make a snap decision, and it was the wrong one. I should have delegated, that time of all times!" He took a long breath. "I helped her pick out a wedding gown. We both talked to the priest." His face hardened. "The priest knew what her damned mother did to us."

"Maria loved her daughter."

"She cost us years!"

"That wouldn't have happened if she hadn't taken you at face value, son," K.C. said. "Even you have to admit that you were a textbook Romeo. She was protecting her daughter."

"I suppose so." He looked worn. He finished the whiskey. "I guess I can give up fieldwork, if I have to. I'm getting too old for it anyway," he added heavily, and he smiled. "Too many gunshot wounds and broken bones over the years. My reaction time is down."

"That's why I had to give it up," K.C. confessed ruefully.

"Well, the baby will make up for that," Rourke chuckled. "He'll provide more than enough excitement on a daily basis."

"You might come home and raise lion cubs for zoos," K.C. mused.

Rourke smiled. "That might not be a bad idea." His face hardened. "But first I have to take care of Sapara and his assassin." His eye narrowed. "I'm going to call in a few favors." He glanced at his father. "Do you still have any of that special ammunition I used to keep handy?"

K.C. nodded solemnly. "And your sniper kit that goes with it." He shook a finger at his son. "You make sure you're sanctioned before you do anything."

"I always do." Rourke grinned. "I don't want to spend the rest of my life hiding from the authorities, in any case. Especially not now, when I've got a family to take care of!"

HE WAS IN Jacobsville two days later, back at Jake's house. The memories had come back with a vengeance. Tat, in his arms in Barrera, afraid of him, loving him.

Saving him from arrest in the bar, when he'd got drunk because she'd told him she was engaged to Ruy. Then when he'd followed her to Manaus, Tat in his arms in bed, loving him, yielding up her innocence to his ardor, wanting him, wanting his child.

Tat loved him. And he'd hurt her, again, just as he'd hurt her in years past. But that had been to protect her, in the old days, because he thought he could never have her. He'd made her hate him, to protect them both from a loss of control that could have had tragic consequences if her mother hadn't lied, if there had actually been a blood relationship between them.

More recently, though, he'd hurt her because he lost all memory of the tenderness, the passion, the commitment they'd made to each other. She'd had his child, thinking he'd never remember any of it. She'd married Ruy. Now he knew why. She was carrying Rourke's child and she was alone. In Manaus, people still remembered her saintly mother. Tat would never have had a child out of wedlock, would never have shamed her family in such a way. She was conventional, just as he was.

So now he had a child, and it carried another man's name.

He groaned inwardly as he realized what he'd given up. Nothing had ever hurt so much. Tat had almost died. She still could, if he didn't find the assassin in time.

He'd called in markers from every federal and international agency he had ties to. He'd already spoken to Eb Scott as well, to make sure he had enough men watching Clarisse. In Jake's guest bedroom, in a second suitcase, was a sniper kit complete with the ammunition he favored. He hadn't told Jake about it. Even though his host had once dealt in covert assassination, he no longer did. He was a minister. He wasn't going to be happy if he knew what his guest was planning.

On the other hand, Jake had loved a woman enough to kill to protect her. He might understand. But Rourke wasn't going to tell him, just the same. Jake had enough on his conscience.

"You said you could recognize Sapara's assassin," Jake said over supper in the kitchen.

"Yes," Rourke replied. "Unless he's wearing a disguise. And he might be. He learned the trade with me, over a decade ago."

"You think he's already here."

"I do," Rourke replied. His eye narrowed as he finished his pizza and washed it down with strong black coffee. "In fact, I have a good idea who he is. Although I didn't connect it until a day ago."

"Who?"

"That cowboy who's always hanging around Tat," he said quietly. "The man I knew wore a beard and mustache, and his hair was longer. But the build and the voice seem the same. I can't be sure, but I'm having him watched."

"By Eb's men?"

Rourke shook his head. Suddenly he frowned, and pulled out an electronic device. He turned it on. Then he relaxed. "Stupid of me not to check for bugs. Just a sec."

He went over the house with it. Sure enough, in Jake's study, under his desk, there was a listening device. He dealt with it efficiently, and then went to sweep the rest of the house.

"Only one," Rourke said. "But one is more than enough when you're dealing in life and death."

"Carlie was here last week and the telephone company sent a man to check a connection in my study," Jake muttered. "I didn't even connect it! And I know enough to check for bugs myself."

"No worries, it's taken care of. But tell Carlie not to let anyone in if you're not here."

"He could get in and plant a bug just the same," Jake replied. "You know how that works."

"All too well. I'll do regular sweeps. Meantime, I won't mention any of the surveillance underway unless we're in a car together. And even then, I'll do a sweep," Rourke chuckled.

"Good idea. I have another one. It wouldn't hurt to do background checks on anyone close to Clarisse," Jake added.

Rourke just smiled. "I'm two steps ahead of you there, mate."

HE WENT TO see Clarisse the next day. He couldn't let her know that his memory had come back. If he did, and she mentioned it, he might accidentally push the assassin into acting before Rourke was ready.

It was difficult. Worse than he'd imagined. She was in the kitchen, nursing the baby. Mariel let him in and led him, smiling, into the bright yellow room.

Clarisse looked up, shocked, and fumbled with a light blanket, trying to cover her bare breast. She flushed with embarrassment. It was new, and disturbing, to have Rourke see her nursing Joshua. She hadn't even known he was back in town.

"Don't do that," Rourke asked softly as he sat down

at the table with her, indicating the blanket. "It's quite beautiful, watching you nurse him."

Clarisse flushed. She glanced at Mariel and smiled, nodding. The woman went back to her chores.

"You said you wouldn't be back," Clarisse faltered.

He shrugged. "My trafficker that I'm watching with my group decided to take a partner," he lied. "So now we're watching two men and hoping for evidence that will convict. I had to come back to oversee the assignment."

"I see."

His eye was intent on the child, suckling at her soft breast, clenching one tiny fist against the creamy skin. He winced. It hurt him, to know that she had his son in her arms and he couldn't even acknowledge that it was his child.

She saw that expression and misunderstood. "You and Charlene should have some of these," she said without looking directly at him. "Babies are nice."

"Are they? Charlene says she's not ready yet."

She was irritated at herself because that gave her hope. Not that it would make a difference. "I'm sorry," she said.

He leaned back in the chair and crossed one ankle over his thigh, smoothing at a wrinkle in the khaki trousers. "She's in love with her father's business partner," he said when he hadn't meant to say anything. "I told her to keep the ring. But we broke up."

Her heart jumped. It was wrong to feel relieved. So wrong. She couldn't let him see how much the statement pleased her.

"Your husband must have been proud of the child," he said in a bland tone.

"He was looking forward to it," she confessed. Her eyes closed. "He died before Joshua was born. He never even got to see him."

"That must have been rough."

She nodded. "Ruy was a good man. I owed him a lot."

So did I, Rourke thought, for taking care of her. But he didn't say it.

"The baby seems much better now," he remarked.

"Dr. Steele is very good," she agreed. "He was doing family practice, but Copper Coltrain was overworked and they needed another surgeon, so he specialized and went back to school."

"He always had a knack for it," Rourke said.

She was thinking about Rourke, with Micah Steele in Africa. "You've always done dangerous jobs. Even when you were a teenager."

"I wanted to be like K.C.," he mused. "I didn't know he was my dad, at the time, but I always admired him. I've had a time trying to keep him out of the field since Mary Luke died. But he's better." He cocked his head, staring with fascination at the baby. "He said I should come home and raise lion cubs for zoos."

"You'd never be able to settle for a life that tame, and you know it," she said, her voice faintly wistful. "You have to have the adrenaline rushes."

He smoothed over the khaki on his knee. "Yes, well, I've been thinking about that. I turned the wrong way and an IED exploded. Shrapnel hit me and did a number on my head. If I'd been home, where I belonged, I wouldn't have lost almost a year of my life."

She looked up at him, her blue eyes wide and sad. His face drew taut. "I do at least remember why I was so cruel to you," he said after a minute. "I thought you were my half sister."

She averted her eyes and her face colored. "Yes."

"Did I tell you that K.C. knocked me over a sofa when I accused him of sleeping with your mother?" he asked with a chuckle. "God, he hits hard!"

"My...mother?" she faltered, wide-eyed.

"Yes. Your mother. That was the gossip."

"My mother was a saint," Tat said quietly. "She would never have cheated on my father in a million years."

"I noticed that when the DNA results came back," he said with a straight face.

She just shrugged.

"The sins keep lining up, don't they, Tat? I vaguely remember telling you once, God knows when, that I'd never hurt you again." He smiled with pure self-contempt as he stared at the baby's small head. "And I've done nothing but hurt you. For years."

She didn't answer him. The baby stopped suckling. She tried to hold him and close the nursing bra, but she couldn't quite manage it.

"Here. Give him to me while you do that," Rourke said gently.

She flushed a little as she lifted Joshua into his arms. She was fumbling with the bra or she might have noticed the exquisite pain on Rourke's face as he looked down into the eyes of his firstborn. He stared into eyes that were already showing signs of being brown instead of blue, at the ears that were like his and K.C.'s.

"He's a sturdy boy, isn't he?" he asked softly, smiling at the child. "I think he may be tall, Tat."

"That's what I thought." She had her blouse back in place, and she started to take the baby when she noticed the expression on Rourke's hard face as he stared down at the little boy in his arms. She hesitated. It was so poignant that tears stung her eyes. Rourke, holding his son, and he didn't know. He'd never know.

She swallowed down the hurt. "He needs to be burped," she said, picking up a diaper.

"Show me how," he said.

She had to reach up to put the diaper over his shoulder. She showed him how to put the baby over his shoulder and rub him gently between the shoulder blades.

"It gets a bit messy sometimes," she warned. "They do spit up…"

"Clothes clean, honey," he said with a tender smile. "It's all right."

She felt the endearment like a soft touch on her bare skin, but she tried to hide the effect it had on her. Rourke didn't seem to realize what he'd said. He was intent on burping his son. A few smooth pats and a big burp came out of the tiny boy.

He laughed with pure delight.

Clarisse smiled tenderly at the picture they made.

He looked up into her soft eyes and his heart jumped right into his throat. He studied her over Joshua's head, intently.

"You're still too thin," he said quietly. "You've been to hell and back. At least you're finally in a place where you have friends. Real friends."

She nodded. "Cash and Tippy have been so kind," she said. "And Eb…" She bit her lip.

"Eb?" he queried, with just the right amount of curiosity.

"Eb Scott," she said. "He and his wife invited me over for supper one night. So did Cy Parks and his wife. They're such nice people."

"Yes, they are. It's a good place to raise a child."

"It is. There are good schools here, too." She looked at the baby on his shoulder. "I've never had a real friend, until Peg Grange. And that was a shameful thing I did to her, while I was spaced out on antianxiety meds. She's a forgiving soul."

"You weren't responsible for your actions," he said. "Any more than I was, just after I was injured."

"It doesn't help a lot," she sighed. "I still feel guilty."

"You made up for it."

"I tried."

He searched her eyes. "Tat, none of us is perfect. We make mistakes. We can't live in the past. Today is all we have, really."

She wrapped her arms around herself. She felt a chill. Sapara was after her and she couldn't tell Rourke. She was nervous and uneasy and afraid.

"What's wrong?" he asked, sensitive to her mood.

"Goose bumps," she lied. "I'm chilly I guess."

He scowled. "Are you still taking quinine?"

"Oh, yes," she replied. "Religiously. It's not malaria. Honest."

He drew in a long breath. "You had a closer call than you told me, Tat," he said. "K.C. told me just how close."

"Neither of us realized it could be malaria," she said simply. "Ruy was overworked and he was treating people with a stomach virus. The symptoms are very similar. I never dreamed..." She stopped before she could add that the mosquitoes had been placed deliberately in the house she shared with Ruy.

"Life happens." He kissed the baby's soft little head. "People die. It's part of life, however tragic. But I'm sorry I said the things I did to you, in the pharmacy that day. I didn't know what the hell I was talking about."

"You didn't remember," she said. "I understood."

That hurt even more. She always forgave him. And this time, she shouldn't have.

"Here, I'll take him now," she said softly, holding out her arms for Joshua. "I put him down for his nap after I feed him."

He handed her the little boy with flattering reluctance. "He's a sweet child," he said quietly. "Does he sleep the night through?"

"Usually. I thought he had colic, and it was a hernia. I didn't even know that babies could get them." She looked up at him. "I'll never forget what you did for him. Giving blood, I mean. It probably saved his life. Micah thought so, at least."

"God couldn't have been that cruel to you, sweetheart," he said gently. "Not after all you've been through."

A tiny smile flared on her lips. "And now I know you've been living with a minister. Because that sounds very much more like Jake Blair than it does like you!"

CHAPTER FOURTEEN

ROURKE REALIZED AFTER a minute that she was teasing, and he grinned. "Well, yes, I'm occupying his spare bedroom. And trying to behave myself. It's not easy."

She smiled back. "He might rub off on you."

"The reverse is more likely."

"He drives a red Ford Cobra," she said. "It isn't exactly the sort of car I'd picture a minister driving, you know?"

He chuckled as he followed her down the hall to the nursery. "He wasn't always a minister."

"Oh? What was he?"

He hesitated. "Probably best not to mention it," he said. "No offense. Small towns, and all."

"I see. He was like you, then."

He lifted an eyebrow. He sobered as he met her soft eyes. "Ya. Just like me, in a lot of ways. He was never the sort to settle down, or so I thought. But now he has a daughter just a few years younger than you, and a grandchild on the way."

She put the sleeping baby into his crib on his side and covered him with a light blanket. "Children change people," she said after a minute.

He stared at her covertly. "I imagine they do," he said. "You look quite natural with a child in your arms, Tat."

She didn't look at him. "Thanks," she said huskily. "If it was a compliment…"

"It was." He moved to stand beside her and look down at the sleeping baby, at his son. His own flesh and blood. Something inside him that had been frozen began to thaw.

"I'm sorry that your engagement didn't work out," she said.

He drew in a breath. "You know why I got engaged, Tat. You won't say it out loud, because you don't want me to feel guilty."

She flushed. "I don't understand."

"I made sure that everyone around me knew about the engagement, so that it would get back to you." His face grew hard and cold. "I don't know how a man can make up for years of cruelty. All I can remember is how badly I've hurt you. I can't even remember why I did it," he lied.

She couldn't look at him. "Maybe it's not a bad thing that you've lost some memories, Stanton," she said at last. "You can start over, start fresh. Charlene might not have been the right woman, but you'll find someone who is." It hurt her to say it, but she was fairly certain that he was unlikely to regain his memory after so long a time.

His heart sank. She wasn't encouraging him. How could he expect her to? He'd done so much damage.

He stuck his hands in the pockets of his slacks. "There's something I wanted to ask you, about Lopez."

She looked up. "Jack Lopez?" she asked, surprised.

"Ya. Is it getting serious?"

Her heart jumped. "Well, not really," she said. "I mean, he picks up things for me at the store sometimes, and I see him at public events. But I haven't invited him here."

"Is there a reason for that?" he asked quietly.

She frowned. "Not a lucid one. He's very nice. He goes out of his way to help me and he seems to like the baby. But there's something…" She laughed suddenly. "I suppose being ill has made me a bit twitchy."

"He makes you nervous. And not in a good way," he replied.

She turned and looked up at him. "How do you know that?"

He lifted his hands to her shoulders and rested them there, looking down at her. "You and I go back a long way. A very long way. I guess I've learned your body language—at least well enough to know when something unsettles you."

"I'm sure it's just my imagination," she said, trying not to let him see how it affected her to have him so close.

His hands framed her face, lifting it to his intent gaze. "I make you nervous, Tat," he said softly. "But not in a way that frightens you."

She swallowed. Her heart was already racing. "Stanton…" she protested.

He moved closer, so that he was right against her, so that she could feel the heat and strength of his body. "I've lost so many memories," he whispered as his head bent. "But I think I remember this…"

His mouth brushed softly over her lips. He expected her to fight him, to draw back, to be angry. But she didn't protest at all. Her breath caught. Her hands, flat against his chest, tightened with a flood of sensation that she hadn't felt in almost a year.

He knew that, too.

"I never touched Charlene," he murmured against her soft mouth. "I haven't touched anyone else, either, since I was wounded."

That was surprising. It was exciting, too. She could taste coffee on his lips. They were warm, and firm, and confident as they teased hers. Her eyes closed on a wave of hunger so strong that she moaned.

"Why does this feel so familiar?" he whispered. "We've done this before, haven't we, Tat?" he whispered, feeling his way. He didn't want to confess what he knew. He didn't dare.

She didn't answer him. But her arms stole up and around his neck so that he could deepen the kiss.

He lifted her against him, so that they were so close that air could hardly pass between them. His mouth opened on her welcoming lips, and he gave in to the hunger that had started to consume him with the return of his memory.

"I don't remember anything recent," he said, deliberately stretching the truth. "But I remember when you were seventeen," he groaned into her mouth. "I was in Manaus on a job and I came by to see you on Christmas Eve. Just an impulse. You were wearing a green dress and I thought I'd never seen any woman so beautiful. I kissed you and it was like starting a brushfire. We were on the sofa, your mother's sofa. We went so far that it was almost impossible to stop, even when we heard your mother coming in the front door."

She gasped. "Yes…"

His hand was behind her head, tangling in her hair. "I wanted you…to the point of madness. Just as I want you now, right now… Kiss me, Tat!"

His mouth was insistent, devouring, on her soft lips. He groaned harshly as one lean hand slid down her back and ground her hips into the arousal he didn't even bother to hide from her. She didn't fight. She couldn't. She pressed closer to him and let the world fall away.

A long time later, he forced himself to draw back. He grimaced. "The stitches... I forgot! I'm so sorry, Tat!"

She was hanging at his lips, her blue eyes open wide, her breath coming in little gasps. "Sorry?" she whispered, dazed.

"The stitches." His hand moved between them to touch, gently, the scar under her cotton slacks on her flat belly.

"Oh. Those stitches. I didn't notice..." She stopped and flushed.

He smiled gently. "And you still don't really know how to kiss, do you, darling?" he teased softly.

"I..." She swallowed, hard. "Well, I haven't..."

His nose brushed against hers. "Not even with your husband?" he asked quietly.

She bit her lip. She didn't dare admit that. He was very quick. He might guess, about Joshua.

"Foolish question. You have a child." He grimaced. "Sorry."

"It's all right."

His fingers brushed lightly over her flushed cheek. "You're so beautiful, Tat," he said in a tone like velvet. "Eyes like cornflowers. Hair like pale silk. But you're too thin. You've had a hell of a bad time, and I haven't helped. If I could go back and change things, I would."

"Life happens," she said simply. "We make choices and then we live with them."

His face went hard. "Sometimes we make stupid choices and other people pay for them, too," he said, thinking back to the assignment he could have refused. If he had, he and Tat would be married. He'd have been with her all through her pregnancy, and Sapara would never have threatened her.

"You still understand Afrikaans, don't you?" he asked abruptly.

"Yes, of course."

He switched to that tongue and gave her a very odd instruction.

"I don't understand," she faltered.

"You don't need to. Things are going on around you that you can't know about. You must trust me. Just this once. Do what I tell you to do. For your sake, and the baby's."

She felt uncomfortable. "You think there are bugs in my house," she said suddenly, still in Afrikaans.

"Yes, I do," he said, without adding that he had other suspicions, as well. "If your cowboy friend comes here unexpectedly, you remember what I said, right?"

"But, why?" she asked.

"Remember when I came and got you out of Ngawa, without telling you why?"

"Yes," she replied.

"It's like that. I know things I can't tell you. But I want nothing more desperately than your safety. So, just do what I say. Okay?"

"Okay." It touched her that he was so concerned, although she wondered why.

He bent and brushed his lips across hers. "You

should lay into me with an iron skillet. Tippy would loan you hers."

She smiled softly. "I don't think she would anymore. You saved Joshua's life," she added. "If you hadn't donated blood, Dr. Steele might not have been able to operate in time."

He thought about that, and it made his stomach drop. His own child, and he hadn't known when he'd gone to donate blood. "Coincidences happen, don't they?" he asked to mislead her.

"They do." She was relieved that he hadn't connected the similarity in blood types between himself and Joshua.

He let her go, reluctantly, and looked down at his child. He felt a surge of pride that hit him right in the heart, but he didn't dare let it show.

"He's a handsome boy," he said gently. "Looks just like you, Tat."

"Yes, he does."

"I'd better go. I have to check in with my squad and make sure they're on the ball." He looked down at her. "You take care of yourself. If you ever need anything at all and you can't reach me, you call K.C., right?"

She nodded. "Right."

"Jake said they're having a potluck supper at the community center Saturday evening. You going?"

"I thought I might."

He smiled. "Thought I might, too. I like to sample other people's cooking skills. I get tired of my own."

"You always did cook better than me," she recalled.

"You do fine, darling. Really you do."

The endearment made her feel warm inside, especially when she recalled the last time he'd used it, in

Manaus. She searched his face, looking for any sign that he might remember. But there was nothing. She had to keep in mind that he could be dead. Even if he never remembered what had happened in Manaus, he was alive.

"You look so sad," he commented.

"I was thinking how much my life has changed in the past two years," she said simply. "I led such a shallow existence."

"Not you," he argued quietly. "If there was a charity or a fund-raiser that needed an expert touch, you always volunteered. You were fierce about things you considered important, things like additions to children's hospitals, orphan relief."

"I get that from my mother," she said sadly. "She was always doing things for other people."

Rourke's face went hard. His one pale brown eye glittered with an emotion he couldn't quite conceal.

She was watching him. That expression registered. Her full lips parted. "Stanton, someone told you we were related," she said softly. "Someone whose word you trusted implicitly." She swallowed. Hard. She drew a breath. "It was my mother, wasn't it?"

He didn't answer her. "I have to go."

She moved closer to him, amazed that it stopped him in his tracks. Why, he was vulnerable! And she'd never realized it. She put her hands flat on his broad chest and watched him struggle to hide his reaction from her.

"You loved your mother," he began.

"Yes, I did, but I wasn't blind to her faults," she said quietly. "She was overly protective of me." She managed a faint laugh. "I hadn't even been on a date, that night in Manaus when I was seventeen. I'd never been kissed at all."

His breath caught. He'd suspected it, but he hadn't known. Not until now. His fingers touched her soft mouth. The feel of her was exquisite. The smell of roses that clung to her delicate skin went to his head. "I knew," he said huskily, "that you were untouched." His jaw tautened. "I should have let you alone, Tat. I should have gone out the door, gone back to Africa…"

Her soft blue eyes looked up into his with an emotion she didn't even try to hide. "I lived on that night for years," she confessed brokenly. "Even when you hated me…!"

His mouth cut off the words. He lifted her against him and kissed her as if he was being led to the guillotine. He groaned harshly as the feel of her aroused him almost to madness. It had been so long since he'd had her in his arms, wanting him. He'd never loved anyone so much, not in his whole life.

She didn't protest. If anything, she incited him. Her mouth opened under his and she clung to his strong neck with all her might as the kiss grew longer, harder, deeper.

Finally, he had to step back. It wasn't the right time. He put her away gently, although his hands were unsteady on her upper arms. He was flushed, as she was, and struggling to breathe normally.

"Sorry," he said roughly. "It's been a long time."

Her mouth was sore, and she didn't care. "You didn't even kiss Charlene?" she wondered aloud, recalling what he'd told her.

"I didn't want Charlene," he said flatly. "I don't want…anyone. Only you."

She was lost for words. She just stared up at him with her heart in her eyes.

He kissed them shut. "I have to go. I don't want to," he added huskily.

She pressed close. "Okay."

His hands smoothed her back. "Eventually things will settle down. Then we might reassess our positions," he said enigmatically.

She drew back, not understanding.

He laughed. "I'm working," he said. "I have a job to get done."

"Oh. Yes."

He searched her eyes. "You should hate me, Tat," he said very softly. He drew in a breath. "But I'm damned glad that you don't."

She shrugged. "I wouldn't really know how," she said after a minute.

He let her go. His pale brown eye went down to the sleeping baby. His son. He knew how K.C. must have felt when he was born, feeling such pride and love, and having to hide them.

Clarisse saw the anguish on his face and didn't understand it, unless perhaps he was territorial about her, and he hated thinking she'd had Ruy's child. She ached to tell him the truth. She didn't dare.

"So. Saturday night? I'll come by and get you. Does the baby come, too?" he added, smiling at the sleeping child in his crib.

His face as he looked at the child was incredibly tender. "Well, it's for adults. I thought I'd leave him with Mariel."

"Leave him with Rory and Tris instead."

She looked worried. "Stanton, what's going on?"

"On?" His eyebrows went up and he smiled. "Why, nothing. I thought Mariel might like to come with us. She hasn't had an evening off since she started working for you, has she?" he added.

She laughed. "Not really, and she's such a treasure."

"Ask her, then. She can ride with us."

"I'll do that. I'll speak to Tippy. Rory is still young, but she may have a regular sitter, just in case there's an emergency."

"You can ask her."

"I will."

He bent and brushed his mouth over hers. "You make beautiful babies, my darling," he whispered. He grinned at her, glanced at the baby and left.

"WOULD YOU LIKE to come?" Clarisse asked Mariel later. "Rourke reminded me that you haven't had a single night off since you started working for me. He said you can ride in with us."

Mariel was flustered. She laughed self-consciously. "I would love to," she exclaimed. "How thoughtful of him!"

"We'll have a good time," she replied, smiling. "Plenty of food, and there's going to be a band. They'll have dancing, as well."

"I have not danced in years," the woman confided. She laughed. "It will be fun!"

"Yes, it will!"

ROURKE WAS TALKING to Cash Grier, in his office, and he told Cash, in Farsi, to wait until he put down a signal jammer first.

"What the hell is your problem?" Cash asked, surprised. "You don't think I check for bugs in my own office?"

"You'd have no reason to think you needed to," Rourke said solemnly. "Here's the deal. Jack Lopez is Sapara's hired assassin. I think he's getting ready to move on Tat. I've got my team in place, and Eb Scott's men are doubling shifts to make sure she and the baby are covered."

Cash let out a sharp breath. "Good God! Right under my damned nose…!"

"Nobody but me ever knew what he looked like," Rourke replied. "I trained with him, years ago, when I started with the company. He thinks my memory is gone, so he's overconfident."

Cash frowned.

Rourke smiled. "It came back, when I went home. I was comparing blood types and making associations." His eye closed on a wave of pain. "AB Negative isn't your garden variety blood type. K.C. has it, I have it… and my son has it." He almost choked with emotion as the words came out. "And I can't tell her that I know. K.C. says that she'd run and Sapara's man might have her to himself and kill her."

Cash was, for once, speechless.

"So I'm pretending," he continued. "I've got men watching Lopez. In fact, there's a legitimate reason for it. He's heavily involved in human trafficking, like his boss Sapara. It's how they funded Sapara's sudden exit from the prison in Barrera." His face went hard. "I can tell you one other thing, as well. When this is over, Sapara will never threaten anyone again. Neither will his man Lopez. It's sanctioned."

"Who did you get for Lopez?" Cash asked, without a single protest.

Rourke lifted his chin. "The only person I'd trust with Clarisse's life. Me."

Cash's eyebrows arched.

"Good God, what do you think I do for a living?" Rourke asked shortly. "I do counterintelligence, but I'm a trained sniper. It's why I spent three years in Argentina undercover. Amazing how many international criminals think it's a good hiding spot."

Cash laughed. "All these years and I never realized…"

"K.C. had his pilot fly me over so that I could carry my own kit with me," he said. "When the time comes, I'll do what I have to. I've spent my life protecting Tat. I'd give it, to keep her and the child safe."

Cash's dark eyes narrowed. He saw the emotion that the other man couldn't hide. He'd been wrong right down the line. Rourke didn't hate Clarisse. Not at all.

"If I can help…"

"No," Rourke said firmly. "You've got a wife and child. Besides that, this is linked to a covert operation that I'm heading. You don't get involved. And not because I think your skills have gone rusty," he added, chuckling.

"You never forget how to use a sniper kit," Cash said heavily. "But it's hard to settle down with some of the memories you have to carry."

"I've had to shoot kids, too, mate," Rourke returned solemnly. "I fought in many covert wars all over Africa when I was still in my teens. In fact, I learned how to be a sniper before I turned ten."

"Ten!"

"My parents were brutally murdered," he said, the pain still in his face. "My father was shot down in the street like a dog by one of the endless factions vying for power in rural areas. My mom was still alive, but she had health issues and she couldn't control me. I went off to fight with one of the local warlords, who taught me the skills I needed to stay alive. My mother was firebombed a couple of years later, during another uprising. I ran wild. Got in with a group of commandos and went hunting for rebels with an AK-47. K.C. was still working in those days, and he didn't find out what had happened for months after my mother was killed. When he did…" He paused and chuckled. "My God, the man's got a temper! He dragged me up before a judge and formally became my guardian. I wasn't very happy about it, and after Tat's family moved in next door, once I sneaked off to do a little fighting. Tat told on me. Hence, her nickname, short for Tattletale" he added ruefully. "God, K.C. gave me hell about that last mission I went on!"

"You didn't know he was your real father at the time?"

Rourke shook his head. "It was a sore spot with me for years, people speculating, gossiping." His chest rose and fell heavily. "I didn't want to think that my mother could have betrayed the man I thought was my father. I had to grow up to understand that even parents make mistakes out of weakness. My mother loved K.C." He hesitated. "Of course, I do, too," he added, chuckling. "We went through the process to have my name legally changed. It was on hold until I got my memory back, but we signed the papers when I was home last."

"K.C. made you toe the line, I gather," Cash chuckled.

"Ya. Made me get an education. I got it in the military, but I got it." He smiled. "I finally realized that if I went off to fight with some insurgent group, Tat would have been two steps behind me. She followed me around like a pup when she was a kid. God, she was brave!"

"I heard about the snakebite."

"Terrified me," Rourke confessed. "I thought I was going to lose her. She was just ten years old, but she wasn't afraid of anything. When she and her parents moved to Manaus, I was alone in a way I hadn't been for years. I mourned her."

"I didn't understand how it was with you two," Cash began.

Rourke held up a hand. "I deserved everything I got," he replied. "Including the side of your lovely wife's tongue." He chuckled. "You brave man, to live with that wildcat!"

Cash just grinned. "A lesser woman would never have managed to take me on," he said. "I settled down, but reluctantly. I wasn't sure I could do it at all." His face went quiet. "I treated her very badly. She miscarried because an assistant director insisted that she do a physical stunt that was dangerous. I thought she put her career first. It was my child, and I'd already lost one…"

Rourke didn't push, but his gaze was intent.

Cash smiled sadly. "I was married before. She wanted my money. She didn't want my child. While I was away on a job, she had a termination."

"I'm sorry," Rourke said. "I can only imagine how that would have felt."

"We all have dark places in our pasts," Cash said. "But some of us get lucky."

"Indeed we do. You and Tippy are coming to the do on Saturday night at the community center, right?"

"Of course." Cash's lips pursed. "We're practicing the tango, so look out."

Rourke chuckled. "Tat's going to ask Tippy if the baby can stay with Rory and Tris while we're away. Do you let Rory babysit or…"

"I've got a man who stays with them when we're gone," Cash interrupted. "He worked for Eb Scott at one time, although he's an independent contractor now. You probably know him. Chet Billings…?"

"My God!"

"Hey, he's good at what he does," Cash chuckled.

"I had to room with him for several days when we were protecting Cappie and her brother Kell Drake from Cappie's old boyfriend. The local vet, Dr. Rydel, had a few issues…"

Cash laughed. "He still does, but he learned very quickly the danger of jumping to conclusions. I understand that he and Cappie are now expecting."

"Lucky devil. I wouldn't mind another child. I'm looking quite forward to getting to know the one I've already got, when things calm down."

"I'd like another child, too," Cash said. "But it doesn't seem likely."

Rourke pursed his lips. "I know a chap back home who's good with charms."

Cash gave him a droll look.

"Sometimes human nature needs a little nudge," Rourke chuckled.

"You can keep your charms," Cash returned.

"I know. You're far too intelligent a man to believe

in hexes and magical things. But I come from Africa. It's hand in hand with the supernatural."

"Your mother was American, wasn't she?" Cash asked.

He nodded. "From Maryland. But her people were Boers. Her father took a job in the States and brought his family over. They went home for a visit and she met the man I thought was my father. He worked for K.C. Fate is fascinating."

"It is, indeed."

CLARISSE WORE A simple white Mexican dress with exquisite embroidery to the potluck supper. It was a warm spring night, and the community center was blazing with light and music and activity.

Mariel was asked to dance almost at once.

Rourke and Clarisse watched the couples on the dance floor while they finished off plates of fried chicken and mashed potatoes.

"At least they're not grits," Rourke mused as he tasted the potatoes.

"What do you have against grits?" she asked with a surprised laugh.

"Nothing personally. In fact, some of my best friends eat them." He leaned forward. "It's the name. Reminds me of pulverized gravel."

She grinned at him.

He stopped eating and just looked at her. She was incredibly beautiful.

She shifted self-consciously.

"Sorry, was I staring?" he teased. "Can't help myself. You're the prettiest woman here, and you're sitting with me."

"You're not bad yourself," she mused.

He chuckled. "Ya, me and my gimpy eye."

She studied him over a sip of coffee. "I never think of it as gimpy."

He searched her eyes. "I know. You took off the eye patch and kissed me there." His face hardened. "You're one of a kind, Tat. Beautiful inside and out."

She was sitting very still. Her blue eyes widened. "You remembered that?" she asked huskily.

He scowled. "Yes." He stared at her. "I never told you how it happened. You sat with me in the hospital at Nairobi, nursed me even when I growled at you and told you to go home. But I never spoke of it."

"I know."

He looked down at his plate. "It was just after your mother told me…what she did. I had plans, Tat," he said with a wistful smile. "It was never what she thought. I was thinking about a house and kids…"

She winced.

"So when she told me…what she told me, I went on a job and got careless. In fact, I didn't care if I came back. I had nothing left, nothing I cared about. When I lost you, as I thought I must, life held no further joy for me. I walked into an ambush." He didn't look at her. "I did it…deliberately."

Tears rolled down her cheeks. She grabbed for a napkin and dabbed at them, but they wouldn't stop.

"Here, now, don't do that," he said huskily. "Tat!"

He left his plate, got up, took her by the hand and led her onto the dance floor. He pulled her close and held her, rocked her to the slow rhythm of the music, his face buried in her throat while she fought tears.

"I'm sorry," he whispered. "I never should have told you…!"

"I know she meant well," Clarisse wept. "But why? Why?"

His arms contracted. "I don't know, baby," he whispered. "Sometimes bad things happen, and we never really understand them. Jake has this philosophy, about life being all lessons and we undergo trials to learn." He sighed. "Maybe he's right."

She pressed closer to him, still dabbing at her eyes.

His lips brushed over her forehead. "Have to stop doing that, or you'll have me in tears, too. What would people think?"

She drew in a shaky breath.

He lifted his head and looked down into her red eyes. "We can't go back. We can only go forward. If you think you can forgive all I've done to you."

The tears came back, in a flood.

"Damn it, woman, there's Tippy over there searching for an iron skillet! You're going to get me killed if you don't stop crying! She'll think I'm at you again!"

She laughed, dabbing at the tears once more. "Sorry."

He lifted his head. "No. I'm sorry. For it all. For everything." He bent and brushed his mouth slowly over her soft lips. "So…very…sorry…!"

After a minute she drew back a little red-faced and hid her forehead against his soft cotton shirt. "People are staring," she laughed.

He chuckled wickedly. "Then let's give them a reason to stare." He lifted his head, caught the bandleader's eye and signaled him. The band stopped playing its blues tune and broke into a tango.

"Hey, Grier, challenge!" Rourke called to Cash.

"Taken!" came the laughing reply. "We've been practicing!" he added as he led Tippy onto the floor.

"Hold on, there. You're not leaving us out!" Matt Caldwell led his pretty wife, Leslie, onto the floor, too. "I invented the tango," he added haughtily with a smug look at the other two men.

"Do your worst there, Caldwell," Rourke invited. He grinned. "And may the best man win!"

Clarisse laughed out loud.

CHAPTER FIFTEEN

IT WAS A very close contest, but most people agreed that Rourke and Clarisse outclassed the other two couples. Temporarily at least.

"We'll have a rematch one day," Matt said drily. "So don't gloat too much."

Rourke just grinned.

Clarisse was talking to Tippy at the snack table when Rourke's phone rang. He excused himself and went outside to answer it.

"Ya," he said curtly, all business. "What's up?"

The caller on the other end relayed the latest information they'd been able to glean in their surveillance. Things were coming to a head. There had been some chatter on an open line that led them to believe Sapara's man was ready to make his move.

"You keep him in sight," Rourke told him firmly. "If anything goes wrong, there won't be a place on the planet where I won't find you."

The other man assured him that he was on the ball.

"Just don't get careless," Rourke said quietly. "More is at stake here than I can even tell you. Keep your eyes open."

He hung up. Then he scrambled the line and called Chet Billings at Cash's house.

"What are you doing back?" Chet asked, surprised.

"I came over to challenge Cash to a tango contest," came the facetious reply. "No, I'm on a job, mate. Anything going on there that I should know about?"

"Yes."

"What?" Rourke asked, worried.

"Cash's brother-in-law just creamed Kilraven in a battleground," Chet said.

"Kilraven? Well! I'll have to tell Cash. It will make his evening."

"I don't doubt it. These guys and their video games. Waste of time if you ask me. Takes away time from hard drinking and gun swapping."

"Listen, you could use a sweet little woman to reform you," Rourke mused. "Someone young and pretty…"

"I don't want someone young and pretty. Or old and ugly. I like living by myself. Nobody tries to take the TV controller away from me," he added firmly.

"Okay. But you don't know what you're missing."

"We heard you were on a job up in San Antonio," Chet said.

"Ya. Something boring," he added, just in case the line was being monitored. You could never tell. "I'll be on my way back home in a few more days."

There was a pause. "Mrs. Carvajal will miss you," Chet said surprisingly.

Rourke's heart jumped. Of course she would. But, then, he wasn't leaving. Not unless he could persuade her to go home with him. It was early days. Still, she loved kissing him. Amazing that she didn't hate him, after what he'd put her through. He thought of making a home with her and his son, having other kids, growing old together. It made him feel warm inside.

"Listen, if you stay with her, you need to think seriously about getting out of fieldwork," Chet said abruptly. "Women don't like the constant upset. They worry. Especially when they know what you do for a living."

Rourke chuckled. "Oh? Somebody worrying about you, is there?"

There was a pause. "Somebody who wants to. She's just a kid, though."

"It's the mileage, mate, not the age," came the quiet reply. "Keep your eyes peeled. I don't know much, but I really am expecting trouble. It may come unexpectedly, and not in the form I'm thinking about."

"I'm always expecting trouble," Chet replied.

"That makes two of us. I'll talk to you again before I leave for home."

"Sure. See you."

Rourke hung up. Then he made one last call. "I want you to check something out for me," he said, and fell into Norwegian as he outlined the information he wanted from his contact.

"How did you know I spoke Norwegian?" the man asked.

"Don't kid me. You specialized in languages. I happen to know you're fluent in about eight of them, and that's one."

There was an amused chuckle. "Well, in my business it does pay to throw the enemy off track. Okay. What do you want to know?"

Rourke told him.

"Good God, not in the States!" came the shocked reply. "Surely not!"

"He isn't here. But his assassin is. I had a contact

working on this info, but he hasn't come through. I need to know if the man has other contacts, ones that aren't obvious. And I need to know quickly. Lives are at stake. That's no bull, mate. That's fact."

"Give me ten minutes. I'll call you back."

"Use this number. I'm carrying a throwaway phone." He called out the number.

"You really don't trust anybody, do you?"

"Comes from years of working covertly," Rourke chuckled. "We get cautious."

"Indeed we do. I'll get back in touch as soon as I can find that information for you."

"I owe you one."

"Yes, you do," came the thoughtful reply. "I won't forget that, either."

Rourke sighed. "Feel free," he said. "You pirate."

There was another chuckle and the line went dead.

THE LAST DANCE was a slow, bluesy tune about lost love. Rourke drew Clarisse close to him and linked her small hand with his.

"All those years we've known each other, and we never danced together," he whispered.

She didn't dare tell him that they had, those magic days in Manaus. "You thought I didn't know how, I expect," she laughed shyly.

He lifted his head and his pale brown eye looked into hers. "I didn't want you to know how vulnerable I was," he corrected, and his expression was solemn. "Just looking at you could arouse me, Tat," he confessed. "It's still that way, all these years later."

Her high cheekbones colored delicately.

"It's nothing to be embarrassed about," he said at her lips. "You're quite beautiful. It's a normal reaction."

"Oh."

His arm contracted around her. "That could have been put better," he said with a soft sigh. "Listen, I was a rounder in my teens and early twenties," he said gently. "I never dated the same woman twice. I was damned lucky that I didn't catch some social disease that would make me untouchable, or even something that could have killed me." His hand smoothed up and down her spine. "But that all ended one Christmas Eve in Manaus," he said, his voice husky with feeling. "I have never wanted anyone the way I wanted you that night. Never, Tat."

She bit her lower lip. "That's just desire…"

He shook his head, very slowly. "No. It's not." His fingers teased their way between hers and he drew her even closer as he made a sharp turn. He felt her shiver at the almost-intimate contact. "I want you very badly. But it's a hell of a lot more than a physical hunger."

She drew in a long breath. "I don't know very much about men," she faltered. Then she flushed, because she'd been married and Rourke thought Joshua was Ruy's son.

"Look at me."

The quiet authority in his deep voice brought her eyes up.

"I know more than you think I do, Tat," he said very quietly. "And when this job is done, and I have time to sit down and talk to you, we're going to make some decisions together."

"What…sort of decisions?"

He bent and brushed his mouth tenderly over her

soft lips. "Permanent decisions," he murmured. "Very permanent."

Her heart began to race. "There are things you don't know," she began sadly.

"And none of them matter." He drew her close, stopped dancing and bent to kiss the breath right out of her. "I am never leaving you again. Not as long as I live." His pale brown eye was flashing with feeling. "My job can go to hell. I've already paid too high a price for it."

Her face colored with faint shock. She looked up at him, all eyes, her heart in her eyes, her young body very still. Did he remember that he'd left her to do one last job, one that nobody else apparently could do? Had his memory returned?

She wanted so badly to ask him. But the music stopped and couples started walking off the dance floor.

He smiled softly. "Time enough for discussions later," he said, kissing the tip of her nose. "Right now, we need to go get Joshua and take you home. You're wilting, my love."

She laughed softly. "I suppose I am."

"You still tire easily," he said. "And you're very thin. We'll work on all that, when I get this job done."

"The job, it isn't dangerous, Stanton?" she worried aloud.

His fingers smoothed over her soft cheek. "No," he lied. "Just intelligence work. We're trying to shut down a human trafficker, that's all. No guns, love," he added, stretching the truth like taffy between two vises. It was all for her own good, of course. He didn't dare tell her the truth, that she was in far more danger than he was right now. "Let's go get your son and get you both to bed, okay?"

She smiled sleepily. "Okay, Stanton."

THEY DROVE TO Cash's house and picked up the baby. Mariel sat with him in the backseat, cooing at him in his baby carrier after it was strapped in.

"Did you have fun?" Clarisse asked the woman.

"It was very nice," she replied. "I can't remember the last time I danced."

"I'm surprised that Jack wasn't there," Clarisse said on the way home, frowning. "I'm sure he told me he'd planned to come. I saw him in the grocery store yesterday. Mariel, you remember—you went with me."

"Yes, he did say he was coming. Perhaps he had a date, yes?" Mariel teased.

"Perhaps so. I had a lovely time," she told Rourke.

He glanced at her warmly. "So did I."

"The two of you dance so beautifully together," Mariel sighed. "I have two left feet."

"You cook like a French chef," Clarisse told her warmly. "We all have things that we're good at."

"True."

Rourke carried the baby inside in the carrier and lifted him out, pausing to kiss one chubby little cheek before he put him down in the crib for his mother.

The baby was still asleep, after all the jostling. Rourke looked down at him with muted hunger. His son. His child. He had to hide the pride and sadness the child kindled in him. It made his face look very somber.

Clarisse turned Joshua on his side and pulled a light blanket over him. Beside her, Rourke was oddly distracted. He'd had a phone call just as Clarisse went in Cash's house with Mariel to get Joshua. Ever since, he'd had a worried expression.

"Is something wrong?" Clarisse asked him when they were on the porch and he was starting to leave.

He touched her cheek gently. "Nothing much. Just something connected with the job. Going to kiss me good-night?" he asked softly.

She flushed. "Don't tease."

"I'm not teasing, baby." He drew her to him hungrily and bent to her mouth. "I'm dead serious..."

The kiss was long, hard, ardent. He wrapped her up against him and groaned. She felt it, too, the anguished hunger for something far more violent, more passionate than the kiss, even if it was as hot as chili peppers.

His hands slid down her back and drew her hips hard against his. "I'm dying for you," he said huskily. "Can you feel it?" he whispered against her soft mouth as he let her feel the power of his arousal.

"I can...feel it," she whispered, a little shy even now with him.

"Oh, God, I want you!" he managed roughly as the kiss grew more insistent.

She shivered as the passion danced through her slender body and made it shiver. "We can't, Stanton," she moaned. "It's a small town. People gossip..."

"I saw a very pretty ring in a jewelry store downtown," he said against her mouth. "I'll bet it's just your size, too."

She was surprised. "A ring?"

"Two rings," he murmured, still kissing her. "Diamonds and sapphires. Blue stones, like your beautiful eyes, Tat."

She stared up at him. "You mean get married?" she faltered. "You want to...marry me?"

He nodded solemnly. "Yes. Get married. It's far too late, at that. It should have happened when you were seventeen. But better late than never."

"You really want to marry me?"

"With all my heart!" He folded her against him and rocked her in his arms, his face buried in her soft throat. A shudder ran through him at the prospect of being her husband, being Joshua's father, raising a family with her. "We can live here, since we have so many friends in town. But we can spend summers at the compound next door to K.C. near Nairobi. The baby can play with my lion." He chuckled. "Well, after he's a bit older anyway."

She was dumbfounded. All her dreams were coming true. "But, you don't remember the past few months..."

He lifted his head. His pale brown eye looked steadily into her blue ones. "I remember that you're my whole world," he said quietly. "That's really all I need to remember. I have no life without you. I have nothing without you!" He brushed his mouth hungrily over hers. "Will you marry me, Tat?" he asked huskily.

Tears rolled down her cheeks. "Yes," she choked. "Oh, yes...!"

He looked down at her with an expression that said far more than words. There was such joy, such hunger in it that he looked like a man who'd won the lottery. He lifted her against him and kissed her until her mouth was sore, and then he kissed her again. His body was in torment. He had to leave or explore alternatives.

"We have to stop," he groaned. A shudder ran through him. "I want you so much that I could have you right here standing up. I have to go back to Jake's house. Right now!"

"No," she moaned. "Not yet!" Her arms clung to him. She lifted her body against him provocatively and drew his head down to hers so that she could kiss him again.

He barely had the willpower to resist her at all. He caught her arms in his hands and gently tugged them down from his neck. "Tat, my darling, I would truly hate for our first time to be standing up against a wall, trying not to let ourselves be overheard," he managed with deathbed humor. He was working around the truth, at that, because he knew it wasn't their first time. He was going to tell her the truth, all of it, but not until they were safely married. And definitely not tonight. He was deliberately giving anyone watching the idea that his mind was on Tat's sweet body, and not on any other single thing.

Clarisse laughed at the outrageous statement, because he sounded so desperate.

She pulled back, reluctantly. "Okay. If you won't let me seduce you, I guess you'll have to go back to Jake's house." She reached up and touched his face with a loving hand. "And I do like sapphires."

He was remembering the emerald ring he'd given her before, his mother's ring. He didn't dare admit that he remembered, or how it hurt him to recall it.

"I like sapphires, myself," he said, smiling as he put her away, reluctantly. "I'll see you in the morning, then," he said. There was an odd note in his voice. It disturbed her, and she didn't know why.

"Is everything all right?" she asked.

"It's fine." He switched to Afrikaans, but smiled so

that anyone looking wouldn't think he was being serious. "Remember what I told you to do if Lopez shows up here. Promise me."

"I will. What's going on?"

"Nothing dire," he lied. He kissed her again and the way he looked at her made her think of warships going out to sea. He looked at her as if he wasn't certain he'd see her again.

"Are you all right?" she asked aloud, concerned.

He framed her face in his hands, bent and kissed her with breathless tenderness. "You are my whole world," he whispered in Afrikaans. "My love. My life."

Tears stung her eyes. "And you are mine," she whispered back in that same tongue.

He drew away at last and took a steadying breath. "I'll see you in the morning," he said softly. "Sleep tight."

She smiled drowsily, deeply in love and happier than she'd been since Rourke left Manaus the last time. "You, too."

"Tot siens," he said in Afrikaans. He winked at her and went down the steps whistling. It was all an act. Tonight, he had a serious and dangerous task to perform. He only hoped everything went as planned.

CLARISSE HAD PUT the baby to bed. Mariel wasn't sleepy, so she said she'd watch a movie and listen for Joshua in case he woke up. She knew Clarisse must be tired. She was still weak from her illness.

"That's sweet of you," Clarisse told the other woman. "Thanks."

"It's no problem," Mariel said. She seemed unusually alert. A minute later, there was a knock on the door.

"I'll go," Clarisse laughed. "It's probably Rourke. He must have forgotten something…"

Mariel walked off down the hall in the middle of the sentence.

Frowning, Clarisse opened the front door. It was Jack Lopez. But he didn't smile. He looked oddly smug. She walked out onto the porch with him, curious.

"Jack," she said. "It's a little late for company…"

"No, actually, it's just the right time," he said with a faint smile as he hand went to his pocket. "You have so much company that it's really been hard trying to get you alone for a minute."

"I don't understand."

"Don't you?" He pulled a pistol out of his pocket. "Sapara says hello," he added with a deep, sarcastic laugh. "So long, Mrs. Carvajal. Tell your late husband he shouldn't have slept with the patio door open. And don't worry about your baby. He'll be joining you very soon."

He raised the pistol.

Clarisse remembered Rourke's warning, the promise she'd made that she hadn't understood until right now.

"You can tell my late husband yourself," she said in a tight, cold voice. And without warning, she dropped to the ground and rolled away from him. She didn't know if it would work, if Rourke even had someone in place watching. But this was the only chance she had, and she took it.

Seconds later, the shocked man standing over her froze and stared down at her with a blank look on his face as the top of his head seemed to explode in a gush of blood. She closed her eyes, because she didn't want to have to see it. She felt a spray of blood fall down on her averted face, smelled the metallic odor of it and tried not to throw up. A fraction of a second later, she heard a crack like the sound of lightning striking and a thud like a melon shattering.

There were running footsteps. Clarisse stayed on the ground. Her mouth was dry. Her heart was racing like a wild thing. She looked up in time to see Rourke running toward her.

"Are you all right?" he asked quickly.

"Yes." Her voice sounded choked. She sobbed, reaction hitting her after the fact. "Rourke!" she cried.

He paused just long enough to put a finger on the neck of the downed man, checking for a pulse that he knew he wouldn't find. The sniper rifle was still in one big hand. He drew Tat up with him, held her very close and bent to kiss her with bruising intensity.

"Thank God you remembered!" he groaned, and he kissed her again, so hungrily that his lips and arms bruised. His powerful body shuddered as he realized how many things could have gone wrong. He could have lost her in an instant. He kissed her even harder. But he drew back almost at once. This wasn't the time.

He jerked out his cell phone and punched in a number. "Well?" he asked in a tone vibrant with anger and relief. His face was solemn. "Ya, that's what I thought. Take the shot. Don't argue with me, damn it, do it now! Right now! Take the shot…! Yes? Yes!" he said with a rough sigh of relief. "No, I can't wait. There's no time. I'll call you." He broke the connection, punched another button, spoke one word into it, turned off the phone and ran into the house, propping the rifle against the wall on the way.

He'd motioned Tat behind him just before he ran down the hall to the baby's room. She followed in his footsteps, wondering why he was in such a hurry. The man lying cold on the ground was no threat anymore, certainly not to Joshua!

When they got to the nursery, Mariel was in the rocking chair holding the baby, just starting to put a bottle to his mouth. Shocked, she looked up at Rourke and then at Clarisse, standing close to him with blood all over her blouse, her face, her throat. The assassin's blood.

"Why, Mrs. Carvajal, you're bleeding!" Mariel exclaimed. "I thought I heard a gunshot! Are you all right?"

"I'm…fine. Why are you giving the baby a bottle?" Clarisse asked. It was strange, because Mariel knew that she nursed Joshua.

"He was hungry and I thought you had gone to bed," Mariel said simply.

"But he was asleep," Clarisse protested, not grasping the situation at all.

Rourke moved forward, as quick as a cat, and took the bottle from her fingers with a gloved hand. "Get up," he said in a voice that rang with authority. "Now!" he added harshly when she hesitated.

"What is wrong?" the woman asked tremulously. "I was only going to feed him!"

Rourke put the bottle on the floor. "Clarisse, take the baby. Do it quick, honey!"

Clarisse didn't hesitate, but she was looking more confused by the minute. She took Joshua from Mariel's arms. She almost had to force him out of them. She stepped back, aware of an odd gleam in Mariel's eyes.

"Check his pulse," Rourke said at once.

She laid her head against the baby's chest. Joshua was awake and looking up at her, not even upset, or so it appeared. "It sounds all right," she faltered. "Rourke, what's going on?"

"Sit down," he told Mariel, because the woman had stood up. When she hesitated, he pulled a .45 Colt ACP smoothly out of its holster and leveled it at her. "I think you've seen gut wounds before," he said in a voice like ice. "They aren't pretty."

"You must be kidding," Mariel gasped, but she sat down. "Señora Carvajal, the man is crazy!"

It did seem that way. For just a second, Clarisse wondered if the head wound had caused Rourke to act out of character. But then she remembered Lopez aiming a pistol at her. He wouldn't be doing this without a good reason.

While she was debating what to say next, sirens came screaming up outside the house. Doors slammed.

Cash Grier came running into the house with two uniformed officers right behind him. His pistol was out as he followed Rourke's curt voice down the hall and into the baby's room.

Cash let out a breath when he saw Clarisse holding Joshua in her arms.

"Thank God," he said heavily. "I was afraid we wouldn't be in time."

"You and me both, mate," Rourke said. His eyes had never left Mariel. "One of my operatives has a dossier on her. We got it from Interpol. She's wanted in more countries than I used to be," he added.

"Any warrants outstanding?" Cash asked.

"Yes. One, in Belgium, for assassination. We've been in touch with authorities there. But you may not want to discuss extradition until you have the contents of that baby bottle screened." He indicated it on the floor beside the rocking chair, and his one brown eye was glittering with fury. "She had it at his lips when I came in. We need to take Joshua to the emergency room and have him checked, just to be sure."

"The bottle…?" Clarisse faltered, holding the baby closer.

"Poison, unless I miss my guess," Rourke said coldly, glaring at the woman, who flushed under the murderous fury of the stare.

Clarisse's horrified gasp was audible in the room. She held Joshua close to her heart and buried her face in his little body. She was shivering as she stared with horror at the woman she'd trusted with his life.

"I admit nothing," Mariel said with faint contempt. "And I might have failed, but this will not be the only attempt…"

"I'm afraid it will be," Rourke replied.

"Señor Sapara will have me bailed out by dawn tomorrow," Mariel assured him with a cold smile while one of Cash's officers read her rights to her.

Rourke pulled out his cell phone and made a call. His face was harder than ever. "Ya. Good job. Yes, I'll tell him." He hung up. The smile he gave the would-be assassin was smug and merciless. "The local police in Manaus have just picked up Arturo Sapara's body," he told her. "Along with those of two of his assistants. He won't be bailing anybody out."

Mariel's face lost color. "You are lying!"

He didn't even answer her. "I left Jack Lopez just outside the front door," Rourke told Cash.

"We noticed." Cash pursed his lips. "I just had a call from Rick Marquez's father-in-law."

Rourke nodded. "It was sanctioned. Even if it hadn't been," he added, looking at Clarisse and the child in her arms with an expression so full of emotion that it burned, "I wouldn't have hesitated. He had a pistol leveled at her."

"I can understand how you felt. How did you know where to find Sapara?" Cash asked as they were all going out the door together. One of his officers had already put Mariel in the back of a patrol car. Rourke had the sniper rifle in his hand.

"I have a man on my team who can track spirits across water," Rourke chuckled. "He has contacts in a number of unmentionable places."

"A blessing," Cash replied.

Rourke put an arm around Clarisse's thin shoulders. "My biggest one today, among many others," he agreed. He kissed Clarisse's hair. "Come on, baby. We need to make sure she didn't get any of that formula into Joshua. I'll drive you."

"I'll need a statement from both of you," Cash said. "But it can wait until morning," he added with a faint smile.

"Thanks, mate," Rourke said with genuine gratitude. "It's been a long night. I wasn't sure of the outcome, either." He glanced at Clarisse. "Thank God you didn't question what I told you to do, and that you remembered when to do it!"

"It sounded very odd at the time, what you told me," she said. "And I didn't understand why you told me in

Afrikaans and refused to let me tell Mariel." She grimaced. "She would have killed the baby…!"

He held her close. "I knew about her, as soon as I knew who Jack Lopez really was. You see, I was the only person we had who'd ever seen him face-to-face. I trained him, in fact, over a decade ago. It was blind luck that I remembered in time."

She wanted to ask if he'd remembered anything else, but he was already herding her toward the car. He locked the sniper rifle in the trunk. Then he let her put Joshua in the backseat, but he watched how she put the baby carrier that doubled as a car seat in place, smiling as he touched the baby's soft little cheek.

"When this is all over, I'm going to have a nervous breakdown," she said huskily when they were pulling up at the emergency room entrance of the hospital.

"When it's over, I'm going to join you," he agreed.

They walked in with the baby. Dr. Copper Coltrain was waiting for them. He did a cursory examination and smiled, because he found no evidence that Mariel had got any of the deadly liquid inside that little mouth.

"Micah's off tonight. So is Lou," he added, referring to his wife, Louise, who was also a physician. "She's in the last stages of pregnancy and having a hard time getting around, so I'm subbing for her. I wish Drew Morris hadn't decided to specialize in radiology, so he'd at least be on call when Lou was incapacitated," he chuckled, referring to their former partner in the practice.

"I hear that Carson Farwalker's planning to fill that spot briefly, until he decides whether or not to become an internist," Rourke mused.

"He is. He's very good. Come on back. We'll draw

blood and check the baby thoroughly." He shook his head, his red hair flaming in the overhead lights. "A woman who'd kill a child for money. I still have a hard time believing there are people like that on the planet."

"So do we," Rourke said, his arm around Clarisse as they walked into the cubicle.

"Let me get one of the lab techs in here to draw blood. It's always better to err on the good side of caution," Coltrain said. "Be right back."

After he left, she looked up at Rourke with soft, loving eyes. "You saved my life," Clarisse said huskily. "And Joshua's. I never even suspected...!" She bit her lower lip. "I have no judgment about people. I'll never hire another housekeeper as long as I live!"

"She was very convincing," he said softly. "You couldn't have known. It was Lopez who put the anopheles mosquitoes in your house in Manaus," he added. "He killed your husband." His face went taut. "He almost killed you, as well."

She tried to find the right words and faltered on them. "You knew about the mosquitoes? But how...? I never told you!"

CHAPTER SIXTEEN

"I KNOW A great many things that you never told me, darling," Rourke said quietly. He bent and touched his mouth to hers while she held Joshua close. Then he bent and kissed the tiny child in her arms. "Dear God, I've never been so terrified in my life! I had a tip that Lopez was on his way to your house. I was in position—I was ready for him. But I was scared to death to take the shot!"

Her lips fell open. "You...you shot him?" she gasped.

"Yes," he said, his eye cold and hard. "I couldn't trust it to anyone else."

Her eyes stared up at him wildly. "You told me to drop and roll," she began.

"Bullets hit bone and ricochet," he said tautly. "Sometimes a sniper accidently kills the victim that way, or an innocent bystander. People have died because snipers know that, and sometimes they hesitate one second too long." He drew the woman and the baby into his arms and bent his head over hers. He could barely get his breath. "I prayed that you'd remember what I said. I've had hell living with a lot of things I did in my life, Tat. But if I'd hit you because my aim was off a hair, they'd have buried me right beside you."

He shuddered. "There is no way in hell I'm staying alive if you don't."

She felt the words. Felt them like silk wrapping around her body. She pressed closer to him, her eyes closed as she drank in the wonder of his feelings for her.

"Stanton, how much do you remember?" she asked without looking at him.

Dr. Coltrain and the nurse walked in just in time to spare him any embarrassing revelations. He would, of course, be obligated to tell her the truth at some point in the near future. But he was going to put it off as long as he could. He still felt enormous guilt at what she'd suffered because of his damned job. And that was another discussion he'd be having with other people very soon.

Joshua was all right. Rourke let out a sigh of delighted relief when Coltrain grinned and handed the baby back to Clarisse.

She kissed his little face and cuddled him.

"He's a lovely child," Coltrain said. "Nice name, too," he chuckled.

"I know, your son is also named Joshua," Clarisse said, blushing a little. "I honestly had no idea…"

"Three of our friends also have sons named Joshua. One is called Joe, one Josh, and ours is Tip."

"We, uh, heard about the train wrecking instincts," Rourke chuckled.

Coltrain just smiled. "So you see, if we all yell Joshua at the same time, only your little boy is likely to come running. Feel better?"

"Much," she confessed. "Thanks."

"Now that you're off the endangered list, are you staying?" Coltrain asked.

"I'd like to," Clarisse said softly. She smiled. "I've never lived in a small town in my life, but I love this one."

"You've made friends here. Besides, Tippy Grier will mourn if you take Joshua away," he laughed. "She's very fond of him. Of both of you."

"It would be nice if she and Cash could have another one," Clarisse said.

Coltrain didn't say a word. He just lifted an eyebrow and changed the subject.

ROURKE TOOK JOSHUA and Clarisse to Jake's house with him.

"But we'll be imposing," she'd protested all the way.

"Honey, you've got a body on your front porch," he pointed out, having taken her out the back door so that she didn't have to see Lopez lying there. He'd also dampened a washcloth and handed it to her before they got in the car to take Joshua to the hospital, so that she could wipe off the blood. "You can't possibly sleep there, and I'm not leaving you alone."

"But you're staying here already…"

"Jake's daughter married Carson Farwalker," he pointed out. "So Jake has a spare bedroom."

"One spare bedroom," she began.

"Just a sec." Rourke pulled a folded piece of paper out of his pocket and handed it to her.

She handed Joshua to him as she read it, standing on Jake Blair's front porch. Her eyes searched Rourke's for a few seconds. "It's a marriage license," she said.

"Ya," he agreed. "We've both had blood work recently. The results are on file. Jake can marry us right now. I even have the ring in my pocket." He cocked his head and he'd never looked more solemn. "We can have a sweet social wedding later on, when we recover from the past few days. But we can be married very quietly, and privately, right here, tonight. If you're willing."

"Of course I'm willing," she faltered. "But you don't remember...things," she added worriedly.

He bent and brushed his mouth over hers very softly. "I remember that I love you," he whispered huskily. He drew back. "What more do I need to remember?"

She flushed. "You love me?" she whispered.

"With all my heart." His face hardened. "More than my own life," he said, and almost choked as he recalled the last time he'd said that to her.

She pressed close to him with a high-pitched little cry and shivered.

Joshua stirred and she laughed as he started searching against her blouse with his tiny mouth.

She drew back. "Someone's hungry again," she teased.

He looked down at the child and smiled warmly. "You'll have time to feed him," he said. "Jake's asked Carlie and Carson to stand with us as witnesses."

"You reprobate," she gasped. "You already had it planned!"

"You bet your life I did," he agreed at once. His face was taut with remembered pain. "This time we're getting married, and my job can go hang. I'll never put it before you again. Not as long as I live, Tat. That's a solemn promise."

Her lips parted on a quick breath. "Stanton..."

Before she could get the question out, the door

opened and Jake Blair gave them an amused smile. "I hear there's going to be a wedding," he chuckled.

"You hear right," Rourke said, smiling. "Darling, this is Jake Blair. He's about the best friend I have in the world."

"I'm very happy to meet you, Reverend," Clarisse said, shaking hands.

"We haven't discussed denominations," Jake began.

"It doesn't really matter," Clarisse said softly. "I like your church very much, from what I've heard about it. And I'd like Joshua to be brought up with a background of faith. It's made all the difference in my own life."

"I've never been much for ceremony," Rourke said solemnly. "But I agree that a child needs a firm foundation to build on. I didn't have that. My father was brutally murdered right in front of me. My mother died in a firebombing a little over two years later. I've lived hard, and I've been bad. I never got that foundation. Except in lectures from her, when she was eight," he added with a glance toward Clarisse. "She was the one who believed in miracles."

"That's because I'm alive because of them," she said simply. She smiled at Reverend Blair. "I'll help you work on him." She indicated Rourke. "It may take more than two of us, however," she added with a resigned sigh.

"I very much doubt it," Rourke replied. He smiled at the baby in her arms, still searching irritably for his bedtime snack.

"I'd better feed him," Clarisse said. "Oh, dear, I don't have a crib…"

"We have one set up in the guest bedroom," Jake said easily. "Rourke called me from the hospital and a kindly parishioner loaned me his spare crib." He grinned. "All the loose ends caught up, and we even have a rocking chair in there waiting for you."

"It's so kind," Clarisse said, and fought tears.

"Dear lady, you're the kind one," Jake replied, and he was serious. "Anybody who could tame that African lion—" he indicated Rourke "—has an overabundance of kindness and patience."

"I've been untamed for a while," Rourke had to agree. Then he grinned at Clarisse. "But I'm becoming more housebroken daily. Feed the baby, darling. Then we'll have a small wedding."

She blushed a little, smiled shyly at Rourke and followed Jake's directions to the guest bedroom upstairs. The men went to drink coffee while she fed Joshua.

CARLIE AND CARSON showed up a few minutes later, holding hands and looking breathlessly happy. Carlie was very pregnant, swollen and heavy, but she looked as if she owned the world.

Clarisse had just put Joshua to bed. She came downstairs smiling. She was introduced to the newcomers and shook hands.

"I couldn't believe it when he told me," Carson said, nodding toward his father-in-law. "I mean, Rourke getting married!"

"Cut it out," Rourke chuckled. "After all, mate, you did it, too."

"They were taking bets down at the police station on whether or not he'd do a flit in the middle of the night the week after the wedding," Carlie said in a stage whisper, indicating her husband.

"Fat chance," Carson said, smiling at her. "I know a good thing when I see it."

"Is it a boy or a girl?" Rourke asked Carson.

"God, I hope so!"

Rourke burst out laughing. "One of the guys in Barrera asked him—" he nodded at Carson "—if Eb Scott's child was a boy or a girl. He said 'yes' and kept walking."

"I have no manners," Carson said easily.

"Yes, you do." Carlie reached up and kissed his chin. "And you're a wonderful doctor. Louise Coltrain sings your praises all the time. Even Copper does!"

"Rare praise indeed," Rourke chuckled. "Copper Coltrain doesn't praise anybody. Ever. From what I hear."

"Well, are we getting married?" Rourke asked after a couple of moments of silence. "I mean, what if she changes her mind in the next five minutes? I have to get her to say the words before she has time to think it through!"

"She'll never change her mind," Clarisse said huskily.

He smiled at her, with his whole heart in the expression. "Fair enough. But let's make it legal."

She moved forward and slid her small hand into his. It was every dream of her life coming true. Since she was seventeen, wearing a green dress on Christmas Eve, this had been all she'd ever wanted.

"Eight years too late, my darling," Rourke said huskily, because he'd been remembering the same thing. "But better late than never."

"Oh, yes!" she exclaimed.

Jake got out his Bible and arranged the couples before him. He smiled. "Dearly beloved," he began.

THE CEREMONY WAS BRIEF, but poignant for all that. Clarisse looked up at Rourke with such love in her expression that he felt warm all over. He bent and kissed her very softly, his lips like a breath against the soft fullness there.

"I will love you," he whispered, "all my life. And I would die to keep you safe. Through wind and storm, gale and thunder, sickness and health and even poverty, I will shelter you from the world. And at the end of my life, when I slip into darkness, I will whisper your name as the last breath leaves my body."

Tears were rolling down her flushed cheeks long before he finished. He bent and tenderly kissed them away.

"I've loved you since I was eight, Stanton," she managed with a wet smile. "And I've never stopped. I never will. Not even when I die."

He drew her into his arms and rocked her, his cheek against hers. "What a long road we've traveled to get here, Tat," he said heavily.

She smiled. "What a sweet rest at the end of that long journey."

"Yes."

He drew away and averted his face for a few seconds to get rid of an annoying and very visible wetness in his eye.

"Well, how about cake?" Jake asked.

They stared at him. "Cake?"

"Cake," he said. "Barbara at the café sent over a wedding cake. She made it herself."

Clarisse's breath sighed out. "Oh, how sweet of her!"

"I love cake," Rourke mused.

"Me, too," Carlie seconded.

Carson grinned. "It's a very big cake. So we thought you might like to share it."

"Share it?" Rourke said vacantly.

Carson went to the door and opened it. Half of Jacobsville poured into the house, including Barbara, Cash and Tippy Grier, and dozens of other people. Rourke pulled Clarisse close and laughed out loud with pure joy.

"I've got five pounds of coffee, too," Jake said with a grin. "I'll start it brewing!"

THE RECEPTION WAS AMAZING. It was the early hours of the morning, but nobody seemed to be sleepy. They drank coffee and ate cake and discussed the events of the night.

Cash pulled Tippy up with an apologetic smile at Rourke and Clarisse. "We have to get home."

"Chet's at my place, watching the kids," Barbara assured him. Her eyes were twinkling. "We'll see you in the morning."

Cash's own dark eyes had a twinkle.

"Tris is at Barbara's?" Tippy began.

"Say good-night, sweetheart," he returned, tugging her toward the door.

"Good night, sweetheart," Tippy said obediently, with a grin, and Cash chuckled as he pulled her out to the car.

Minutes later, he locked them in the bedroom of their home and tossed Tippy a small bottle of pills.

"What are these?" she asked.

"Baby pills." He undressed and then undressed her.

"Baby pills?" she began. He turned around and she gasped as she saw him. Not since a night long ago in New York had he looked so formidable.

"Impressive, isn't it?" he mused. "I've had a little too much pressure, and we've had a lot less privacy than we've needed. So Coltrain took care of one problem, and Barbara took care of another. It's just one night." His lips pursed as his eyes slid over her beautiful nude body. "But what a night it's going to be!"

Her eyes lit up. "Baby pills?" she teased.

He pushed her back down into the mattress, his eyes full of loving good humor. "You'll see in a few weeks. Now move this leg, just like this, honey, and hold on tight...!"

She tried to laugh, but his mouth was on hers and the joy she felt melted into the most awesome bout of passion she'd ever experienced in her life.

ROURKE TOOK CLARISSE and Joshua to church the next morning. She was amazed at how good he was with the baby. He already knew how to strap the baby into the backseat of the Jaguar. Clarisse stared over the back of her seat at him.

"Just a little ride, Joshua, honest," she promised, cooing at him.

"Damned distance," Rourke mused. "I don't like having the child in the backseat away from us like that."

"Neither do I. But air bags are very dangerous for babies."

"When I was eleven, K.C. used to put me right up

front with him in that old Land Rover and take me places. In fact, he was still driving it when you moved next door."

"I remember." Her heart was in her eyes as she studied him. "I can't believe we're actually married," she said huskily.

"It's my damned fault we weren't, when you were pregnant with Joshua," he said in a voice vibrant with regret. "So much pain. All because I put my job before you. Never again. I swear it. I've already turned over this last assignment to another agent, and I had a long talk with them. I'll be administrative, or I'll quit. I can afford to. The game park makes more than enough revenue to take care of both of us into old age and manage college for Joshua and any brothers and sisters we might give him. So no more fieldwork. Ever."

She'd wondered about his memory returning. She gazed at him curiously.

He glanced at her. "We'll talk when we get back from church. Okay?"

"Okay."

He winked and pulled into the church parking lot.

ROURKE HAD NEVER felt anything as profound as the way he felt at that first church service. He shared Joshua with Clarisse, holding him when he fussed to relieve her, because even though the incision had healed, she was still somewhat fragile.

"You're very good with him," Clarisse murmured when they were walking into Barbara's Café for Sunday dinner, along with half of Jacobsville.

Rourke put his lips against the baby's forehead.

"He's a treasure. Like you, my darling," he said huskily, glancing at her.

She flushed and laughed. "You thought I was a plague until a year ago," she recalled.

"Not true." He bent to brush his lips across hers as they waited in line to get into the building. "You know why I tried to make you hate me, Tat," he added huskily. "One lie, and the ripples spread out for years." His face hardened. "I understand why your mother did it. But she cheated us, Tat. She cost us years."

She moved closer to him, her head just coming to his shoulder. "I know. I'm so sorry."

"So am I, honey." He cuddled Joshua closer. "At least we have a future now." His eye closed on an inward groan. "Dear God, what that decision cost me!"

"Accepting the last job?" she asked.

He looked down at her with anguish on his hard face. "Yes. You meant everything to me, but when the call came to move into action, I agreed. It was a terrible mistake."

"But we're together now. That is all that matters."

"I'd lived wild and free all my life. But I was scared to death that you might actually marry Carvajal," he added in a rough undertone. "You threatened me with him in Barrera at the awards ceremony. I went out and got drunk and wrecked a bar. Did you ever figure out why?" he added suddenly.

She frowned. "No."

"Because I knew if you cared at all, even a little, you'd come and save me from myself," he said, and his smile was like sunshine itself. "That was when I knew I still had a chance to keep you in my life. I'd never been so happy." The smile faded. "But it all went wrong in Manaus, when I left you," he added on a long breath.

Her face colored. "You remember," she said unsteadily.

"Yes. I remembered when I went home to see about K.C.," he said. "It was the blood type. Joshua's blood type. My son's…blood type." His voice was vibrant with pride and affection as he looked down at the child in his arms. "My son," he whispered. His face contorted. "I almost lost him. I almost lost both of you." His pale brown eye was tormented as it met hers. "I tossed you out of my house, and you had my child under your heart," he added on a harsh breath. "Dear God, everything I got, I deserved."

She didn't know what to say. She hadn't realized that his memory had come back. "Stanton," she began softly, "we can't go back and change what was. We can only go forward."

"Carvajal married you to spare you the shame of having a child out of wedlock, in a city where your mother was so well-known," he said huskily. "Yes?"

"Yes. He was kind to me. You see, he had an injury that robbed him of his manhood. He…couldn't. He knew he could never marry. But when he married me, people assumed the child was his. He was so happy." She bit her lip. "I felt sorry for him. But more than that, I was grateful. I didn't know what to do. I couldn't give up my baby…"

He pulled her close, wrapping her up tight against him. "I've given you nothing but hell," he said quietly. "I'm so sorry, my darling. So very, very sorry, for every harsh word. If there was any way I could undo the past eight years…"

She reached up and put her fingers across his hard mouth. "We have a little boy to raise," she said with a warm, quiet smile. "The past doesn't matter. Not anymore."

"K.C. had photos of you in the hospital when Joshua was born," he said gently. "I never would have thought K.C. would take to being a grandfather. He really loves Joshua."

"Joshua will love him, too. Just as he'll love you," she added softly, searching his face with loving eyes. "Just as I love you. I never stopped."

His eye closed on a grinding pain. "I don't deserve that."

"You didn't remember, Stanton," she said. "That wasn't your fault."

"If I hadn't agreed to that job…!"

"If, if, if," she chided. She reached up and kissed his chin. "Let's have a nice lunch and then we can go and sit in the park, if you like."

He searched her soft eyes. "I know something I'd rather do," he said huskily.

Her face colored.

"Jake had a cleaning crew go over to your house when the crime scene unit left. We can go home tonight, if you want to."

She couldn't quite meet his eyes. "That would be… nice."

"Oh, better than nice," he murmured at her ear. His lips smoothed over her earlobe. "I'll have to stop by the pharmacy first, however. Unless you're taking something…?"

She looked up at him with her heart in her eyes. "I'm not. I don't want to," she whispered.

His face tautened. "I missed it all," he said. "Knowing you were pregnant, watching you carry my son, being there when he was born... I missed everything," he ground out.

She put her fingers over his hard mouth. "There will be another time."

He caught her hand and held her palm to his lips. His eye held hers. "It's too soon," he said unsteadily.

She felt her heart racing. "Joshua is almost two months," she said unsteadily. "We could...if you wanted to."

His face went scarlet, at just the thought of it. "I wanted to make you pregnant in Manaus. I told you that I did." His jaw tautened. "But this time, if it happens, there is no way I'm leaving you. Not even for a day!"

She pressed close to his side. "Not even for a day, my darling," she whispered.

Her heart soared. She'd never felt such happiness in her whole life.

THAT NIGHT, HE loved her to sleep in her own bed, his body slow and tender, his mouth touching and lifting and teasing her until she thought she'd go mad.

"I thought I remembered how good this felt," he murmured against her breasts, chuckling.

"I remembered." She reached up and kissed his wounded eye. She'd teased him out of the patch already. He gave in with good grace. He didn't really mind letting her see the injury. She loved him so much that she never even noticed it, and he realized that.

He moved slowly on her yielding body, enjoying the soft little cries that pulsed from her throat, the way her

short nails dug into his hips as he lifted and fell against
her. The whole time, he watched her face, enjoyed the
intimacy of being with her, all over again.

"I didn't think...you could be so patient," she whispered brokenly.

"Why? Because you think I had other women
while my memory was gone?" he teased unsteadily.
"I couldn't touch another woman, not even Charlene,"
he murmured at her lips. "I didn't want anyone else. I
couldn't understand why, until I ran headlong into you
in the Jacobsville pharmacy. My God, what a shock! I
was so aroused that I attacked you," he groaned.

She gasped. "Aroused?"

"Aroused." He moved harder against her. "I hadn't
felt it since the wound. I just looked at you and went
rigid." His mouth ground into hers. "Lift your legs
around me, darling," he whispered as he shifted, making her moan even louder. "That's it. Yes...like that...
hold on, baby. Hold on. Hold on. Hold on...!"

The words echoed with every hard, deep motion of
his hips. The rhythm went wild all at once. His hands
tightened at either side of her head and his face mir-
rored the sweet torment of what he was beginning to
feel.

"Oh, God, Tat...!" he cried out and began to shudder rhythmically.

She went with him, her body arching, lifting, grinding up into his as the fever melted them together like
molten steel. At the end, she cried out and sobbed
against his shoulder, giving in to a wave of pleasure
that threatened to kill her. She almost lost conscious-
ness, it was so violent.

She felt his heartbeat shaking her. She felt the beloved weight of his warm, damp body on hers as they both gasped at breath.

"I died," he murmured against her soft breast. "I died."

"So did I," she whispered, still shivering.

"I got you pregnant the first time we made love," he said huskily. "I wanted it, so much!"

"Me, too," she whispered, holding him closer.

"If only," he managed, lifting his head to look down into her soft, sated eyes.

She touched his cheek with the tips of her fingers. "If only."

"We've had a hell of a rocky ride to the altar," he said drowsily. "But maybe, with a little luck, it will be smooth sailing from now on."

"I hope so," she agreed. She smoothed her hands over his broad, hair-covered chest. "You're so beautiful, Stanton," she whispered. "I never get tired of looking at you."

"That's my line," he argued, laughing as he bent to her mouth. "My lovely Tat."

She sighed and pulled him closer. "Now I'm sleepy."

"Me, too." He rolled over, pulling her with him. "Do you have the monitor on in Joshua's room?"

"Yes, of course," she murmured. She grimaced. "I still can't believe I trusted Mariel with him." She shivered. "I was so stupid…!"

"You had no reason to believe she meant you any harm." He traced her eyebrows. "I'm so sorry, for the pain you've endured because of me. I'm sorry about Carvajal, as well. Not that I wouldn't have done everything in my power to get you and my son away from him, if he'd survived the malaria," he added darkly.

"He wouldn't have tried to make me stay. He knew how I felt about you," she added sadly. "He'd been in love, himself. He never told her after the accident. He said she deserved a full life."

"He was a good man," he said reluctantly.

"So are you," she replied, tracing his hard mouth. "And I love you insanely."

He laughed softly and kissed her back. "I love you insanely. Otherwise, I assure you, I wouldn't have gone eight damned long years without a woman!"

She wreathed her arms around his neck and leaned over him. "I'll make it all up to you," she murmured against his mouth.

"You will?" he teased.

"Oh, yes. I can start right away, too." Her long, soft leg smoothed in between his hair-roughened ones. "Do you like this?"

"Like it?" he groaned, arching. "I love it!"

"In that case, suppose I do this, too...!"

He rolled her over onto her back and groaned as he found her mouth. For a long, long time, they didn't say another word.

JOSHUA WAS CHRISTENED at the age of four months in Jake Blair's church. His name had already been changed to Kantor, just as Rourke's had. Clarisse had felt a pang of conscience at first, but it wasn't right to keep the name of a man who wasn't Joshua's father. She knew that Ruy would understand.

Joshua's proud parents stood with the Griers, Cash and Tippy, who were to be his godparents. On the other side was K.C., his grandfather, who released the honor of godparent to one not of the family. There was a crowd for the event.

The reception was held at the fellowship hall, but just as a buffet lunch was being served, Tippy left Tris with her brother, Rory, and Clarisse left Joshua with his father and grandfather, and both women made a sudden beeline for the ladies' room.

As they bathed their faces shortly afterward, they exchanged looks of unholy amusement.

"I know, it's too soon, but we really wanted another one," Clarisse began.

Tippy was laughing through tears. "I wasn't convinced that I could get pregnant again," she confessed. "Cash is going to be shocked!"

SHOCKED WASN'T THE WORD. Cash picked her up in his arms and carried her around the fellowship hall, kissing her nonstop the whole time. Rourke was similarly involved with his own wife.

"Must be the water," Jake Blair murmured, glancing at his daughter, who was almost ready to deliver.

Her husband, Carson, just grinned.

MANY MONTHS LATER, Rourke and Cash were pacing the waiting room while their wives were admitted and taken into the delivery room.

"I want to be in there with her," Cash muttered as the obstetrician, a woman, came into the seated area.

"So do I," Rourke added. "We did the natural childbirth thing…"

"Mrs. Grier went into labor almost before we could get her prepped," she told Cash with a big smile. "You have a son, Chief Grier. A fine, healthy little boy."

"A boy." Cash's face went white. "A boy! Tippy, is Tippy all right?" he added quickly.

"She's just fine. You can go in and see her. Marie, will you take the chief back to his wife and son?" she added, motioning to a nurse.

"My pleasure. Come along, Chief Grier," Marie said.

"What about Tat?" Rourke asked, beside himself.

"We had to do a C-section. It's all right—she's doing very well," the doctor assured him. She laughed. "I know you were hoping for a matched set, but it's another boy."

Rourke just smiled. "I was hoping for a healthy baby," he corrected. "I'd have been happy with either, as long as my sweetheart is okay." That concern showed.

"She's doing fine. Come along. I'll take you back myself." She shook her head. She laughed. "Maybe it really is the water."

ROURKE STOOD OVER the bed where Tat, pale but happy, was holding the newest addition to their family. He bent and touched the tiny head with his fingertips. There was a wetness in his good eye.

"All my life, I've felt as if I never had a place where I truly belonged. Now I do," he said, lifting his gaze to her rapt face. "I could die of happiness right now."

She smiled softly. "So could I, my darling."

"K.C. is on his way over. He's bought out half a toy store for Joshua, and he's bringing a bag full of things for the new baby."

"I'd like to call him Kent," she said gently. "For K.C." It was Rourke's father's real first name.

His face softened. "He'd be very proud."

"And Morrison for my father. It was his middle name."

"Kent Morrison Kantor it is," he said softly. He bent and kissed her eyes. "Have I told you today how much I love you, Mrs. Kantor?" he whispered.

"Only ten times," she murmured, drawing his face down so that she could kiss him warmly. "Not nearly enough."

He chuckled. "I love you madly."

"I love you madly back," she said against his mouth.

"Forever," he whispered, and his face was so radiant with love that it almost blinded her.

She brushed his lips with hers, fighting tears that felt like a watery overflow of happiness. Her mind was drifting back, over the long barren years with glimpses of terror and pain and sadness. All that, and now this. Heaven.

"Don't cry," he whispered, kissing her eyelids, sipping away the tears. "I'll never leave you again. Never."

She managed a watery smile. "I know, my darling," she whispered softly, overcome with joy. "I know."

Rourke kissed his son's little head. "After the storm, the sunlight," he said under his breath, in Afrikaans.

She nodded. "And it's blinding—it's so beautiful!" she whispered.

"Beautiful," he agreed, but he was looking at her lovely face.

She looked down at the child in her arms and drew in a long breath. "Better call K.C.," she told Rourke.

He chuckled, pulled out his cell phone, took a selfie of the three of them, and sent it off to his father.

An instant later, there was a reply. There, on the

screen, was K.C., with a grin like a Cheshire cat, wearing a long red cap with a white ball on the end, waving a small soccer ball and a stuffed lion. There was a text message underneath.

On my way, with the contents of another toy shop. Harnessing the reindeer as we speak!

"My God, it's Christmas tomorrow," Rourke exclaimed.

"Yes, and you didn't believe in Santa Claus, you silly man," Clarisse chided. "But look what he brought you!" she added, indicating the child in her arms.

He bent and brushed his mouth over hers, and then over the child's head. "I must have been a very, very good boy this year!"

She pursed her lips. "Oooooh, yes," she drawled, and gave him a steamy appraisal.

Cash Grier poked his head in the door. "I'm going for coffee. Want some?" he asked Rourke.

"Yes," Rourke said. "I'll go help you carry it. Back in a jiffy," he promised his wife, grinning.

"What did you name him?" Clarisse asked.

"Marcus Gilbert Rourke Grier."

Rourke caught his breath. He looked oddly flushed.

Cash grinned. "We'd have added Cassius, but Carson's got that on his side of the family. So we thought we should have Rourke for yours." He put an affectionate arm around Rourke. "After all, that's what Jacobsville is. A family. Right?"

Rourke was trying not to show the emotion he felt. He looked at his wife, his newest child and thought of K.C. on the way to join them. "Ya," he said after a minute, when he'd composed himself. "A big family."

Clarisse's eyes were brimming over with joy. "Hey," she teased, "bring me back a steak, could you?"

Rourke made a face at her. "I'd be hung from the ceiling with IV tubes, my darling," he confessed. "Sorry. But you can have a teddy bear."

"A lion," she corrected, her eyes soft with love. "We'll name him Lou, after yours back home."

"I'll see what I can do." He winked at her and went out the door with Cash, whistling softly.

Clarisse drew in a breath. She had the world. The whole world. She kissed her little boy's head and closed her eyes. Life was sweet. Sweeter than dreams.

* * * * *

*Be sure to check out
Diana Palmer's next book in her beloved
LONG, TALL TEXANS series,
DEFENDER.*

*The man who shattered Isabel Grayling's
trust is back to protect her.
Can she trust Paul Fiore not to break
her heart once again?*

*Turn the page to get a glimpse of
DEFENDER.*

CHAPTER ONE

ISABEL GRAYLING STUCK her head around the study door and peered in. The big desk was empty. The chair hadn't been moved from its position, carefully pushed underneath. Everything on the oak surface was neatly placed; not a pencil wasn't neatly in a cup; not a scrap of paper was out of line. She let out a breath. Her father wasn't home, but the desk kept the fanatical order he insisted on, even when he wasn't here.

She darted out of the office with a relieved sigh and pushed back the long tangle of her reddish-gold hair. Pale blue eyes were filled with relief. She wrinkled her straight nose, where just a tiny line of freckles ran over its bridge. Her name was Isabel, but only Paul Fiore called her that. To everyone else, she was Sari, just as her sister, Meredith, was always called Merrie.

"Well?" her younger sister, Merrie, asked in a whisper.

Sari turned. The other girl was slender, like herself, but Merrie had hair almost platinum blond, straight and to her waist in back. Her eyes, like Sari's, were blue, but paler, more the color of a winter sky. Both girls looked like their late mother, who was pretty but not beautiful.

"Gone!" Sari said with a wicked grin.

Merrie let out a sigh of relief. "Paul said that Daddy

was going to Germany for a few weeks. Maybe he'll find some other people to harass once he's in Europe."

Sari went up to the shorter girl and hugged her. "It will be all right."

Merrie fought tears. "I only wanted to have my hair trimmed, not cut. Honestly, Sari, he's so unreasonable…!"

"I know." She didn't dare say more. Paul had told her things in confidence that she couldn't bear to share with her baby sister. Their father was far more dangerous than either of them had known.

To any outsider, the Grayling sisters had everything. Their father was rich beyond any dream. They lived in a gray stone mansion on acres and acres of land in Comanche Wells, Texas, where their father kept Thoroughbred horses. Rather, his foreman kept them. The old man was carefully maneuvered away from the livestock by the foreman, who'd once had to save a horse from the man. Darwin Grayling had beaten animals before. It was rumored that he'd beaten his wife. She died of a massive concussion, but Grayling swore that she'd fallen. Not many people in Comanche Wells or nearby Jacobsville, Texas, wanted to argue with a man who could buy and sell anybody in the state.

That hadn't stopped local physician Jeb "Copper" Coltrain from asking for a coroner's inquest and making accusations that Grayling's description of the accident didn't match the head injuries. But Copper had been called out of town on an emergency by a friend and when he returned, the coroner's inquest was over and "accidental death" had been put on the death certificate. Case closed.

The Grayling girls didn't know what had truly happened. Sari had been in high school, Merrie in grammar school, when their mother died. They knew only what their father had told them. They were much too afraid of him to ask questions.

Now, Merrie was in her last year of high school and Sari was a senior in college. Sari had majored in history in preparation for a law degree. She went to school in San Antonio but wasn't allowed to live on campus. Her father had her driven back and forth every day. It was the same with Merrie. Darwin wasn't having either of his daughters around other people. He'd fought and won when Sari tried to move onto the college campus. He was wealthy and his children were targets, he'd said implacably, and they weren't going anywhere without one of his security people.

Which was why Sari and Paul Fiore, head of security for the Grayling Corporation, were such good friends. They'd known each other since Paul moved down from New Jersey to take the job while Sari was in her last year of high school. Paul drove the girls to school every day.

He'd wondered, but only to Sari, why her father hadn't placed them both in private schools. Sari knew, but she didn't dare say. It was because her father didn't want them out of his sight, where they might say something that he didn't approve of. They knew too much about him, about his business, about the way he treated animals and people.

He was paranoid about his private life. He had women, Sari was certain of it, but never around the house. He had a mistress. She worked for the federal government. Paul had told her, in confidence. He wasn't afraid of Darwin Grayling—Paul wasn't afraid of anyone. But he liked his job and he didn't want to go back to the FBI. He'd worked for the Bureau years ago. Nobody knew why he'd suddenly given up a lucrative government job to become a rent-a-cop for a Texas millionaire in a small town at the back of beyond. Paul never said, either.

Sari touched Merrie's slightly bruised cheek and winced. "I warned you about talking back, honey," she said worriedly. "I'm so sorry!"

"My mouth and my brain don't stay connected." Merrie laughed, but bitterly. Her blue eyes met her sister's. "If we could just tell somebody!"

"We could, and Daddy would make sure they never worked again," Sari said. "That's why I've never told Paul anything..." She bit her lip.

But Merrie knew already. She hugged the taller girl. "I won't tell him. I know how you feel about Paul."

"I wish he felt something for me," Sari said with a long sigh. "He's always been affectionate with me. He takes good care of me. But it's... I don't know how to say it. Impersonal?" She drew away, her expression sad. "He just doesn't get close to people. He dated that out-of-town auditor two years ago, remember? She called here over and over, and he wouldn't talk to her. He said he just wanted someone to go to the movies with, and she was looking at wedding rings." She laughed involuntarily. She shook her head. "He won't get involved."

"Maybe he was involved, and something happened," her sister said softly. "He looks like the sort of person who dives into things headfirst. You know, all or nothing. Maybe he lost somebody he loved, Sari."

"I guess that would explain a lot." She moved away,

grimacing. "It's just my luck, to go loopy over a man who thinks a special relationship is something you have with a vehicle."

"It's a very nice vehicle," Merrie began.

"It's a truck, Merrie!" she interrupted, throwing up her hands. "Gosh, you'd think it was a child the way he takes care of it. Special mats, taking it to the car wash once a week. He even waxes it himself." She glowered. "It's a truck!"

"I like trucks," Merrie said. "That cowboy who worked for us last year had a fancy black one. He wanted to take me to a movie." She shivered. "I thought Daddy was going to kill him."

"So did I." Sari swallowed, hard. She wrapped her arms around her chest. "The cowboy went all the way to Arizona, they said, to make sure Daddy didn't have him followed. He was scared."

"So was I," Merrie confessed. "You know, I'm seventeen years old and I've never gone on a date with a real boy. I've never been kissed, except on the cheek."

"Join the club." Sari laughed softly. "Well, one day we'll break out of here. We'll escape!" she said dramatically. "I'll hire a team of mercenaries to hide us from Daddy!"

"With what money?" Merrie asked sadly. "Neither of us has a dime. Daddy makes sure we can't even get a part-time job to make money. You can't even live at your college campus. I'll bet that gets you talked about."

"It does," Sari confided. "But they figure our father is just eccentric because he's so rich, and they let it go. I don't have any real friends, anyway."

"Just me," Merrie teased.

Sari hugged her. "Just you. You're my best friend, Merrie."

"You're mine, too, even if you are my sister."

Sari drew back. "One day, things will change."

"You've been saying that since we were in grammar school. It hasn't."

"It will."

Merrie touched her cheek and winced. "I told Paul I fell down the steps," she said, when she noticed her sister's worried expression.

"I wonder if he believed you," Sari replied solemnly. "He's not afraid of Daddy."

"He should be. I've heard Daddy has this friend back East," Merrie told her. "He's in with some underworld group. They say he's killed people, that he'll do anything for money." She bit her lower lip. "I don't want Paul hurt any more than you do. The less he knows about what goes on here when he's off duty, the better. He couldn't save us, anyway. He could only be dragged down with us."

"He wouldn't let Daddy hurt us, if he knew," Sari replied.

"So he won't know."

"Someone else might tell him," Sari began.

"Not anybody who works here." Merrie sighed. "Mandy's kept house for over twenty years, since before you were born. She knows stuff, but she's afraid to tell. She has a brother who does illegal things. Daddy told her he could have her brother sent to prison if she ever opened her mouth. She's afraid of him." She looked up. "I'm afraid of him."

Sari winced. "Yes. Me, too."

"I don't ever want to get married, Sari," the younger woman said huskily. "Not ever!"

"One day, you might, if the right man comes along."

Merrie laughed. "He's not likely to come along while Daddy's around, or he'll be leaving in a body bag in the back of a pickup truck."

The dark humor in that statement sent them both into gales of laughter.

PAUL FIORE WAS ITALIAN. He also had a Greek grandmother. It accounted for his olive complexion and thick jet-black hair and large brown eyes. He was handsome, too, tall and broad-shouldered, muscular without making a point of it. He walked like a panther, light on his feet, and he had a quick mind. He'd been in law enforcement most of his life until he took the job with the Grayling Corporation. He'd wanted to get as far away from federal work—and New Jersey—as he could. Jacobsville, Texas, came close to his ideal place.

He was fond of the girls, Merrie and Sari, and he took charge of the house when Mr. Grayling was out of the country. He could handle any problem that came up. His main responsibility was to keep the girls safe, but he also kept a close watch on the property, especially the very expensive Thoroughbreds Grayling raised for sale.

The housekeeper, Mandy Swilling, was fond of him. She was always baking him the cinnamon cookies he liked so much, and tucking little surprises into his truck when he had to be away on business.

"You've got me ruined," he accused her one morning. "I'll be so spoiled that I'll never be able to get along in the world if I ever get fired from here."

"Mr. Darwin will never fire you," Mandy said confidently. "You keep your mouth shut and you don't ask questions."

His eyes narrowed. "Odd reason to keep a man on, isn't it?"

"Not around here," she said heavily.

He stared at her, his dark eyes twinkling. "You know where all the bodies are buried, huh? That why you still have work?"

She didn't laugh, as he'd expected her to. She just glanced at him and winced. "Don't even joke about things like that, Mr. Paul."

He groaned at her form of addressing him.

"Now, now," she said. "I've always called the boss Mr. Darwin, just like I call the foreman Mr. Edward. It's a way of speaking that Southern folk are raised with. You, being a Yankee…" She stopped and grinned. "Sorry. I meant to say, you, being a northerner, wouldn't know about that."

"I guess so."

"You still sound like a person born up north."

He shrugged and grinned back at her. "We are what we are."

"I suppose so."

He watched her work at making rolls for lunch. She wasn't much to look at. She was about fifty pounds overweight, had short silver hair and dark eyes, and she was slightly stooped over from years of working in gardens with a hoe. But she could cook! The woman was a magician in the kitchen. Paul remembered his tiny little grandmother, making ravioli and antipasto when he was a child, the scent of flour and oil that always seemed to cling to her. Kitchens were comforting to a child who had no real home. His father had worked for a local mob boss and done all sorts of illegal things, like most of the rest of his family. His mother had died miserable, watching her husband run around with an endless parade of other women, shuddering every time the big boss or law enforcement came to the front door. After his mother died and his father went to jail for the twentieth time, Paul went to live with his little Greek grandmother. He and his cousin Mikey had stayed with her until they were almost grown. Paul watched Mikey go the same route his father had, attached like a tick to the local big crime boss. His father never came around. In fact, he couldn't remember seeing his father more than a dozen times before the man died in a shoot-out with a rival mob.

It was why he'd gone into law enforcement at seventeen, fresh out of high school. He hated the hold crime had on his family. He hoped he could make a difference, help clean up his old neighborhood and free it from the talons of organized crime. He went from local police right up into the FBI. He'd felt that he was unstoppable, that he could fight crime and win. Pride had blinded him to the reality of life. It had cost him everything.

Still, he missed the Bureau sometimes. But the memories had been lethal. He couldn't face them, not even now, years after the tragedy that had sent him running from New Jersey to Texas on a job tip from a coworker. He'd given up dreams of a home and all the things that went with it. Now, it was just the job, doing the job. He didn't look forward. Ever. One Day at a Time was his credo.

"Why are you hiding in here?" Mandy asked suddenly, breaking into his thoughts.

"It's that obvious, huh?" he asked, the New Jersey accent still prevalent even after the years he'd spent in Texas.

"Yes, it is."

He sipped the black coffee she'd placed in front of him at the table. "Livestock foreman's got a daughter. She came with him today."

"Oh, dear," Mandy replied.

He shrugged. "I took her to lunch at Barbara's Cafe a few weeks ago, just a casual thing. I met her at the courthouse. She works there. She decided that I was looking for a meaningful relationship. So now she's over here every Saturday like clockwork, hanging out with her dad."

"That will end when Mr. Darwin comes back," she said with feeling. "He doesn't like strangers on the place, even strangers related to people who work here."

He smiled sadly. "Or it will end when I lose my temper and start cursing in Italian."

"You look Italian," she said, studying him.

He chuckled. "You should see my cousin Mikey. He could have auditioned for *The Godfather*. I've got Greek in me, too. My grandmother was from a little town near Athens. She could barely speak English at all. But could she cook! Kind of like you," he added with twinkling eyes. "She'd have liked you, Mandy."

Her hard face softened. "You never speak of your parents."

"I try not to think about them too much. Funny, how we carry our childhoods around on our backs."

She nodded. She was making rolls for lunch and they had to have time to rise. Her hands were floury as she kneaded the soft dough. She nodded toward the rest of the house. "Neither of those poor girls has had a childhood. He keeps them locked up all the time. No parties, no dancing and especially no boys."

He scowled. "I noticed that. I asked the boss once why he didn't let the girls go out occasionally." He took a sip of his coffee.

"What did he tell you?"

"That the last employee who asked him that question is now waiting tables in a little town in the Yukon Territory."

She shook her head. "That's probably true. A cowboy who tried to take Merrie out on a date once got a job in Arizona. They say he's still looking behind him for hired assassins." Her hands stilled in the dough. "Don't you ever mention that outside the house," she advised. "Or to Mr. Darwin. I kind of like having you around," she added with a smile and went back to her chore.

"I like this job. No big-city noise, no pressure, no pressing deadlines on cases."

She glanced up at him, then back down to the bowl again. "We've never talked about it, but you were in law enforcement once, weren't you?"

He scowled. "How did you know that?"

"Small towns. Cash Grier let something slip to a friend, who told Barbara at the café, who told her cook, who told me."

"Our police chief knew I was in law enforcement? How?" he wondered aloud, feeling insecure. He didn't want his past widely known here.

She laughed softly. "Nobody knows how he finds out things. But he worked for the government once." She glanced at him. "He was a high-level assassin."

His eyes widened. "The police chief?" he exclaimed.

She nodded. "Then he was a Texas Ranger—that ended when he slugged the temporary captain and got fired. Afterward he worked for the DA in San Antonio, and then he came here."

He whistled. "Slugged the captain." He chuckled. "He's still a pretty tough customer, despite the gorgeous wife and two little kids."

"That's what everyone says. We're pretty protective of him. Our late mayor—who was heavily into drug smuggling on the side—tried to fire Chief Grier, and the whole city police force and fire department, and all our city employees, said they'd quit on the spot if he did."

"Obviously he wasn't fired."

She smiled. "Not hardly. It turns out that the state attorney general, Simon Hart, is Cash Grier's cousin. He showed up, along with some reporters, at the hearing they had to discuss the firing of the chief's patrol officers. They arrested a drunk politician and he told the mayor to fire them. The chief said over his dead body."

"I've been here for years, and I heard gossip about it, but that's the first time I've heard the whole story."

"An amazing man, our chief."

"Oh, yes." He finished his coffee. "Nobody makes coffee like you do, Mandy. Never weak and pitiful, always strong and robust!"

"Yes, and the coffee usually comes out that way, too!" she said with a wicked grin.

He laughed as he got up from the table and went back to work.

THAT NIGHT HE WAS researching a story about an attempted Texas Thoroughbred kidnapping on the internet when Sari walked in the open door. He was perched on the bed in just his pajama bottoms with the laptop beside him. Sari had on a long blue cotton nightgown with a thick, ruffled matching housecoat buttoned way up to the throat. She jumped onto the bed with him, her long hair in a braid, her eyes twinkling as she crossed her legs under the voluminous garment.

"Do that when your dad comes home, and we'll both be sitting on the front lawn with the door locked," he teased.

"You know I never do it when he's home. What are you looking up?"

"Remember that story last week about the so-called traveling horse groomer who turned up at the White Stables in Lexington, Kentucky, and walked off with a Thoroughbred in the middle of the night?"

"Yes, I do."

"Well, just in case he headed south when he jumped bail, I'm checking out similar attempts. I found one in Texas that happened two weeks ago. So I'm reading about his possible MO."

She frowned. "MO?"

"Modus operandi," he said. "It's Latin. It means…"

"Please," she said. "I know Latin. It means method of operation."

"Close enough," he said with a gentle smile. His eyes went back to the computer screen. "Generally speaking, once a criminal finds a method that works, he uses it over and over until he's caught. I want to make sure that he doesn't sashay in here while your dad's gone and make off with Grayling's Pride."

"Sashay?" she teased.

He wrinkled his nose. "You're a bad influence on me," he mused, his eyes still on the computer screen. "That's one of your favorite words."

"It's just a useful one. *Snit* is my favorite one."

He raised an eyebrow at her.

"And lately you're in a snit more than you're not," she pointed out.

He managed a smile. "Bad memories. Anniversaries hit hard."

She bit her tongue. She'd never discussed really personal things with him. She'd tried once and he'd closed up immediately. So she smiled impersonally. "So they say," she said instead of posing the question she was dying to.

He admired her tact. He didn't say so, of course. She couldn't know the memories that tormented him, that had him up walking the floor late at night. She couldn't know the guilt that ate at him night and day because he was in the wrong place at the wrong time when it really mattered.

"Are you okay?" she asked suddenly.

His dark eyebrows went up. "What?"

She shrugged. "You looked wounded just then."

She was more perceptive than he'd realized. He scrolled down the story he was reading online. "*Wounded.* Odd choice of words there, Isabel."

"You're the only person who ever calls me that."

"What? Isabel?" He looked up, studying her softly rounded face, her lovely complexion, her blue, blue eyes. "You look like an Isabel."

"Is that a compliment or something else?"

"Definitely a compliment." He looked back at the

computer screen. "I used to love to read about your namesake. She was queen of Spain in the fifteenth century. She and her husband led a crusade to push foreigners out of their country. They succeeded in 1492."

Her lips parted. "Isabella la Catolica."

His chiseled lips pursed. "My God. You know your history."

She laughed softly. "I'm a history major," she reminded him. "Also a Spanish scholar. I'm doing a semester of Spanish immersion. English isn't spoken in the classroom, ever. And we read some of the classic novels in Spanish."

He chuckled softly. "My favorite was Pío Baroja. He was Basque, something of a legend in the early twentieth century."

"Mine was *Sangre y Arena*."

"Blasco Ibáñez," he shot back. "*Blood and Sand*. Bullfighting?" he added in a surprised tone.

She laughed. "Yes, well, I didn't realize what the book would be about until I got into it, and then I couldn't put it down."

"They made a movie about it back in the forties, I think it was," he told her. "It starred Tyrone Power and Rita Hayworth. Painful, bittersweet story. He ran around on his saintly wife with a woman who was little more than a prostitute."

"I suppose saintly women weren't much in demand in some circles in those days. And especially not today," she added with a wistful little sigh. "Men want experienced women."

"Not all of them," he said, looking away from her.

"Really?"

He forced himself to keep his eyes on the computer screen. "Think about it. A man would have to be crazy to risk STDs or HIV for an hour's pleasure with a woman who knew her way around bedrooms."

She fought a blush and lost.

He saw it and laughed. "Honey, you aren't worldly at all, are you?"

"I'm alternately backward or unliberated, to hear my classmates tell it. But mostly they tolerate my odd point of view. I think one of them actually feels sorry for me."

"Twenty years down the road, they may wish they'd had your sterling morals," he replied. He looked up, into her eyes, and for a few endless seconds, he didn't look away. She felt her body glowing, burning with sensations she'd never felt before. But just when she thought she'd go crazy if she didn't do something, footsteps sounded in the hall.

"So there you are," Mandy exclaimed. "I've looked everywhere." She stared at them.

Paul made a face. "Do I look like a suicidal man looking for the unemployment line to you?" he asked sourly.

Both women laughed.

"All the same, don't do that when your dad's home," she told Sari firmly.

"I never would, you know that," Sari said gently. "Why were you looking for me?"

"That girl at college who can't ever find her history notes wants to talk to you about tomorrow's test."

"Nancy," she groaned. "Honestly, I don't know how she passed anything until I came along! She actually called up one of our professors at night and asked if he could give her the high points of his lecture. He hung up on her."

"I'm not surprised," Paul said. "Better go answer the questions, tidbit," he added to Sari.

"I guess so," she said. She got off the bed, reluctantly. The way he'd looked at her had made her feel shaky inside. She wanted him to do it again. But he was already buried in his computer screen.

"There was an attempted horse heist just two days ago up near San Antonio," he was muttering. "I think I'll call the DA up there and see if he's made any arrests."

"Good night, Paul," Sari said as she left the room.

"Night, sprout. Sleep well."

"You, too."

MANDY LED HER into the kitchen and pointed to the phone.

"Hello, Nancy?" Sari said.

"Oh, thank goodness," the other girl rushed. "I'm in such a mess! I can't find my notes, and I'll fail the test…!"

"No worries. Let me get mine and I'll read them to you."

"You could fax them…"

"You'd never read my handwriting." Sari laughed. "Besides, it will help me remember what I need for tomorrow's test."

"In that case, thanks," Nancy said.

"You're welcome. Give me your number and I'll call you back. I'll have to hunt up my own notes."

Nancy gave it to her and hung up.

Sari came back down with the notes she'd retrieved

from her bulky book bag. She phoned Nancy from the kitchen, where Mandy was cleaning up, and read the notes to her. It didn't take long.

"I'll see you in class," Nancy said. "And thanks! You've saved my life!" She hung up.

"She says I saved her life," Sari said, chuckling.

Mandy gave her a glance. "If you want to save two lives, you'll stay out of Mr. Paul's bedroom."

"Mandy, it's perfectly innocent. The door's always open when I'm in there."

"You don't understand. It's how it looks, that easy familiarity between you two. It will carry over to other times, in daylight. If your father sees it, even *thinks* that there might be something going on…"

"I don't do it when he's here."

"I know that. It's just…" She grimaced. "I don't know where he put all the cameras."

Sari's heart jumped. "What cameras?"

"He had it done while you girls were at school. He had three security cameras installed. He sent me out of the house on an errand while they were put in place. I don't know where they are."

"Surely he wouldn't have them put in our bedrooms," Sari began worriedly.

"There's no telling," Mandy said. "I only know that he didn't put one in here. I'd have noticed if anything was moved or displaced. Nothing was."

Sari chewed on a fingernail. "Gosh, now I'll worry if I talk in my sleep!"

"The cameras are why you should stay out of Mr. Paul's bedroom. Besides that," she added under her breath, "you're tempting fate."

"I am? How?" Sari asked blankly.

"Honey, Mr. Paul takes a woman out for a sandwich or a quick dinner. He never goes home with them."

Sari flushed with sudden pleasure.

"My point is," the older woman went on, "that he's a man starved of…well…satisfaction." She faltered. "You might say something or do something to tempt him, is what I'm trying to say."

Sari sighed and rested her hands on her palms, propped on her elbows. "That would be a fine thing," she mused. "He's never even touched me except to help me out of a car," she added on a wistful sigh.

"If he ever did touch you, your father would be sure to hear about it. And I don't like to think of the consequences. He's a violent man, Sari," she added gently.

"I know that." Her face showed her misery. She was too innocent to hide her responses.

"So, don't tempt fate," Mandy said softly. She hugged the younger woman tight. "I know how you feel about him. But if you start something, he'll be out on his ear. And what your father would do to you…" She drew back with a grimace. "I love Mr. Paul," she added. "He's the kindest man I know. You don't want to get him fired."

"Of course I don't," Sari replied. "I promise I'll behave."

"You always have," Mandy said with a tender smile. "It all ends, you know," she said suddenly.

"Ends?"

"Misery. Unrequited love. Even life. It all ends. We live in pieces of emotion. Pieces of life. It doesn't all get put together until we're old and ready for the long sleep."

"Okay, when you get philosophical, I know it's past my bedtime," Sari teased.

Mandy hugged her one last time. "You're a sweet child. Go to bed. Sleep well."

"You, too." She went to the doorway and paused. She turned. "Thanks."

"What for?"

"Caring about me and Merrie," Sari said gently. "Nobody else has, since Mama died."

"It's because I care that I sometimes say things you don't want to hear, my darling."

Sari smiled. "I know." She turned and left the room.

MANDY, OLDER AND WISER, saw what Sari and Paul really felt for each other, and she worried at the possible consequences if that tsunami of emotion ever turned loose in them.

She went back to her chores, closing the kitchen up for the night.

CHAPTER TWO

WHEN ISABEL WALKED past Paul's bedroom after she called Nancy, she noticed his door was closed and the lights were off.

She went into her own room, climbed into bed and extinguished the single bedroom lamp in the room.

She recalled what Mandy had said, about the dangers of getting too close to him, with sadness. Yes, of course, her father would fire him if anything indiscreet came to light. She also recalled the pain she felt when the older woman spoke of Paul going on dates with other women.

He didn't take them to bed, that much was clear. But it also indicated that he wasn't ready to get serious about a woman, that he wasn't interested in marriage and kids. And Isabel was. She'd gladly have given up college to end up in Paul's arms with a baby of her own.

But that seemed more unlikely by the day. She was living in pipe dreams. Paul was content to have her at arm's length. He didn't want her. At least, he didn't want her the way she wanted him. She cared more for him than she'd ever cared for anyone, except her mother and sister.

As Paul liked to remind her, though, she hadn't been out in the world long enough to know what she really wanted. That amused her. He seemed to think she was still the seventeen-year-old he'd taken to school every day in the limo. She was twenty-one, almost twenty-two now. She'd graduate from college in a few months. That made her, in the eyes of the world, an adult. Not to Paul, though. Never to Paul.

She had to start thinking about what she was going to do with her life after college. Law had always fascinated her. She'd been hanging around the courthouse after school, grilling one of District Attorney Blake Kemp's assistant DAs about what it was like to practice in a courtroom. Glory Ramirez was happy to talk to her, filling her head with thoughts of working in the DA's office.

"Blake knows how much time you spend here, on my lunch hour and after work," Glory teased.

"Oh, no," Sari began.

Glory held up a hand. "He doesn't mind. There aren't that many people blazing paths up the street to the courthouse to solicit work in the DA's office." She sobered. "It's hard work, Sari, with long hours. Sometimes defendants' families target us because they think we've been unfair. Sometimes the defendants themselves try to attack us when they get out. Those instances are rare, but they do happen. Family life is hard." She smiled gently. "I'm qualified to know that, because my husband and I have a son who's almost four years old. Rodrigo still works for the DEA and I'm at the courthouse all hours. Sometimes we have to have the Pendletons babysit." The Pendletons were Glory's adoptive family. Jason's father had been Glory, and Gracie's, guardian.

"I don't really think they mind," Sari teased, because it was well-known that although Jason and Gracie Pendleton had a son and daughter of their own now, they still loved to watch their nephew. All the kids had enough toys to stock a nursery.

"Of course not." Glory laughed. "But I'm still missing out on time with my family to do this job. I love it," she added gently. "It's a special thing, to help keep people safe, to make sure people who do terrible things are punished and off the streets. That's why I do it."

"I...would do it for that reason, as well," Sari said, not adding that her terror of a father was one of her own motivations. He was the sort of person who should have been sitting in a jail cell, but never would, because of his wealth. "Justice shouldn't be dealt according to who has money and who doesn't," she added absently.

Glory, who had some idea of Darwin Grayling's illegal dealings, only nodded her head.

"Anyway, what about those courses you mentioned?" she asked, bringing Glory back to the present.

Glory laughed. "Okay. Here's what you need to consider in law school..."

SARI WAS FULL of fire for the fall semester in law school, after she got her undergraduate degree. Her cumulative grades assured that she would graduate, the finals from each class notwithstanding. She already had a graduate school picked out. Law school in San Antonio.

"You'll have to drive me, of course," Sari told Paul with a sigh when she outlined the courses Glory had told her about. "There's no way Daddy will ever let me drive myself. I don't even have a driver's license."

He scowled. "Surely not."

She shrugged. "He holds the purse strings, you

know. Either I do it his way or I don't do it," she said with the complacency of a woman who'd lived such a sheltered life. "So I do it."

"Haven't you ever wanted to break out?" he asked suddenly.

She grinned at him across a plate of cookies, which they were sharing with cups of coffee at the small kitchen table. "You offering to help me?" she teased. "Got a helicopter and a couple of guys wearing ninja suits?"

He chuckled. "Not quite. I used to know a couple of guys like that, though, in the old days."

"Oh, please," she said, munching a cookie. "You aren't old enough to be remembering 'the old days.'"

His eyebrows rose. "You need glasses, kid. I've got gray hair already."

She eyed him. He was so gorgeous. Black wavy hair, deep-set warm brown eyes, high cheekbones, chiseled mouth; he was any woman's dream guy. "Gray hair, my left elbow."

"No kidding. Right here." He indicated a spot at his temple.

"Oh, that one. Sure. You're old, all right. You've got one whole gray hair."

He grinned, as she'd expected him to. "Well, maybe a few more than that. I'm like my grandfather. His hair never turned gray. He had a few silver hairs when he died, at the age of eighty."

"Do you look like him?" she asked, sipping coffee.

"No. I look like my grandmother. Everybody else was Italian. She was tiny and Greek and she had a mouth like a mob boss." He chuckled. "Do something wrong, and that gnarled little hand came out of no-where to grab your ear." He made a face.

"So that's why your ears are so big," she mused, looking at them.

"Hey, I was never that bad," he argued. He glowered at her. "And my ears aren't that big."

"If you say so," she said, hiding the gleam in her eyes.

"You little termagant," he said, exasperated.

"Where do you get all those big words?" she asked.

"College."

"Really? You never told me you went to college."

He shrugged. "I don't like talking about the past."

"I noticed."

"We could talk about your past," he invited.

"And after those forty-five seconds, we could go back to yours," she teased, blue eyes twinkling. "Come on, what did you study?"

"Law." His face hardened with the memories. "Criminal law."

She frowned. "That was before you came to work for Daddy, yes?"

She was killing him and she didn't know it. His hand, on the thick white mug, was almost white with the pressure he was exerting. "A long time before that."

"Then, what..."

Mandy came into the room like a chubby whirlwind. "Where did you put the ribbons I was saving to wrap the holiday cookies with?" she demanded from Sari.

"Oh, my gosh, I was working on homemade Christmas cards and I borrowed them. I'm sorry!"

"Go get them," Mandy ordered with all the authority of a drill sergeant. "Right now!"

Sari left in a whirlwind, and Mandy turned to Paul, who was paler than normal. His hand around the mug was just beginning to loosen its grip.

He gave her a suspicious look.

"Sari doesn't think," Mandy said quietly. "She's curious and she asks questions, because she doesn't think."

He didn't admit anything. He took a deep breath. "Thanks," he bit off.

"We all have dark memories that we never share, Mr. Paul," she said gently. She patted his shoulder as she walked behind him. "Age diminishes the sting a bit. But you're much too young for that just yet," she added with a soft chuckle.

"You're a tonic, girl."

"I haven't been a girl for forty years, you sweet man, but now I feel like one!"

He laughed, the pain washing away in good humor.

"There. That's better," she said, smiling at him. "You just keep putting one foot in front of the other, and it gets easier."

"It's been almost five years."

"Thirty years for me," Mandy said surprisingly. "And it's much easier now."

He drew in a breath and finished his coffee. "Maybe in twenty-five years, I'll forget it all, then."

She looked at him with a somber little smile. "It would do an injustice to the people we love to forget them," she said softly. "Pain comes with the memories, sure. But the memories become less painful in time."

He scowled. "You should have been a philosopher."

"And then who'd bake cookies for you and Miss Sari and Miss Merrie?" she asked.

"Well, if we had to depend on Sari's cooking, I expect we'd all starve," he said deliberately when he heard Sari coming.

She stopped in the doorway, gasping and glaring. "That is so unfair!" she exclaimed. "Heavens, I made an almost-edible, barely scorched potato casserole just last week!"

"That's true," Mandy agreed.

Paul glowered. "*Almost* being the operative word."

"And I didn't even mention that I saw you pushing yours out the back door while I was trying to pry open one of my biscuits so I could butter it!"

Sari sighed. "I guess they were pretty good substitute for bricks," she added. "Maybe I'll learn to cook one day."

"You're doing just fine, darlin'," Mandy said encouragingly. "It takes time to learn." She shot Paul a glance. "And a lot of encouragement."

"Damn, Sari, I almost got one of those biscuits pried open to put butter in!" He glanced at Mandy. "How's that?"

"Why don't you go patrol the backyard?" Sari muttered.

"She's picking on me again, Mandy," he complained.

"Don't you be mean to Mr. Paul, young lady." Mandy took his part at once.

"He says terrible things about me, and you never chastise him!" Sari accused.

"Well, darlin', I may be old, but I can still appreciate a handsome man." She grinned at them.

Sari threw up her hands. Paul gave her a handsome bow, winked and walked out the back door.

"You always take his side," Sari groaned.

Mandy chuckled. "He really is handsome," she said defensively.

"Yes. Too handsome. And too standoffish. He'll never look at me as anything but the kid I was when he came here."

"You've got law school to get through," Mandy reminded her. She sobered. "And you know how your dad feels about you getting involved with anyone."

"Yes, I know," Sari said miserably. "Especially anybody who works for him." Shivering softly, she said, "It's just, I'm getting older. I'm a grown woman. And I can't even drive myself to San Antonio to go shopping or invite friends over."

"You don't have any friends," Mandy countered.

"I don't dare. Neither does Merrie," she added solemnly. "We're young, with the whole world out there waiting for us, and we have to get permission to leave the house. Why?" she exclaimed.

Mandy ground her teeth. "You know how your dad guards his privacy. He's afraid one of you might let something slip."

"Like what? We don't know anything about his business, or even his private life," Sari exclaimed.

"And you're both safe as long as it's kept that way," Mandy said without thinking, then slapped a hand across her mouth.

Sari bit her lower lip. She moved closer. "What do *you* know?"

"Things I'll die before I'll tell you," the older woman replied, turning pale.

"How do you know them?"

Mandy ignored her.

"Your brother, right?" she whispered. "He knows people who know things."

"Don't you ever say that out loud," she cautioned the younger woman, looking hunted until Sari reassured her that she'd never do any such thing.

"It's like living in a combat zone," Sari muttered.

"A satin-cushioned one," came the droll reply. "If you want an apple pie, here's a do-it-yourself kit." She put a basin of apples in front of the younger woman. "So get busy and peel."

Sari started to argue. But then she recalled the delicious pies Mandy could make, so she shut up and started peeling.

GRADUATION CAME ALL too soon. The household, except for Darwin Grayling, who was in Europe at the time, went to Merrie's first at the high school and took enough pictures to fill an album. Then, only a few days later, it was Isabel's graduation from college. Merrie kept fussing with Sari's high collar.

"It's okay," her older sibling protested.

"It's not! There's a wrinkle, and I can't get it smoothed out!" Merrie grumbled.

"It will be hidden under my robes," Sari said gently, turning. She smiled at her younger sister. She shook her head. With her long blond hair like a curtain down her back, wearing a fluffy blue dress, Merrie looked like a picture of Alice in Wonderland that Sari had seen in a book. "I like your hair like that," she said.

Merrie laughed, her pale blue eyes lighting up. "I look like Alice. Go ahead. Say it. You're thinking it," she accused.

Sari wrinkled her nose.

Merrie sighed. "He decides what we'll wear, where we'll go, what we'll do when we get there," she said under her breath, her eyes on their father, standing with Paul near the front door. "Sari, normal women don't live like this! The girls I go to school with have dates, go shopping…!"

"Stop, or I won't get to graduate at all," the older sister muttered under her breath when Darwin Grayling shot an irritated glance toward them at Merrie's slightly raised tone.

Merrie drew in a deep breath. "It's Sari's collar," she called to her father. "I can't get the wrinkle out!"

"Leave it be," he shot back. He looked at his watch. "We need to leave now. I have meetings with my board of directors in Dallas in three hours."

"That's your graduation, sandwiched in between breakfast and a board meeting," Merrie teased under her breath. "At least he came home for your graduation," she added a little bitterly.

Sari kissed her sister's cheek. "I was there at yours. So were Mandy and Paul. Now shut up or I'll never graduate," came the whispered reply. "Let's go!" She smoothed down her very discreet black dress, regardless of her own wishes, and started toward the door. She noticed Paul's faint wince as he saw how she was dressed, like someone out of a very old Bette Davis movie instead of a young woman ready to start graduate school.

She didn't answer that look. It might have been fatal to his employment if she had.

GRADUATION WAS BOISTEROUS and fun, despite her father, who sat through the entire ceremony texting on his phone and then conducting a business call the minute the graduates filed out into the spring sunshine.

"Maybe it's glued to him," Merrie teased as she and Sari were briefly alone.

"Attached by invisible cords," Sari replied. "Hi, Grace, happy graduation!" Sari called to a fellow graduate.

"Thanks, Sari! You off to law school in the fall?" she asked.

"Yes. You?"

"I'm moving in with my boyfriend." Grace sighed, indicating a tall, gangly boy talking to another boy. "We're both going to the University of Tennessee."

"Oh, I see," Sari said, still not comfortable with modern ideas and choices.

Grace made a face. "Honestly, Sari, you need to buy normal clothes and go out with boys," Grace said, loud enough for Sari's father to hear.

He hung up his phone and moved to join them, looking expensive and coldly angry. "Are you ready to go, Isabel?" he asked curtly. His eyes never left Grace. He looked at her as if she were some disease he was afraid his daughters might catch.

"Uh, congrats, Sari. See you around," Grace said, red-faced, and went back to her boyfriend.

"Slut," Darwin said, just loud enough for his voice to carry and Grace to look both ruffled and insulted. "Let's go." He took Sari by the arm and almost dragged her to the waiting limousine, with a flustered Merrie running to catch up.

"I'll have Paul watching," Darwin said as Paul put the girls into the back of the limo and stood aside, holding the door, so that Darwin could slide into the seat facing them. The door closed. "I'll expect you to associate with decent girls. Do you understand? That goes for you, too, Meredith!"

"Yes, Daddy," Sari said.

"I understand," Merrie added with a sigh.

The sisters didn't dare look at each other. It would have been fatal.

THE DINNER DARWIN had referred to was obviously going to be prepared by Mandy and just for the two women. Darwin had Paul drive him to the airport where his corporate jet was waiting. Sari and Merrie changed clothes and sat down to a lovely chicken casserole with homemade rolls and even a chocolate cake.

"It's delicious, Mandy," Sari said halfway through the meal. "Thanks!"

"Yes, it's wonderful!" Merrie enthused.

"Some graduation," Mandy muttered. "Should have gone out with your classmates and had fun, not be stuck here with me and an empty house."

"You know how Daddy is," Sari said quietly. "He doesn't think..."

"He doesn't care," Merrie interrupted coolly. "It's the truth, Sari, you just don't want to admit it. He doesn't want us going out with men because we might get involved and tell somebody something he doesn't want known. He doesn't want us getting married because we'd be out from under his thumb! Besides, some of that money might go outside the family!"

"I suppose you're right," Sari said, tasting her cake. "It's just, you get used to a routine. You don't even realize that it really is a routine." Her eyes twinkled. "Honestly, I thought Daddy was going to have a coronary when Grace talked about moving in with her boyfriend!"

Merrie chuckled. "I know! At least four of my classmates live with boys. They say it's very exciting…"

"Don't you even think about it," Mandy told them, waving a spoon in their direction. "There's enough wild-eyed girls out there already. You two are going to get married and live happily ever after."

"You make it sound like a fairy tale," Sari accused.

"Maybe, but I want more for you than being some man's temporary bed partner while he climbs the ladder to success," Mandy murmured. "Your mother wanted that, too. She went to church every Sunday. She believed that people have a purpose, that life has a purpose. She was an idealist."

"Yes, well, she waited to get married and she found Daddy," Sari said quietly. "So there goes your fairy-tale ending. I remember her more than Merrie does. She was unhappy. She tried not to let it show, but it did. Sometimes I found her crying when she thought nobody was looking. And she had bruises…"

"Don't ever speak of that where Mr. Darwin or even Mr. Paul could hear you," Mandy cautioned, looking frightened.

"I never would," Sari assured her. She grimaced. "But it's like living in prison," she muttered.

"A prison with silk hangings and Persian carpets," Mandy said mischievously.

"You know what she means, Mandy," Merrie piped in as she finished the last of her cake. "We aren't even allowed to date. One of my friends thinks our father is nuts."

"Merrie!"

"It's okay, he's from Wyoming," Merrie said, grinning. "He's in private school up north somewhere, but he visits a cousin here during the summer. His name is Randall. He's really nice."

"Don't you dare," Mandy began.

"Oh, it's not like that. We're just *friends*." She emphasized the word. "He goes through girls like some people go through candy. I'd never want somebody like that! But he's very easy to talk to, and he listens to me. I like him a lot."

"As long as you don't tell him things you shouldn't," Mandy replied.

Merrie's eyes fell. "I'd never do that."

Sari put down her fork with a sigh. "Well, it was a very nice lunch, even if it didn't come with scores of well-wishers and dancing." She frowned. "Come to think of it, I don't know how to dance. I've never been anywhere that I could learn."

"We went to that Latin restaurant once, where they had the flamenco dancers," Merrie said, tongue in cheek.

"Oh, sure, and I could have gotten up on a table and practiced the steps," came the sardonic reply.

Suddenly a door slammed. Paul came into the dining room with his hands deep in his pockets. His thick, wavy black hair was damp and there were droplets on the shoulders of his suit coat. "Well, it's raining." He sighed. "At least it held off until after the graduation ceremony."

"At least," Sari replied. "There's plenty left." She indicated the remnants of the lovely meal. "And lots of cake."

He chuckled. "I'm sorry."

"About what?" Sari asked.

"You should have gone out with your friends for a real celebration," he said, dropping into a chair. "With balloons and music and drinks…"

"Drinks?" Sari asked with raised eyebrows. "What are those?"

"I had balloons at my fifth birthday party, when Mama was still alive," Merrie added.

"Music. Hmm," Mandy said, thinking. "I went to a concert in the park last week. They had tubas and saxophones…"

Paul threw up his hands. "You people are hopeless!"

"We live in hopeless times," Sari said. She stood up and adopted a pose. "But someday, people will put aside their differences and raise balloons in tribute to those who have given their all so that we can have drinks and tubas…"

The rest of them started laughing.

She chuckled and sat back down. "Well, it was a nice thought. Daddy doesn't like us being around normal people, Paul," she added. "He thinks we'll be corrupted."

"That would be a choice," he replied. "I don't think you get one if you live here."

"Shh!" Sari said at once. "Don't say that out loud or they'll find you floating down some river in an oil drum!"

His eyes twinkled. "We found a guy like that once, back when I was a kid. Me and some other guys were goofing off near the river, in Jersey, and we saw this oil drum just floating, near the shore. One of the older boys was curious. He and a friend went and pried off the lid." He made a horrible face. "We set new land speed records getting out of there! It was a body inside!"

"Did you get the police?" Merrie asked curiously.

He gave her a long look. "Honey, if we'd done that, we'd probably have ended up in matching oil drums ourselves! You don't mess with the mob."

"Mob? You mean, real mob...mobsters?" Merrie asked, her eyes as big as saucers.

"Yeah," he replied, grinning. "I grew up in a rough neighborhood. Almost all of the kids I knew back then ended up in prison."

"But not you," Sari said, with more tenderness in her tone than she realized.

"Not me," Paul agreed. He smiled. "How about a plate?" he asked Mandy. "I've fought traffic all the way from San Antonio and I'm starved!"

"You had the nice big breakfast that I made you this morning," Mandy taunted.

"Yeah, but all of it got used up listening to that guy who spoke at Sari's graduation ceremony. Who was he again?" he teased.

"That was one of the finer politicians this state has produced," Sari informed him haughtily. "In fact, he's your US senator."

"In that case, may he return to Washington, DC, with best possible speed and stay there from now on!" he said. "Gosh, imagine having to listen to him drone on for hours in Congress!"

"It beats having him drone on at somebody's graduation," Merrie said under her breath. "Oh, sorry!" she told her sister, but she ruined her apologetic tone by grinning.

Sari laughed, too. "I think there's some basic rule

that people who speak at graduation ceremonies have to bore people to death."

"It would seem so."

"Who spoke at your graduation?" Sari asked Paul.

"The director of the FBI," he replied without thinking. His fingers, on the fork he was holding, went white.

"That must have been an interesting speech," Sari said. Not looking at Paul, she didn't see the effect the words were having on him.

"I'll bet he bored Paul out of his mind," Merrie teased.

Paul snapped out of it. He glanced at her and laughed. "Well, not completely. He had a sense of humor, at least."

"What did he... Oh!"

Mandy turned over the cream pitcher as Sari was about to ask Paul something else about his graduation.

"I'm getting so clumsy in my old age! My poor fingers just won't hold things anymore! Get us a rag, will you, darlin'?" she asked Sari.

"Of course." She paused to hug the older woman. "And you're not getting old!"

After Mandy mopped up the spill, the girls went to change out of their finery into casual clothes.

"Saved my bacon. Again. Thanks," Paul said to Mandy when they were alone.

She sat down beside him. "Whatever it is, you haven't really faced it, have you, dear?" she asked gently, laying a hand over his big one.

His lips compressed. "I came south," he said. "I couldn't stay where I was, doing the job I was doing. I wanted to get away, do something different, be around people I didn't know." He shrugged. "It seemed the best thing at the time, but I'm not sure it was. You don't face problems by running away from them."

"No," she said softly. "You never do. They just come along for the ride." She patted his hand again and got up. "But, that being said, there's no need to go rushing back to deal with them, either," she added with a smile. "We've gotten used to having you around."

"I like it here," he confessed, leaning back in his chair. "I didn't expect to. I mean, a south Texas ranch, cowboys all over the place, people with thick accents who wouldn't know a dissertation from a dessert." He glanced at her. "I got a surprise."

She laughed. "A lot of those drawling people with accents have degrees, in all sorts of surprising subjects," she translated. "And a slow voice doesn't equate to a slow mind."

He nodded. "The Grier boys changed my mind about a lot of things. You don't expect to find somebody like Cash Grier working as a small-town police chief. Or a guy who worked with the FBI's Hostage Rescue Team, like his brother Garon, heading up a local FBI office."

"Cash has been a constant surprise," Mandy said. "None of us really expected him to settle down here. He was going around with Christabel Gaines before she married his friend Judd Dunn. Then, all of a sudden, he's married to a former supermodel and he's got two kids."

He laughed. "I know what you mean." He leaned over his coffee cup. "But the big surprise was finding Eb Scott here with a counterterrorism school. I knew him years ago. He worked as an independent contractor when I was overseas, in the Middle East."

"In the military?"

He nodded. "Spec ops. Green Berets," he added with twinkling eyes. "Eb saved my life. He went on to bigger and better things."

"So did you."

"Me? No, I'm just private security," he said, pausing to sip coffee.

"Not what you were before, though," Mandy said.

He glanced at her, frowning.

"My brother." She averted her eyes. "He…pretty much stays in trouble. He lived in New Jersey for a long time, working for some…well, some people you probably knew in the old days. I mentioned your name. Not deliberately, just in passing." She swallowed. "He knew about you."

His face went hard. Very hard. He looked up at her with cold dark eyes.

"I never tell anything I know to anybody, Mr. Paul," she said quietly. "And shame on you for thinking I would."

He grimaced. "Sorry."

"You don't know me. Not really." She sat back down beside him. "Our parents died when we were young. Grady took care of me. He worked odd jobs, did some questionable things, but he kept us together and put food on the table. When I graduated high school, I got a job working for Mr. Darwin, here. Grady figured I could take care of myself, so he went north, looking for better pay. He found it." She drew in a breath. "I keep thinking I'll hear one day that he's been found in an oil drum," she added with a wan smile. "I can't stop him from doing what he pleases. The best I can hope for is to make sure Mr. Darwin doesn't ever have a reason to turn him in to the authorities."

He scowled. "Would he?"

"You know he would," she replied quietly. Her eyes met his levelly. "It's why I never tell anything I know. And you'd better make sure you do the same. You may not have people he can blackmail you with, but Mr. Darwin could plant evidence and have you put away. It wouldn't be the first time," she added in a whisper, her eyes looking all around.

"There's no surveillance equipment in here," he whispered back.

"Would you care to bet on it?" she returned.

Don't miss
DEFENDER
by New York Times *bestselling author*
Diana Palmer,
available June 2016 wherever
HQN Books books and ebooks are sold.
www.Harlequin.com

**Tough, rugged and oh-so-sexy...
There's just something about those Western men!**

From Wyoming to Oregon, Texas to Montana, let today's
top-selling masters of Western romance sweep you away with
this sneak peek at ten brand-new novels.

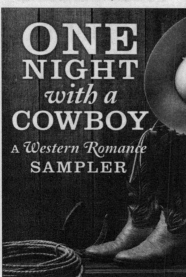

FEATURING EXTENDED
EXCERPTS FROM

Once a Rancher
by Linda Lael Miller

Untamed
by Diana Palmer

One Night Charmer
by Maisey Yates

Rustler's Moon
by Jodi Thomas

Home on the Ranch
by Trish Milburn

Hard Rain
by B.J. Daniels

Texas on My Mind
by Delores Fossen

Texas Rebels: Jude
by Linda Warren

Out Rider
by Lindsay McKenna

Hard Silence
by Mia Kay

The West has never been wilder!

Download your free copy today!

Available wherever ebooks are sold.

Be sure to connect with us at:
Harlequin.com/Newsletters
Facebook.com/HarlequinBooks
Twitter.com/HQNBooks

HQN™

www.HQNBooks.com

PHLLM579

Wrangle Your Friends for the Ultimate Ranch Girls' Getaway

Win an all-expenses-paid 3-night luxurious stay for you and your 3 guests at The Resort at Paws Up in Greenough, Montana.

Retail Value $10,000

A TOAST TO FRIENDSHIP, AN ADVENTURE OF A LIFETIME!

Learn more at
www.Harlequinranchgetaway.com

Sweepstakes ends August 31, 2016

WCHMR

Same great stories, new name!

In July 2016,
the HARLEQUIN®
AMERICAN ROMANCE® series
will become
the HARLEQUIN®
WESTERN ROMANCE series.

Connect with us to find your next great read, special offers and more.

 /HarlequinBooks

 @HarlequinBooks

www.HarlequinBlog.com

www.Harlequin.com/Newsletters

HARLEQUIN®

A *Romance* FOR EVERY MOOD™

www.Harlequin.com

HWR2016

REQUEST YOUR FREE BOOKS!

2 FREE NOVELS
FROM THE ROMANCE COLLECTION
PLUS 2 FREE GIFTS!

YES! Please send me 2 FREE novels from the Romance Collection and my 2 FREE gifts (gifts are worth about $10). After receiving them, if I don't wish to receive any more books, I can return the shipping statement marked "cancel." If I don't cancel, I will receive 4 brand-new novels every month and be billed just $6.49 per book in the U.S. or $6.99 per book in Canada. That's a savings of at least 19% off the cover price. It's quite a bargain! Shipping and handling is just 50¢ per book in the U.S. and 75¢ per book in Canada.* I understand that accepting the 2 free books and gifts places me under no obligation to buy anything. I can always return a shipment and cancel at any time. Even if I never buy another book, the two free books and gifts are mine to keep forever.

194/394 MDN GH4D

Name	(PLEASE PRINT)	
Address		Apt. #
City	State/Prov.	Zip/Postal Code

Signature (if under 18, a parent or guardian must sign)

Mail to the **Reader Service:**
IN U.S.A.: P.O. Box 1867, Buffalo, NY 14240-1867
IN CANADA: P.O. Box 609, Fort Erie, Ontario L2A 5X3

Want to try two free books from another line?
Call 1-800-873-8635 or visit www.ReaderService.com.

* Terms and prices subject to change without notice. Prices do not include applicable taxes. Sales tax applicable in N.Y. Canadian residents will be charged applicable taxes. Offer not valid in Quebec. This offer is limited to one order per household. Not valid for current subscribers to the Romance Collection or the Romance/Suspense Collection. All orders subject to credit approval. Credit or debit balances in a customer's account(s) may be offset by any other outstanding balance owed by or to the customer. Please allow 4 to 6 weeks for delivery. Offer available while quantities last.

Your Privacy—The Reader Service is committed to protecting your privacy. Our Privacy Policy is available online at www.ReaderService.com or upon request from the Reader Service.

We make a portion of our mailing list available to reputable third parties that offer products we believe may interest you. If you prefer that we not exchange your name with third parties, or if you wish to clarify or modify your communication preferences, please visit us at www.ReaderService.com/consumerschoice or write to us at Reader Service Preference Service, P.O. Box 9062, Buffalo, NY 14240-9062. Include your complete name and address.

DIANA PALMER